PROOF OF GUILT

ALSO BY CHARLES TODD

THE IAN RUTLEDGE MYSTERIES

THE BESS CRAWFORD MYSTERIES

OTHER FICTION

PROOF OF GUILT

Charles Todd

wm WILLIAM MORROW
An Imprint of HarperCollins*Publishers*

PROOF OF GUILT. Copyright © 2013 by Charles Todd. All rights reserved. Printed in the United States of America. No part of this book may be used or reproduced in any manner whatsoever without written permission except in the case of brief quotations embodied in critical articles and reviews. For information address HarperCollins Publishers, 10 East 53rd Street, New York, NY 10022.

HarperCollins books may be purchased for educational, business, or sales promotional use. For information please write: Special Markets Department, HarperCollins Publishers, 10 East 53rd Street, New York, NY 10022.

FIRST EDITION

Library of Congress Cataloging-in-Publication Data has been applied for.

ISBN 978-0-06-201568-6 (hardcover)
ISBN 978-0-06-225026-1 (international edition)

13 14 15 16 17   OV/RRD   10 9 8 7 6 5 4 3 2 1

For Otto Penzler
and everyone at
The Mysterious Bookshop

For all you've done for the Mystery, for mystery writers,
and for mystery fans everywhere.
Here's to you!

Chapter One

Funchal Harbor, Madeira
3 December 1916

He couldn't remember, later, what had taken him down to the harbor.

Now, staring out at the masts of the CS *Dacia,* the British cable-laying ship, he found himself thinking about England.

Dacia was said to be diverting the overseas cable, in an attempt to deny the Germans access to it. Whether it was true or not, he didn't know. But she and the French gunboat *Surprise* had brought the war home to him in an unexpected and unwelcome fashion.

England had been at war since August 1914. But Portugal and, by extension, Madeira had remained neutral in spite of a centuries' old alliance with Britain. In spite, as well, of clashes with Germany in the Portuguese Colony of Angola, in Africa. Neutrality was one of the reasons he'd decided to live here. His grandmother had been a Quaker by conviction, and he himself held strong views about war and the waste it brought in its wake.

He turned to look upward. Madeira was volcanic, its climate temperate, and its soil fertile. A paradise of flowers, which his mother had loved. Clouds were beetling down the mountainside, concealing the heights, but on a promontory to the far side of the bay, he could still see the tower of his house. Three stories, like most in Funchal, and in his eyes far more handsome than the house where he'd grown up in Essex. It was his late grandfather Howard French, his mother's father, who had introduced him to the wine business here. He'd come as a boy and stayed as a man. An exile, but a happy one.

A flash spun him around to stare at the harbor just as an explosion amidships sent a column of black smoke rising from *Dacia.* He was trying to think what could have happened aboard when another explosion rocked *Surprise,* and just above him, from the vantage point of the Grand Hotel grounds, someone was pointing and shouting.

"There—look, it's a submarine!"

The voice carried clearly, this close to the water.

He didn't lose time trying to see. He began to run, turning his back on the harbor as other explosions shook it. People were coming out of doorways, stopping in the streets to stare, calling to one another, unable to believe the evidence of their own eyes. He risked a glance over his shoulder and saw pillars of black smoke rising from *Dacia,* which had been hit again, and *Surprise,* and even *Kangaroo,* a third ship near them.

Someone in the water was screaming, and he could hear other cries as the heavy smell of burning timbers wafted inland on the onshore breeze, making him cough.

His offices were on the street just above the harbor. French, French & Traynor, Exporters, handled Madeira, the fortified wine that had made the island famous. And if this shelling of the ships in the harbor was a precursor to an invasion, there was work to be done in a hurry.

Sprinting across the street, where a few motorcars were halted, and several carriages and drays had pulled up, their occupants transfixed by the burning ships, he passed a wild-eyed horse rearing in its traces, the odor of smoke terrifying it.

In the doorway of the export house stood most of his employees, and those who couldn't crowd into the narrow space were at the windows, their faces nearly as shocked as he felt.

"Mr. Traynor!" his foreman shouted in English. "What are they doing?"

"I don't know." He pushed his way inside and ordered his people to follow him.

His own office was in the front, overlooking the street. Behind the offices was the long space where the shop stood and the heavy drays were kept. Above and beyond that the cavernous rooms where great barrels of Madeira, coded by age and type, rested on their sides. And the high-ceilinged rooms with the kettles and vats and gauges that heated the wine, along with the smaller room where all the tools collected through centuries of winemaking were displayed. And at the very back, the long room where employees ate their meals, walls hand-painted by them down the generations and a source of much pride.

Wood, all of them, and they were all vulnerable to fire.

He stopped short, suddenly overwhelmed.

What to do? It would take days—and at best would be a very risky task—to move the wine, and as for the equipment, more days to disengage the pipes and lines that connected kettles to vats. An impossible task.

Even if he managed it, where could he take an entire building to safety?

Matthew Traynor stood there, feeling helpless.

Damn the Germans. And damn the war.

Someone was asking him if Portugal had been attacked—if it had fallen—if this was a prelude to invasion. Others were pleading with him to allow them to leave, to reach their families before it was too late.

Torn, feeling for the first time in his life that he didn't know how to answer, he tried to collect his wits and act.

Just as he was about to speak, someone poked his head into the doorway behind Traynor and shouted, "The U-boat. She's surfacing."

He went to the door to see for himself, and there was the U-boat, in plain view, water still spilling across her hull, gun crews clambering out of the tower, racing across to the deck guns. The fort's harbor batteries, such as they were, hadn't opened up. By the time he looked back at the submarine, men had reached the guns, swung them around, and the shelling began.

Not of the harbor, but of Funchal itself.

He realized then that it was too late. "Go home. While you can," he told the employees waiting anxiously behind him. "If this is an invasion, stay at home. Don't do anything rash."

"What about the wine?" his foreman asked. "What are we to do?"

Traynor took a deep breath. "We'll just have to pray it survives. Now go, take the back streets. *Hurry*. No, not this way, out through the rear door."

He could hear the shells exploding now, picture in his mind the damage being done, the cost in property and lives. People were screaming, running in every direction, panicked.

His secretary, a young Portuguese man he'd hired last year, was tugging at his sleeve. "Come, you must go too. Look how the shells are falling!"

And Matt Traynor let himself be led to his own rear door, his mind numbed by shock and a terrible anger he couldn't control. Around him the building shuddered as a shell landed not more than three houses away.

Years of work. *Years*. And there was nothing he could do.

The shelling lasted all of two hours. The harbor guns, ineffectual at best, could do little to stop the ravaging of the capital. Runners had been sent to other towns on the island, asking if there had been landings of German troops, but no reports came back.

And then, as suddenly as it had begun, the shelling stopped. The submarine decks cleared, the hatch was closed, and she slipped quietly beneath the harbor waves, leaving behind two burning vessels, the *Dacia* already sunk, and countless lives lost. In the town itself, shells accounted for other deaths, falling masonry and timbers for more wounded and dying.

Matt Traynor, hurrying by horseback into Funchal again, saw to his utter amazement that the firm's windows had been blown out, glazing everywhere, but the building was still standing and appeared to be sound. Still, there were the casks, the great barrels, and the shaking they must have sustained, seals broken, staves sprung. The new wine the vats held, which would either be all right or a total loss, nothing in between. Weeks would pass—months—before he learned what the cost of the shelling would actually be. And there were the glaziers, to replace the glass. They would be busy—he must contact them at once, today, to protect the building from looters come for the wine. Meanwhile, he must hire more night watchmen to stand guard until the House of French, French & Traynor was secure once more.

Dismounting, he stood there for a moment, staring around him at the destruction that had changed this familiar street into a nightmare, masonry everywhere, trees shattered, the pavement itself pocked and broken.

And then, taking a deep breath, he prepared himself for what he'd find inside.

Someone was running down the littered street, calling his name. It was a maid from the house of his fiancée. He felt his heart turn over. "What is it?" he shouted to Manuela and stood where he was, rooted to the spot.

"It's the Senhorita," she cried, and he wanted to cover his ears.

Please, God, nothing more. I can't face anything more.

The bleeding of war-torn France, the endless lists of dead, wounded, and missing from Ypres and the Somme, the suffering in England—none of these had touched him. But this was different. This was his own safe, happy world.

"She's dead," Manuela was saying, tears streaming down her red face, and he could read her lips even though the words refused to register. "The beam in her bedroom—she was praying before the Madonna, and it— She's dead."

He heard himself say, "But—that's not possible. Her house was out of range, it was *safe*."

"It was the shaking, Senhor. It went on and on, and the plaster gave way . . ."

A week later, his affairs set in order, his fiancée and her mother buried in the hillside cemetery where scarlet bougainvillea spilled luxuriantly over the wall, a brightness that hurt the eyes, he set sail for Portugal. To enlist there.

Chapter Two

Edgar Billings had stopped at the small pub for a late lunch, lingering over the remnants of his pudding in spite of the glances cast his way by the proprietor, eager to see him off and clear away the noontime meal.

It was nearly two o'clock when the outer door of the pub crashed open and a man dressed in worn corduroy trousers and Wellingtons came quickly inside, calling for Constable Means.

"He's not here," the proprietor said. "I expect he went home for his meal. What's happened, then?"

"A body. Washed up on the shale below Dungeness Light. I thought he'd want to know."

"A body?" the proprietor repeated. "Not someone we know?"

The Pelican was some distance from Dungeness, but a good many of the fishermen along the coast stopped in there from time to time.

The man shook his head. "Didn't recognize him."

"Aye, well, that's something to be grateful for."

Billings had risen from his table and walked toward the two men, reaching into his pocket for his money.

He paid his account and went out the door. The man who had brought the news looked after him. "Stranger?"

"Yes," the proprietor said. "Passing through. He said."

"Well, then, I'll be off to find Means." The man nodded.

Billings, in the yard outside the pub, was already in his motorcar. "Give you a lift?" he asked the man.

"Thanks, no, I'm just off up the road."

Billings had already cranked the motor, and he let in the clutch, turning toward the coast.

Watching him drive on, the man said to himself, "Now what's his interest in the body?"

He set out at a trot for the constable's small house.

B illings found the lighthouse with no trouble. It stood out across the flat land along this part of the coast. But there was no direct way to reach it. The track into it wandered past the rough houses of fishermen, skirted patches of wind-beaten grass, and finally came to an end above the long shelf of shale that began by the light and covered the quarter mile to the sea itself. After reversing the motorcar to face the way he'd come, he got out.

Walking was difficult through the shale. Each step seemed to spread a dozen stones into thousands, with no good purchase for his shoes, like walking in sand but harder, and by the time he was in sight of the sea, he was winded.

From here he could see the body lying just above the tide line. A lone fisherman kept watch, and the smell of his pipe tobacco reached Billings from where the man squatted by the corpse.

Billings plodded on, under the eye of the fisherman, and soon reached the body.

The dead man was dressed in a well-tailored shirt, summer-weight trousers, no shoes. Hair too dark and muddied with seawater to judge its color, his face scraped by the stones where he must have tossed and turned with the incoming tide before being washed up far enough to come to rest at the edge of the tide line, too heavy now in his sodden clothing to be carried out again.

Like a discarded piece of driftwood the sea didn't want any longer.

The fisherman stood up as Billings approached.

"Stranger," he said with a nod.

"I was at the pub when someone brought news of a dead man."

"That'ud be Burton," the fisherman said, still watching Billings with suspicion in his eyes.

"Burton? Yes, I expect it was," Billings said easily. "I thought I'd have a look for myself."

"Curious about a dead man?" the fisherman asked.

"I've been searching this coast for days, looking for a certain man. I thought perhaps this might be he."

"Looking to find—or to drown?"

Billings smiled and took out his identification. "Scotland Yard."

The fisherman scrutinized it. Billings wondered if the man could read.

Finally satisfied, the fisherman nodded. "Right, then. Have a look. Constable Means will be along soon. He might not care to have the Yard meddling in his patch." It was said with an overtone of venom, as if the fisherman and Means didn't get along.

Billings came forward, careful where he stepped, but there was nothing here that could tell him where the man had died or why. And there were no stains on the shirt to indicate a wound washed clean by the sea.

Squatting, as the fisherman had done, he peered into the dead face. It wasn't his quarry. He was sure of it. "Any identification on him?"

The fisherman shook his head. "Burton looked."

"Did he take anything away from the corpse?"

"He's an honest bloke, Burton. I doubt he'd rob the dead."

"Yes, well, honest men have their price." Billings rose to his feet. "My compliments to Constable Means. The corpse is all his." He turned to leave, then thought of something else. "Your name? For the record, since you've kept the man company for some time."

The fisherman hesitated, then said, "Henderson. George Henderson."

Billings nodded. "Good day, Henderson."

The wind from the sea buffeted him as he walked back to where he'd left his motorcar, making the going even harder. A sudden gust nearly knocked him off his feet, and he was glad, finally, when he'd gained the shelter of his vehicle.

He sat there for a time, in the shadow of the lighthouse, as the sun went in and out briefly and then retired from the fray altogether. And then, with decision, he got out, turned the crank, and drove back the way he'd come.

Chapter Three

London, Late Summer 1920

It wasn't an inquiry that Rutledge relished. A man had been killed in Chelsea, not far from the house where Meredith Channing had lived.

It was closed now. Had been since he'd escorted her to Bruges, in Belgium, where the man she believed to be her husband—he'd gone missing in the war—had been discovered, ill and unable to care for or even name himself. Rutledge had not been convinced that she was certain the man was Channing. She'd been searching a very long time, and her need to believe it was and make her peace with her husband had been stronger than her usual sound judgment. He'd had no choice but to walk away and leave her there, cutting short whatever closeness might have bloomed between them in different circumstances. The attraction had been there. He himself had tried to pretend it hadn't.

She was in Belgium still, although he was the only person who knew her whereabouts. Most of her friends assumed she was visiting in Scotland—or Yorkshire—or possibly Devon. It was not his charge to enlighten them.

He had been sent to the scene by the Acting Chief Superintendent with the comment "Bloody motorcars. The sixth death in London this month, by my reckoning. And not likely to be the last."

"I should think a traffic death would be handled by the Metropolitan Police," Rutledge had answered.

"As a rule," the Acting Chief Superintendent had agreed. "But Constable Meadows felt the circumstances were a little odd. For one thing, the vehicle didn't stop. For another, there are no witnesses. Not even a milk van, mind you."

Someone should have seen or heard something, in spite of the fact that the accident had occurred in the predawn hours. The motorcar braking suddenly, the force of the bonnet or the wing striking the victim, even if there had been no time for him to cry out.

Sergeant Gibson, just coming up the stairs as Rutledge was leaving, greeted him with a nod and then said, "The doctor's been and gone."

"What did he have to say?"

"Injuries consistent with being struck by a motorcar, but he put the time of death closer to midnight than dawn."

Rutledge thanked the sergeant and went on his way. He had noticed, but had said nothing about it, that Gibson was himself again. And he was happy to see it.

Chief Superintendent Bowles's sudden illness had caused drastic upheaval at the Yard, compounded by frantic jockeying to fill his shoes and the temporary assignment of several Acting Chief Superintendents until Bowles's condition had been clarified. When the new man had been brought in from Yorkshire and appointed to take his place for the foreseeable future, there had been a settling out.

As shocked as anyone about what had happened, Gibson had

withdrawn into a strictly by-the-book mode that had made him prickly and unhelpful, as if by holding himself to Bowles's standards now, he believed he could assure that no one would guess his true feeling about the man or the number of times he'd gone behind the Chief Superintendent's back. But like good resolutions at any time, this one had been short-lived. Everyone was weighing the new man, but no one had uttered an opinion. Rutledge had already formed his own.

Constable Meadows was still standing guard over the body, waiting for the undertaker to arrive. Behind him, Rutledge could see two more constables, brought in for the purpose, canvassing either side of the quiet street. If the neighbors were curious, they were keeping indoors and watching events from their windows. But then Huntingdon was not the sort of street where residents or servants stood and gawked.

Meadows was a thin, quiet man of perhaps thirty-five, and he said as Rutledge approached, "Scotland Yard?"

"Inspector Rutledge."

"Yes, sir. I was asked to wait until someone arrived."

"I understand you felt the circumstances surrounding this accident were odd?" Rutledge stooped to lift the blanket that had been placed over the victim's body. The man appeared to be in his late twenties or early thirties, slim and well dressed, brown hair matted with blood from the wound where the back of his skull must have struck the uneven edge of the street, one arm at an angle that would be unnatural in life, and trousers torn at the ankle.

Meadows reached down and turned the body a little so that Rutledge could see where the man's coat was torn near the collar and covered with dust and bits of stone and grass. There was a long scrape down one side of his face. "It appeared that he was dragged some distance. The doctor's estimate was close to ten feet, until the coat or even that edge of his trousers tore away. But if you look in the road there's no sign of anything dragged."

Rutledge let the blanket fall back into place and rose. Looking back down the road, the direction in which the body would have been carried by the motorcar, he had to agree with the constable. No sign at all, although the man was not slight, and even a sack of coal would have left some impression in the soft summer dust.

Meadows was saying, "For another thing, sir, the doctor told me he'd been dead longer than I'd thought. I walk this street at least once every hour on my rounds, and he wasn't here before half after four. I'd swear to that. For another, there's nothing in his pockets to show who he is. And you'd expect to find a wallet, if he was coming home at this hour."

"Was he robbed, do you think?"

"Sir, no. No sign of that that I could see. Pockets weren't turned out. And there's a watch in his vest pocket. Rather a nice one. French, at a guess. No one would miss it, even in the dark. There's a nice chain on it as well." He held out his hand, and in the palm lay the watch and chain.

They were expensive. Rutledge could see that for himself, both case and chain well made and of smooth, heavy gold. They matched what he had seen of the man's clothing.

Flicking open the case, he looked for an inscription, but there was none. "The jeweler or watchmaker who sold this might have a record of it," he said. "Before the war, I should think. And you're right, the face appears to be French."

"I'll see that's passed on, sir."

"Better still, I'll ask a jeweler I know what he makes of it. And then the Yard can begin a search for the owner."

Just then the undertaker arrived, and Meadows stepped forward to speak to the driver.

At the sound of a door closing, Rutledge looked up the street. A constable was coming down the steps of a house near the corner, and he turned in Rutledge's direction.

Rutledge went to meet the man, leaving Meadows to deal with the removal of the body.

"Constable," he said. "Found a witness, I hope?"

"Sir, not precisely. But the footman in the house with the iron railings above the door was waiting up for the owner to return from a dinner party, and I spoke to the gentleman as well. When he came home at a quarter past twelve, he saw nothing in the street. He's willing to give a statement to that effect."

"Was he driving? Could he have knocked the man down?"

"I'm to look at his motorcar, sir. The footman has gone to bring it around. But I'd say Mr. Belford was unlikely to have been the one we're looking for." The constable cleared his throat. "He's a rather formidable gentleman, sir."

"Perhaps I should have a word with him. After we've looked at his motorcar. He was driving himself? There was no one else with him?"

"No, sir, he was alone."

"Could he have been too drunk to realize what he'd done?"

"According to the footman, Mr. Belford isn't one for the drink."

"Indeed. Ah, here comes the motorcar. Let's have a look."

The footman was an older man, to Rutledge's surprise. As a rule it was a position for younger ones. He drew up in the street next to the two policemen and said, "Here you are, Constable Doyle. Have a look." He nodded to Rutledge. "Sir."

But they could see straightaway that the meticulously maintained motor had not been involved in any street accident. It could have rolled out of the showroom door only yesterday, it was in such excellent condition. As he was examining it, Rutledge saw the footman take out a handkerchief and briskly rub an edge of the near-side headlamp where Constable Doyle had briefly rested his hand as he bent to look more closely at the frame. The frown on the man's face as he polished away the offending print indicated that the motorcar was in his charge and his joy.

Rutledge turned to Constable Doyle. "I'd like to speak to Mr. Belford. Will you tell Constable Meadows that I'll be back shortly? He's not to leave until I return."

Doyle, still minutely examining the motorcar, said, "Yes, sir, I'll pass the word."

Rutledge walked on to the Belford house and knocked at the door. A housemaid answered and showed him into a small parlor. It was rather formal: dark blue and cream, the drapes dark, lined with the lighter color, the carpet the reverse, cream with a dark blue pattern, the chairs covered in a shade that complemented the drapes. Still, it had the appearance of being well used, as if the owner preferred it in the evening to the drawing room.

Within less than a minute after the housemaid had left Rutledge there, Belford came into the room.

He was a man of medium height, with iron gray hair and a trim mustache. There was an air about him that would have suited an earl, and he said without waiting for Rutledge to speak, "I've told Constable Doyle all I can about last night and sent out Miller with my motorcar. What is it now?"

There was neither irritation not curiosity in his voice, only impatience.

"I'm Inspector Rutledge, Scotland Yard," he answered easily. "I understand that you saw nothing unusual when you returned to your house last night a little after midnight."

"That's true."

"The dead man was lying on the far side of the road. Could you have missed him? You were driving yourself, I understand."

"I was. And I would most certainly have noticed a corpse on my street."

"And your footman returned the motorcar to the mews where you keep it?"

"Yes, of course."

"Can you be certain that he didn't strike the man?"

"Miller? He would have told me."

But would he have? Still, there was no damage to the vehicle.

"Before the body is taken away, I'd like to have you look at the victim and tell me if you recognize him. He could well be a neighbor, although Constable Meadows didn't know him."

"Very well." Belford turned on his heel, led the way out the door and through the foyer to the street, not waiting to see if Rutledge was following. The body had just been put into the rear of the van when Belford reached it, and he said, "Show me the man."

The driver hesitated, looked over his shoulder at Rutledge, who nodded once, and then uncovered the face of the corpse.

Belford peered at it intently, as if to memorize the dead man's features, then turned to Rutledge. "I have never seen him before. I can be quite sure about that."

"Can you?" Rutledge asked as the hearse's driver waited for permission to cover the body again.

"Absolutely. He does not live on this street, he did not serve under me in the war, he does not move in circles that I frequent, and I can think of no other occasion when he should have come to my attention."

"Thank you, Mr. Belford." Rutledge gestured to the driver, who nodded, dealt with the corpse, and shut the doors of the hearse.

Belford stepped to one side, waited until the hearse was driving away, and then said, "I should like to know what he was doing here, on this street."

"There is no identification on the body," Rutledge said. "We have no idea who the man is, where he lives, or what brought him here."

"Then I can be of no further service to you." With a brisk nod, Belford walked away. But he'd taken no more than a half-dozen steps when he turned and said, "Constable Doyle said the man was dragged some ten feet. I should think that would indicate an intent on the driver's part to see his victim dead."

"We haven't determined whether he was or not," Rutledge replied. "Constable Meadows could find no evidence of dragging after he discovered the body. But judging from the scrapes on the man's face and the state of his clothing, it struck him as very likely."

"Then you must take your inquiry elsewhere," Belford said with some satisfaction. "Because the likelihood is that the dead man was not killed on this street at all, but brought here and left for someone to find."

Rutledge studied Belford for a moment. "That's an interesting supposition. What evidence is there to support it?"

"See for yourself, Inspector. He appeared to have been dragged after he was struck by the motorcar, but you can find no marks on the street, no tracks where his heels dug in or his body disturbed the dust. Nor does there appear to be any blood where he was found. Therefore he must have been dead for some time before he was left here. He's not a resident of this street, and he couldn't have been leaving a dinner party at that hour because he isn't dressed for dining out. Those are more country clothes, in my opinion. Your men are going house to house, and if you came to call on me, then asked me to identify the victim if I could, you have had no success thus far. My motorcar bears out the fact that I have not run anyone down. Nor, clearly, has my footman. The question you must now ask yourself is, who wanted this man dead, and who brought him here after killing him elsewhere? I have no enemies who could have done that to embarrass me, and I think you'll find that this will also hold true for my neighbors, when you have interviewed the remaining residents here and those in the streets on either side of this one. Now I have other matters to attend to, and I will leave you to your own work."

Rutledge took out the watch. "This was in his vest pocket." He held it by the chain, and it twisted for a moment before stopping, the early morning sun reflecting from the gold case. "Is there anything about it that strikes you?"

Belford reached out to touch the watch with the tip of his finger, turning the face his way. "You've looked inside for an inscription?"

"Yes."

"It's French, of course. And expensive. A gentleman's watch, I should think, possibly inherited, because of its age. That's all I can tell you."

This time when he turned away, Belford continued to walk on toward his house without looking back, shoulders straight, head high, like the officer he must have been in the war. Rutledge had met officers like him, disciplined, fair, but strict observers of the rules. He found it interesting that the man had chosen not to use the honorific of his rank after returning to civilian life. For that matter, it would be interesting to know just what rank he'd held in the war.

Behind Rutledge, Constable Meadows was saying, "He makes a very good point, sir."

He did, Rutledge thought. Observant, concise in his interpretation of what he'd seen, Belford had told Scotland Yard how to proceed. But Rutledge himself had reached the same conclusion. If the dead man had not been lying here by the side of the street when Mr. Belford returned home, he must certainly have been killed elsewhere, and someone had had time before daylight to rid himself of the body.

No identification. No business, as Belford had put it, in this street. And no sign of blood in the roadway to show where he'd died.

But Belford had driven here from somewhere. He could have brought the body this far, and left it to be found by a neighbor or the constable on his rounds. A cloth could wipe away any bloodstains on the leather seats. But that brought Rutledge back to the condition of the motorcar's exterior.

Rutledge turned to Meadows. "How well do you know Mr. Belford?"

"He keeps himself to himself. Money—there's a staff there, footman, two maids, cook, housekeeper, and valet. And never a minute's trouble. I should know, I've been here ten years myself."

"Which isn't to say that Mr. Belford doesn't have another life outside Chelsea."

"True enough, I expect. But I've never got wind of it."

Rutledge nodded. "The first order of business is to identify our body. Only then can we be certain he has had no interaction with Mr. Belford. When you and the other constables have finished speaking to everyone on this street, and you have no more information than you possess right now, begin on the adjacent streets, working your way toward the river. If there's a connection with this part of London, we must find it before going farther afield. If there isn't, then perhaps the watch will open up other avenues."

"Yes, sir, I'll see to it."

Rutledge went out into the middle of the street and walked up and down for some twenty yards in either direction from where the body had been discovered, but keen as his eyes were, sharp as the morning light was, he still could find no evidence to show that the victim had been dragged here. Or that such signs had been brushed away, in an attempt to point the police in a different direction.

He was forced to agree with Belford, although it would have been more satisfying on general principles to find the man wrong. He smiled at himself. It would most certainly have made his task easier. Wherever the victim had died, it wasn't here.

Had this site been chosen at random? Or was it meant as a message to someone who lived on this street? For that matter, the killer could have got the address wrong.

"You cover several streets on your rounds," he said to the constable as he came to stand beside him again. "Have you seen anything, heard any gossip that might indicate someone else in this area was engaged in activities that could have resulted in a rather nasty warning?"

"I was wondering that myself, sir, but I can't think of anyone who isn't respectable. There's an artist or two, and one famous actor. But they live as quietly as anyone as far as I can tell."

Finally satisfied that he could do no more here, Rutledge left, asking Constable Meadows to see that statements were copied and sent along to the Yard.

He was glad to be out of Chelsea, and drove directly to Galloway and Sons, a jeweler on Bond Street. As a young policeman, Rutledge had found the man who had broken into the shop one Saturday evening, and recovered most of the stolen items as well. Galloway had been in his debt ever since.

He greeted Rutledge warmly, and when he had finished his business with the young couple already in the shop, he turned to the Inspector.

"You've neglected us of late," he said, smiling. "I should have thought by now you'd be purchasing a ring for a young lady."

"One day perhaps," Rutledge answered. "Today I'm here on police business. Would you take a look at this watch and tell me what you can about it?"

He passed the watch to Galloway, who studied it carefully before opening it.

"Is this connected in any way with a crime?" the jeweler asked as he worked.

"It would be helpful to learn the identity of the owner."

"To be sure." After inspecting the back of the watch, Galloway finally turned to Rutledge. "I thought at first that this was a French timepiece. Well, of course it is, but it was sold in Lisbon. The jeweler left his mark just there, do you see? On the frame. At a guess, it was not a presentation piece—a coming of age or advancement, that sort of thing—but bought to use every day. Some slight signs of wear, but maintained beautifully. I'd put the date at perhaps 1890, 1895?"

"Interesting," Rutledge said. "Anything else?"

"I'm afraid not. I do have a connection in Lisbon. Would you like me to make inquiries? Quietly, of course."

"Yes, that would be very helpful."

Galloway jotted down his observations and returned the timepiece to Rutledge.

"Contact you through the Yard, as usual?"

"Please, yes."

Rutledge walked back to his motorcar with his mind on the inquiry.

A voice said, "I see you've no time for old friends."

He came back to the present to find former Chief Inspector Cummins standing in front of him. Smiling, he said, "Sorry! I was debating with myself whether this latest inquiry is a murder or an accident someone tried to cover up. What brings you to London?"

"My daughter and my wife are looking at wedding gowns. I've been cast adrift and told not to return for at least an hour. It's nearly up. I'm glad I ran into you. A pity about Bowles's heart attack, but I daresay there were many who were surprised to learn he even had one. Myself among them. What do you think of the new man? Markham?"

It occurred to Rutledge that if Cummins had been still at the Yard, he would have been in the running for the position of Acting Chief Superintendent. It was a loss to the Yard that he wasn't.

"A dark horse. So far he's been reasonable enough to work with, but his reputation precedes him. He doesn't care for leaps of intuition and is a stickler for regulations."

"The new broom sweeping clean, yet?"

Rutledge considered the question. "He's too new. Time will tell."

"One school seems to think Bowles is mending and will have his old position back or know the reason why. Another thinks he's stepped on too many toes and that he'll be asked to retire, if the Home Office finds a satisfactory replacement."

Rumors that Rutledge hadn't heard. "Thank you for the warning." *Better the devil you know?* He wasn't sure.

"Good to see you again, Ian. Keep your head down, and you'll be all right."

But Rutledge stopped him. "Do you miss it? The Yard?" He hadn't intended to ask the question. It was too personal for one thing, and none of his affair for another.

After the clinic, he had used his return to the Yard to stop himself from sliding into irreversible madness, and he had fought to hold on to that in the face of Bowles's intransigence and the fearsome darkness occupying his mind. He had survived, because he had never dared to look beyond the Yard. Never dared to contemplate what would become of him if his work were suddenly taken away. As it had been for this man.

"I do," Cummins said, and Rutledge felt cold. And then Cummins added, "But not as much as I'd expected to. Does that make sense?"

Rutledge could only say, "Yes."

At the Yard, Rutledge's first order of business was to ask Gibson to find out whatever he could about the helpful Mr. Belford. In his office with the door shut, he sat down at his desk, turned his chair toward the dusty window, and looked out. He was grateful for this glimpse of the outside, even if it consisted mostly of trees and a part of the road below. His claustrophobia, a relic of the trenches, hadn't gone away with time, as the doctors had suggested it might. And it helped him to think, staring out at green leaves and tree trunks that hadn't been blighted by artillery and turned into churned-up mud, bone, blood, and lost hopes.

The Acting Chief Superintendent would be impatiently awaiting his report, but Rutledge wasn't quite satisfied with what he'd seen in that street in Chelsea.

The victim was still wearing both shoes. Surely if he'd been dragged ten feet, one of them would have fallen off. Had someone replaced them? And while his coat showed every sign of dragging, no attempt had been made to simulate a track in the dust of a Chelsea street. Rutledge found that interesting. Where, then, had the man come from? And why was he brought to London? Because it was large and anonymous, or because this was the place where he needed to be?

"Because where he died would point to the killer," Hamish suggested in the back of his mind, answering so clearly his voice seemed to come from just behind Rutledge's shoulder.

He should be used to it by now. That voice, neither specter nor friend nor rational thought.

Whatever had brought the dead man to Chelsea, it would be necessary now to circulate a description of him to large cities all over the country. And hope that inspectors there would pass the word to the smaller towns and villages in their patches. If the Yard was very lucky, a constable somewhere would recognize the man and put a name to him.

Rutledge had been warned that the Acting Chief Superintendent didn't care for inquiries with loose ends.

He was more optimistic about the watch. It was expensive enough that jewelers in England, like Galloway, would have kept a record of such a purchase and a satisfied client, in the expectation of future business. But would that be true in Portugal?

Why had the killer overlooked that watch when he—or she—had emptied the dead man's pockets?

By accident? Or by design?

The only other chance for an early identification was for a family member, a neighbor, an employer to report the victim as missing.

Rutledge turned around to his desk, wrote a description of the dead man, and carried it to Sergeant Gibson.

"We don't have the doctor's final report yet. Once we do, this should be sent out to your list of county police stations," he told the sergeant.

"All of them, sir?" Gibson asked, already calculating the work involved.

"The victim could have come from Cornwall or Northumberland or any county in between. I'm afraid it's all of them."

With a nod, he went on to speak to the Acting Chief Superintendent, who grunted when Rutledge had finished, then commented morosely, "I've always said nothing good would ever come of a gasoline-propelled vehicle."

Rutledge wasn't sure whether the remark was intended as dark humor or whether the Acting Chief Superintendent was thinking about distances that could be covered more quickly.

It was late the next morning before the report arrived from the doctor who had examined the body.

Dr. Parker wrote:

My first estimate of the time of death still stands, as does the fact that the victim was dragged. Male, in his very early thirties, no distinguishing marks on the body, no indication of livelihood from his hands or his clothing. Possibly a gentleman of independent means, judging from the quality of said clothing. Internal injuries consistent with being struck by a motorcar. Broken left arm. No war wounds.

War wounds had become a factor in identification.

Rutledge passed the report on to Sergeant Gibson, and then read through the interviews from the constables canvassing the streets on either side of the one in which the body was found. The upshot was that everyone was accounted for in each of the houses that had been visited, and no one had had guests on that particular evening.

Hamish said, "Ye'll no' have any luck with this one."

Rutledge was beginning to think he was right.

Chapter Four

Rutledge was in his office finishing a report on another case when Sergeant Gibson walked in.

"We've received three responses about your dead man," he said, "but there's not much to choose from between them." He passed the sheets across the desk to Rutledge, who gestured to one of the chairs.

Scanning the three pages, he had to agree with the sergeant.

The first was in regard to a husband missing for the past two years. The constable reporting had added at the bottom of the sheet, *Mrs. Trumbull being somewhat of a termagant, I expect Mr. Trumbull would have gladly thrown himself under the wheels of any motorcar to escape being returned to Derbyshire.*

Rutledge said, "The man was a butcher. If it was the only trade he knew, then there's probably no connection with our victim. Butchers generally don't have the hands and nails of a gentleman. Still, we'll keep an open mind."

Moving on to the second sheet, he frowned. "A schoolmaster from Kent. It's possible."

No comment had been added here, but Gibson said as Rutledge finished reading, "I took the liberty of putting in a call to Kent. I happen to know Constable Parry from the war—a case having to do with the report of a spy at the Chatham Shipyard. False alarm, as most of them were. He tells me the schoolmaster recently lost a child and he's not been sober a day since then."

"Our man hadn't been drinking, according to the doctor."

"True, sir. But still . . . we'll keep an open mind."

The third was also a possibility. An Inspector from Norfolk wrote, *I've no reason to think that your corpse is that of Gerald Standish, for he hasn't been missing for any length of time. On the other hand, I must tell you that he has tended to wander off without notice since he came home from France. He was seen by his daily walking toward the edge of town one evening, apparently out for the exercise, for he greeted her quite naturally. His bed was not slept in that night, but she made no report as he generally reappeared in a day or so. This time was the exception. The constable in Moresley has had no word from or about him since.*

"Did you speak to the Inspector?" Rutledge asked Gibson.

"Sir, there isn't a telephone where I can reach him."

"Then we'll wait a few more days to see if the watch can tell us anything before taking these queries any further. There's something more. What have you discovered about Mr. Belford in number 20?"

"I'm waiting for a reply from the War Office. He's not known to the Metropolitan Police or to us." Gibson cleared his throat. "Reading the report from Constable Meadows, I gathered Mr. Belford was cleared of any involvement."

"So far. But he knew rather too much—or guessed more than he should have done—to strike him off the list just yet." Belford's manner hadn't rankled—Rutledge was always grateful for whatever a potential witness could contribute, for it was impossible to know and see everything in a neighborhood he didn't himself live in. Still, there had been something in the man's brisk reconstruction of events that had been very different from the usual shocked response the police were accustomed to dealing with in the face of sudden death.

It was next afternoon when Gibson returned with a puzzled look on his face and handed Rutledge a sheet of paper without comment.

He scanned it, then slowly reread what was printed there.

As far as anyone could determine, Mr. Belford was precisely what he seemed to be—a helpful neighbor. There were few details added to that—the household staff had been with him for at least ten years and in two cases for fifteen. He had never been in trouble with the law. His military career had been exemplary, and he had risen to the rank of Captain. He had seen action at Mons, Passchendaele, the Somme, and Amiens, was wounded three times, and returned to active duty as soon as he was cleared by his doctors.

Rutledge had never encountered Belford in France, but that wasn't too surprising. What was, was the fact that he'd never heard the man's name mentioned. When new companies were being transferred in, there was usually information about where they'd come from, what regiment they had served with, and the name of the officer in charge of their sector.

Gibson said, "That's all there is. The War Office was too quick to answer our questions. Makes you wonder."

Pulling information out of the War Office was generally an exercise in patience, as all records were handwritten and the filing system was archaic. Sometimes it was also a matter of obfuscation. When Rutledge needed to know something urgently, he was forced to call in favors to speed up the search.

"As he hasn't been shot at dawn, he can't be a German spy living among us," Rutledge said wryly.

Gibson answered, "Indeed, sir. When Constable Meadows asked the servants on either side of his house, they said he was an ornament to the neighborhood."

"Good God," Rutledge said blankly. "How did he achieve such a distinction?"

"The constable was told that he gives generously to any charitable cause."

"Ah."

"Always anonymously."

"Interesting. Then we'll keep Mr. Belford in the backs of our minds until we know more about the dead man."

Two other reports came in from the description that had been sent out. One from Cornwall, the other from Chester.

Gibson followed them up.

The Cornishman had gone for a walk on Exmoor and hadn't been seen since. He had a history of shell shock, and his actions were not, according to Constable Tilly, predictable. Still, the man had been missing for three weeks. In that length of time he could reasonably have reached London, if he had traveled by train or even on an accommodating lorry headed anywhere.

Rutledge, wincing at the mention of shell shock, said, "We'll have to keep this man in mind. What's his name?"

"Fulton, sir. He's from Nottingham. Married a Cornish girl before the war, and the pair have been living in a cottage on her father's farm."

"He could have made his way to Nottingham," Rutledge said. "If he was determined enough."

The man from Chester was unlikely to be their victim. He'd been wounded in the war and his arm had been badly fractured. According to the police there, he had never regained full use of it.

"And the postmortem didn't show a bad arm," Gibson reminded Rutledge. "Only wounds that caused his death."

"Did you tell Chester that we don't have their man?"

"I did. There's still the missing man in Norfolk."

"We're back to the watch," Rutledge said. "And I should have heard something by now."

"What if it was stolen?" the ever-dour Gibson wanted to know.

"I rather think, considering the quality of the dead man's clothing, that it must have belonged to him."

But Gibson wasn't convinced. "More than one pickpocket dresses like a gentleman. Best way to pass unnoticed at a gathering where the pickings are good."

I t had been nearly a week since the body was discovered when Galloway came himself to see Rutledge at the Yard.

He was escorted to Rutledge's office by Constable Thomas, and as he came through the doorway, he said, "Patience has its reward. I've something here I thought you ought to know at once."

"That's good news, I hope," Rutledge said, rising to greet Galloway. "What does your contact have to say?"

"The watch in question was actually one of a pair ordered from the jeweler in Lisbon in 1891. They were presented by a Mr. Howard French to his son and his son-in-law on the occasions of their marriage and, in due course, were returned to Lisbon for cleaning and polishing by the owners before being given to grandsons on reaching their majority."

"Why were they purchased in Lisbon rather than in London or Paris?"

"It seems that French was part owner of a winery on Madeira, and he visited Lisbon often on business matters. Before he was forty, he was sole owner of the firm and had bought land on Madeira where he could grow his own grapes. It was an experiment that succeeded beyond his wildest dreams. So I was told."

"Does the firm have an English address here in London?"

"There's an office here, but strictly for the importing and selling of wine. The jeweler in Lisbon tells me that the family owned vineyards in Portugal, but it was the ones on Madeira that gave their wines such a recognizable quality. Quite extraordinary, in fact. I fancy a glass of

Madeira wine myself, after a good meal. And it's usually from the cellars of French, French, and Traynor." He shook his head. "Imagine that."

Madeira wine was fortified and then aged. Rutledge's father had enjoyed a five-year-old Madeira, although there had been several bottles in his cellar much older than that—one crusty forty-year-old, in fact, that *his* father had put down.

"Then the place to start is here in London. I don't see the Yard paying for a jaunt to Madeira."

The jeweler smiled thinly. "Not at public expense. But I daresay it would be a very pleasant holiday."

Rutledge thanked Galloway and saw him out.

Sergeant Gibson, he was told as he returned to his office, was closeted with the Acting Chief Superintendent. And so he searched out Sergeant Fielding. Five minutes later, armed with the information Fielding had given him, Rutledge was on his way to the City and the firm of French, French & Traynor.

Neither of the principals was in, he was told by a junior clerk when he arrived at the handsome building near Leadenhall that housed the firm. It was three stories high, with an ornate façade that could have been designed by Wren. It was the right age. Above the door was a gilded sign with the name picked out and nothing more.

He opened the door and stepped into a small reception room. The paneling was well polished, the chairs were Queen Anne, and the thick carpet was Turkish, the rich colors in its pattern gleaming like dark jewels. The impression was of a well-established firm accustomed to serving the best clientele.

The junior clerk who had greeted him and asked his business deferred to a more senior clerk, and the man who then came out to speak to him would have been at home in a solicitor's chambers: tall, graying, with a high forehead and still-black eyebrows that gave his face an air of dignity and authority.

He also knew how to sum up a visitor in one swift glance.

"Mr. Rutledge? I'm the senior clerk. Gooding is my name. Frederick Gooding."

"Do you know where I can find Mr. French? I'd like very much to speak to him."

"I'm afraid he's not in today. I'll be happy to help you in any way I can."

"Mr. Traynor, then. Where will I find him?"

Mr. Gooding's eyebrows rose. "The senior Mr. French was killed in the war. The younger Mr. French is presently in Essex. Mr. Traynor handles the firm's business on Madeira."

Rutledge brought out the watch and set it on the table beside him, where the lamplight caught the gold of the case and the chain. "Have you seen this watch before?"

"It looks very like the one that the senior Mr. French inherited from his father. It went to the younger Mr. French at his brother's death. Returned from the Front in his kit." He touched it lightly, turning the face toward him. "Yes, indeed. I could almost believe that it is one and the same." Glancing up at Rutledge, he said, "How did Scotland Yard come by it? Can you tell me?"

"By chance," Rutledge answered. "I've been told that a grandfather founded the firm, passed it to his son and son-in-law, and they passed their shares to their own sons. Is this correct?"

"The French family has been in the wine business for centuries. Shakespeare records that the Duke of Clarence was drowned in a butt of Malmsey. If this is true, then very likely it was a wine provided to the Court by the French family. The grandfather, as you describe him, decided to go into the business of growing the grapes and producing his own wine, instead of merely importing it. He had a son—that would be Mr. Laurence—and a daughter, who married a Mr. David Traynor, who was then brought in by Mr. Howard French as a partner. Their son is the Mr. Matthew Traynor who presently lives on Madeira. Mr. Laurence had two sons of his own, Michael, who was killed in the war, and his brother, the present member of the family in charge of the firm." Gooding had been concise, deferential, and yet obstructive.

"Where in Essex can I find Mr. French the Younger?"

Gooding smiled slightly. "Mr. Lewis French has a home in a village in Essex just north of Dedham. A village called Stratford St. Hilary."

Constable country, near the Suffolk border, where the artist's most famous scenes were painted. Rutledge's grandmother had been particularly fond of Constable's work.

Rutledge asked, "When did you last speak to Mr. French?"

The clerk pursed his lips. "Friday of last week, I believe. He telephoned me to ask if I'd received final word of his cousin's travel plans. I hadn't, and he was not pleased. But then Mr. Traynor had business in Lisbon as well, and that could have taken longer than he'd expected."

That would have been the Friday before the body was found on Monday morning.

"Does Mr. French usually reside in this village and commute to London?"

"No, no, he has a house in London. He wanted to be sure the ancestral home, as it were, was ready for Mr. Traynor's arrival."

Rutledge considered asking the clerk to view the body of the accident victim, then changed his mind. He didn't relish having the news precede him if this was, by any chance, French the Younger. Lewis, he corrected himself.

"Is there a staff at the Essex house when Mr. French is in London?"

"Oh, yes. And his sister lives there. Miss Agnes French. She keeps house for her brother and her cousin."

"Both men are single?"

"Mr. Traynor lost his fiancée during the war, and Mr. French has recently announced his engagement." Something in the clerk's face changed. "There's to be a Christmas wedding," he added, as if he disapproved.

"Does his fiancée live here in London?" If the dead man was French, then he might well have been on his way to call on her.

"She lives with her parents in Dedham, I believe."

Which shot down that possibility. Unless there was another woman in the picture. But Rutledge rather thought Gooding wouldn't tell him even if there were.

The door behind the clerk stood ajar, as if he had expected his business with Rutledge to be brief. Rutledge could just see the edge of a heavy gold-leaf frame, the sort favored by firms that choose to display portraits of founders or benefactors.

He walked around Gooding, saying, "I'd like to see the portraits in the passage there, if you don't mind."

Surprised, the clerk said, "The portraits?" He turned. "Ah. Mr. French and Mr. Traynor."

He reached the door before Rutledge in a swift but discreet movement and held it open for him to enter, with the air that looking at the paintings had been his own idea, not Rutledge's.

The passage was quite wide, and there were two larger-than-life portraits hung on the dark walnut paneling between doors to what must be private offices.

"Both were painted by artists of the Royal Academy," Gooding was saying. "This is Mr. David Traynor. He was perhaps fifty when this was done."

Rutledge recognized the name of the artist in the lower-left-hand corner.

Traynor appeared to be of medium height, his fair hair combed in the style of the day, and his sober expression that of a successful man who knew his own worth but had earned it. One hand rested on a large crate of wine with the firm's name emblazoned on the side, and the other seemed to point to a map lying on the table next to him, showing Portugal and the island of Madeira some distance away.

There was no resemblance to the victim lying in the hospital mortuary.

Rutledge moved down the passage to the next portrait as Gooding said, "This of course is Mr. Howard French, the original founder. I have often felt there was a likeness to the present Mr. French. More so than to his elder brother, who closely resembled their mother."

"There is no portrait of Mr. Laurence, Mr. Howard's son."

"It hangs in the office of the present head of the firm, Mr. Lewis. He is quite fond of the painting."

The man also appeared to be of medium height, his hair a medium shade of brown, his eyes a medium shade of blue. But there was no mistaking the fact that there was nothing "medium" about the shape and thrust of his jaw. While Traynor celebrated for posterity his rise to new heights of wealth and prestige, there was no doubt that his father-in-law was the force behind the firm's changing fortunes.

Nor was there any doubt that the dead man bore enough of a likeness to the portrait that he could very well be a relative of the founder, even though he didn't possess that thrusting jaw or air of power. It was mainly in coloring and size, the ordinary nose, the shape of the head. Not conclusive, of course.

But that likeness, coupled with the watch, was convincing evidence that Mr. French the Younger was dead.

Now the question must be *why?* And where had he been killed?

Chapter Five

I t was time to speak to the Acting Chief Superintendent again.

Rutledge thanked Frederick Gooding for his assistance and turned to go. But he had a feeling, as the clerk politely accompanied him to the door and closed it almost silently behind him, that the man was more than curious about this visit from Scotland Yard and was busily speculating about what had precipitated it.

Then why had he not pressed for more information? Shown more concern? He had maintained the reserve that made chief clerks a formidable presence in any firm, giving Rutledge the French family genealogy but not much else in the way of real information. Was it an attempt to protect the head of the firm with silence until Gooding could find out for himself why the watch was in the hands of Scotland Yard? Or did he already know—or guess—how it had got there? Some indiscretion that would reflect unpleasantly on the firm's good name and reputation?

What sort of man was Lewis French?

Certainly the firm was not accustomed to receiving representatives of Scotland Yard. The police had no file on it. The question was, would Gooding himself try to locate Lewis French to warn him of the Yard's visit and possession of the watch?

Rutledge wished he had known enough beforehand not to have shown the watch to Gooding at all. But it had been the only lead he'd had when he knocked on the firm's door.

The Acting Chief Superintendent was in his office when Rutledge returned to the Yard, and according to Gibson, there was no one in there with him.

Rutledge knocked at the door, then opened it as Markham called, "Come."

Joel Markham had come through the ranks as Bowles had done but so far seemed to hold no grudge against men who had been to University. He was a burly man, fair hair beginning to recede, rather avuncular in appearance, but it would have been a mistake to think his easy manner was weakness. His hard green eyes told another story.

He considered Rutledge as he gestured to a chair. "I expect you have something to tell me about that accident in Chelsea. Just this morning I was asking Sergeant Gibson if we were to be favored with word on the result of your inquiry."

Rutledge smiled. "I've only just found the last piece of the puzzle regarding the dead man. And I am forced to the conclusion that he was murdered, his body brought to Chelsea, and left there on the street without identification in the hope that he might not be identified either in the near future or ever, depending on how clever the police were in learning more about him."

He went on to explain about the watch and the queries from other parts of the country, and finally his visit to the wine merchants.

"And no one had reported this man French as missing?"

"He was in Essex, according to the clerk. He may have come to town on a personal matter. He was recently engaged; it could have had something to do with a ring or other arrangements. Whatever it was, no one appears to have had any reason to worry until now."

"Then you'd best get yourself to Essex before they do miss the man. Catch them before they hear the news from someone else." Markham considered Rutledge. "You drive your own motorcar, I hear. Why is that? Why not the train like everyone else?"

Rutledge could feel himself stiffening. How to answer this man without telling more than he wished to be generally known?

"The war, sir." It was curt almost to the point of rudeness, but he was still struggling with the question.

"The war?" Markham prompted.

He'd been buried alive when a shell landed too near his sector, and all that had saved him was the dead man's body flung on top of him. Only, the dead man was Hamish MacLeod, whom he'd just been forced to execute for disobeying an order under fire. He'd never quite got over owing his life to the man to whom he'd delivered the coup de grâce mere seconds before the shell exploded. The young Scottish corporal had not wanted to die. But he would not lead his men back into the teeth of a German machine-gun nest when they'd lost so many already in futile attempts to silence it. Rutledge had wanted to spare him—but his corporal's very public refusal had left him no options. The claustrophobia he'd endured since then had been nearly unbearable. Nor had he been able to free himself of Hamish or that memory.

He said after a moment, "I took too many trains then. Packed with frightened men on their way to be slaughtered. Hours of watching them struggle to be brave. Watching them write last letters, pray to whatever God they believed in, or simply sit, staring at their own fate. I swore I'd never take another one again if I could help it."

It was as close to the truth as he could come. He waited for the Acting Chief Superintendent to react.

Markham studied him closely for a moment, then nodded. "I appreciate your candor. All right, drive if it suits you. What I want is results. I don't care, within reason, how you go about getting them."

Rutledge managed to thank him and get himself out of the office. It had begun to close in on him, making him want to stand up and fight his way out, away from those all-seeing green eyes and the feeling that he couldn't breathe. The panic of being cornered with no possible escape and disgracing himself into the bargain.

Once in the passage, he took as deep a breath as he could manage and tried to steady himself. He could feel the perspiration breaking out on his forehead, his mouth dry as a desert.

And then as swiftly as it had come, his anxiety dissipated as he walked on to his office, grateful not to encounter anyone along the way. But he could feel his heart still hammering in his chest for several minutes afterward.

Essex. He forced himself to think about the journey ahead. He began to collect what he would need to take with him, and that steadied him. Markham had come too close to the truth. For an instant, Rutledge had wondered if Bowles had said something to Markham. Or if the Acting Chief Superintendent had found something in his file. Rutledge had always suspected there must be something there.

He shook himself. His own imagination had made more of the situation that it had warranted.

Walking out the door, Rutledge located Gibson and told him where he was going and why. The sergeant listened and then asked, "Should I advise the Inspector in Norfolk that you'll be looking into his missing man while you're in Essex?"

"It will depend on what I discover about French. So far no one seems to be alarmed about him. If he's as busy a man as he appears to be, it's odd that a week has passed without someone needing to contact him. But then his senior clerk is perfectly competent."

Gibson nodded. "Then I'll hold off."

Rutledge started down the stairs. And stopped to add, "I'd like you to look into Frederick Gooding, the clerk at French, French, and Traynor."

"Any particular reason?" Gibson asked.

Rutledge considered the question. There was nothing he could put his finger on except for that one change in the man's demeanor. "Thoroughness," he said finally and continued on his way down the stairs.

He went home, packed his valise, wrote a note to his sister, Frances, to drop into a postbox on his way, and set out for Essex.

He had friends on the Thetford Road outside Bury St. Edmunds, so he knew a good bit about the general area. Dedham had been listed in the Domesday Book as a Saxon town, its history even older than that by several centuries. Situated on the River Stour with a year-round ford, it had prospered as an agricultural community and from an influx of Flemish weavers. Wool had made it rich, like so many towns, and when wool was no longer king, it had settled into genteel obscurity. But the town had produced one famous son, the artist John Constable.

Traffic was light, and Rutledge crossed the Thames before stopping for a cup of tea and a sandwich. He'd had nothing since breakfast, and the pub was pleasant, with a terrace in back that ran down to a little stream. The sun was warm, the air benevolent, and he was tempted to stay longer. But it was important to reach Dedham before news of his visit to the clerk in London came to their ears. The firm had a telephone, and it was not unlikely for the family to have a way of contacting London when French was in Essex.

The shortening of the summer days caught up with Rutledge, and it was dusk before he drove through Dedham and found the French property well outside the town. At the turning, he looked to see if there was another village beyond the house where he could stop for the night. But if there was, he couldn't pick out lights through the wood that extended in that direction.

A large scrolled *F* adorned the graceful wrought-iron gates, and griffins stood watch on the tall stone posts, their wings folded.

The gates stood open, and he drove up the long, looping drive until he came to the house. It was not as large as he'd expected, but the size was perfect for the proportions. The dark red brick, faced with white stone, was illuminated by his headlamps as he swung into the loop of the drive. Lamps were lit on either side of the door, and the knocker he saw, as he got out and walked up the two shallow steps, was in the shape of a tropical flower. Hibiscus?

He lifted it and let it fall. After a time, an older woman dressed in black opened the door to him and asked his business.

Rutledge said, "I've come to speak to Mr. French. Mr. Rutledge."

"I'm afraid you've missed him. He returned to London ten days ago."

"I'm sorry to hear that. Is there anyone else in the family in residence at the moment?"

"Miss French is here. Shall I ask if she's receiving visitors?"

"Yes, thank you." He smiled.

She was not taken in and left him standing there, the door ajar.

From where he stood, Rutledge could see part of a polished wood floor that ran down the left side of a staircase—the carved mahogany newel post was just visible. A painting graced the wall between two closed doors, and the table beneath it was Queen Anne, he thought. The painting itself appeared to be modern rather than the usual Italianate landscape. As in the style of the French Impressionists, the subject was not the French countryside but a vast grassy slope, grazing sheep in the distance, and in the foreground, an old man dressed in what appeared to be a hooded cape, leaning on a shepherd's crook. There was something about the figure that spoke of such utter loneliness that Rutledge turned away.

It seemed that Howard French and his descendants had not flaunted their newfound wealth by renovating and enlarging their country house. No grand lobby with marble floors and statuary, to awe the visitor. He wondered if that indicated how little they used this house, or if they preferred to be comfortable here and entertained in London. An interesting insight into the man who had given his heirs a timepiece to be passed down to posterity. Solid, dependable, useful.

The maid returned to tell him that Miss French would receive him in the sitting room.

He followed her to a door down the passage. She tapped lightly and then opened it to announce him.

And the sitting room showed that he'd been right about the house. It was comfortable and well used, although the carpet and furnishings were of the best quality.

The woman standing by the hearth didn't resemble the portraits he'd seen in London in any way except for her coloring. Her features were—he couldn't be kinder than that—plain. And the dress she wore, a dark blue that made her skin appear sallow, did nothing for her appearance.

She said, in a pleasant but cool voice, "Mr. Rutledge." And waited for him to speak.

"I apologize for coming to call at such a late hour," he said. "I need to speak to your brother, Mr. French."

"As I think you were told, he left for London last week."

"Yes, which surprises me, as he wasn't at the firm's offices on Leadenhall Street."

"It was a private matter that took him to the city." She waited again, but when he didn't fill the silence, she added, "I was not best pleased, I can tell you. He left me with the final preparations for our cousin's arrival."

"Was he expecting to meet anyone in particular?"

"I have no idea." He could read the annoyance in her eyes. "If you want the truth, he often leaves me to finish whatever needs to be done. He finds household matters infinitely boring. His words, not mine.

I would not at all be surprised if his pressing matter was merely an excuse. May I ask what brings you all the way to Essex? You aren't carrying news of our cousin's instant arrival, I hope. We've not yet aired the beds."

"I'm afraid not." They had remained standing, and he said, "Could we be seated, Miss French? This will take a little time to explain."

He thought at first she was going to refuse. Then after the briefest hesitation, she offered him a chair and took the one opposite his.

"If this is a business matter," she warned him, "I know nothing about wine, Madeira, or shipping. You've wasted your journey."

He took the watch out of his pocket and showed it to her. "Do you recognize this, by any chance?"

She did, he could see that. But she took it from him and looked at it more closely. "If I didn't know better I would say that this belonged to my brother. But he was wearing his when he left. I'd swear to it." She passed it back to him, then said with severity, "Just what do you expect to gain by coming here? Are you suggesting that I should buy this watch back from you? I'm not a fool, Mr. Rutledge, and I think it's time you left."

She was on the point of rising to reach for the bellpull when he said, "I'm from Scotland Yard, Miss French."

Sinking down again into her chair, she stared at him.

"I gave my name as Rutledge. It's Inspector Rutledge." He showed her his identification, but she didn't take it. Her eyes were riveted on his.

"What has he done? My brother? Are we insolvent? Has he been embezzling, or does this have to do with my cousin's visit? Is he involved?"

"I have no idea," Rutledge answered. "We were called to Chelsea some days ago to investigate a body that had been discovered in Huntingdon Street. There was no identification on the body, but we did find the watch—"

She was on her feet before he could finish, pacing to the hearth, her face set.

"If a dead man had that watch," she said huskily, "then something has happened to my brother. He would not part with it willingly. Don't leave me in suspense. Did this man kill my brother? Is that what you are trying to tell me? Please—"

Rutledge hadn't considered theft of the watch from French himself. It had seemed to him that the watch had been overlooked when the dead man's pockets had been emptied.

Still, there was the faint likeness to the portrait he'd seen in the firm's office.

Hamish, suddenly there again in Rutledge's mind, said, "There's more here than ye knew."

"We feared," Rutledge said carefully, "that the dead man was the victim, not the attacker."

"My brother wouldn't kill anyone. Why should he? He has everything he has ever needed." Was there bitterness behind those words?

This time she did reach for the bellpull and in her agitation jerked it hard. "How did you come here, Inspector? By train, I should imagine."

"I have my own motorcar with me."

"So much the better. You will drive me to London, if you please, and we'll get to the bottom of this business."

"Miss French. There's the possibility that your brother was the man we found in the street," he said, trying to prepare her.

But she ignored him. "Nonsense. He didn't have an enemy in the world. Well, at least not in London."

And what did she mean by that? The interview was not going in the direction he'd anticipated.

"You are telling me that there is someone in Dedham who wishes him ill?"

"Not in Dedham," she retorted impatiently. "In the village here.

Did you not come through it on your way to the house? There was a Dominican abbey here, and when it was torn down by Henry the Eighth, a hamlet sprang up in the ruins. Servants from the abbey, dispossessed brothers— Ah, Nan, there you are. Would you please pack a small valise for me? I'm needed in London at once."

When Nan had gone, Miss French turned to Rutledge again. "Where was I? Oh, the village. My brother was engaged to a young woman who lived close by the church, and then he jilted her for someone else. She didn't take that very well. If he'd been attacked here, I'd have pointed the finger at her. But in London? I don't believe it."

"She could have followed him there," Rutledge pointed out.

"Yes, yes, I know, but how likely is it? She doesn't have a motorcar and she doesn't know the city."

She looked at the mantel clock. "If you'll excuse me, I'll ask the kitchen staff to put up sandwiches and a Thermos of tea."

And she was gone.

Shock took people in many different ways, Rutledge thought. And Miss French needed to be busy now, demonstrating that she was in control of the situation. He had a feeling she would fall apart if she was called on to identify the dead man and realized that it was indeed her brother.

Or had he jumped to conclusions based on a likeness that was not very strong?

On the whole, he didn't believe he'd missed his identification. The man's clothing had been that of a gentleman, and in the dark, the watch might easily have been overlooked by a killer in a hurry to rid himself of a corpse.

"Or was too well known to be of any value," Hamish put in.

And that was true as well. But first things first. If Miss French was determined to travel to London, then so be it. He'd drive her. The body had to be identified.

Twenty minutes later, dressed in traveling clothes and followed by

Nan hurrying after her with a valise in one hand and a picnic basket in the other, Miss French opened the sitting room door and said, "Thank you, Nan, I'll telephone you from London. I'm ready, Inspector."

She had very little to say on the long journey, and he was tired, in no mood to make light conversation. In the reflected light of the headlamps he could see only her profile, and it was set, as if her thoughts were already in London, facing whatever dreadful thing she might find there.

He could understand, but she had been determined not to listen, and he had had no choice but to let her have her way. And it was far better to put off the final shock until they reached the city. She would have long enough to mourn afterward.

It was very late when they drove into London. They had only stopped for petrol and to eat the sandwiches, drink the tea. Miss French said, rousing herself, "I didn't call the house to tell them I'm coming. They'd have had it ready for my brother anyway. If you will take me there, I'll be waiting at whatever time you suggest in the morn-ing. I don't feel up to doing more tonight."

"Yes, that makes good sense," he told her. "Will nine be too early?"

"Thank you. I doubt I'll sleep, but at least I—at least I shan't spend what's left of the night having nightmares."

He carried the valise and the picnic basket to the door as she pulled the bell.

The house was in a handsome square, although as in Essex it was not pretentious. Rutledge was beginning to understand Howard French. The founder of the present firm had inherited a business that was centuries old, even if he'd given it a new and very prosperous direction. But he appeared to have preferred to be thought of as old money and refrained from showing off his newfound wealth. Even the pocket watches passed down to the present generation had been elegant and expensive, but in perfect taste. Rutledge found himself wondering if the man had had hopes of a title from the Queen or at the very least from Edward VII. George V, the present king, hadn't consorted with wealthy men in quite the same way his father had.

The door opened finally, and a young man stood there, his clothes hastily thrown on and his face reflecting his shock at seeing Miss French on the doorstep, much less, Rutledge thought, at this late hour of the night and with a valise, no maid, and a stranger in tow.

"M-Miss French," he stammered, then got himself under control. "Is everything— I mean, please, come in."

They stepped into the entrance hall, and Rutledge handed over the valise and basket.

"I'm sorry to disturb you at this hour, Robert, but I need to speak to my brother. Is he here?"

"No, Miss—er—he's in Essex, I was told, and not expected back in London until this Friday."

She turned to glance at Rutledge, willing him not to speak. Then she said to Robert, "Well, then, I've come ahead. I'll be spending the night, what's left of it, and possibly tomorrow night as well. If you'll tell Mrs. Rule. I don't require much in the way of food, but as she will remember, I do like it on time."

"Yes, Miss, I'll tell her. Is there anything else you need? Shall I wake up Nell and ask her to attend you?"

"No. I'm not used to a lady's maid at home, and I don't need one in London," she said briskly, then thanked him for thinking about Nell. Turning to Rutledge, she held out her hand. "Nine o'clock then, Mr. Rutledge."

It was dismissal, and he was glad to go now that he'd heard for himself that French wasn't staying at the London address.

He turned and left. Robert had followed him to the door and locked it behind him.

Back in the motorcar, Rutledge let in the clutch and drove off, making his way to his own flat.

He wondered how much longer Miss French could sustain the pretense that all was well. Too many factors pointed to her brother's disappearance, if not to his death. He wasn't in London or in Essex; the watch was in the possession of the Yard; and even Gooding could give them no information regarding French's whereabouts. Or did the clerk know something that Rutledge did not?

It was an interesting possibility. Whatever French had decided to do with himself, it was unlikely that he would cut off ties with his firm.

With that thought in his mind, Rutledge walked through the door of the flat and went directly to his bedroom.

For a mercy he fell asleep almost at once and did not dream for what was left of his night. It was a measure of how long his day had been.

He did not think, when he handed Miss French into the motorcar the next morning at nine o'clock on the dot, that she had slept at all.

There were puffy rings under her eyes, making her appear even plainer, and the effort to keep herself calm showed in the tension in her jaw.

"Please. Let's get this over with as quickly as possible. I'll agree to anything, just let it be done," she said to him.

He drove to the hospital, where earlier he had made arrangements for the body to be viewed, and led her into the bowels of the building to the unmarked door halfway down the long poorly lit corridor.

He opened the door for Miss French, but she pulled back, her hands shaking. "I— Let me have a moment."

Rutledge let the door swing to and waited. He thought she might faint, she was so pale. But she managed to collect herself finally, her breathing still a little rapid, her eyes already filling with nervous tears. With a nod, she indicated she was ready, and he took her inside the large, chilly room that smelled of formaldehyde.

Ignoring his hand at her elbow, she marched across to the lone table, where a sheet-shrouded body lay under a stark lamp. It was easy to see the human outline—the peaked tent of the feet, the amorphous shape of a skull. She swallowed hard, her head jerking with the effort.

A middle-aged man appeared from another room and came to remove the sheet from the dead man's face.

Miss French reached the table just as he gently placed the last fold across the throat, showing only the face. The dust and stones that had been caught in the flesh and the hair had been washed away. Save for the abrasions, like little freckles down the ridges of the forehead, cheekbone, and chin, the skin was clear.

She was clutching her handbag now as if it were a lifeline. Glancing down at her, Rutledge realized that her eyes were closed, probably had been as they had walked across the room. After a moment she opened them, and then she swayed, and he touched her arm to steady her.

"Oh, dear God," she said in a voice that was barely audible. "Oh, my God."

"Is this your brother, Miss French?"

She leaned against him for an instant, and then recovered, moving away as if embarrassed by such brief weakness.

"You must tell me, Miss French. So that the attendant and I can hear your statement clearly," Rutledge prompted.

"No. No, it is not my brother Lewis." Her voice echoed around them, high pitched, as if she couldn't control it.

And then she did faint.

Chapter Six

Rutledge carried Miss French into a small waiting room that the attendant pointed out to him, and it was not long before she came to.

Her statement had taken him completely by surprise. But he didn't press her for more information until her color had returned and she seemed to be aware of her surroundings again. She wheeled around, as if expecting to see the table with the covered body somewhere just behind her.

"It's all right," he said quietly. "This is a private room. We can stay here as long as you like."

She relaxed and closed her eyes again. After a moment she said, "Michael was buried in France. My elder brother. I didn't— We never saw him."

"But you saw Lewis just now?" He wasn't convinced she knew what she was saying.

She opened her eyes, a little of her spirit evident again. "I have told you. That was not Lewis. Although at first—the scratches on his face—I saw those first. But it wasn't my brother."

"You are absolutely certain then."

"Absolutely." She saw the glass of water he was holding, took it, then gave it back to him, her hand shaking too much to try to sip it. "Could we leave, please? I seem to smell that odor still. It's making me quite ill."

Other witnesses had said much the same thing. Rutledge himself had become inured to it. But he had never become inured to the dead, even after four years in France, where bodies had been almost as common as the rats underfoot.

He gave her his arm, and they walked together down the long passage back to the motorcar. Once there she seemed to revive completely, pulling on her gloves and fiddling a little with the buttons at the wrists as if to distract her thoughts.

When they had left the hospital behind, she said, "I can't understand why you thought that man might be Lewis."

"The watch, of course, which sent me to French, French and Traynor. The clerk there identified it, and he told me Lewis French was in Essex. I went there to find out. And he's not at the London house. Where, then, is he?"

"I have no idea. My brother has been his own man since he left for University."

"Was he in the war?"

"No. He's subject to seizures. The Army wanted no part of him. He might as well have had the plague. It bothered him more than he was willing to admit."

Which meant there were no war wounds to use for identification purposes. Rutledge was still not satisfied that the dead man was not French.

There was also the likeness to the portrait of Howard French.

As if she sensed his reaction, Miss French said, "My father had a mistress, I think. I was never told, of course, but I remember my mother crying sometimes when he seemed to be too busy to come home. It wasn't until much later that I understood why his absences upset her. And when he died—he outlived my mother—there was a woman's photograph in his desk. It had one of those hidden compartments, and I found it quite by accident. Perhaps my mother had found it as well. I can't say. I did wonder— I'd look sometimes at the village children, searching for a likeness. But of course if he'd been involved with someone locally, it would have been the height of foolishness. Gossip would have ferreted out the truth, wouldn't it? Perhaps she lived in London. I don't know."

"You are telling me that the man in the mortuary could be your illegitimate half brother?"

She took a deep breath. "Women do have children out of wedlock." And then without warning, she began to cry. "It could have been Lewis lying there. I haven't got over Michael's death. What if I'd lost Lewis as well?" She fumbled in her bag for a handkerchief and buried her face in it.

They had almost reached the London house when she said, her voice thick with tears, "I'm so sorry. It's the shock of everything. And I parted with Lewis on bad terms. Over *airing bedrooms*. I was so angry— I know I haven't married, I know I haven't got a house of my own, but I'm not a servant, and I couldn't bear to be treated as one."

He was glad to hand her over Robert. Between them they got her into the house, and as the door swung shut behind the footman and the woman on the verge of collapse, Rutledge could hear the harried young man's voice saying, "I'll call Mrs. Rule, shall I? She'll know what to do."

H e was to dine with Frances that night, and he was twenty minutes late.

As soon as he'd left Miss French in the hands of her brother's household, Rutledge had returned to the wine merchant's offices in the City. Frederick Gooding came to collect him after he'd been greeted by another young clerk, this one named Simmons. Gooding conducted him past the portraits and into an office where bills of lading, orders, and ships' manifests nearly covered the top of a large partners desk.

"I've been going over the books," he said in apology. "That's one of my duties. The late Mr. French, Mr. Lewis's father, believed that a quarterly review of accounts discouraged embezzlement and gave him a clear picture of where the firm stood. Where the wine was going, who had purchased it, what bottoms we were shipping it in, and what the output of the vineyards was, as well as the status of wine being aged in the main office, in Funchal."

"And how does the firm's business stand?"

"Quite well, as a matter of fact. Since the end of the war we've been very fortunate in rebuilding our clientele and finding ships that can carry our wares. Shipping took a terrible blow, what with submarines and raiders attacking convoys. But I daresay the newer vessels have a faster turnaround rate than the old ones. There's always a silver lining." Shifting the subject, he said, "And have you been to Essex? Have you spoken to Mr. French?"

"He was not in Essex," Rutledge said. "Nor is he in the house in London. His sister is in residence there now. She has no suggestions for finding him. I was hoping that you might help me."

Gooding frowned. "This is most unusual. When he's away, Mr. French is always careful to tell me precisely where he will be at any given time—within reason, of course—so that I can reach him if there is an emergency. If he says he's in Essex, then he is in Essex."

"Unless of course he'd dead."

Gooding's face paled. "Don't even say that. There is no one to take over the English half of the firm if something happens to Mr. French."

"There's his sister."

"Sadly, I don't believe she knows enough about the business to make sound judgments." He studied Rutledge's face for a moment. "You aren't— You had Mr. French's watch. He is never without it. Is there something you haven't told me?"

Rutledge said, "Before I go into that, there's something else I need to discuss with you. I'm told that Mr. French's father had a second family, one that his wife and children were not aware of. Is this true?"

If he'd suggested that the late Mr. Laurence French had possessed two heads and was born a Hottentot, Gooding couldn't have looked more astonished.

"If the Mr. French I served was engaged in such an affair," he said after a moment, "he would not have confided in me. If you are after such details about his private life, I suggest you speak to his solicitors. The firm of Hayes and Hayes."

But the Mr. French the clerk had served was an older man—and a junior clerk would have been the last person he'd have confided in. Still, this meant that there was no gossip in the firm about the man. He had been very discreet. Not surprising if he was expecting his son and his nephew to come into the business at some future date.

"I had reason to believe that Mr. French was killed last week in a motorcar accident," Rutledge said. "Miss French went this morning to identify the body. She didn't know the man."

"Then it wasn't her brother. I should think she knows him better than anyone."

"Will you go with me to look at the body?"

"No," Gooding said firmly. "If I disagreed with her for any reason at all, whose word would you take?"

"I should be forced to take hers. But I should continue to search for Lewis French."

"Then my word would be superfluous."

And Gooding wouldn't budge from that position.

In the end, Rutledge went to the Inns of Court and found the street where Hayes and Hayes had their chambers. The elder Mr. Hayes agreed to see him. Rutledge said nothing about the dead man. Instead he began with the late Mr. French's will.

"I should like to know if he made any provisions for a second family, one that his wife and children knew nothing about."

Hayes regarded him with what Rutledge could only describe as hooded eyes, although the impression came from the second fold of skin that age had deposited on the lids. His eyes were a cold gray, deep set. Bristling gray brows like an overgrown thicket jutted out above them. Rutledge found himself thinking that such a fierce scowl would be a very effective weapon in a courtroom.

"I could of course show you a copy of the will," Hayes said finally. "But I can assure you that there was no mention made in it of a mistress or children born out of wedlock." Rutledge was about to speak, but Hayes held up a blue-veined hand. "Nor was there a codicil setting out such an arrangement. Why should you believe that such a provision existed?"

"Miss French went with me this morning to look at a dead man I believed to be her brother. It was very difficult for her. I was already fairly certain that it was Lewis French. She assured me it was not. And she told me later that her mother had been very concerned about the elder Mr. French's fidelity. It would account for a resemblance I'd noticed between the dead man and a portrait at the wine merchant's, if the victim had been her father's child by a mistress."

"Then she is greatly mistaken. Her father as far as I know was faithful to his wife. It was *his* father, Mr. Howard French, who had an affair before he was married with a young woman who died in childbirth. The child was adopted by one of *his* father's servants. We have no other information about that child. Presumably he was never told of his true parentage."

Which would explain, Rutledge thought, why a nervous and rather insecure wife might imagine her own husband had strayed.

He said, pursuing that thought, "Was Lewis French's mother wealthy?"

"She was very wealthy. Her father had made a fortune in shipping, and with the marriage came a very satisfactory arrangement for the French and Traynor wines to be carried around the world in that firm's bottoms."

Small wonder the woman was insecure, more especially if she had been as plain as her daughter.

"Then the man in the mortuary could well have been a descendant of Howard French's—er—indiscretion."

"It is entirely possible. Although highly unlikely."

But how did he come by that watch? And where was Lewis French?

"Do you know the name of the family that was given the child to foster?"

"There is no record to my knowledge. Mr. Howard French provided for them at the time, and no bequests were made at his death or that of his son. Lewis French's father."

It was the ideal way to handle such a youthful indiscretion. The servants would be given a tidy sum to move elsewhere and take the child with them. A gamekeeper, a groom, a coachman, a head gardener. No one would think anything about a family suddenly coming into a small inheritance from a distant relative and deciding to move to the cottage in Wales or Kent or Cumberland that had been left to them. And it would be surprising to find anyone who remembered such an obscure event so long afterward.

"The baptismal record? Was there one?"

"The child would have been baptized in whatever village the family chose. Or not, as the case may be."

If the servants were Chapel, then it would be almost impossible to find any record at all.

A dead end. And Rutledge disliked dead ends.

"If the man in the mortuary is not Lewis French, then where is he? And why is he not in Essex or in his London home?"

"I can't answer that," Mr. Hayes replied. "Not from any reluctance on my part. Simply the fact that we don't know the answer. But if there was something he wished to do without his sister's knowledge, then it's his business and not that of Scotland Yard."

Rutledge left soon after. His experience of dealing with solicitors had long been one of accepting that they would answer the questions put to them precisely and generally quite truthfully, with very little additional information volunteered, unless giving that was also to their advantage. For all he knew, Mr. Hayes held in the firm's boxes the solution to his inquiry—but to unlock that bit of information would require a prodigious leap of imagination on Rutledge's part to come up with the right question. He smiled to himself at the thought. Still, Hayes was not concealing information concerning the whereabouts of Lewis French. Of that Rutledge was nearly sure.

He carried this knotty problem with him to dinner, although he tried to hide his distraction from his sister. Frances was all too perceptive when it came to her brother, and she soon had him in a better frame of mind.

But as he drove home at the end of the evening, he had come to accept Miss French's statement as the final word on the identity of the man who had been left on Huntingdon Street in Chelsea. Whether he was satisfied or not, there was no alternative.

The next morning Rutledge gave an oral report to the Acting Chief Superintendent.

Markham listened, nodding from time to time, until Rutledge had finished. Then he leaned forward in his chair, his brows drawn together in a frown.

"You've told me who our inconvenient corpse is not. You can't tell me who killed him or why he possessed a watch he had no right to. What's more, you've lost its lawful owner, Lewis French."

Rutledge took a deep breath. "French has a fiancée in Essex. I'd like to speak to her before Miss French returns from London. There was no reason to call on her during my first visit. French may have confided his intentions to her rather than to his sister."

"They weren't on good terms, the brother and sister?"

"I have a feeling that French imposed on his sister. She maintains the family home, and she was in the midst of preparing for a cousin's arrival. She was rather angry with French for leaving when she could have used his help."

Markham linked his fingers, stretched them, then uncoupled them. "The dead man's not the cousin?"

"I should think Miss French would have recognized him. The wine merchant's clerk is awaiting news of Traynor's travel arrangements. He's returning to England from the firm's office in Funchal."

"And what is Funchal when it's at home?" Markham asked testily.

"The principal city on the Portuguese island of Madeira. It's where French, French and Traynor have done business for three generations. Apparently before that, they were solely London importers of wines and spirits."

Markham considered Rutledge with raised eyebrows. "You aren't telling me you wish to travel there, are you?"

Rutledge smiled inwardly, remembering that Yorkshiremen were notoriously tightfisted. "I'm sure any information I need can come through the police there."

Markham sat back in his chair, his face clearing. "Off to Essex with you, then. And bring back results, if you please."

An hour later, Rutledge was on the road again, heading toward Dedham.

What results? he asked himself as he drove through London traffic and turned east, then north.

Hamish, restless in the back of his mind, reflecting Rutledge's own unsettled mood, said, "Ye ken, ye canna' return now withoot something."

* * *

His first duty was to look for the nearest local police station and speak to the constable there. On his earlier visit, there had been no need to pay a courtesy call, but now there was, and Rutledge was hoping not to have to deal with the larger force in Dedham. Smaller police stations, often with a single constable on duty, generally knew the people in their villages better. Nor was there that tendency toward resentment of the Yard infringing on another man's turf.

Passing the French house, Rutledge found the village of Stratford St. Hilary less than a mile beyond. There was no sign of the Dominican abbey, although a wide green could well have been the site of the order's church and outbuildings. If so, then this had been no more than a satellite community rather than a major branch of the order. Clustered around the green were a number of rather handsome houses and shops, and a small, ancient building that was a pub now—The Tun and Turtle, according to the sign—which could have been here in coaching days. Too small for a hotel, it probably offered a room or two to visitors when necessary. He could just see a stream running past the back garden and winding away among a thin stand of trees. On the far side of the stream he glimpsed the chimney pots of another large house. He wondered if wool had built the small church or if it had been a private chapel in the days of the abbey, for without it the village was no more than large hamlet.

Rutledge found the police station sandwiched between a stationer's shop and a narrow-fronted bakery. The bakery was already closed, but as he passed the door, the faint smell of yeast breads and cinnamon lingered in the warm evening air.

The constable was not in. But he'd left a message on a small board by the door for anyone who needed him. It read:

AT HOME

There was no indication where HOME might be.

Rutledge had counted on the constable to give him the name and direction of French's fiancée. The other source for information was of course the rector.

He left the motorcar where it was and walked toward the church. It sat on a slight knoll, and in the churchyard that sloped down to the street he could see mossy and lichen-etched stones leaning crazily in front of much later ones that marched up the slope to disappear around the apse before reappearing at the far side.

The French family monument was ornate, and in the shadow of the tower. But there were a number of other grand mausoleums and weeping angels in the centers of family plots. As he stepped out of the motorcar, Rutledge could see TRAYNOR incised in the base of a stone, the shaft broken and draped with mourning in a very Victorian concept.

The Rectory was a modest house up a lane overlooking the churchyard.

Rutledge walked there as the sun dropped behind the yews that encircled three sides of the low wall.

A man in shirtsleeves was standing on a high ladder, painting the house trim.

Rutledge called to him as he came up the path, "Is the rector in?"

The man looked down at him. "Sadly he is out. Is there something I can do for you?"

"I'm looking for Lewis French. He isn't at home. Nor is his sister—"

The man spilled a great dollop of paint as he lifted his brush out of the jar without wiping it. "Drat!" he exclaimed. Then to Rutledge he went on: "Miss French isn't at home?"

"I believe she's still in London."

"London? Is something wrong?"

"Should there be?" Rutledge asked.

The man came down the ladder. "She never leaves St. Hilary. Well.

Only to visit the shops in Dedham." He looked ruefully at his paint-stained fingers. "I can't offer to shake hands. But we don't run to rectors here. I'm the curate. Williams is my name."

He was fairly young, thirty perhaps, and he walked with a limp. When he saw Rutledge had noticed it, he grimaced. "The war. I was a soldier and then a chaplain after I was invalided out. But what's this about Agnes French going to London?"

"She was looking for her brother. She didn't find him. I thought perhaps his fiancée might know where he went after he left the house nearly a fortnight ago. Apparently he hadn't confided in his sister."

"He seldom does," Williams replied with a shake of the head.

"They don't get on?" Rutledge asked with interest.

"I wouldn't put it that strongly. Both of the brothers—that's Michael, who died in the war, and Lewis—were often in London with their father, being introduced to the firm. Agnes was a homebody. She never went anywhere."

"By choice or by lack of invitation?"

"I don't really know," Williams said, considering the question, his head to one side. "I wasn't here then, of course. I've been told that she looked after her mother throughout her last illness and then took care of her father after his stroke. It's what daughters do. Unmarried ones, most particularly."

"Had the sons—Lewis and Michael—visited Madeira?" Rutledge asked.

"Yes, from a very early age—twelve, I've been told. But Agnes never showed an interest in travel."

"Or pretended she had none," Rutledge said, "after being excluded."

"She never gave the impression she felt excluded."

But then, Rutledge thought, she wouldn't have shown how she felt, if it had hurt her. Her general disposition spoke volumes.

"Lewis is responsible for the management of the London office,

I understand." When Williams nodded as he cleaned paint from his fingers with a cloth that was already saturated, Rutledge went on. "Would Miss French take a position in the firm if anything happened to her brother?"

"Oh, I'm sure she wouldn't. She's had no training, you see. There's the cousin, Traynor, of course. It's not as if there's no one at the helm." He gestured over their heads. "The last time Traynor was in England he paid for the Rectory chimneys to be repaired. Before that the house was nearly uninhabitable for weeks, with smoke filling the rooms. I wasn't here then, it was before the war, but my predecessor told me what we owed to his generosity. Sorry. I've wandered off the subject. Why should Miss French be looking for her brother?"

"You must ask her when she returns. Meanwhile, I'd like to find Lewis French's fiancée."

"Yes, of course. Mary Ellen Townsend lives in Dedham. There's a house not far from the church. You can't miss it, there's a plate on the door just before it—her father's the local doctor and that's his surgery." He glanced up at his own house. "I've lost the light, haven't I? Well, I can't say that I'm sorry. I really can't abide painting, but there's no one else, is there? I'm sorry, I don't believe I caught your name?"

He hadn't given it. "Rutledge."

"I'll bid you a good day, Mr. Rutledge. I hope you enjoy your stay in St. Hilary."

Rutledge walked back to the motorcar, listening to Hamish in the back of his mind.

"Ye didna' tell him the whole truth. Or who you are," the soft Scottish voice said from behind Rutledge's left shoulder, where he'd so often been standing in the trenches. He wasn't there, of course. But Rutledge had never had the courage to look and see if he was when Hamish MacLeod was speaking.

"Sometimes the whole truth is not the best choice," Rutledge answered aloud and earned himself a stare from the man walking a small dog. He hadn't seen them in the gathering dusk.

He drove back to Dedham and quickly found his way to the surgery, avoiding construction in the square.

It was located in a smaller brick building adjacent to the three-story house where Townsend and his family lived. Leaving his motorcar just down the High Street, Rutledge walked back to knock at the house door.

A maid answered, and he asked for Miss Townsend.

"Your name, sir?"

"Rutledge," he said. "I'm looking for Lewis—Lewis French. He isn't at his house, and it was suggested that he might be here or that Miss Townsend knew where he was going. It's urgent that I find him. A matter of business."

"One moment, sir."

Two minutes later, a young woman came to the door. She was fair, with blue eyes—and quite pretty.

"I'm told you're looking for Lewis. I thought he'd left for London. Is something wrong?"

He looked up the street where an elderly couple was strolling in their direction, enjoying the warm evening. "May I come in?" he asked.

"Yes, of course."

She ushered him into a formal room where she offered him a seat, and then she hesitated before taking one herself, as if doing so would encourage him to stay longer than he should.

"I was told at the firm in London that I could find Lewis French here in Essex. But apparently he'd already left some days ago. His sister couldn't help me, but she thought you might know his plans."

That seemed to surprise her. "Did she? Well, I'm afraid I don't know anything myself. He was here on the Thursday before he left, for lunch, and he told me that he expected to get an early start for London the next day. He needed to reach his cousin in Madeira. He said something had come up that he wanted to discuss with Mr. Traynor."

"I'd heard that Mr. Traynor was on his way to England."

"Yes, but his travel plans were indefinite, and Lewis didn't want to wait for his arrival."

"Did he seem upset about whatever it was he needed to discuss with his cousin?"

"Not—upset. I had the feeling he was more annoyed, out of patience. He said he'd always wondered how he was going to solve the problem if it ever came up, and now that it was actually here, he could see he needed help. The clerk Gooding seemed to be the person Lewis always went to when he wanted advice, and I suggested that he telephone London rather than make the trip. But he shook his head and said that even Gooding couldn't work any magic here. Then he changed the subject, and we talked about other things."

. . . he'd always wondered how he was going to solve the problem if it ever came up, and now that it was actually here, he could see he needed help . . .

It would be easy to jump to the conclusion that what had disturbed Lewis was the sudden appearance of a member of the illegitimate line of the family. And if his mother had indeed been fearful that her husband was a philanderer, then he would have been primed to believe whatever he was told.

Had he met this man? What had happened? If the other man was dead, had Lewis French killed him and then disappeared?

Except for the watch, there would have been nothing to connect the French family with the dead man.

On the other hand, Lewis's problem could be a question of dealing with a shipping firm that was no longer satisfactory or changing bank managers. A matter in which the partners themselves would have to make a decision.

Hamish said, "Or how to deal wi' his sister, and her increasing outrage."

An interesting point. She herself had told Rutledge that she had quarreled with her brother before he set out for London.

Miss Townsend was still speaking. "Are you a friend of Lewis's? I don't believe I've heard him mention your name."

"I'm not surprised," Rutledge said. "I've only known him . . . officially."

Her face was lit by a smile. "I know very little about the business side," she admitted. "I don't think I've ever tasted Port or Madeira. My father doesn't care for wine or spirits."

"Yet you are marrying a man whose livelihood is wine."

"My father understands that. Of course he does. His feelings are personal."

Rutledge had run into this sort of thing before. He'd have been willing to bet that someone in the elder Townsend's family had been a drunkard.

"I'm so sorry I couldn't help you," Miss Townsend was saying.

It was dismissal, but he'd learned more than he'd counted on.

"Do you know if Mr. French was wearing his watch when you had lunch with him?"

"His watch?" She was completely lost. "Should I have had a reason to notice it?"

"No, not at all. I was thinking that perhaps he'd mislaid it—it could explain why he'd missed our appointment."

She smiled, her face clearing. "Lewis is always on time. No, there must have been some other reason."

He was just preparing to thank her and take his leave when the door opened and a portly man with fair hair and a mustache came into the room.

"Mary, I was told someone called."

"Papa, this is Mr. Rutledge. He's looking for Lewis. Something to do with the firm."

"Indeed."

"Thank you for your help, Miss Townsend. It's possible I just missed him in London. I'll try again. Good evening, sir."

Rutledge made his escape before Townsend could ask more questions than he was prepared to answer. And as he was opening the outer door, he heard the man's voice saying, "You have no business entertaining a stranger without a member of the family present. Furthermore, I shall tell French that he's not to send his business acquaintances—" The rest was cut off as Rutledge stepped outside.

As he walked back to the motorcar, he swore under his breath. Neither fish nor fowl nor good red herring . . . Why did the dead man have that watch? Or to turn it around another way, why was Lewis not wearing the watch? It was a symbol of who and what he was. Not something he was likely to give up easily.

Hamish said, "Unless it was no' for verra' long."

It occurred to Rutledge that French had palmed the man off with the watch and then looked for a chance to run him down. Then why hadn't he recovered the watch first thing? Had he been interrupted?

And that brought up another missing piece of property—Lewis French's motorcar. Had there been enough damage to make it impossible to drive into London without questions being asked? Was it somewhere in England where an unwitting smith was making repairs so that French could reappear? It would be impossible even for Gibson to trace such a small shop.

Rutledge drove back to the Sun, once an old coaching inn, and took a room for the night. It was too late to return to London anyway, and he could put the morning hours to very good use here.

I t was nine o'clock when he rang the bell at the French house. Nan opened the door and at once looked beyond Rutledge, as if expecting to see her mistress alighting from the motorcar.

He said, "I'm afraid Miss French has decided to stay in London for a few days. I've come to ask—did Mr. French leave his motorcar here or take it with him to London?"

She stared at him.

"The problem is, we can't seem to find him in London. If the motorcar is still here, perhaps he took a train."

Her face cleared. "I believe he drove himself, sir. He usually preferred it."

"Then very likely he stopped off to visit a friend."

"He could have. He wasn't expected in London for several days."

"And you saw him leave?"

She looked away and then back at him. "He left in the evening. He and Miss French had had words about readying the house for Mr. Traynor. I heard the door slam, and Miss French went out after him. Then she came back, dismissed me for the night, and went into her room. I thought she'd been crying and didn't want me to see."

"Did they often quarrel? Miss French and her brother?"

"Not often, sir. But she felt sometimes that he was unappreciative of all she did. And I must say, it was true. She told me once that she didn't envy Miss Townsend."

"Where were they to live when they married? Here? Or in London?"

"I expect in London."

He thanked her and left.

Coming out of the drive, Rutledge saw the curate, Mr. Williams, peddling his way. He waited for him, and Williams pulled up by the iron gates.

"Did you find what you were looking for?" the curate asked.

"Yes, thank you. Are you going into Dedham? I'll give you a lift."

"Nice of you! Shall I lash the bicycle to the boot?"

"Yes, you'll find rope in there." When Williams had finished and joined him in the motorcar, Rutledge said, "I haven't known Lewis French long. What sort of person is he?"

"Nice enough chap. I think the elder brother, Michael, was the pick of the family. Everyone had high hopes for him. But then he didn't come home from the war, more's the pity. Lewis has made a go of the firm, and his fits seem to have lessened with age."

Rutledge had forgot that Miss French had mentioned her brother's seizures. "Were they severe?"

"Not as a rule. But a time or two they were very bad. If he were very upset, the spells were worse. Dr. Townsend had to be called in once. French had bit his tongue rather badly. You've been asking a good many questions about the family, and French in particular. And you listen, which encourages confidences. Perhaps it's time to ask who you are?"

There was nothing for it but to give the curate a fair answer.

"My name is in fact Rutledge. And I'm an Inspector at Scotland Yard."

There was stunned silence. His companion turned to look at him, then stared straight ahead.

He could see the curate remembering everything he'd told Rutledge. A lonely man—there had been no sign of a wife—he'd talked freely, trusting that his instinct about people was right, and this stranger was what he seemed.

"Forgive me. I hope I have done no one any harm," he said at last, then paused. "If the Yard is involved, then we must be dealing with murder. Are you here about the victim? Or the killer? And what does the French family have to do with this business?"

"A dead man turned up on a quiet street in London. There was no identification, and we were at a loss to explain how he got there, where he'd died, and most urgent of all, who he was. But he was carrying a rather unusual timepiece. Somehow, whoever emptied his pockets missed it. Or for all we know, left it there on purpose. We investigated the watch, and it turned out the owner was one Lewis French. We thought we had identified our man. He was not French, as it happened. Still, we needed to know how he'd come by French's watch. But we haven't been able to find Mr. French. Or the motorcar in which he left his house over a fortnight ago."

"Dear God." As the whole of what he'd been told sank in, Williams shook his head.

"I'm afraid I can't help you. But have you spoken to Miss Townsend? Could she tell you where French had gone? Surely he wouldn't hare off on a whim without saying something to her. It's my understanding that he had planned to be here at least a week. That was the impression he gave when he came to services that first Sunday morning after he arrived from London. He told me there was a problem at one of the farms on the estate. Worm, he thought, and he was to speak to a man in Dedham about replacing the infected wood."

"And did he, do you know?"

"I expect he must have done, as later in the week I saw the carpenter's dray turning into the farm lane as I was coming back from visiting one of our parishioners."

That was the thing—in a village as small as St. Hilary, there were eyes everywhere. But if he was returning to London, French would have gone in the opposite direction, through Dedham.

"The assumption is that he stopped off to visit a friend on the way to London, and since he wasn't expected to return to French, French and Traynor straightaway, he didn't think to tell anyone his plans. But that seems odd to me. Gooding, the senior clerk in London, hasn't heard from him, and French had had a telephone put in at the house here expressly to allow him to stay in touch with his clerk whenever he was in Essex."

"I don't like the sound of this. Not at all."

"Precisely why the Yard has sent me here. Until now I've been very careful not to raise any alarms. But it's important to start a search now. He could have been set on and robbed. He could be injured or unable to report what happened."

"Have you spoken to our constable here in St. Hilary?"

"I stopped at the station yesterday. He wasn't in."

"I don't know that he'll be much help," Williams said skeptically.

"He knows his patch, and if anything had happened to French near St. Hilary, he'd have heard something by now. He keeps his ear to the ground. But he hasn't said anything, has he?"

"He would have no reason to be looking for French. I have to begin where he was last seen." He let the silence between them lengthen. He didn't think the curate had ever encountered murder, for he still appeared to be taking it all in. Then he asked, "Was French's father—or grandfather for that matter—ever involved with other women?"

"Involved with—not to my knowledge. And I've heard no gossip in that direction. How does this fit into murder?"

"Sometimes people left out of a will are vindictive. I understand that that watch has some significance in the family. Perhaps it has more value in that direction than if it were sold. If a thief tried to sell it, many jewelers would be suspicious."

"I see where you're going here. Still, why had your London victim been stripped of his identity?"

"There's the possibility that someone else hired him to steal the watch. And when it came to turning it over, the thief got suddenly greedy."

Or whoever killed him had decided that he knew too much?

"Then why did the thief's killer leave it?"

"Because it was now tainted. Most especially if anything had happened to the owner, Lewis French."

"Oh dear. I quite see now why you've been reluctant to raise the alarm until now. And I also understand what took Agnes French all the way to London. If her brother wasn't here, he had to be in London. I'll be happy to help in any way I can. But I must ask to see your identification. You will understand why."

Rutledge pulled to the verge. They were nearly into Dedham, and this was the widest place in the road. He took out his identification and passed it to Williams. The curate examined it with care, then handed it back to Rutledge.

"Thank you. I don't believe I've ever encountered anyone from Scotland Yard before this."

Rutledge could see that Williams wasn't certain whether to consider this an honor or a curse.

After a moment the curate added, "To be honest with you, I can't think of anything I might know that would be helpful to you. None of my parishioners has any deep dark secret that might lead to murder."

Rutledge found himself thinking that if there were secrets, no one would consider confiding them to Williams. He was rather naïve for a man who had fought in the war and then turned to the church for his livelihood.

"There must be someone else who knows the family well." Rutledge reached for the brake and let in the clutch, moving out in the sporadic traffic on its way into Dedham.

"I never knew Michael, of course. But his tutor is still alive, and he lives in a small house here. He was also Lewis's tutor, I believe. And there's Miss French's governess, but her mind isn't what it once was. Sad, really, but she's up in years. Michael French went to call on the tutor whenever he was on leave, or so Miss French told me. But Lewis finds him too dull to visit, I'm afraid. Sorry."

"Still, I'll keep the tutor in mind, if this inquiry isn't closed one way or another soon."

"With French dead? God save us, I hope not."

It wasn't until Rutledge was waiting for the curate to remove his bicycle from the boot that Williams said, "There *is* someone. I should have thought—she was engaged to Michael, and then to Lewis. Only she broke off the engagement quite suddenly. She's known the family for years. She might be able to help you."

Chapter Seven

The name Williams gave him was Valerie Whitman. She lived in the village of St. Hilary, and according to the curate her house was easy to find, just across from the church.

Agnes French had mentioned another woman when first Rutledge had called at the house, telling him that if something had happened to her brother in St. Hilary, she would look first at his jilted fiancée. At that point, Rutledge had still believed French was dead in a London hospital.

Now Williams was telling him that Miss Whitman herself, not French, had ended the engagement abruptly.

He was more inclined to believe the curate than Agnes French, whose view of the broken engagement would have been colored by her brother's feelings. Still, jealousy had been the motive for murder in more than one instance. And who had or hadn't ended the engagement didn't matter. What had come after that did.

Rutledge was fairly certain he'd noticed the Whitman house earlier, a pretty cottage with roses clambering up the sunny wall and
overhanging the porch. Nothing to compare with the Townsend
house in Dedham, but large and comfortable enough to indicate that
Miss Whitman was Lewis's equal. And he found it easily.

But the quandary was, while he had been able to approach Miss
Townsend and Miss French's maid, even the curate, using the excuse
that he was trying to find French, Rutledge could hardly ask Miss
Whitman if she knew where he'd got to. The general assumption
would be that they had had no contact since the broken engagement.
And he had no idea on what terms they had parted or how she felt
about French now.

If he believed Agnes French, her feelings had been murderous.

He wasn't happy with the plan of knocking at the door in official
inquiry until he knew a little more.

And so he left the motorcar by the empty Rectory and walked
in the St. Hilary churchyard while keeping an eye on the Whitman
house.

His vigilance was rewarded. A young woman came out the door
with cut flowers in her hand and walked down the path to the garden
gate.

There was no certainty that this was Valerie Whitman. He had neglected to ask Williams if there were sisters. But it was a place to begin.

She continued down the road to a cottage near where the High
Street made a slight turn to accommodate the Common and went
up to knock at the door. He moved to the far side of the churchyard
so that he could keep watch. She was admitted, and she stayed the
proper fifteen minutes, returning without the flowers.

He was ready. Leaving his place of concealment under the heavy,
drooping leaves of an old maple and timing his approach perfectly, he
met her before she had reached her house.

Taking off his hat, he smiled and said, "My name is Rutledge. I'm
from Scotland Yard."

Her hair was a light brown with highlights of honey gold in the sun, and her eyes were hazel, green overlaid with flecks of brown and purest gold. She was not conventionally pretty in the way that Miss Townsend was, but he found himself staring, nevertheless. There was something about her that would still be attractive when she was old.

"Scotland Yard? I can't imagine why you should wish to speak to me." She moved past him, opened the gate, and was walking up the path to her door before he could stop her.

"Miss Whitman?"

She turned quickly, her eyes wary. "How did you know my name?"

"I told you. I'm a policeman. It's my business to know such things."

"Then what is it that you want?"

"I'm trying to find Lewis French. It's urgent that I speak to him as soon as possible. It could even be that he's in some trouble. I might be able to help him, if he is."

"If he's in trouble, I'm the last person he'd turn to. I can't think why, if you know my name, you would believe I could tell you anything. His sister lives between here and Dedham. You should speak to her."

"She's in London at present. I asked the curate, Mr. Williams, if there was anyone else who knew the family well. He gave me your name."

"But he knows I've been—estranged from the French family." She shook her head.

"You were close at one time. You've been engaged to both brothers."

"Michael was going off to war. We'd known each other for ages, and it seemed natural to make promises. I can't tell you now if it was love or just the need to cling to something sane in a mad world. In any event, when Michael was killed, I think Lewis proposed because he'd always wanted anything his brother had. Once he had it—in this case me—he tired of it quickly."

"But you accepted his proposal, did you not?"

"Michael was dead, it came as a shock, and I was silly enough to think my life was over. My grandfather told me I'd be happy with Lewis, and certainly he was kind and caring and *there*. So many of my friends were killed. Men I'd known from childhood. Like Michael they'd marched off to war as if it were a great adventure. Then they began to fall, one by one. Mons, Ypres, the Somme, it was horrible, and no end in sight. Three of my friends were already widows—"

She broke off, staring at him. "Why am I telling you these things? They won't help you find Lewis."

"You said, once he had something of Michael's, he tired of it quickly. Did that include the firm?" That could easily explain Lewis French's disappearance.

Miss Whitman considered the question. "It was still a new toy at that time. Now? I couldn't tell you. Ask Miss Townsend."

"I've spoken to her. French appeared to be himself, the last time she saw him. Perhaps he's tired of her as well."

"I doubt it. She never belonged to Michael." A smile flitted across her face, warming her eyes. "I doubt he could jilt her, anyway. You haven't met her father."

But he had. Another possible reason behind a sudden disappearance?

That would also mean giving up position and his wealth. It might be easier to wed Miss Townsend, relegate her to Dedham, and go on with his life in London as he pleased. Would it be as easy to relegate a wife as it was a sister? The answer to that would lie in the strength of mind of Miss Townsend. Or whether her father would be pleased to keep her close by.

Miss Whitman had turned to go inside. He wanted to keep her there talking, but his concentration had been broken by the question of the relationship between Lewis French and his fiancée.

Hamish said, "Yon dead man."

Rutledge began, more bluntly than he'd intended, "I drove Miss

French to London because we'd found a man dead on a street in Chelsea. We had every reason to believe it was French."

Valerie Whitman turned back to face him.

"Was it Lewis?" Her expression was unreadable. Her hat shadowed her eyes now, and he couldn't see their color, whether the green had changed to brown.

Was there a need to know—the fear of what he would answer? Or only curiosity?

"She very courageously went with me to the hospital morgue. Because you see, he had no identification, but he was carrying Lewis French's watch in his pocket." He took a deep breath. "It was not her brother."

After a moment, Miss Whitman asked, "Then why was he carrying the watch? I don't understand. Is this the trouble you think Lewis might have got himself into? Do you think he had something to do with this man's death?"

"I don't know. Yet. Miss French told me that her mother had always suspected her father of affairs with other women—"

"She did. I remember it," Miss Whitman interrupted.

She stood there, the sunlight on her hair under that summer hat, her teeth catching the edge of her lower lip as she considered him.

Rutledge waited.

And then she said, "I won't invite you in. But I will walk in the churchyard with you."

Surprised, he opened her gate and held it for her to pass through. They crossed the road in silence and went through the gate in the wall, where trees offered a little respite from the sun.

"Let me see your identification," she said, and he gave it to her.

Handing it back to him, she said, "I will talk to you for Agnes's sake, but not for Lewis's. I knew Agnes French very well once upon a time. She took care of her mother even when Mrs. French couldn't recognize her own daughter. Strangely enough, she could always remember her sons. She was a woman of nervous disposition who gave her husband and her children a very difficult time. Mr. French was away a good deal, of course. And she imagined that he must be having an affair. In London, in Madeira, even in Lisbon, where he went some-times on business. I never believed it could be true. Surprisingly, he was devoted to her."

"That's interesting in light of something I'd heard, suggesting it was her father-in-law, Howard French, who had had an affair when he was quite young. There was a child of the union, who was adopted elsewhere. Which has led me to wonder if the dead man could have been a descendant of that child. There was a slight resemblance to the portrait of Howard French that hangs in the offices of French, French and Traynor. In fact, it was that likeness coupled with a watch that does belong to French that sent us searching for him. But he's missing. And so is his motorcar."

"Well, of course, wherever he is, he must be driving. He hated trains. The fact that you can't find the motorcar surely means he's off on a personal errand of some sort."

They had walked as far as the French mausoleum. She stood look-ing at it with sadness in her eyes, and he could feel her slip away from him, her mind elsewhere.

"It would be nice if things were that simple," he said, answering her suggestion about the errand. "You mentioned a grandfather. Do you have any other family?"

"I didn't agree to talk about myself," she said sharply, turning toward him.

"You told me that you'd been close to Agnes French 'once upon a time.' What caused the breach between you?"

When she didn't answer, he went on. "Was it the engagement to Michael—or the breaking off of your engagement to Lewis?"

Miss Whitman shook her head. "I don't know. It was a sudden coldness. I wondered if Lewis had said something. I tried to put as good a face on it as I could, but I was jilted, you see. Yes, Lewis was a gentleman, he let me cry off. He walked into the cottage one afternoon, stood there in front of me, and said, 'I've changed my mind. I don't think we'll suit after all. Besides, there's someone else. I leave it to you to think of a reason why we should no longer wish to marry.' He waited only long enough to hear me say, 'Yes, all right, if that's how you feel.' He replied, 'It is.' I handed him his ring, he thanked me with a cool little bow, and that was that."

Rutledge found himself thinking that Lewis French was a fool.

And he was reminded all at once of his own bitter memories. Jean had been eager to leave him. She had broken off their engagement without even telling him, although he'd known he couldn't marry her as he'd been in the spring of 1919. And she had been in such a hurry to leave the clinic after seeing him there for the first—and only—time. It had turned out for the best, but it had been impossible for him to accept that when, suffering from shell shock to the point that he couldn't eat or sleep or think, he had needed an anchor, a connection to reality.

He would have given much to know whether it had only been Valerie Whitman's pride that had been hurt. Or had the pain gone deeper? He had known that too, when Meredith Channing had traveled to Belgium to nurse the ruin of a man she believed to be her missing husband.

"A woman scorned . . ." Hamish's voice startled him. Rutledge glanced quickly at Miss Whitman to see if she had heard it too. But she was staring up at the church tower, where a pair of rooks were circling and calling.

"There's a pair that lives in the tower," she said, changing the subject. Then: "I really must go." And she turned back toward the High Street.

"I'll walk with you as far as your gate," he said, following her, although his motorcar was in the opposite direction. "If you think of anything that might be useful in discovering the whereabouts of Lewis French, please send word to the Sun Inn in Dedham."

"I'm not likely to. I've already told you. Speak to Miss Townsend." This time he could hear anger behind her words.

They continued in silence to her gate, which he opened for her to pass through. As he was closing it again, she said, "I'd rather not let it be known that I spoke to you. I have no right to discuss the French family with anyone."

"There's no need," he said. "For anyone else to know."

"Not even Mr. Williams," she said, after considering the matter, her head to one side, the sun touching those honey gold lights in her hair. Rutledge wondered if she knew how she looked in the sunlight. "He sometimes forgets that a priest's duty to his parishioners extends beyond the secrets of the confessional."

And he had indeed forgot, Hamish reminded Rutledge. Because the man from London had been such a good listener . . .

Why had Miss Whitman told him so much? For reasons of her own?

Without another word, she was gone, walking briskly up the path and into the house. She didn't look back.

He watched until the door closed and then stood there at the gate a moment longer.

On his way to the motorcar, he surprised himself thinking again that he wouldn't have chosen Miss Townsend over Miss Whitman. If he had been Lewis French.

The inn in Dedham was on the telephone, and Rutledge shut himself into the tiny closet to put through a call to the Yard.

When Gibson had been found and brought to the instrument, he said to Rutledge, "You'll be interested to hear Mr. Belford's background." Without waiting for a reply, he went on. "He was in the Military Foot Police. An officer."

Which explained his easy recapitulation of the evidence surrounding the dead man. He was accustomed to setting out the facts in an orderly manner, for an inquiry.

"Anything else?"

"Not so far. His record was exemplary, according to my sources. And he doesn't appear to have any connection with French, French and Traynor. Although he's been to Lisbon, oddly enough. Something to do with deserters."

That was food for thought, although Rutledge wasn't prepared to see a connection. Yet. But if Belford was behind the death of the man on his street, it would have been to his advantage to try to lead the Yard astray.

And he hadn't.

Unless he had lied about recognizing the body. If so, where had the dead man come by the watch?

"Has French turned up at his London house or at the wine importers?"

"We've asked the constables in each street to keep an eye open for him, and they report daily. No sighting so far. And the constable in the City by the wine importers sometimes stops in at the neighboring firm to see a friend there. According to this friend, the chief clerk has been trying to contact Mr. Traynor to tell him what's happening here. And Mr. Traynor hasn't responded. The clerk has been that upset."

Mr. Gooding had a great deal of responsibility on his shoulders. He would prefer to have some sort of direction, but he would not have been the one to gossip. Someone in his office must be talking to the neighbor. Gooding would not be pleased. Still, it gave the constable access to information.

"Any new information for me?" Rutledge asked.

"There's been another query from Norfolk, asking if we know anything about their man. He's still missing. And we had a new name sent in by the police in south Devon. It doesn't appear to be very promising."

"Just now there's more than enough to keep me busy here."

He rang off, then walked out of the inn directly into the path of Miss French.

She had taken an early train, he guessed, because she was still dressed for traveling. A motorcar for hire had just deposited her in front of the inn's door.

Looking up as Rutledge's shadow fell across her path, she said, "Oh. It's you." As if she had been expecting to find someone else waiting for her. "Have you found my brother?"

"Not yet."

A look of irritation crossed her face. "It's so like Lewis to leave everyone waiting on his convenience. He's probably stopped to see Henry Jessup. They were at Cambridge together, and Henry's getting married in November. Lewis had expected Henry to ask him to stand up with him."

"Where can I find Henry Jessup?"

She frowned. "I believe he lives near Hatfield. He's a solicitor. Lewis told me he wasn't a very clever one. Still, he's joined his father in a partnership, and so it probably won't matter whether he's clever or not."

"Have you met this man?"

"No, Lewis seldom brought his friends home. My parents were very ill toward the ends of their lives, and it couldn't have been pleasant for young men looking for a country weekend to have to tiptoe about for fear of waking the invalid. And there's no shooting here to amuse them." She looked around. "I've missed my breakfast—I can't eat anything on a train the way it bounces about. And Nan isn't expecting me."

With a nod she walked past him and into the inn.

It took him twenty minutes to run down the firm of Jessup and Jessup. It was indeed on the outskirts of Hatfield. A woman answered the telephone, asking his business.

Without giving his name, he asked to speak to the younger Mr. Jessup.

"He's just come in. A moment, please."

And then Jessup was on the line, a deep voice that sounded as if the speaker was recovering from a summer chill.

"I'm trying to locate Lewis French on an urgent matter. Is he by any chance with you?"

"Gooding? Is that you? You don't sound like yourself," Jessup replied.

"The name is Rutledge."

"Ah. Well, I must tell you that French isn't here. Nor has he been for some weeks."

"There was a possibility that he had stopped over with a friend on his way back to London from Essex without telling either Mr. Gooding or his sister of his plans."

"I see. Yes, that does present a problem, doesn't it? I wish you luck. And I'm sorry I couldn't be more helpful."

Rutledge put up the receiver. He didn't think Jessup was lying. So where, then, was French?

As he was leaving the telephone closet, he glimpsed Miss French in the dining room. She had called the waiter to her table and was pointing to something on her plate. He realized that she always seemed unhappy with her lot in life, and as the waiter carried away her plate, she sat there looking at her teacup with a frown, as if it too had failed to satisfy her.

He considered asking her for the names of other friends, and then she looked up and saw him through the glass doors.

She beckoned to him, and he went into the dining room to speak to her.

"Did you find Henry Jessup? Was Lewis there?"

"I located Jessup," Rutledge answered, "but he hadn't seen your brother in several weeks."

"He must be lying. I can't think why, except that Lewis was angry with me when he left, and he has probably told Mr. Jessup not to let on that he was there."

"I rather thought he was telling the truth."

She sighed. "It's so typical. He's left me to make all the decisions about our cousin's visit. I don't even know when to expect him or how long he's to stay with us. It's really unfair."

Just then the waiter returned with her Scotch eggs. She inspected them closely and then nodded in resignation, as if she couldn't expect any better of the cook.

Rutledge waited until the man had left and then asked, "Is there anyone else he might have visited?"

"How can I know? I told you, I haven't met most of his friends. Michael at least wasn't so selfish, he'd bring friends home from Cambridge sometimes." That brought a shadow to her eyes, and she said sharply, "My breakfast is getting cold. Please leave me alone."

He thanked her and was turning away when she added, "It's not a friend, is it? He— There's a woman somewhere. He jilted Miss Whitman for Miss Townsend. Not surprising, of course. Miss Townsend is the daughter of a doctor, after all. But he can't seem to settle." She viciously stabbed her Scotch eggs. "There must be someone else, and he doesn't want anyone to know!"

"What will become of you, if he marries and brings a bride home?"

Tears stood in her eyes. "He's not that mean. I'll have a home. He's told me so. For as long as I live."

Rutledge left then, walking out of the dining room, through Reception and out to the motorcar.

Telling Miss French that she would have a home as long as she lived was tantamount to telling her she would very likely spend those years as a spinster, with no hope of marriage. And who would she meet if her brother never brought home any eligible men?

The information he was gathering about Lewis French did not paint a pleasant picture.

If there was indeed a third woman involved in the man's disappearance, it would be impossible to track her down unless she was related to one of Lewis's friends. She couldn't be in St. Hilary, or in Dedham, surely, where gossip would quickly have found her out by this time. Lewis French was too well known.

Essex was wide, as was England. Rutledge sighed. Whatever Markham would have to say about progress, this inquiry wouldn't be closed very soon.

There was nothing more to be gained by staying here. The Yard was patient, it could wait until Lewis French surfaced. Markham permitting.

Still, there was one more thing Rutledge wanted to do before he left.

The local man. He hadn't spoken to him, and it would be just as well to have eyes here after he'd returned to London.

He went back to St. Hilary and the narrow little building that housed the police station.

This time the door was open, and Rutledge walked from the sunshine into the dim interior, almost colliding with a man coming out.

The man apologized and went on his way. Behind him at an old wooden desk that must have served the first constable here in St. Hilary was a man in uniform. The small board in front of him read CONSTABLE BROOKS. It was neatly hand-lettered in black.

"Good morning, sir. How can I help you? Directions, most likely."

He smiled, an affable man with a black patch over one eye.

Rutledge presented his credentials. "Not directions, precisely. Information."

He went on to outline the circumstances that had brought him here. Brooks listened carefully until he'd finished.

"I can't tell you much about Mr. French. He's hardly been here often enough for me to get to know him. And then I was gone for most of the war. He was a man when I got back, and generally in London. A well-spoken gentleman, polite, his main interest his work. It seems to absorb him. Or else he finds London more to his liking than St. Hilary."

"Yet he found time enough here to become engaged twice."

Constable Brooks frowned. "He'd known Miss Whitman most of his life. I had the feeling that he wanted to marry her because everyone thought she was to marry Mr. Michael."

"And what did Miss Whitman think about that?"

"Gossip didn't say. Still, she accepted Mr. French's proposal of marriage," Brooks replied, his voice deliberately neutral. "She could have done better ten times over, in my view."

"It was comfortable, what she knew," Rutledge suggested.

"As to that, I'm not sure it wasn't her old grandfather who encouraged her there. The French family could give her everything, couldn't it?"

"And then she broke off the engagement."

Brooks nodded curtly. "So they say. But in regard to Mr. French, if he's not here and not in London, where is he?"

"Is there any place around St. Hilary—or even Dedham—where a motorcar could be concealed for a long period of time?"

"Not the River Stour—it's too busy, is it? And we've no bogs where it could disappear, like. Nor old sheds, derelict buildings, or thick woods."

The constable would know, Rutledge thought, glad to be spared a long, muddy tramp along the river's banks or through fallow fields.

"No, if it's anywhere, it's with Mr. French." Brooks nodded in agreement with himself when Rutledge didn't respond at once.

"Will you keep a lookout for the man—and send word to London at once if he reappears? And search for that motorcar. You know your patch better than we do."

"Yes, sir, that's not a problem. But are you thinking *Mr. French* has killed this man you found in the road? It doesn't make any sense."

"Or perhaps the man has killed French, to take his watch."

"I'd sooner believe that, sir, not that I want to."

"I've met Miss Townsend's father. What would he think of a black sheep suddenly appearing in St. Hilary?"

"Black sheep? Whose, sir?"

"For the sake of argument, let's say someone the French family would wish to keep out of the public eye."

"Well, he's rather a stickler, is Mr. Townsend. But I don't see the French family having anything to hide. And Mr. Lewis is not a devious man. That I can be sure of. If he set out for London, then he set out, intending to go there."

R utledge left the Sun Inn an hour later, heading toward London. He'd asked questions—and yet the answers he was looking for had eluded him. Because he'd asked the wrong questions? Or because he hadn't recognized the right answers?

Hamish said, "Aye. It smacks of failure."

And for the rest of the journey Hamish seemed to hover just behind his shoulder, commenting on everything that Rutledge preferred to set aside. He could not conquer the past, the war. He couldn't put it out of his mind. He had forced himself to come to barely tolerable terms with it, and the way that he'd forged was littered with deep pits of despair.

Only now, the war over, he couldn't pray for a German bullet to put an end to the misery.

Which was why he had kept his service revolver locked away, beyond reach when the darkness came down.

Chapter Eight

When Rutledge made his report to Chief Superintendent Markham, the Yorkshireman gave him his full attention, then nodded as he finished.

"He can't disappear forever, can he now? Not with French, French and Traynor to run. It's a grand business, it's where most people purchasing Port wine and Madeira for their cellars go to buy it. Half London wouldn't know what to do with themselves without it. What's more, the firm has never been scandal prone until now. What's changed?"

"A very good question," Rutledge agreed. "His encounter with the dead man? So far that's the only change in his routine. And he must have encountered him, there's the watch. But was that meeting happenstance? Contrived? Related to business? To family matters? Did it have anything to do with the upcoming visit by the other partner,

Traynor? We don't even know enough to speculate. And who got the better of the encounter? So far, the man without a name is dead, but we can't be certain French killed him. Or if he killed French, then was run down to silence him in turn."

Markham frowned. "You make it far too complicated. Look closer to home, man. What about the woman? Miss Whitman? It would seem to me that she had the best reason to do away with Lewis. And for all we know, the poor bastard found in Chelsea had happened on the corpse and helped himself to yon watch. Or she hired him to kill for her, then ran him down before he could think about blackmail."

"Then let's consider that line of inquiry. What has she done with French's motorcar? That too is missing."

Markham waved a large hand. "That's for the local police to discover. This Constable Brooks for one, in St. Hilary."

Rutledge took a deep breath. "Indeed."

"Then drive yourself back to Essex and see what you can learn about this young woman."

"I should think it would also help to circulate a photograph of the dead man and see what comes of it."

Markham peered at him. "Is she pretty, this Miss Whitman?"

Taken aback by the unexpected question, Rutledge said, "Miss Townsend is far prettier."

"Ah, you've noticed, then, have you?" Markham sat back, his mouth smiling in satisfaction, but his eyes cold.

"I'm trained to observe," Rutledge replied, only just preventing himself from snapping, feeling that he'd been trapped into an admission that suited Markham's purpose.

"And being not as pretty could rankle. Are you certain she wasn't jilted?"

Rutledge hadn't told Markham that. The Acting Chief Superintendant had leapt to the conclusion.

"A man doesn't leave the prettier girl for a less attractive one unless there's more money to be had in the bargain. In fact, he did just the opposite, didn't he? A prettier girl with greater social standing, a doctor's daughter."

Rutledge wanted to say that he couldn't imagine Miss Townsend killing anyone, under her father's thumb as she was. But that would leave Miss Whitman open to the obvious comparison. And it would feed Markham's theory.

"I'd still like to circulate that photograph," Rutledge answered, fighting a losing rearguard action. "Whether he has anything to do with Lewis French's disappearance or not, he's a victim. And if we can connect him to Miss Whitman, we could prove your theory. That he was hired to do the deed, turned greedy, and was killed."

"Yes, yes, I take your point. Put Gibson onto it, then, or Constable Graham. They can sort through responses for you. Once we have a name and a place to begin, we'll send someone to interview this fellow's friends and family. The mystery now is what became of French, and what's the connection with this young woman."

Rutledge wasn't particularly happy with the thought of another inspector muddling whatever links there might be between French and the victim. Or between the victim and Miss Whitman. Legwork, yes, that was always helpful. But if conclusions were to be drawn, he wanted to do interviews himself. To know what was said, and how and why.

Markham picked up a file, then set it down again, a preliminary to dismissal.

"You've finished your paperwork on the Devon inquiry?"

"It's in the hands of Sergeant Griffin."

"Good. Then there's nothing to keep you in London."

Rutledge went back to his flat, repacked his valise, and then set it aside.

Chief Superintendent Bowles had been a master at keeping Rutledge out of the way if there was a major inquiry beginning in London. Wherever undeserved credit could be garnered to himself, he preferred not to have Rutledge as a witness to it. And if Rutledge happened to finish a highly publicized case, Bowles barely offered grudging congratulations.

Markham had so far not shown himself to be in the same mold as the man he was temporarily replacing. But this latest meeting had raised alarms in Rutledge's mind. First the query regarding the use of his motorcar rather than public transportation, and now this business with Miss Whitman. Markham was a hard man to read.

Sergeant Gibson had known Bowles for years before Rutledge joined the Yard, and Inspector Cummins among others had dealt with him as well. But Markham had been brought in from outside, no track record, no gossip to make it easier to penetrate his dour Yorkshire demeanor.

But there was nothing to be done. Even if Markham had been as easy to read as newspaper through a clear glass, it wouldn't matter. His wishes were law and not to be argued with.

There was still the connection—if any—between Belford and the dead man. Why had Belford, even with his background in policing, offered his own view of the victim's death? It had been unnecessary, with the Yard in charge. Was it a habit that even now he couldn't break? Or had he wished to be sure the Yard saw the circumstances in the right light?

Leaving his valise where it was, Rutledge drove back to Chelsea.

Belford was at home, he was told, and after several minutes, the man walked into the sitting room, saying, "Good afternoon, Inspector."

It was the opening that Rutledge had expected. Giving away nothing, waiting for the other person to lead the conversation.

"I've come to ask a few more questions about the body found in the street here."

Belford gestured to chairs by the open window, and the two men sat down. Belford seemed to be at his ease, politely waiting for Rutledge to continue.

Smiling inwardly, Rutledge said, "I understand you were an officer in the Military Foot Police. I'd been curious to know why you so expertly set out the evidence for us. The three conclusions I might have drawn were an unusually keen eye, police experience, or an attempt to lead us up the garden path."

The man betrayed himself with a tightening of the lips. Otherwise his face remained impassive. After a moment—to be sure he had himself under control?—he said, "I was not happy to see trouble on this street. I've lived quietly and comfortably here for some time. I didn't wish that to change."

Mr. Belford had enemies, then. And he had surveyed the scene to protect himself, and viewed the dead man's face with the same concern in mind.

"I've come to ask what conclusions *you* drew. Other than those pointed out at the time."

Surprised, Belford said, "Then you have not found out the identity of this man, nor have you learned where he came from and how he was left here. Certainly not where he died."

"We've found out who he is not. There was a resemblance to a member of a merchant family in the city. But he was not that man. Even though he was carrying that man's watch in his pocket."

"Ah. The watch. Yes, I thought that might lead somewhere."

"It was a family heirloom, traced easily enough."

"Perhaps someone wished to have you believe that the dead man was the owner of the watch. To buy a little time."

"To what end?"

"To see to it that any remaining evidence of the man's true identity was successfully destroyed."

"That's possible. But how did he come by the watch to create the illusion that this was the owner?"

"A clever pickpocket could have done the trick."

An interesting possibility. But pickpockets were ten a penny. It would be impossible to question a quarter of them.

"Is a young woman's honor at stake?"

The question caught Rutledge off guard. "What makes you ask that?"

Belford shrugged. "Even a hundred years ago, an unwelcome suitor could end up in the river. The police are more thorough now. And so one must be more clever in making an unpleasant annoyance disappear. And better for him to disappear, you see, than to be found dead, questions asked, fingers pointed, and all that."

In the circumstances, it was not a suggestion that Rutledge appreciated, but he had to accept the merits of it.

"The man the dead man was supposed to impersonate is missing. His motorcar with him."

"Indeed." Belford frowned. "That puts an entirely different complexion on the watch, doesn't it?"

"In what way?"

"I don't really know."

"Was a mistake made in the first death?"

"Now there's an interesting prospect." Belford seemed suddenly keen, his mind already considering and rejecting possibilities.

Rutledge said, "What's done in anger . . ."

"Yes, of course, it would have to be that, wouldn't it? And when the head is cooler, one is faced with an extra corpse. But the watch—again, how did the killer come by it?"

"A family member. In this case a sister." Rutledge thought that over, then shook his head. "Unless of course, all this preparation is to put blame on that sister and rid the killer of her as well as her brother."

"It won't be the first time."

Rutledge rose. "This has been a very interesting conversation. It doesn't mean that you've been struck off the list of suspects. You're clever enough to have killed the man if in some way he threatened you."

Belford stood as well. "Like you, I've seen a great deal of tragedy. It doesn't mean that we have been corrupted by it. Good day, Mr. Rutledge."

And he stayed where he was as Rutledge went to the door.

Driving to Essex, Rutledge mulled over what Belford had told him.

Speculations, all of them. Some of them he'd already considered as he'd driven back to London from Dedham to report to the Yard. But where was the evidence to link any one of the possibilities to the missing Lewis French or the dead man in London?

"Are ye certain of the identification?" Hamish asked. "It could be wrong."

"My point," Rutledge said aloud before he thought, "when I asked for the photograph to be sent round to local police stations. Someone ought to recognize him."

"There's Norfolk," Hamish reminded him.

"I know. That's where I'm going first. Norfolk. And if need be, we'll look at Cornwall next. What was that man's name? Fulton."

The village of Moresley was in the middle of the county, small and ordinary, famous only for the twisted remains of a tree still standing on the narrow green. It had sheltered Nelson on his way south to take up his first command. Whether that story was true or false, the locals had built a small wicker cage around the trunk to protect it from grazing cattle or sheep. The village shared a constable with its nearest neighbor, and Rutledge was fortunate to catch him in Moresley late that evening as he turned into the High Street.

The constable was just mounting his bicycle to finish his rounds.

Rutledge pulled up beside him, identified himself, and said, "I've come about the missing man report. One Gerald Standish."

"Mr. Standish, sir?" The constable considered that. "Is he a Yard matter after all? What's become of him, then?"

"We don't know. You reported him missing after we sent round a sheet describing a dead man in London."

"Sir, there was no answer to my query. Inspector Johnson in Norfolk and I thought perhaps the dead man had already been identified."

"There were several other avenues to explore before I could get here. Tell me a little about Standish."

"His grandmother lived here. When her son died young, his widow married again, and she didn't see much of the boy. Still, she left the cottage to him. He came to Moresley after he was demobbed in 1919. Quiet, kept to himself, no trouble. 'Twas his daily, sir, that came to me to say his bed hadn't been slept in for three nights. She was worried. He hasn't stayed away this long before. Usually just a day or two, and he comes back tired, confused."

"Does he own a motorcar?"

"No, sir, he usually gets about by bicycle. But it's still behind the cottage."

"Then he can't have gone too far. Do you know anything about Standish's background before the war?"

"Just bits and bobs of conversation. He had a little money, and he was careful with it. Inherited from his father, he said, who was an estate manager in Worcestershire. I don't think he cared much for his stepfather, not unusual in a boy who loses his own father young."

"Does he receive any mail?"

"As to that, I don't know, sir. You'd have to ask the postmistress. The post office is in the greengrocer's shop. I daresay it's closed now."

"Where can I find her?"

"She's the greengrocer's wife. Mrs. Lessor. They live in that house with the white gate."

"I'll have a word with her. Will you come with me?"

Rutledge could see that the constable was torn between arriving home in time for his tea and accompanying Scotland Yard on an interview. Duty won. The constable hesitated for a few seconds and then propped his bicycle against the wall of the ironmonger's shop before getting into the motorcar.

They drove the short distance to the greengrocer's small house. Lamplight spilling from a front window lit the path for them as they walked up to the door.

The greengrocer, a bluff man, short and portly, answered their knock.

"Constable Denton," he said, then turned to look Rutledge up and down before asking Denton, "What's this about, then?"

Rutledge left explanations to the constable.

"Inspector Rutledge is looking into the disappearance of Mr. Standish. He's come to ask Mrs. Lessor if Mr. Standish ever received any mail."

"She's setting out our tea," Lessor responded.

"I'm sure it won't take more than five minutes of her time." Rutledge's voice was polite, but it left no doubt that he was not to be put off.

Lessor looked at him again, decided that the Londoner intended to have his way, and, with a sigh, called to his wife.

She was a little flustered when she came to the door. A trim woman in her middle years, she was still wearing her apron, and she seemed to remember it only after she stopped by her husband's side.

"Um, Constable," she said. "Is anything wrong?"

Rutledge took charge. "I'm sorry to delay your tea, Mrs. Lessor." He smiled, and went on to show her his identification and to ask his question.

She looked at her husband, and he nodded. "Well. I don't believe Mr. Standish has received more than two or three letters in all the time he's lived in Moresley. I make a point not to look at anything but the name on the front of the envelope. It's a small village, and I have to be careful, you see. Everyone has secrets . . ."

It was an admirable attitude, but hardly helpful.

"He never said, as you handed him his mail, 'Ah, that's from my aunt—my brother—a friend from France'?"

"He did mention when the first one arrived that it was the deed to the cottage. He seemed to be very happy about that. He never said anything about the others."

Rutledge was getting nowhere.

"Does anyone in Moresley have a connection with a family called French?"

Mrs. Lessor shook her head. "I've never heard anyone speak of such a connection. Do they live in Norfolk? You might ask in the town. The Inspector there might know of them."

Rutledge tried another direction.

"What about his grandmother? She lived here. What does local gossip remember about her?"

Mrs. Lessor glanced again at her husband, as if to be sure she could speak freely. Whatever she read in his expression, it was reassuring. She turned back to Rutledge.

"Mrs. Standish lived alone. She said once that she'd had a falling-out with her son's wife. My mother told me that she remembered when Mrs. Standish first came here. She was still quite pretty at fifty, with the loveliest hair. We didn't know until she'd died that there was a grandson. She left a handwritten will leaving the cottage to him. But he was still in France and it was a while before he could be reached. Didn't Constable Denton tell you?"

He hadn't. But then Rutledge hadn't asked about the grandmother, and he doubted if Denton would have remembered the details that Mrs. Lessor had given.

Lessor cleared his throat. His tea was waiting.

Rutledge thanked the man and his wife, and with Constable Denton at his heels, he went to the motorcar.

"Where's the cottage? I'd like to have a look inside."

Denton said, "I don't know if it's proper. We can't be sure yet anything has happened to Mr. Standish. He could come home tomorrow."

"But he hasn't in a good many tomorrows. If the Yard is investigating his disappearance, then the Yard can have a look at his house."

The cottage was just down the street, set back under a large tree, rather a pretty place in its day but sadly untended now, the front garden a tangle of late flowers and weeds.

"Mr. Standish wasn't much of a gardener," Denton said as they walked to the cottage door. "His grandmother, now, she had a way with growing things."

The door wasn't locked, and inside it was quite dark, now that the sun was setting. What's more, the tree's shadow prevented the last rays from reaching the front room's windows. At length Rutledge found a lamp and lit it. As the light bloomed he could see that the cottage was furnished in a style at least a generation earlier, Victorian and rather heavy. But it wasn't cluttered, save for books scattered everywhere, as if the owner had begun one, then stopped reading that one and picked up another in its place.

A pattern, Hamish was telling him, of a restless mind. For in the month between his release from the clinic and his return to the Yard, Rutledge had done much the same thing, unable to settle to anything.

He felt a coldness as he looked around the cottage. As if he could sense the despair in the owner, and a darkness that wouldn't lift even when the sun rose.

Hamish said, "Ye'll find him deid. Whoever he may be."

And Rutledge thought it was very likely.

There was no private correspondence in the desk, and not much of anything else that would define the character of Gerald Standish or his grandmother. There were no pictures anywhere, but on the wall by the worn chair that stood under the window was a miniature, the ivory oval in its silver frame catching his eye. Rutledge brought the lamp nearer, and decided that the young girl who stared back at him must have been the grandmother, for the style of clothing was early Victorian. He thought she must have just put her hair up, and the occasion was marked by this likeness. She had dark hair, dark, smooth brows in an oval face, high cheekbones that gave him a glimpse of how she must have looked in maturity, and very dark blue eyes. She was too young for her face to show her character, only her loveliness. But whatever life had brought to her, it had ended in a lonely old age.

Rutledge wondered why she had had a falling-out with her son's wife, but he suspected it very likely had to do with the woman's marrying again. Looking around him, he thought the elder Mrs. Standish had only enough money to live comfortably in a small village. Or she had been frugal for reasons of her own.

"Sad," Rutledge said aloud, more to Hamish than to Denton.

The constable came to stand behind him, looking over his shoulder. "Is that Mrs. Standish? Her face was lined and her hair gray when I came to Moresley."

"Only Gerald Standish can tell us who she is. But it's likely, I should think."

Rutledge spent another ten minutes looking through the cottage, upstairs and down. He discovered that the clothes in the cupboard in the bedroom were of good quality with well-known labels. He couldn't be sure whether they were hand-me-downs or had been purchased new before the war. Nevertheless, Standish had seen to it that they were carefully maintained and well brushed. Denton, coming again to look over his shoulder, commented that Mr. Standish had taken time over his appearance.

"Not vain or anything. It was just the way he had. As if it mattered to him."

In the end, Rutledge had learned very little, less of it helpful. He even looked at the flyleaves of books, to see if there were dedications.

An enigma, Mr. Gerald Standish. Rutledge returned to the miniature just as he was leaving.

Miniatures were an art. Painting a portrait on ivory with a brush that had only one or two hairs took skill and patience and a great eye for detail that could capture the subject in a few strokes. The artist might be known, although Rutledge could see only initials at the edge the sitter's shoulder.

"I'll give you a receipt for this, in the event Standish returns. But I'd like to find the artist. That might tell us the name of the subject."

He crossed to the desk and began searching for paper and pen, writing out a brief message and signing it.

"But wouldn't the artist be long dead, sir?" Denton asked.

"I've no doubt of it. But anyone this good will be known in art circles, and there's nowhere else to look for information."

They left the cottage as they'd found it, Rutledge putting out the lamp, and they saw as they stepped outside that night had fallen in earnest, dark clouds beginning to blot out the stars. The air smelled of thunder.

The village street was deserted save for a dog making its way home, trotting purposefully down the middle until it came to a bungalow. It went to the door, scratched on a panel, and was admitted by the time Rutledge and the constable had caught up with it.

Denton said, "It's late, sir. If you wouldn't mind dropping me off in the next village, I'd be obliged."

Rutledge said after the constable had lashed his bicycle to the boot, "Do you have much trouble in this part of the county?"

"None to speak of, sir. Neither of my villages are rich enough to tempt trouble, and the poor are not destitute. The church and the Women's Institute see that everyone has food on the table and a roof over our heads. Mind you, I don't lack for occupation, there's always keeping the hotheads amongst the young lads from doing something they'll live to regret, but we don't run to real crime. That's why I contacted Norfolk when Mr. Standish went missing, and Inspector Johnson passed the report on to the Yard."

"What's your best guess about Standish? Will we find him, do you think?"

"I fear he may be dead, sir. By his own hand."

It was very late when Rutledge reached Dedham, and he was glad to find a room at the Sun.

The next morning, he set out to find the St. Hilary curate. In most villages he would have paid a call on the doctor, but he rather thought Dr. Townsend would be less than helpful in any matter relating to the French family.

Williams had finished painting the trim along the front of the Rectory, and he was just now clinging precariously to his ladder with one hand as he tried to reach the corner on the west side.

Hearing the motorcar pull into the yard, he glanced over his shoulder, nodded in acknowledgment of a visitor, and put the last touches to the corner before coming down the ladder.

"Sorry. But I knew you wouldn't mind waiting a bit," he said in greeting.

"There's something I want to show you," Rutledge said and drew out his handkerchief with the miniature cradled carefully inside. "Do you recognize this woman?"

"When was it painted?" Williams started to reach for the ivory, realized his hands were spattered in paint, and hastily withdrew them. He leaned forward instead.

"Sixty years ago? Seventy?"

"Well, it's not really possible to tell, is it? She's what? Sixteen in this painting? And even if it's an accurate likeness, her face would have changed as she aged."

"Study it, all the same."

The curate peered at it. "Lovely child, isn't she? She would have been a lovely woman as well. But I don't recognize her. Should I?"

Rutledge returned the miniature to his pocket. "No. Although I'd hoped you might. You've been a guest at the French house. You've very likely called on the Townsends in your pastoral capacity. And Miss Whitman, for that matter. If there was one portrait painted, there could have been another—or even a photograph."

"Yes, I see. Of course. I'm sorry to say I can't help you at all. I've seen nothing like that."

"Is Standish a name that's common in this part of Essex?"

"It's not common, no, but there's at least one family in Dedham. The youngest daughter sings in the church choir there. A very nice voice. What's more, the family is quite fair with ruddy complexions. Not dark at all."

"Any connection with the French family?"

"I don't believe so. I've never heard one mentioned. And someone surely would have, I think. After all, they're probably the wealthiest family around."

Rutledge let it go. "Does Miss Whitman know how to drive?"

"Actually she's a good driver. During the war, she volunteered. Mostly in the city of Norfolk, I was told."

Norfolk. Not that far from Moresley. But Gerald Standish had been in France at that time.

Rutledge thanked Williams, asked directions to the house of the former tutor to the French sons, and made his way to a comfortable cottage overlooking the green.

Mr. MacFarland was older than Rutledge had expected. He must have been middle-aged when he taught Michael and Lewis French. White hair rose from a high forehead, but the skin of his face was still smooth, his blue eyes alert. His Highland accent was pronounced, and Rutledge had to suppress the memories it brought back in a surge of images. Faces of the men who had served under him, their voices soft in the quiet of the trenches before an attack, calling encouragement to one another as they charged through the German fire, begging him to hold their hands as they lay dying. Of Hamish, steadfastly refusing to lead his exhausted company into the teeth of the machine-gun nest, close to breaking but strong and determined to put his men first, no matter the cost.

MacFarland said, concern on his face, "Are you all right, man?"

Rutledge clamped down on the past, bringing all his will to bear. "A headache coming on," he replied as calmly as he could and identi-fied himself, explaining that he was interested in two of MacFarland's former pupils.

"Come in, then, and have something cool to drink while we talk." He ushered Rutledge into the front room, cluttered with books and compositions for the elderly harpsichord in one corner.

While he was fetching the water, Rutledge had an opportunity to recover, crossing to a window and looking out on the quiet, pleasant green. Behind the house, the wood closed in, thickening as it marched toward the walls of the park that surrounded the French house.

MacFarland came back with a tray and two glasses of water, saying, "Move those books from the chair and sit down."

Rutledge did and took the glass held out to him. "How do you keep the instrument tuned?"

"They say the Elizabethans enjoyed the harpsichord, and their castles were damper and gloomier than my house. But I doubt we either of us hear it as it really sounds." He grimaced. "But I persevere. I've always enjoyed music, and it's the only instrument I learned to play, save for the pipes. And my neighbors aren't too fond of them, I can tell you."

Rutledge laughed. "Nor were the Germans."

"I can't imagine why you should be interested in any of my former pupils. They all grew up, as far as I know, to be upstanding young men. I lost seven in the war, sadly, but that's what war is about—young men. Which ones brought you here?"

"The French children. Michael and Lewis."

"Ah, yes. Michael was one of my seven. And the most promising of all." He took a deep breath, his blue eyes focused on the past. "I can't complain of either of my pupils. They were bright and well behaved. Lewis had seizures occasionally, but they seemed to become less frequent as he grew older. Still, he was as active as his brother."

"Grand mal seizures?"

"Nothing so dramatic. He would just fade away for a moment or two, and then go on as if nothing had happened."

"There was no trouble between the brothers? Or between the brothers and their sister, Agnes?"

"They got along well enough. Mrs. French was the greatest threat to discipline. She had spells of anxiety and uncertainty, and this kept the household in turmoil. It was sad, really, because the children were neither spoiled nor sheltered and a pleasure to teach."

"I've been told that Lewis was jealous of his brother."

"Perhaps. Certainly no more so than any younger brother when his elder is all that he'd like to be. On the other hand, when he went away to school, Lewis found his own feet quickly. I like to think that I contributed a little to that by treating him as I treated Michael, in spite of the handicap of seizures."

"Does the French family—or the Traynors for that matter—have any enemies?"

"That's a strange question for a tutor. Not to my knowledge. The cousin, young Matthew, was a frequent visitor to the house. His family lived on the other side of the village. When his parents died, he let the house for several years. He was living in Madeira, you see. A pity it is standing empty now. Never good for a house. Back to Traynor—he's a fine young man, like his cousins."

"I understand Miss Whitman was also a frequent visitor."

"Yes, the loveliest girl. She was a friend of Agnes's, and often at the house. I don't know what happened to the friendship. Suddenly it was over."

"What was Agnes French like as a child?"

"Often dissatisfied. Not surprisingly, as the only daughter, it was her lot to look after her parents when they were elderly and infirm. And she nursed them faithfully, difficult as it was dealing with her mother. Her father as well, after his stroke. While her brothers were off in Portugal with their father, she was left to care for the house. It seemed to me that she should have been asked to go with them, at least after her mother's death. Her brothers came home filled with stories about toboggan rides down a mountainside on a stone chute, going up into the volcanic peaks by horseback, or boating around the island, swimming in the sea. It couldn't have been easy for her."

Rutledge could understand what MacFarland was saying in a polite way, that the daughter was ignored and, being a plain child, she understood all too well why she was left out. And then MacFarland underscored Rutledge's viewpoint.

"I couldn't help but think that if Agnes had been as pretty and as lively as young Valerie, she would have been treated very differently."

"Did Miss Whitman try to usurp Agnes French's place, do you think?"

"Never deliberately so. She was just a child, father absent, lonely and looking for an ordinary family life."

"Absent?"

"Yes, her father was Royal Navy. Her mother died in childbirth, and she was left with her nurse when he went back to sea. He could hardly take her with him. And to tell truth, I think Valerie was happy enough as it was, running in and out of the house, playing with the French children. She never seemed to notice that she lacked a mother, or that her father was generally away. Everyone made a pet of her, and her sunny disposition, her sweet nature, endeared her to the staff as well."

Rutledge took out the miniature now, and showed it to MacFarland. But while the tutor admired it, he said, "I don't know who the sitter is. Sadly. A lovely child."

Rutledge was on the point of thanking him and leaving when Mac-Farland said, "You know, I had nearly forgot. Something happened years ago. I expect the children never knew about it because they were upstairs in the Nursery asleep. I was talking to Mr. Laurence French. I'd come to be interviewed for the position of tutor, you see, and after dinner, we left Mr. Howard French in the drawing room and withdrew to the study to finish our conversation about my experience and references. Suddenly a man came bursting into the house. He shoved aside the maid who'd answered the door, and he ran up and down the passage, flinging open inner doors, shouting for Mr. French. Mr. Laurence and I hurried out into the passage to find this strange man with his hands around Mr. Howard's throat, on the point of throttling him. Mr. Howard backed up, forcing us into the study again, and I entered the fray, trying to pull the man off him. I'd just succeeded, with Mr. Laurence's help, when the man broke away from us and pulled out a knife. He lunged at Mr. Howard, but Mr. Laurence threw himself in the way and was stabbed in the chest. Mr. Howard cried out in fury, and between the two of us we were able to disarm the man without anyone else getting hurt. I can tell you I was in a state of shock, I'd never dealt with anything like that. Anyone could have been downstairs—Mrs. French—the children—guests, if there had been any—right in the midst of the brawl. Someone would have got badly hurt."

"What happened next?"

"I sent the housemaid who had opened the door for the footman and the coachman while Mr. French attended his son. Thank God the wound scored his ribs but did no greater damage. All this while, the intruder was babbling in a language I didn't know, but Mr. French said it was Portuguese and he began questioning him. It was quite dramatic, couldn't have lasted more than five minutes from start to finish. But I felt I had battled with that man for hours."

"Did anyone summon the police?"

"Just the doctor. Mr. Howard French had a cut over one eye, the intruder had a split lip, and Mr. Laurence French was bleeding from that chest wound. I was luckier: only my hands were badly bruised."

"Was this Dr. Townsend?"

"His predecessor. And he gave the man something that made him more manageable. I was asked to stay the night, and in the morning the man was gone. I don't know what became of him. When I asked, I was told the incident had been handled by the police. But no one ever questioned me."

"Did French tell you why this man was so angry?"

"Apparently his father—Howard French—had decided to grow his own grapes in Madeira and bought a large farm for the purpose. The previous owner had lost his wife to cholera and he didn't have the heart to go on. He sold the land to Mr. French for what was then considered to be a fair sum. But the owner's son, who was in prison in Portugal, felt that he had been cheated. When he was released, he came to Madeira, nearly killed his father, and threatened Howard French. He was tried and convicted but escaped when he was on his way to a Portuguese prison. Somehow he traced the family to England, and he came to Essex demanding justice. He must be dead by now. He was about forty years old when he came to Dedham."

"Still, he could have passed his feeling that he was cheated on to another member of the family. Do you know, was the vineyard where the farm had been more valuable?"

"I have no idea. I shouldn't be surprised. It was probably what the man wanted, to be paid the difference. If he'd been intent on killing French, he could have done it more efficiently with a knife or a pistol. Instead he went for his throat."

"Do you remember if you ever heard the intruder's name?"

"I could have done and never realized it. I don't believe he spoke any English. Or if he did, I never heard him. At any rate, I was hired on the spot, for what I'd done to try to help Mr. French fight him off. Something good came of a rather nasty shock."

"And Mrs. French—was she aware of what had happened?"

"She was upstairs resting. She hadn't come down to dinner, in fact. But she must have heard the uproar, because the housekeeper later told me she was convinced an irate husband had come to the house. At any rate, she went to bed for a week, refusing to see anyone, even the children. It was given out that she was suffering from a migraine. Naturally I kept my mouth shut. It was a good position, one I was happy to have." MacFarland shook his head. "I'm sure this has nothing to do with present problems. Perhaps I shouldn't have mentioned it to you. But it came rushing back, the way memories sometimes do."

"And you're quite sure the children were unaware of the intruder?"

"Absolutely. Michael never spoke of it. Lewis heard something, most likely the carriage being brought around, but had no idea what it was all about. If the man had appeared an hour earlier, he would have found the children downstairs saying good night to their father. I shudder to think about that."

"Did you wonder what had become of the man?"

"Yes, I'm as curious as the next person. But there was my position, you see. I couldn't ask. Since nothing more was said, I assumed he was taken to London and dealt with there. It would have been the best way to avoid gossip. Besides, the man was as mad as a hatter."

Rutledge wondered if that was why MacFarland had been hired on the spot, rather than for his resourcefulness in coming to French's aid—to prevent him from gossiping.

He thanked the tutor and took his leave. Hamish was saying in the back of his mind, "The person to ask is yon clerk. Gooding."

It was a very good idea.

Rutledge was walking back to fetch his motorcar when the local constable came peddling toward him.

"There you are, sir!" he called out with evident relief. "There's been a summons from London." As Rutledge turned to wait for him, Constable Brooks added, "A Sergeant Gibson, sir."

The constable slowed, got off his bicycle, and fell in step with Rutledge. "The Yard telephoned the inn. They were fairly certain you were out, but the sergeant was insistent. The inn sent for the police, and when Dedham didn't have any luck finding you, Sergeant Gibson told the constable to look in St. Hilary. He came to me, and we went off in different directions, looking for you. I saw your motorcar in the Rectory yard, but I didn't know which way you'd gone from there."

"I'm to call the sergeant? Or return directly to London?" Rutledge couldn't believe that Chief Superintendent Markham had grown that impatient. But it was the only reason he could think of that Gibson hadn't left any message.

There was nothing for it but to go back to Dedham and put in a call to London. The two men walked toward the church together, Brooks leading his bicycle. As he was passing the Whitman cottage, Rutledge glanced that way. He could have sworn that he saw a curtain twitch in one of the front windows.

Had Miss Whitman also seen the motorcar on Church Lane and kept an eye out for him, to be forewarned if he came knocking at her door again? He'd waited for her in the churchyard the last time.

Rutledge encountered the constable from Dedham near the gates to the French estate and offered him a lift back to Dedham.

But the man couldn't tell him any more than Brooks had.

They reached the inn, and Rutledge went directly to the telephone closet. When the call was put through to London, Sergeant Gibson answered almost at once.

"Rutledge here."

"Sir, there's been a development. The Chief Superintendent wants you back here to have a look."

"You can't give me more information?"

"Sir, I was told not to. Ears."

The telephone exchange. Then it had something to do with St. Hilary.

"I'll leave at once."

"Thank you, sir, and I'll tell the Acting Chief Superintendent that."

Rutledge fetched his valise from his room, settled his account, and went on his way.

It was late when he reached the Yard, but the sergeant was waiting for him.

Without a word, Gibson handed him a folder.

Rutledge read it through, then looked up. "When was it found? Lewis French's motorcar? Are you sure it's his?"

"We were told not to take any steps until you were back in London. The Surrey police found it in a chalk quarry yesterday morning around dawn. Light reflected from the bonnet, and the constable went to investigate. Lads sometimes go to that quarry to drink, and there had been a fight or two recently. He found the motorcar instead."

"Had it been tampered with?"

"Not as far as he could tell. But he thought it had been there for some time. He checks the quarry most days, but doesn't go deep inside unless he sees signs that someone has been prowling about again."

"How did he identify it?"

"He didn't. His first thought was that the owner had come there to take his own life. It had happened once before. And so he searched a bit. Finally he went to find a telephone and put in a call to the Yard."

"Did he, by God! Good man."

"The Acting Chief Superintendent sent me along to have a look. It fit the description we had of Mr. French's motorcar. Chassis number, and so on. And there was a dent in the near-side wing. After I'd had a look at the vehicle, we searched the quarry more thoroughly, but there was no sign of a body. To tell the truth, I'd expected to find one. It seemed to me that whoever put the vehicle there hoped the Yard would still be looking in London for the motorcar until the corpse had decomposed. Once I was satisfied, the local man put a constable on to watch the site, and I came back to London to tell you what had been discovered." Gibson hesitated. "Only, when I tried to reach you last evening at the inn, they told me you weren't a guest there. Sir."

"I'd gone first to Norfolk. No answers there. Standish hasn't come back and there's been no word from him."

"I don't think the Acting Chief Superintendent will be best pleased. He seems to have his heart set on finding French somewhere in Stratford St. Hilary."

It was a warning.

"Yes, I know. He was certain the motorcar was there as well. Most particularly, he's pointing toward one of the women. In my view, Agnes French could hardly disappear from her home long enough to dispose of her brother, take a dead man to Chelsea, and then leave the motorcar in Surrey. What's more, she'd have to find her way from Surrey back to Essex. Her household would know if she had gone away without warning."

Hamish said, "It wasna' the sister yon Acting Chief Superintendent believes is guilty."

Rutledge nearly answered him aloud, biting off the retort at the last second and covering it with a cough.

Gibson made no comment. Norfolk had seemed a reasonable line of inquiry to him as well. Now he was having second thoughts.

On the other hand, the Acting Chief Superintendent was new and an unknown quantity, and Gibson's first loyalty was to himself. He and Rutledge had always had an uneasy truce, both men doing the best they could under the capricious Bowles, both of them well aware that they couldn't afford friendship. Bowles would have seen that as collusion, and it would have cost both men dearly.

With only a few hours' sleep, Rutledge was back at the Yard before eight the next morning, to find Gibson waiting for him on the street, as arranged. The sergeant had very little to say, getting into Rutledge's motorcar with a grunt and settling down for the drive.

The silence lengthened, lasting until they reached the Surrey chalk quarry. It was well off the main road, down a muddy lane that was overgrown. At the end of it, the great white face loomed above a bed of rubble. It appeared to have been a hill once, before this side had gradually been cut away.

"According to the local man, the quarry was abandoned because it was increasingly unstable. A workman was killed scaling the face."

The constable guarding the site recognized Gibson and let them through. And the motorcar bounced and jolted over the rubble to where the other vehicle stood.

It was covered with a light dusting of chalk, like summer snow. Rutledge realized that the intent of whoever had brought the motorcar here was to drive it as close as possible to the high face, so that the next major collapse would cover the vehicle. But there must have been a minor fall as the driver was maneuvering the motorcar into position, for the idea had hastily been abandoned. On the whole, Rutledge couldn't judge just how long the motorcar had been there. From the start? Only a few days?

They got out and clambered over the hummocky chalk. Much of it was darker, more the color of dingy cream, but there were newer, whiter bits as well. As they got closer, their shoes collected the white dust, and Rutledge noted ruefully that his trouser legs were not far behind.

He could see the long dent in the wing well before he reached it.

Rutledge carefully examined it, but the sergeant had been right, there was nothing linking the motorcar to the victim except for that dent.

He got down on one knee, looking up at the undercarriage, scanning the linkages. "Sergeant, my torch from the motorcar, please."

Gibson went to fetch it and brought it to him as Rutledge, ignoring the damage to his clothing, was inching his way under the chassis. He went over every projection and rough edge he could see, touching each one with his gloved fingers. Nothing hooked or caught, nothing jammed. Just black metal.

He was about to push himself out again when he spotted it, where the housing of the motor was bolted to the frame. It was on the far side from where he'd been lying, almost invisible. But his torch beam had cast a shadow, just an outline that seemed irregular. He edged in that direction, swearing at the uneven chalk bed beneath his shoulders, and saw that a tiny square of cloth had been caught by and then wedged against the bolt.

Unless the motorcar had been put on an overhead rack, it would have been missed, and even then, dark as the cloth was, dark as the paint was just there, it would have been difficult to pick out.

It didn't want to give up its hold on the bolt. Almost, Rutledge thought, as if it had been glued in place. A measure of the weight pulling against it as a man was dragged, jamming it there.

He slowly worked it loose, careful not to damage it further. He swore again at a lump of chalk digging into his shoulder, a little deeper with every movement he made.

Gibson, bending over to try to see what Rutledge was doing, said, "Any luck?"

Without warning, the tiny fragment of cloth fell, fluttering across his face. Rutledge almost lost it, barking his wrist against the undercarriage as he reached for it before it could drift into the uneven bed of chalk by his head.

Securing his find, he began to wriggle out from underneath the motorcar. It had been too claustrophobic by far, caught there between the heavy vehicle and the chalk, and he could feel his heart pounding now as he saw release coming.

By this time Gibson was on his hands and knees, his face alight with curiosity. He straightened, offered Rutledge a hand up once he was clear of the chassis, and said, "You found something then."

Rutledge pulled off his driving glove, and there was the small dark square, the weave stretched and twisted from the stress put on it as it snagged.

Gibson said, "Ah," and poked it with a finger. "Will it match the dead man's clothing, do you think? There were several tears, as I remember."

Rutledge dropped the bit of cloth into his handkerchief for safekeeping, folded it, and put it carefully back into his pocket. Using his gloves to dust his coat and trousers, flecking off the worst but unable to budge most of the finer particles, he said, "Did you search the interior?"

"Cursorily, to see if we could find anything to tell us who it belonged to. I told you. The Acting Chief Superintendent ordered us to wait for you."

Rutledge gave up, putting his gloves back on. "I'll do that, and afterward we'll take it to London. I want Gooding, the wine merchant's clerk, to give us a positive identification. It might shake his complacency."

Opening the motorcar's door, he began to examine the interior, looking anywhere that something could have fallen and escaped the killer's attention.

He thought at first his search was a waste of time. There were no bloodstains or scuff marks to show that a body had been transported any distance in the rear seat. But then a clever killer would have come prepared with a blanket or tarp. Still proceeding methodically from back to front, he asked Gibson look in the boot.

The sergeant had just called to say that it was empty but for the tools usually kept there when Rutledge put his hand beneath the driver's seat. He pulled out the chamois used to keep the motorcar clean, and something else came with it.

He saw that it was a woman's handkerchief, lace edged and embroidered with a pretty design of pansies in one corner. It was smudged, as if someone had cleaned his or her fingers on it, then shoved it under the seat out of sight while he or she drove.

He held it up for Gibson to see.

"Do you think a woman could be our killer?" the sergeant asked.

Rutledge had been thinking just that. He said, "How would she lift the dead weight of a man's body into the motorcar?"

"She has an accomplice," Gibson answered promptly.

Standish?

Rutledge went on searching, brushing his gloved fingers over the carpets in the hope of bringing to light any small clue that the killer had missed.

The motorcar was clean.

The French household, like Belford's, would have a chauffeur or a footman in charge of seeing that the motorcar was kept running and ready whenever the owner called for it. If that handkerchief had been there before French's disappearance, it would have been removed, laundered, carefully pressed by one of the maids, and presented to French to return to its owner—or not, as he saw fit.

The thought was depressing.

"We've done what we can," Rutledge said finally, looking up at the sky as he got out of the motorcar. The sun was disappearing behind clouds, and he thought it best to start for London as soon as possible. "Can you drive this one back to London? It will save some time."

"I think the Surrey police would be just as glad to be shut of it." Gibson went to speak to the constable at the entrance.

Watching him go, Rutledge pulled out the handkerchief and looked at it again. It was too clean and fresh to have been under that seat for any length of time. And there were three women in Lewis French's life who could have left it there. Or a fourth, if Agnes French was right, that her brother had found someone else. He still couldn't picture Miss Townsend as a murderess, and she would surely have been in the motorcar as a passenger. Agnes French could argue the same, that she'd driven out with her brother during his stay in Essex.

Which left him with Miss Whitman, who claimed she hadn't seen French since the engagement had been broken off.

And Markham was prepared to put his money on Miss Whitman.

Rutledge glanced up to see that another man had joined Gibson and the local constable. Dressed in street clothes, he looked like an inspector. Gibson had reached the constable on duty, and the other man stepped forward to join the conversation. Then Gibson was thanking them, shaking hands, answering a final question put to him by the newcomer. He appeared to be satisfied when the sergeant had finished speaking, giving him a nod. Without turning even to glance Rutledge's way, the newcomer walked off, taking his constable with him.

Gibson came back to say, "They've no complaint. But they'd appreciate a copy of the final report on the motorcar and the inquiry regarding it."

A standard courtesy.

Rutledge took the crank in hand and reached down to insert it and turn it. He said, "I'll follow you. If you have any trouble, signal me, and I'll pull over."

He made certain that Gibson could manage the extraction from the quarry, told him what he wished to do, then led the way out of the gates to the nearest road as thunder rolled in the distance, like the guns in France. Rutledge was grateful that he had his own motorcar to himself.

Gibson pulled up as close to the wine merchant's door as he could, and Rutledge stopped just beyond him. The rain had held off, but only just.

He went inside, leaving Gibson with the two motorcars, and asked for Gooding.

When the senior clerk came into the room, Rutledge said, "Will you step outside for a moment?"

Gooding frowned. "Do you have more information, Mr. Rutledge? You can speak freely here."

"That will depend on what you can tell me first." He turned and held the door. Gooding had no choice but to precede him outside.

The wind had picked up. Gooding looked first to his right, as if expecting to see someone standing by the door, and only then to his left. His frown deepened as he recognized the vehicle, his gaze moving on to Sergeant Gibson behind the wheel.

"That's Mr. French's motorcar." He hesitated, then asked, "Will you please tell me what it is you know?" His voice was strained. "Why is a policeman driving, and not Mr. French?"

"The motorcar was reported abandoned. By the Surrey police."

"*Surrey?* Has there been an accident? Is Mr. French all right?" Gooding began to walk toward the motorcar, his eyes going directly to the deep indentation in the wing.

"It was found just as it is in an unused quarry. Was it damaged that way when last you saw Mr. French driving it? There, on the wing?"

"No—no, it wasn't. He stopped by here to sign some papers regarding a shipment, and I walked out with him afterward. But what was he doing in *Surrey?*" He might as well have said "the antipodes."

"And you would be willing to swear that this is indeed Mr. French's motor?"

"Yes, I assure you," Gooding replied testily. He looked at Rutledge. "What is it you aren't telling me? Do you know where Mr. French is?"

"I wish I did," Rutledge told him somberly. "I have another call on my time this afternoon. But if you will accompany Sergeant Gibson, there's a body I want you to see. And this time, like it or not, you'll view it for Scotland Yard."

"Dear God. But surely— Are you telling me Mr. French is dead?"

"We don't know," Rutledge said. And he stayed with Gooding while he told the junior clerks that he would be away for an hour, helping the police with their inquiries, then saw him off with Gibson.

When they were out of sight, Rutledge got into his own motorcar and drove to the house where Lewis French lived in London.

Chapter Nine

Rutledge had not questioned the London household until now. He was fairly certain that Agnes French had told them very little—and learned even less. French had last been seen in Essex, after all, and when Miss French arrived in London, the staff not only had been surprised to see her there but were totally unprepared to receive her. Now, with the motorcar surfacing in Surrey, so close to London, the complexion of the case had changed.

It was still a fashionable address, although Mulholland Square had been built years before the turn of the century. Rutledge, looking up at the mansard roof and the stone facings at the windows, decided that if Howard French had bought the property as an investment, it had been very sound. And it spoke of old money, settled and respectable.

He lifted the knocker and let it fall.

The middle-aged woman who answered the door opened it wide for him to enter when he told her he was from Scotland Yard.

Miss French had stayed here, but she hadn't felt at home here. The staff was her brother's, not her own, and it was now his principal residence. She had taken the train back to Essex rather than wait for news of him here. That, then, was Rutledge's starting point.

The woman said. "I'm Mrs. Rule, housekeeper to Mr. French. Is there a problem, Inspector?"

"It would be best if we spoke in private," he replied with a glance toward the staircase. He could just hear someone using a carpet sweeper on the first floor.

She too glanced over her shoulder toward the stairs, then took him to a small parlor, where he was offered a seat. Still standing, she waited for him to begin, her hands clasped lightly in front of her as if to calm her rising concern. He could see the tension around her eyes.

"When was the last time you saw Mr. French?" he began.

She looked at the painting on the wall behind him as if it could give her the date. "It's three weeks now, almost. He drove to Essex to visit his fiancée and to prepare the house in Dedham for his cousin's visit."

"When do you expect Mr. Traynor to arrive in England?"

"Any day now, I should think. Mr. French was expecting him last week, but apparently it has been difficult to arrange passage. Quite frustrating, he said, but then Mr. Traynor did speak the language."

"Why was it difficult?"

"Mr. French didn't say, only that Mr. Traynor had had to travel to Lisbon first, then take passage from there, rather than come directly from Madeira. I believe there are packets that bring wine and messages to the City on a regular schedule. Mr. Gooding—he's the senior clerk in the firm—is to notify me as soon as he learns a date. Word will come to him, as he must know where and when to meet the ship."

"And Mr. Gooding hasn't contacted you?"

"No, sir, not yet. I did ask Miss French when she came to the house if she had heard any news, but she said she hadn't, that she wasn't privy to her brother's arrangements. I'd thought at first that she had come down to greet Mr. Traynor. She was always fond of him."

"She didn't tell you why she visited London so unexpectedly?"

"No, sir, she was in a fractious mood when she came, meaning no disrespect to her, and she spent most of her time in her room, even taking her meals there."

"Does Mr. French usually drive himself?"

"Yes, sir, he prefers it."

"Who maintains the motorcar for him?"

"He sees no reason to keep a chauffeur. We have a footman who sees to it. He's quite good with mechanical things."

"Has there been any recent damage to the motorcar?"

"I haven't been told if there was. George would have said something. He's very particular about it, you see."

"I'd like to speak to him later."

"Yes, sir. Has something happened to Mr. French, sir? Seeing that you're from Scotland Yard . . ." She let her voice trail off as if afraid to put what she was thinking into words.

"We don't know. He left Essex some days ago, and we haven't been able to locate him."

"That's unlike him, sir. Mr. French generally keeps Mr. Gooding informed of his whereabouts. Have you spoken to *him*?"

"He hasn't been contacted by Mr. French. Have you met Miss Townsend?"

"She and her parents came to dinner here on their last visit to London, just before the engagement was to be announced."

"Tell me about her parents."

She said, "I don't wish to speak out of turn, sir."

"You won't be. Not to a policeman."

"Well, there's little to tell. Her father is a doctor and rather—" She searched for the right word. "He's a man who knows his own mind," she ended.

Rutledge interpreted that to mean he was hard to please.

"Her mother is such a kind lady, very quiet but with a surprising sense of humor. It was a pleasure to serve her."

"Dr. Townsend is very strict where his daughter is concerned," Rutledge commented and watched her brows go up in surprise.

He wondered if she would have used another word. But she said only, "She's such a lovely young lady. I'm sure he means well."

"Did you meet the young woman Mr. French was engaged to before he met Miss Townsend?"

"Miss Whitman," she replied warily. "She came to dinner a few times. The staff liked her very much. I was sorry to hear that she had broken off their engagement."

"How did Mr. French take it?"

"He was not as upset as I'd expected. More philosophical, you might say."

Rutledge could just imagine that he was.

"He left for Newmarket the very same day, expecting to meet friends there. Dr. Townsend was also invited. I happened to hear Mr. French tell another of his friends that the doctor would arrive for the weekend. I expect that's how he came to know Miss Townsend."

Or he was already intending to court her father, and then her.

As if she'd heard his thoughts, Mrs. Rule said, "It did seem that his broken heart mended very quickly. But young men will be young men."

Rutledge took out the handkerchief that he'd retrieved from under the seat in the motorcar. "We found this in Mr. French's motorcar, in Surrey. A lady's handkerchief, I should think. Do you by any chance know the owner?"

"I would have no way of knowing, sir. Except that Miss French favors handkerchiefs with her initials in the corner. Did you say you'd found the motorcar—but not Mr. French?"

"I'm afraid so."

She was shaken. "When I saw a policeman at the door, I knew

something was wrong. Is—is there bad news? Was there . . . a crash on the road?"

He said, "We have very little information at all. That's why I'm here. Did Mr. French often visit friends in Surrey?"

But Mrs. Rule knew very little about her employer's personal life and could say only "I don't know that I've heard him mention visiting anyone in Surrey. Certainly we've not entertained guests from there in return." Her eyes began to fill with unshed tears. "I do hope there's nothing wrong."

When she had recovered a little from her shock, Rutledge asked to speak to George.

He was directed to the mews, where the motorcar was kept.

George as it happened had been an aircraft mechanic during the war, and he had taken the position of footman because he would also be in charge of the motorcar. When Rutledge asked him if there had been any dents or scratches on the chassis of French's motorcar, he was indignant.

"It's in perfect condition," he said. "And no one can say any different."

"You'd swear to that?"

"I would, sir, yes. That's to say, when it left here it was. But Mr. French is a careful driver, and he wouldn't bring it back to me in any shape but the one he'd found it in."

Rutledge said, "Where do you keep the chamois you use when cleaning the vehicle?"

"Under the front seat, sir. Mr. French likes to see the headlamps and other chrome bright. I leave one there for him."

"Anything else?"

"No, sir."

"A lady's handkerchief?"

"No, sir, never. Why should I have done that? Has Mr. French made a complaint, sir?"

"He hasn't. But we found the motorcar in Surrey, and we haven't been able to speak to Mr. French so far."

"He can't be far away. Here, you haven't left him without it?"

It was all Rutledge could do to prevent George from claiming the motorcar in the name of Lewis French and driving it to Surrey to search for him, even though he couldn't think where to start. "It could have been a malicious prank, sir, and he'll be quite angry."

Rutledge had to tell the footman that no prank was involved.

When he left, George was standing in the door of the mews, looking like a man who had lost a friend.

And Hamish was hammering away at the back of Rutledge's mind, reminding him that the dent in the wing wasn't evidence until the dead man's clothing had been shown to match the bit of cloth found on the frame.

Gibson had returned to the Yard by the time Rutledge got there. He encountered the sergeant in the passage beyond the stairs.

"What did Gooding have to say when he saw the body?"

"He didn't know who it was. Certainly not Mr. French. He worried me, did Mr. Gooding. His hands were shaking so he could hardly get out of the motorcar when I took him back to the wine merchant's."

"He thought it was going to be Mr. French?"

"I expect he did, the Yard finding the motorcar and then calling on him for news of his employer."

"Was the body Mr. Traynor, by any chance?" It was only a wild guess.

"I didn't ask. But he knows Mr. Traynor, and he'd have said as much when I asked him if he could identify the body."

That was true.

"Did you feel he was telling the truth?"

"He appeared to be. What's to be done with the motorcar now, sir?"

Rutledge gave him instructions to return it to the Mulholland Square mews, and Gibson nodded.

"I'll see to it, sir. Meanwhile, while I was at the morgue, I took the liberty to bring back the packet with the dead man's effects in it, including his clothing."

"Let's have a look." As they walked back toward Rutledge's office, he told Sergeant Gibson what he'd learned at the French family's London house.

It was Gibson's turn to ask, "Did you believe the housekeeper and the footman?"

"On the whole, I think I did. There's no reason for them to lie. They have good positions, and Mr. French doesn't appear to be a difficult employer." He opened the door to his office.

A large brown parcel bound in string covered his desk.

He cut the string and opened the paper. It yielded shoes, stockings, undergarments, trousers, suspenders, a shirt and tie, and a coat.

Rutledge set most of the smaller items aside and looked at the shoes first.

The toe of one and the side of the other were scuffed, adding further proof, if it was needed, that the dead man had been dragged.

Then he spread the trousers out across his desk, where he could examine them carefully. There were rents in one cuff, snags here and there, but as far as he could see, there were no places where a piece of the cloth was missing.

He turned from that to the coat. At first he couldn't find what he was looking for. The front and one arm had suffered from being dragged—threads pulled here and there, bits of gravel and dirt lodged in the fabric, and the back seam had opened up near the collar. It wasn't until he had lifted the collar that he saw the hole.

He took out his handkerchief, unfolded it, and held the contents up next to the coat.

The pattern matched perfectly, although the bit of cloth from the

motorcar was stretched and distorted from having been ripped forc-
ibly from the coat.

Rutledge put his finger gently into the tear. It went through the
lining, although the shirt, when he checked that, had no matching rip.

Had the man's neck snapped as the coat snagged, ripped, and then
with the weight of the body, pulled free, leaving behind only a tiny
telltale bit?

"It's murder, isn't it, sir?" Gibson asked, looking over his shoulder.

"Or the driver panicked and tried to cover up what had happened."

"Then who was driving, sir? It couldn't have been this man. It
must have been Mr. French. And that's why the motorcar had to be
disposed of. With that dented wing, the evidence was too strong, once
we'd connected the dead man to Essex."

"If it was French, why didn't he simply report an accident?" He
could have told any tale that suited the circumstances, and Lewis
French, of Dedham, would have been believed.

Rutledge's mind made the leap before Gibson could answer his
question.

The tutor had told him about a man bursting into the house and
threatening the family. That was decades ago. What had become of
the intruder?

If he'd been in prison until now, if he'd been released, finally,
having served his sentence for attacking Howard French and his son
with a knife, he could have come back to Essex with murder—or
blackmail—in his heart.

Was this the troublesome thing that French needed to discuss with
Matthew Traynor? Had an approach been made?

What if the killer, thwarted in his intentions, had resorted to
murder and had got the wrong man? It would explain why French—
without his motorcar and uncertain where to turn—had gone to
ground. Was he waiting for his cousin to reach England before coming
out of hiding and demanding that the police do something? If he'd

been injured in the struggle, he might very well have found sanctuary until he had healed sufficiently to deal with the situation.

That would also explain how French came to lose his watch.

Hamish spoke, his deep voice with its soft Scots accent echoing in the room so loudly that Rutledge expected Sergeant Gibson to stare about looking for the source.

"The man was killed with French's ain motorcar. Wha' else but French couldha' been driving?"

And the only answer that Rutledge could think of was *Someone he trusted.*

Which brought him back to the lady's handkerchief with the little embroidered pansies in the corner.

Pansies. For remembrance.

Eager as he was to drive straight through to Dedham, while in London, Rutledge made a detour to the shop of the jeweler.

Galloway was pleased to see him, asking immediately if the pocket watch had been helpful in bringing in a murderer.

"The inquiry is still open, but yes, it's proved immensely helpful," Rutledge replied. "Now there's another small matter I'd like to explore."

He brought out the miniature and set it on the counter in front of Galloway.

"Well, well. What an exquisite little ivory," the jeweler said, leaning forward to admire it. "Certainly fine workmanship, and the sitter is quite lovely. How did you come by it?"

Rutledge was prepared with a portion of the truth. "There's another man in this inquiry besides the owner of the watch. He lives alone, his family having predeceased him. This miniature was in the house his grandmother had left to him, and we rather think the image may be hers. Her son was an estate manager in Worcestershire. It would be helpful if we could learn more about her grandson and about his family. This is the only clue I have. If we could find out who the artist was, we might discover who the grandmother was."

"Have you tried Somerset House?"

"I'm afraid the sorts of records I'd like to uncover wouldn't be there. For instance, who were the true parents of this young man? And does he have any connection with the family who presented the watch? The public record can tell me when he was born, and who is officially listed as his mother and father. The Yard can find out if the father had ever been in prison or suspected of any crime. If he served in the Army. Known facts. Not gossip. It could well be that the grandmother was the child I am looking for. There was money at one time, enough to have this painted when she came of age. Did she marry well? Poorly? What did she tell her son and grandson about her past? What, for that matter, did she even know to tell them?"

Galloway nodded. "I take your point. As you know, I have a brother with connections in the art world. If he can't tell me more about this little painting, then I'll be very surprised."

Rutledge smiled. "Thank you. When we've finished with it, I shall have to return it to its rightful owner. Meanwhile, I leave it in your care."

The call on Galloway had not taken an inordinate amount of time. When he reached Dedham, the shops were still open and Rutledge went in search of one that sold embroidered handkerchiefs. The first two carried only initialed, Irish linen, or lace edged. Hand embroidery, he was told, was hard to come by since the war, most people accepting the inferior machine-made handkerchiefs for lack of a better choice.

The third was a shop called Mary's. The window was decorated with paper flowers, children's pinafores, and an assortment of gloves.

A middle-aged customer was gossiping with the woman behind the counter, regaling her with a story in a low voice that indicated how salacious it was. She broke off in some confusion as Rutledge came through the door, and hastily bade the younger woman a good day before hurrying out.

There were no other customers in the shop, and the woman behind the counter turned to Rutledge with a polite "Could I help you with anything, sir?"

He took the handkerchief out and placed it on the counter, so that the embroidered corner was uppermost. "I'm looking for something like this for my sister."

She didn't need to examine it. He could tell that she had recognized it at once.

Smiling sadly, she said, "I'm afraid we don't carry these any longer. The woman who embroidered them for us died in the spring. She was quite elderly, but her fingers were as nimble as a girl's. My customers bought them as a kindness, because this was her only income, but also because they were so charming. Flowers, birds, puppies, kittens." Shaking her head, she added, "I could have sold dozens of them, but of course she could turn out only so many."

"Who bought them?"

She frowned. "I don't talk about the people who come to my shop."

He took out his identification and set it on the counter next to the handkerchief.

She stared at it, then looked back at him. "Why are you here? Not for a lady's handkerchief, surely."

"It's precisely why I'm here. Did other shops carry this particular line of embroidery?"

"They were exclusive to Mary's. Because Miss Delaney could only provide so many a week."

"Did Miss French, for example, purchase the pansies?"

"She preferred roses. Miss Whitman and Mrs. Harris bought pansies."

"Who is Mrs. Harris?"

"She's the sister of the owner of the Marlborough Head."

This was the inn just down the High Street from the Sun.

"Was there a large market for the birds?"

"Yes, they were quite popular. The chats and the tits were quite lovely. My mother was fond of the puppies. Could you tell me why you're asking these questions? Has it to do with Mary's?"

"This handkerchief was found in Surrey. I don't know how it came to be there. Or why. If this handkerchief was exclusive to your shop, I needn't waste my time in London or Hatfield."

She appeared to be relieved. "Yes, of course. I can tell you that this particular example was indeed embroidered by Miss Delaney because of the delicacy of the stitches. See for yourself." She went to a drawer along the back wall of the shop and took out several handkerchiefs. Bringing them to Rutledge, she pointed to a nosegay of violets. "Compare these to the pansies."

"Yes, I do see," he replied. The difference was noticeable. He found himself thinking that Miss Delaney must have had extraordinary eyesight to take such tiny stitches, giving the colors almost a three-dimensional quality. "Thank you." He picked up the handkerchief and returned it to his pocket. "I must caution you not to discuss my visit with anyone. It's police business at the moment."

"Yes, of course, I do understand."

The door behind him opened, and two women came in, chatting and laughing. He used their presence to make his escape without having to answer more questions.

His next call was at the Dedham police station. The constable behind the desk looked up from the forms in front of him, realized that Rutledge was a stranger, and asked, "Yes, sir. Could I help you?"

Rutledge identified himself. "I'm here about an old case that might—or might not—have a connection with an event in St. Hilary some fifteen or twenty years ago. You're too young to remember. Is there anyone who might recall the event?"

The constable's face brightened. "That would be Sergeant Terrill. He's only just retired. You'll find him in Laurel Cottage on the St. Hilary road." He gave Rutledge directions, adding, "If there's more we can do, Inspector Thompkins will be in shortly."

Terrill's cottage stood in a small open space just before a copse of trees. Both the house and the gardens were in such good condition that it was clear the sergeant had found time heavy on his hands after his retirement to civilian life.

Rutledge ran him down in the back garden, cultivating between rows of vegetables, sleeves rolled up and his forehead creased with the effort.

Terrill looked up, straightened quickly, and said, "I don't believe I know you."

"You don't," Rutledge replied. "Inspector Rutledge, Scotland Yard. The constable on duty in Dedham told me how to find you."

Terrill visibly relaxed, saying, "And what brings you to Essex, sir?"

"Curiosity," Rutledge told him. "I have heard that, some years ago, a madman broke into the house belonging to the French family and made threats. But he was quickly apprehended and sent away to be locked up. Had you joined the police by that time?"

"I had, a green constable who hardly knew his arse from his elbow. But how did you come to know about this?"

"A tutor had just arrived to be interviewed for a position teaching the two French boys. He was in the house at the time."

"Was he, by God. We were never told about that. Someone would have interviewed him."

"I don't think the family wanted that. And I find that curious. Will you tell me what happened?"

Terrill led Rutledge to a pair of benches under a tree.

"One of the household, a maid, came running into the police station in St. Hilary, where I was posted at the time. She was frightened out of her wits, and I sent her along to Dedham on my bicycle, to find Inspector Wade. I got to the house first, of course, being closer. It was already dark, and the door stood open to the night. From inside I heard raised voices, and I was that glad to see the Inspector arriving on my heels. The maid had run into him coming out of his house after his dinner. He set me to watch the door and charged inside. There was even more of an uproar, and he shouted for me. I ran in to help. In the drawing room, it was a sight. Overturned tables and chairs, the elder Mr. French standing there like something carved from stone, and the Inspector trying to handcuff a dark-haired man who was so red in the face, I thought he would have an apoplexy. I added my weight to that of the Inspector, and we finally got the fellow under control, wrestling him into a chair while French watched."

"French. Which member of the family was he? The father or the grandfather of the present Mr. French?"

"Lewis French's grandfather. Mr. Howard French. He had just come up from London. His son was lying on the floor, blood on his face and murder in his eyes if I ever saw it. I went to help him, and he shook me off with an oath, stood up on his own, swaying a little. The doctor was there; he'd been attending to Mr. Laurence, and next he went to look at Mr. Howard's lip. I could see a bloody knife on the floor, kicked to one side."

"Go on."

"The elder Mr. French didn't seem best pleased to see us. He told us that the man was out of his head and that he wanted him dragged off to the nearest asylum, not to gaol. I didn't doubt he was right. The man was still cursing and yelling in a foreign tongue that we were later told was Portuguese. Both Mr. French and his father spoke it. We asked the elder Mr. French to translate, but he got fed up and turned to tell us that there was no reasoning with the man. He said that the intruder accused the family of theft, and it was clear that he would have to be shut up, or he'd come back to finish what he'd begun. Even

I could see it was true. It was as if the man was obsessed, shouting abuse and threats even with the police standing right there. That's when the doctor gave him something to settle him down. Inspector Wade wasn't happy about that, but I couldn't see what else to do."

"That was the end of it?"

"Mr. Howard spoke up, then. He said he felt sorry for the poor devil—his words—and that he was a stranger in a strange land, and he himself would pay for whatever was needful. His care, whatever treatment was required. The Inspector still wanted to know what the fuss was about, and the younger Mr. French said the man's father had sold a certain property in Madeira to the family, and his son, who had a history of mental disturbance, had taken it into his head that the farm had been stolen from him and that the father had had no right to act without his knowledge. The son had, in fact, been in prison at the time for violent protests against the Portuguese government."

"Was this true? Was there any legal proof offered to you?"

"It wasn't for me to ask, and it seemed that the Inspector believed Mr. French. In the circumstances, there was the evidence of our own eyes that the man was mad, and even with the drug he'd been given, you could read his face. He wanted blood. It was as simple as that."

"Was the intruder taken to the police station and kept in custody?"

"Mr. French asked the doctor for his opinion, and the doctor said that he didn't think custody was the answer, that the man was too violent and would have to be kept sedated if we expected to handle him. There was also the language problem."

"This was Dr. Townsend?" Rutledge had been given the answer by MacFarland, but he wanted to be sure.

"No, the doctor before him. I can tell you, I didn't relish the idea of having to feed and take care of someone all but foaming at the mouth with madness. They discussed it a bit between them, and the doctor suggested a private asylum near Cambridge. I didn't know anything about it, but Inspector Wade had heard of it. The question was, who would pay for such care? Mr. French said he felt responsible and would see to it that the man wanted for nothing. The doctor replied that it was very generous of him. And it was. He could have had the man up for attempted murder."

"What then?"

"Mr. French contacted Cambridge. They asked if the patient could be brought to them for observation. There was nothing they could do until they had seen the lay of the land, like. And so Mr. Howard French and the doctor bundled the man into a carriage, and they set out for Cambridge then and there. Inspector Wade wanted me to take statements from everyone first, but as Mr. French was not pressing charges, it was agreed that the matter was no longer the concern of the police."

"And Wade was satisfied with that?"

"He was. He said that if the man had behaved properly, coming to the house and speaking to Mr. French about his belief that his father had been cheated, rather than forcing his way in and attacking Mr. French, he'd have insisted on giving him a hearing. But he couldn't speak the language, all the evidence in the case was in a foreign land, and the man was in no mood to be reasoned with. Mr. Laurence reminded everyone there were women and young children in that house, and if the intruder got loose, next time there might be far more serious consequences."

"Did you learn this man's name?"

"I did. And I was not likely to forget it. Ever. Afonso Diaz."

"Was he committed to the asylum for the rest of his life?"

"Yes, of course he was. But there's new thinking now on such cases. I discovered quite by chance that he was released two years ago. A broken man, the doctors at the asylum said, and no threat to himself or anyone else."

"Was he sent back to Portugal?"

"No, sir, he had learned a trade and was content to stay in England."

"What trade?" Rutledge could hear the echo of Hamish's voice: What trade for a man like Afonso Diaz, who had come to England to commit murder?

"Gardening. He'd spent the last ten years tending the asylum gardens. He talked to the plants, I was told, but was meek as a lamb otherwise. A very modern doctor, it seems, who didn't believe in keeping such a man under lock and key, judged him cured." There was doubt in the sergeant's voice.

"Where did he choose to go to live after leaving the asylum?"

"He went to Surrey, I was told."

The question was, could this old man be a threat to the family now? Could he have plotted to kill Lewis French, only a child when Diaz had gone to the French house, and something, somehow had gone wrong? How could he have driven French's motorcar all the way to that quarry? Where indeed had he learned to drive? He would not have forgot where to find the French family, whatever else he could or could not do.

Rutledge could see that he had no choice but to look into Afonso Diaz's movements in the last few weeks. But it seemed that the sergeant was right. After all, the asylum had chosen to free him, and there was his age, to boot. Still, the Yard couldn't ignore the connection with the French family.

Terrill was saying, "One good thing came of that night. I was promoted out of St. Hilary the very next week, and another man was brought in from Suffolk. Inspector Wade found himself in the Cambridge constabulary. And the housemaid who had come screaming to my door was told never to speak of that night again, on pain of instant dismissal. She was a clever girl, she knew better than to embarrass the family."

And so all evidence that Afonso Diaz had ever come to St. Hilary had been expunged. Except in the memories of a tutor and a policeman.

Rutledge found himself wondering if the family had done that out of guilt or out of a care for the firm's good name. If the land that had made French, French & Traynor famous for its fine wines had once belonged to the Diaz family, and the sale was questionable, the repercussions could have been formidable. Howard French had saved his family—and his firm—by his quick actions.

On the whole, Rutledge believed that French had been telling the truth. He was too good a businessman to cheat a rival.

Hamish said, "Gossip doesna' hear the truth."

This was pressing new information. He ought to go directly to Surrey. But there was the matter of the handkerchief still to be dealt with. Until he could learn more about Diaz, the evidence still pointed directly at Valerie Whitman.

And before he left Essex, he would have to call on her.

Chapter Ten

This time Rutledge didn't watch for Miss Whitman to leave her house.

He knocked on the door and stood there patiently waiting.

After several minutes, she opened the door herself, and he asked if he could come in.

"Must you?" she responded.

"I don't think what I have to say is something you want your neighbors gossiping about behind your back."

She stared at him. But he could see that she was torn between telling him to go away and hearing whatever it was he had to say.

Finally she opened the door and let him inside.

The cottage was furnished with lovely old pieces that must have been inherited, and the colors of the curtains, the carpets, and the chair coverings were pleasing. The room to which she took him was done up in pale greens and creams, and several of the paintings on the wall were quite good.

Offering him a chair, she stood by the hearth, indicating her intention to keep the interview short.

He could see again how different she was from Miss Townsend. In manner, appearance, temperament. And he regretted having to show her the handkerchief and question her about it.

Then he changed his mind, holding it out to her. "I believe this belongs to you," he said simply.

She came to take it from him and looked at it. He could read her face, and he knew before she answered what she was going to say.

"Wherever did you find this?" she asked warily.

"I believe it was embroidered by Miss Delaney."

"Yes, yes," she said impatiently. "But where did you find it?"

"It was found beneath the driver's seat of Lewis French's motorcar."

"*Where?* Why should Lewis have my handkerchief?"

"I don't know that he did. It was found under the seat. He might not have seen it there."

"Well, then, if you've located his motorcar, you can ask him." She gave the handkerchief back to him.

"I told you that we had the motorcar. So far we don't have Mr. French."

"Oh." She digested that, then said after a moment, "Are you saying that you believe I had something to do with his disappearance?"

"As you can see, the handkerchief is relatively fresh. It couldn't have been where it was for months. For that matter, the man who sees to the motorcar for French tells me he cleans it thoroughly whenever it is taken out. He would have found the handkerchief long ago."

"Then Lewis put it there. For some ridiculous reason of his own. I didn't. I will swear to that."

"If he's engaged to another woman, why should he have kept your handkerchief?"

"I didn't say that he did. I'm not always at home. The house is unlocked. The shop sells these to other customers. You must ask him these questions. I can't answer them."

"Miss Whitman, if you will help me, I'll be better able to help you."

"I don't need your help. I don't need anyone's help."

"The Yard is going to find the person who used Lewis French's motorcar to run down and kill a man. Someone who may've thought he was killing French himself. And if French is still alive, he may well find him and not bungle his murder a second time. In some quarters, you appear to have a very good motive for killing French—for all we know, it was you who got the wrong man. The Yard will be looking closely at you and at how your engagement to French ended. At any hard feelings you may still harbor. Tell me what you know—or what you suspect has happened. It will save you a great deal of grief. Believe me."

She considered him. "Do you really think I could have killed anyone?" Her voice began to shake at the start, and then she brought it under control.

"Sadly, for the police there is nothing that marks a murderer. Nothing that allows us to look at you and know whether you are guilty or innocent."

"I've killed no one," she said huskily. "Please go. Please."

Cursing himself for what he'd had to say, he rose. "If you need help, send for me. I must go to London straightaway, and you can reach me through Sergeant Gibson at the Yard. Will you promise me to call?"

He waited, but she said nothing more, her gaze turned away from him, her face half in shadow so that he couldn't read her expression or see the color of her eyes. He had no choice. He left the house.

As he walked back to his motorcar, Hamish spoke unexpectedly.

"Ye ken, if she tried to kill him, and instead killed the wrong man, he couldha' helped her dispose of the corpse."

Men had done stranger things, but Rutledge couldn't picture

Lewis French being cajoled into doing it. Unless he'd found it the only way out.

"Then why did he disappear afterward?" Rutledge asked, speaking aloud.

"Because he's had second thoughts about the wisdom of marrying the other lass."

It held together too well for comfort. Lewis French could have disposed of the corpse by driving it to Chelsea, and then left the motorcar in the quarry to throw off the police. If true, this would most certainly explain why the dead man was carrying Lewis French's watch. After all, French would eventually get it back after the police had finished their inquiry.

But where was he now? Why hadn't he come forward with a tale of being robbed, his motorcar taken away, leaving him too dazed to find his way home again until now?

And why was Hamish suddenly defending Valerie Whitman?

Rutledge stopped at the French house to ask Agnes French if she had heard from her brother.

As he expected, she had not.

She said waspishly, "He never thinks of anyone but himself. Michael was never as selfish as Lewis. But then my parents spoiled him because of his seizures. He expects me to treat him the same way. And I refuse to cater to his whims."

"If you hear from him, will you let the Yard know where he is and where he's been?"

"If you want to know my brother's whereabouts, look for him yourself. I won't be made my brother's keeper even for Scotland Yard."

Rutledge left it at that and set out for Cambridge.

The asylum on the outskirts of town was, he discovered, a small private clinic for the mentally ill. It struck him as he drove up the short drive that it had been very wise of Howard French or his son

Laurence, whoever had made this decision, to put their problem into an isolated private clinic where he could be successfully hidden away. With no family or friends in England, Diaz would have no way of leaving on his own.

Rutledge wondered if Michael or Lewis French had unwittingly neglected to pay for the man's keep, which had allowed the doctor in charge to decide to release him without letting the family know. If there had been no provision for the fees in the late Laurence French's will, and the sons knew nothing about the intruder in the house, it would be understandable. For that matter, the elder French, after his stroke, could have forgot the man existed.

The manor house was well kept, the grounds pleasant, and no fences spoiled the image of a private country estate. A place where unwanted family problems could be discreetly kept out of the public eye. Even the King had allowed young Prince John to be locked away until he had been all but lost to public view.

Hardly the place one would expect to find a Portuguese farmer's troublesome son.

Rutledge opened the door into a lobby where a woman was seated behind a small but very pretty cherry desk.

She greeted him pleasantly and asked if he was a visitor.

"I've come to speak to one of your doctors about a man who used to be a patient here. My name is Rutledge. Scotland Yard."

The smile slipped a little, but the woman said, "If you'll be seated, Mr. Rutledge, I'll ask if Dr. Milton is available."

She turned and stepped through the door just behind where she was seated. And she was gone for some time.

He was on the point of following her when she finally came back, held the door open, and an elderly man preceded her into Reception.

"Mr. Rutledge? I'm Dr. Milton. Senior medical staff."

They shook hands, and then Dr. Milton suggested, "Perhaps a stroll in the grounds would be best. You can speak freely there."

Or, Rutledge thought, the doctor himself could.

They went out into the sunlight, crossed the drive, and set off across the lawn.

"I understand you wish to see me about a patient. Is he—or she—in trouble with the law, or is it something else?"

"As far as I know, there's no problem with the law. The patient is Afonso Diaz. Or at least that's the name he was using."

"Ah. I see. A rather . . . unusual case, as I recall."

"You treated him?"

"I tried to. I'm not sure whether I succeeded in helping him or he simply grew tired of carrying the burden of anger for so many years."

"Why was he angry?"

"It's a long story. We cobbled it together from what Diaz told us and from what the Portuguese police had to say. They had no interest in him—he'd served his time and they more or less washed their hands of him. Apparently he was a student in Lisbon, sent there from Madeira by his father. It seems he joined a rather radical group of student agitators, and in the end he was arrested, tried, and sentenced. He remained in prison for some ten years. When he was finally released, he learned that his father, rather than wait for him to return one day to Madeira, had sold the family estate to outsiders—in fact, to the firm of French, French and Traynor. I don't know how the young Diaz was treated in prison. There were indications of brutality, but he could have brought that on himself in the beginning. Apparently he had suffered in silence, was set free, and blamed everyone but himself for his troubles. I expect the truth of the matter was, his father had given up hope and decided that his son would never settle down to the land. Perhaps he was right, because shortly after his release his son had sworn vengeance against the friends he thought had betrayed him to the police. He nearly got himself arrested again, this time on far more serious charges. He fled to Madeira, only to discover what his father had done in his absence. I imagine the father never found the courage to write and explain to his son why he'd sold the land. Perhaps he was even afraid of him. At any rate, Diaz was convinced that the wine merchants had tricked his father into selling."

"And Diaz waited for his chance to avenge himself against Howard French. The grandfather of the present family."

"Precisely." Dr. Milton nodded. "By that time, apparently, the elder French was no longer traveling to Madeira. He'd left that to his son. It took some time for Diaz to find the money for his passage to England—his own father was dead now, and his second wife, whom he'd married while Afonso was in prison, was not about to share her inheritance with the black sheep of the family. But he finally reached England some twenty years ago, bent on revenge, his mind absorbed by it to the point of excluding everything else. Howard French was the cause of all his problems, and Howard French would pay for that."

"Was he armed when he came to the house in St. Hilary?"

"He was, although Howard's son had managed to disarm him before the police arrived. A rather nasty-looking knife. He was declared mentally unfit to be tried for assault, trespass, and attempted murder. Instead he was brought here."

"And where did he go when he was released?"

"He was growing infirm physically, but he loved to garden, and I found a family in Surrey, the Bennetts, who would take him on as an undergardener. I didn't think he was capable of carrying out his revenge—after all, both Howard French and his son were dead by this time. And Diaz had earned the right to leave."

"He's still with the family in Surrey?"

"Yes, of course. I receive monthly reports."

"Did he make friends when he was here?"

"Not really. There was one man he seemed to like. But I couldn't describe it as a friendship. It was more the sense that both were outcasts, unwanted, unwelcomed in society as a whole."

"I'd like to speak to this man."

"He died in the influenza epidemic. Quite a few of our patients did. It swept through the clinic like wildfire and was as quickly gone. Many of them had physical as well as mental deficiencies, and they were vulnerable."

"Is that all you can tell me about Afonso Diaz?"

"Yes. He was an odd case, I never really got to know him. The language barrier, for one thing, and the way he nursed his belief that his life was ruined by others. But that faded with age, leaving a shell of the man he once was. The fires of hate consume some people, and in the end there's little left because the person never filled the void with anything else."

"And yet you felt that he was safe enough to be let out into a population that knew nothing of his history."

"But the Bennetts do," Dr. Milton said. "They have always felt strongly that we have a duty to the less fortunate, and they have taken in many of our patients as well as a few of the criminally insane who are declared cured. And in all this time, they've never been proved wrong."

Rutledge thought that Dr. Milton was more than a little naïve. Once out of his care, people could revert to their true selves. Could connive and plot and inveigle and even kill. And by the time the good doctor learned he'd been wrong, someone else would have paid the price.

He thanked Dr. Milton and left the clinic. But he carried one thing away with him. The address where the Bennett family lived in Surrey.

He slept in his own bed that night, and in the morning, despite a slow drizzle of rain as he set out, he drove into Surrey. The sun found him there, the rain clouds moving northeast.

The Bennett family owned a sprawling property along the Berkshire–Surrey border. The drive led through an overgrown wood, but the grounds near the house were well manicured, the flowers in the two borders planted with an eye to coordinating colors. The effect was like a rainbow.

The door to the house stood wide, sunlight spilling into the flagged hall. Rutledge saw no bell, and he was about to knock when a voice from the corner called, "Help you, sir?"

"I'm looking for Mr. or Mrs. Bennett." He turned to see a skeleton-thin boy standing there.

"Mrs. Bennett is sitting on the terrace watching a croquet match."

"Show me the way, if you please."

The boy nodded and waited for Rutledge to come up to him at the corner of the house. "I'm Luke," he said. "I'm recovering from tuberculosis."

"Are you indeed?" Rutledge replied, not giving his name, although he was fairly certain the boy had expected him to.

"Yes. Fresh air and good food. That's the ticket," he responded. "I drink a lot of milk."

Along the west front of the house, a terrace looked out over a grassy lawn where a fierce game of croquet was in progress. The woman sitting in a chair under a black umbrella looked up. "You were right, Luke. A motorcar. Wonderful. And who is this?"

Rutledge reached the terrace steps and paused. "The name is Rutledge."

The woman frowned. "I thought they were sending someone named Martin. Well, of course I might have misheard. Now then, Mr. Rutledge, you can see that we occasionally play croquet together. It promotes a sense of cooperation and provides exercise."

Looking at the croquet game, Rutledge thought it promoted a competitive spirit that bordered on warfare. The players were all men of various ages, from fifteen to sixty, if he was any judge. Sweating in the sun, they must have been thirsty and uncomfortable.

Mrs. Bennett herself was closer to fifty than forty, her hair already streaked with gray, her clothing more classical than cool, despite the umbrella. It was then he noticed the twisted foot under the hem of her skirt.

"I can see that it does," Rutledge said. "Could I speak with you in private, please?"

"I'm not ready to go inside," she told him. "And I'm sure you'll want to interview my staff."

"Interview?"

"You *are* from the *Times,* are you not?"

"I'm afraid not."

"Drat," she said in annoyance, and then to the croquet players she called, "Shall we take a break? This was not the gentleman I expected."

The men broke off their game with alacrity and went to sit in the shade of the nearest tree. All but Luke, who still stood just behind Rutledge.

"Perhaps Luke would be happier in the shade as well," Rutledge suggested.

"Luke, would you stay by the door, in the event Mr. Martin appears? There's a dear boy."

Luke reluctantly walked off, and Mrs. Bennett turned to Rutledge. "There, we are quite alone. What is your business with me, Mr. Rutledge?"

"I've come to speak to you about one of your staff. A gardener named Diaz."

"And what is it you need to know about him?"

"Is he still in your employ?"

"Of course. Sadly he suffers from rheumatism, which makes getting down on his knees even more difficult, but he has a marvelous eye for color, and so he instructs the undergardener, who does the actual work."

"Where do you find most of your staff, Mrs. Bennett?"

"There's the problem, you see. We could no longer afford to keep a staff. The war has made life difficult for everyone, and so we decided that perhaps we could help those in need of help and still make life bearable for ourselves. In a small way, we are striving for a brighter world. No one labeled, no one treated with less than courtesy, everyone contributing in the best way he or she can. Call it an experiment in kindness."

He rather thought that her kindness was self-serving, but the boy Luke appeared to be happy enough, and certainly if he was well fed and cared for, he would regain his health here more quickly than in a crowded tenement.

"Where do you find your staff?" he asked again.

"We contact various institutions, asking if they have inmates who would benefit from a second chance. Luke Simmons suffers from tuberculosis, he grew up in the worst slums in Manchester, and what he needed was country air, which we have in great plenty. We have a man from a mental institution—Afonso Diaz—who as you know is our gardener, with the help of Bob Rawlings, who is also interested in growing things. Sam Henry drives the motorcar for me—as you can see, I'm crippled. Harry Bray is a wonder in the kitchen. He and Davy Evans 252 keep us fed. Evans had been in prison so long he forgot how to live a normal life without bars and locks and warders. He wandered the grounds for days, simply looking at freedom. It was very touching. He was the two hundred and fifty-second prisoner by the name of Evans in the Welsh jail, and he likes his number used even in conversation."

"Do your staff keep in touch with the world they lived in before they were—er—incarcerated?"

"Most of them have no one other than us. That's why they're here. Bob sometimes writes to his brother, but I gather they have little in common. Bob told me once that they had different fathers." She smoothed her skirts with her fingertips. "Can you tell me why you are curious about our little family?"

"Has anyone on your staff left the house recently? For an extended period of time?"

"Harry does our marketing, of course, since I can't. Sam takes the motorcar for petrol. I don't see that that's a problem. They are never away for more than half an hour."

"And Afonso Diaz?"

"I don't believe he's set foot outside the gates since he arrived. There's a language barrier, you know." She smiled. "The flowers and vegetables don't seem to care."

But just how strong a barrier was it?

"I'd like to speak to him, if that's possible."

She turned to one of the men beneath the tree. "Would you fetch Afonso, please? Mr. Rutledge would like to speak to him."

"I'd prefer it if Luke took me to find him," Rutledge interjected.

"Yes, of course. It will save Afonso walking back to us. How kind of you."

Rutledge went to the front of the house and gave Luke the message regarding Diaz.

The boy set off at a trot, and Rutledge followed. They walked away from the house and toward a shrubbery that he could see in the distance. Beyond was an orchard that was heavy with fruit. So heavy, he discovered when he'd gone through the gate, that several branches had been broken by a storm, their leaves already drying.

A man stood on the ground shading his eyes, looking up at a younger man, who was doing the pruning. The saw bit through the limb, and it came crashing down.

The younger man said, "A pity. They're nearly ripe, those apples. I'll have one when I'm off this ladder—" He broke off as he saw Luke coming down the break between lines of trees, leading Rutledge toward them. "Who the hell's that?" he demanded, starting down the ladder.

The other man turned to see and said something under his breath.

Rutledge reached them, nodded to the younger man, then said to the elder, "Mr. Diaz?"

There was a pause, then the man said, "I am," in a deep voice that was heavily accented. But Rutledge had a feeling his English was better than he was willing to admit. He'd had twenty years to learn in an environment where Portuguese was never spoken, and at times he'd communicated with his doctor. What's more, he'd been to university; he wasn't an untaught farmer's son who could hardly read or write in any language.

"Will you walk with me a little way? I'd like to speak to you privately."

"Does Mrs. Bennett know you're here?" his companion demanded, his eyes narrowed. "She doesn't care for strangers coming into her property."

Luke said helpfully, "That's Bob."

"It was Mrs. Bennett who asked Luke to take me to you." He considered Bob, a short man with strong, broad shoulders and the belligerent nature of an undersize bulldog. "How long have you been working for her?"

"Four years, if it's any of your business."

"Actually, it is my business." Reaching into his pocket, Rutledge took out his identification, holding it so that both men could see it clearly.

Luke whistled. "Cor! Scotland Yard."

"I think Mrs. Bennett is expecting you," Rutledge said to the boy. "The photographer? I'll have no trouble finding my way back to the house."

"Oh. Yes." Luke, obviously torn between duty and curiosity, hesitated for a few seconds, then turned away. He walked slowly, scuffing in the thick grass under the trees.

Rutledge waited until he was out of earshot, then repeated, "Mr. Diaz? If you will walk with me?"

Diaz glanced at Rawlings, then without a word followed Rutledge back toward the gate.

Diaz was not what Rutledge had expected. The image he'd had of a man bursting into the French house, threatening the French family with a knife, and then being wrestled to the ground and disarmed was far from the reality.

A small, wiry man with a naturally dark complexion and nearly white hair, he had deep-set, black-lashed, dark eyes that struck Rutledge as still young in spite of the hands and elbows knotted with rheumatism. His back was straight, and his clothes smelled of applewood smoke.

When they reached the gate, he regarded Rutledge, then said with resignation, "Am I being returned to the clinic?"

"Mrs. Bennett appears to be very happy with your work. I've come to ask you how you feel today about the firm of French, French and Traynor."

"That was long ago. Today I am old, tired. They will not let me return to Madeira to die. I would like that very much. It is all that matters to me now."

Hamish said, "But he didna' live there verra' long."

It was a good point. The boy Afonso had gone to the Portuguese mainland to school, had got himself into trouble there and served out his prison sentence there.

And for a man who purportedly knew very little English, he had circumvented Rutledge's question very neatly.

There was, Rutledge thought, more to Afonso Diaz than met the eye.

But suspicion was not proof of any wrongdoing. The question remained—had his years in an asylum changed him for the better? Or the worse? He had not been mad, not in the accepted sense. But he had been shut up with the mad.

"Have you had any contact—directly or indirectly—with the French family since your release?"

"I don't understand 'directly or indirectly.'"

Rutledge waited for a beat before rephrasing the question. He would have wagered that Diaz knew perfectly well what the words meant. "Have you written, spoken to—even on the telephone—or seen a male member of the French family since your release?"

"I can think of no reason to do this."

"Have you asked anyone else to write, speak to, or call on any member of the family for you?"

"I know no one in England, except for the Senhora and the people at the asylum. Who would I ask to do such things?"

Rutledge changed tactics. "Do you hold Lewis French to blame for his grandfather's decision to purchase your father's land?"

"I do not know this Lewis French."

Which was true, in the literal sense. Diaz had never seen the French children when he came uninvited to the house. But he could have made it his business, since his release, to find out what had become of the senior members of the family. The Bennetts must read the London papers. And at some point, French's name would have been mentioned in connection with a charity event or business meetings on exports and imports, or even a social gathering.

"If it could be arranged for you to return to Madeira, would you be willing to leave England straightaway?"

Something stirred in the back of the man's eyes. Rutledge could have sworn it was a smile.

"Yes."

Because his work was done? French was dead?

There had been a Portuguese contingent in the last two years of the war, but Rutledge had had no personal contact with them. He had been told that they were good men but that their music had been dark and fatalistic.

It offered him no key to this man standing patiently waiting for his next question.

Diaz had come to England alone, knowing very little of the language, and yet he'd found his way to Dedham to demand what he believed was his right.

"When your father died, did he leave you any of the money he'd been given for the farm in Madeira?"

"When I went to prison, he told me he owed me nothing."

Now that, Rutledge thought, was interesting. If Diaz had lost his inheritance because of his fall from grace, it was well before the family vineyards had been sold to the English firm. It was possible that he had come to England for a very different reason from the one everyone had believed. Of course there was the language barrier at that time, but Rutledge was fairly sure the French family must speak Portuguese fluently in order to do business in Madeira and on the mainland. Whatever the doctor and the police were told, Howard and Laurence French would have understood what was driving this man. The land had been taken away before he'd had a chance to redeem himself in his father's eyes. And his father, after the sale, had remained adamant about an inheritance.

Why hadn't Howard French or his son told the authorities the whole truth?

Attempted murder—attempted revenge—would have brought Diaz into the courtroom to face trial. But they had chosen to send him to the asylum.

Rutledge realized that they must have been very afraid of him—and afraid to trust the courts to keep him away from them. The only safety lay in putting him somewhere they could rely on his being locked up for good.

And as far as Rutledge was concerned, studying the closed face in front of him, this man had a better motive for killing Lewis French than anyone he'd interviewed in St. Hilary.

The problem was going to be proving it.

How had Diaz managed to leave this estate without his absence being noted and reported to the clinic by the Bennetts?

Or would they have done so? Their experiment was succeeding against the odds. If one of their staff was involved in any crime, it would mean the end of their comfort.

Diaz was still waiting for the next question, clearly in no haste to end their conversation.

Rutledge nodded. "Thank you. I'll come back if there are any more questions."

"I have nothing to hide," Diaz said, then as an afterthought, he added "Sir."

The game was over when Rutledge reached the lawn again. Mrs. Bennett was closeted with the photographer and was not to be disturbed.

Rutledge turned to Luke. "Do the members of the staff leave the estate for any reason?"

"No, sir. Even the doctor comes here when he's needed."

"What's his name?"

"Dr. Burgess."

"Do any of the inmates send or receive letters?"

"Most of us have no one to write to," the boy said. "Much less anyone who cares enough to write to us. Mrs. Bennett always tells us that we are her family now. We don't need anyone else."

"That's very kind."

"I think," the boy said, practical as well as honest, "it's not kindness so much as knowing we don't have anywhere else to go."

Chapter Eleven

Rutledge had said nothing to Mrs. Bennett about calling on Dr. Burgess. And so he had not asked her where the doctor's surgery could be found, assuming it must be in the nearest village.

To his surprise when he pulled up in front of the first surgery he came to, the name on the board was not Burgess. He went inside anyway and asked the woman behind the desk if she could direct him to the right place.

She frowned as if displeased by his question, saying only, "He lives on Blackwell Street, just off the High, next to the shoemaker's shop."

Rutledge thanked her and went to find Blackwell. It was more a lane than a proper street, narrow and running off at an angle several streets past the square. He found the shoemaker easily enough but was surprised to see that Burgess lived in a modest house with no surgery attached.

He knocked at the door, and after a time it was opened by a slender, once-handsome man whose bloodshot blue eyes and overlong, graying hair told their own tale. But his voice was not slurred as he said, "What is it you want?"

"I'm looking for Dr. Burgess," he said.

"And I am he. I no longer practice medicine in this community. If you need care, see Dr. Preston. He's on the High, you can't miss his surgery."

"Are you still able to practice medicine?"

"That, sir, is my business and not yours. I bid you good day."

But Rutledge had his boot in the door and said, "I was just at Mrs. Bennett's house."

Burgess paused. "We had an agreement, she and I. I would treat her staff, as Dr. Preston would not, but no one else. Neither friend— nor foe."

"Why did Dr. Preston refuse to serve her staff?"

"If you've been there, I don't have to tell you that the good doctor suggested to her that convicted felons and madmen caused his other patients some disquiet. Poppycock. He's afraid of them himself."

"I've come to your door because I need to talk to you about one of her staff."

Burgess made to close the door again. "I cannot discuss my patients."

"You can discuss your personal relationships with them. My name is Rutledge, and I'm from Scotland Yard."

Burgess stared at him. "Are you, indeed. Well, come in, then. We'll see whether you're right or I am."

Rutledge followed him into a comfortable sitting room. It was clearly kept tidy for visitors, but in the passage leading to it, there was the lingering odor of stale whisky. Hamish said, "It's no' good whisky. He canna' afford the best."

Taking the chair that Burgess casually pointed out, Rutledge said,

"I'm not particularly interested in the health and well-being of your patients. What I should like to ask is whether without Mrs. Bennett's knowledge you have carried messages or made telephone calls for any one of them."

"For one thing, I'm not on the telephone. And for another, I am not employed to deliver the post. I deal with the physical needs of my patients. Their connections with anyone outside the walls of the Bennett house are not my concern."

"But they are mine," Rutledge told him flatly. "Afonso Diaz had an altercation with two male members of a prominent family. He was carrying a knife at the time, and used it on one of the men in the room before he was disarmed. The son of that man has disappeared—since Mr. Diaz was released from the clinic and given employment with Mrs. Bennett. Mr. Diaz has the best motive to harm the son—now an adult—and it's my duty to find out if he is indeed responsible. Mrs. Bennett tells me that Mr. Diaz has not left the premises. Still, I'm of the opinion that he could very well have engaged someone else to carry out his revenge for him."

"Diaz, is it? Odd little man." Burgess frowned thoughtfully. "I can't tell you whether he's responsible or not. I most certainly haven't been a go-between for him and anyone else. I've carried no messages, made no contacts."

"Then who in that household could have done so?"

"Ah. It's Mrs. Bennett's belief that there is ultimate good in all of us. And that given a chance, a man will choose the right path as opposed to the wrong. It's an admirable belief. I don't subscribe to it myself. I've seen the best and the worst of human nature during my years as a doctor. I've seen depravity and despair and outright cruelty. I served in the trenches as a regular soldier until His Majesty's Government in its greater wisdom decided that medical men might be more useful in caring for the wounded. And I came home with nothing to help me forget but a bottle of spirits. Followed by a second and a third until

I have lost count. There are one or two of Mrs. Bennett's staff who could probably cut her throat without hesitation. And Diaz—when he chooses to speak English—is so devious he exhausts me when we talk. I strive to keep them healthy enough to do the tasks assigned to them. Beyond that, I am neither a father confessor nor a policeman, and most certainly not a nanny."

"Mrs. Bennett told me that this arrangement of hers was the solution to the problem of finding suitable servants. Is that true?"

"As far as I know, it is. She's an invalid herself, as you may have noticed, and requires assistance."

"I didn't meet Mr. Bennett. What can you tell me about him?"

"There's little to tell. He apparently adores his wife, for he does whatever she feels is right, and he's probably writing a treatise on the entire enterprise."

"She was expecting a photographer when I called."

"Good lord. The woman's run mad. It's one thing to convince herself that this foolish premise of hers works, but quite another to broadcast it to the world."

"Perhaps she still needs to convince herself."

Burgess considered that. "God help us," he said and rose to indicate that the interview was finished. "But I am not her keeper. I bid you good day, Mr. Rutledge."

Outside in the motorcar once more, Hamish said, "He's no' the first doctor to seek solace in whisky."

It was true enough. But what concerned Rutledge more than the doctor's mental collapse was his rather cavalier attitude toward Mrs. Bennett and his patients. He treated them as needed, but washed his hands of any responsibility. He knew that some of the men could be dangerous, and he ignored that.

But on the whole, Rutledge thought the doctor hadn't been involved in carrying messages between Diaz and someone else. He would make a point not to involve himself, not because of any moral scruples but because his own pain demanded all the energy and re-sources he had.

"No' so verra' different from your ain life," Hamish told him bluntly.

But Rutledge knew that his sense of duty and his responsibility to a victim—however good or bad that person might have been in life—outweighed hiding. Or he would never have had the courage to return to the Yard.

The question now, he reminded himself on the road north toward London, was what to do about Afonso Diaz. If the man was indeed innocent, then Rutledge could not in good conscience take him into custody without a great deal more evidence than he now possessed. Evidence that could link Diaz directly to Lewis French or evidence that he had persuaded someone else to carry out his acts of revenge.

The question was, how would Markham view this new development?

Rutledge was to find out sooner rather than later.

Markham had left word with Sergeant Gibson to send Rutledge to his office as soon as he came in.

Rutledge made his report as objectively as he could, bringing in what he had learned about Diaz, what he'd discovered in the French motorcar, and what conclusions he'd drawn from the facts available to him.

Markham listened without interrupting, his face unreadable. When Rutledge had finished, the Acting Chief Superintendent leaned forward in his chair and said, "I told you that motorcar of yours would lead you down the primrose path. Here you've been haring all over England, and there's nothing to show for it but an old man with a past. What about the woman in St. Hilary whose handkerchief you found under the seat of the motorcar? That's a great deal more damning than this nonsense about the mental patient."

"I can't see how she could have killed the man we found in Chelsea, put him into Lewis French's motorcar, driven him to London, and then left the motorcar in a quarry in Surrey before making her way back to Essex."

"There's an invention called the bicycle, man. She could have made her way to the nearest railway station or even into London for that matter, taken a train north, and got off a station before her own. Have you looked into that?"

Rutledge had not.

"Well, then, be about it. Put Gibson onto it or Fielding, or one of the other men at your disposal. It's critical to learn if she was on that train or not. If she was, she's damned."

"I'll see to it at once," Rutledge told him, "but meanwhile, I'd like to check the prison records of the men who live in Mrs. Bennett's house. Diaz couldn't just hire a killer from a costermonger's wares. He has to have someone who could point him in the right direction. Who knew someone who would be willing to kill."

"Precisely why we investigate the trains first, Rutledge." Markham lifted a file from the five or six at his elbow. "Report to me as soon as you have."

Dismissal.

Rutledge left with a nod, walking down the passage to his own office, listening to Hamish rampant in his mind, listening to his own doubts.

Gibson was busy. Rutledge went to Fielding, a steady man with long years of experience in deploying people to search out information. For it would take a contingent to do what Markham wanted.

Fielding listened to Rutledge's information, taking notes, rubbing the top of his bald head as if it would help him plan, then finally looked up with a nod.

"Yes. I agree that she's not likely to take a train in Surrey, not if that's where she left the motorcar. A small station, never very crowded? Someone is likely to remember her, especially if she's young and pretty. London is bigger, people everywhere, the stationmasters and their minions busy. She could slip through unnoticed. And you're right, it's some little distance from Surrey, on a bicycle. But men who drive lorries will take pity on a damsel in distress, trying to arrive home before her mother knows she's been out with a young lad. Or perhaps she claimed her mother was ill, and she had to go to her. Finding this lorry driver will be needle and haystack work. My suggestion is, we begin in London, and if we can spot her here, then we'll worry about the lorry driver later. Now then, experience leads me to believe it would be helpful to know the name of the dead man. We could cast a wider net."

"We don't have it."

"Is she a strong enough woman to pedal a bicycle for miles?"

"The ground is relatively flat."

"Indeed. And what's become of the bicycle?"

"Abandoned, at a guess. Or she may have decided to take it along. To account for it later."

"Absolutely. Yes. And now her description, if you please."

Rutledge gave it. Fielding raised his eyebrows. "A pretty young woman. Yes, very helpful, that. And where will you be meanwhile?"

"I'm going back to St. Hilary. There are some loose ends to clear away." Rutledge gave Fielding the name of the inn in Dedham.

"I remember Dedham. Such a pleasant town. Hard to believe it could harbor a murderess."

When Rutledge reached Dedham, it was very late. He had to rouse the night clerk to beg a room, and it was on an upper floor, eaves sloping down to the windows, giving it the feeling of walls closing in. He opened a window to let in the cool night air, tried to shut out Hamish from his mind, and settled himself to sleep through what little was left of the night. But the deep Scots voice, unrelenting and intolerable, kept him awake. In the end, he got up and sat in a chair by the window listening to the night sounds of the town until he fell asleep as a false dawn brought color back into the world.

There was one question that he needed to put to Miss Whitman: who else had been in her cottage the night that someone was killed with Lewis French's motorcar?

He found her coming back from market, a basket of early apples over her arm.

She slowed as she saw him waiting in the churchyard, near the wall, where she couldn't miss him.

"You again," she said, her voice carrying to him where he stood.

"Yes, I'm afraid so."

"You've found Lewis, then. And he's dead."

"What makes you believe that?"

"It's the only reason I can think of that would bring you back to the churchyard."

He stepped over the wall and was walking toward her. "He's still missing."

Miss Whitman frowned. "That's not like him. He's always busy."

"It's possible he struck the man we found dead. And he's afraid the police will be waiting to take him up."

She shook her head. "That doesn't sound like Lewis, either. If it was an accident, he'd have said so."

"And if it wasn't? If it was deliberate?"

"No, he has no enemies. Why should he have killed that man?"

But he did have an enemy, Hamish was pointing out. And if the man had tried to kill Lewis first, he'd have been justified in running him down.

That still didn't explain Lewis's disappearance.

Rutledge took a deep breath. "Do you live alone, Miss Whitman?"

"I have for some time."

"Do you have servants?"

"A daily who comes three times a week. A woman who prepares

my lunch and my dinner. I am perfectly capable of cooking my own breakfast."

"And can they swear that you were at home the night that Lewis French went missing?"

She looked away then. "I doubt it. The women are sisters. They live here in St. Hilary. Their brother took ill in Thetford, and they asked to go to him. They were away for the weekend, and for most of the week that followed, taking turns nursing him. Very inconvenient for me, isn't it?"

"I'm afraid so."

"Why should anyone think I would kill Lewis French?" She was suddenly angry. "I didn't love him, you know. I don't know that I loved Michael. He went to war so long ago that sometimes I have trouble remembering how I felt."

"Then why did you agree to marry him?"

"It was expected, I think. Even the Queen was engaged to one brother and married the other." Her voice was strained.

"Pride can be hurt as quickly as one's heart."

She turned back to him. "Yes. Pride."

He probed a little deeper, aware of some undercurrent that he couldn't quite put a finger on. She had all but grown up with the French family, and yet she lived here in this modest cottage with only a daily and a cook. She had been engaged to both brothers, which meant she had the blessing of the family. And yet a doctor's daughter was more socially prominent.

"Are you related to the family? A cousin, perhaps?"

She smiled. "Not at all."

Against his will, he said, "Because of the handkerchief, the Yard is nearly convinced that you are in some way responsible for Lewis French's disappearance and the death of a man whose body was found in Chelsea."

Her head to one side, she studied him. "You're a policeman. You must have dealt with the very worst sort of person. Do you really believe I'm capable of murder?"

Hamish's voice was loud in his ears, drowning out the bells in the church tower marking the hour. "'Ware!"

And Rutledge heeded the warning.

"I've told you. There's no mark of Cain to guide us in finding a killer."

She turned, walking away. "Then come and take me into custody when you're ready."

He watched her go, and just as she reached for the latch to open her door, he asked in a quiet voice that would carry to her and not to the neighbors, "Afonso Diaz. Do you by any chance know the name?"

She had said all she intended to say to him. She shut the door firmly behind her, leaving him with no choice but to return to his motorcar and drive away.

There was another call he intended to make this morning.

Miss French was in her garden, he was told when he arrived at her house, and Nan, the maid, had answered his knock.

And he found her there, a pinafore over her dress to protect it as she worked among the roses in a garden shaped like a half-moon.

Looking up, she recognized him and said quickly, "Well? Have you found my brother?"

"Not yet. We've located his motorcar. It was in Surrey."

"Surrey?" She frowned. "We don't know anyone there."

"As far as I can tell, it wasn't your brother who abandoned his motorcar in a chalk quarry."

"Aband— I think he cared more for that motorcar than for me. I don't believe you."

"Nevertheless, it's true. And I'm afraid I must ask you a few questions as a result."

She wiped her forehead with the back of her wrist, pushing away her hair, and said, "The summerhouse. Over there."

He followed her to a round Greek temple set on a slight rise that enabled her to view the garden in comfort. Cushioned bench seats followed the rail, and she took one side, offering him the other. From this vantage point he could see that there was a ten-foot section only just added to one side of the garden. The earth was different there, indicating that it had been plowed recently.

"This must be a spectacular view when all the plants are in bloom," he commented.

"Yes, I've worked on it since I was twelve or thirteen. But you aren't here to admire my roses, are you? What is it you want to ask? And please hurry, I'd like to finish my work here before the day grows too warm."

"Are you sure there's no one in Surrey? Someone—perhaps a girl—your brother knew and you did not."

"It's quite possible. But I have no idea where he met her or who she may be. It won't be as easy to jilt Mary Ellen Townsend. Her father has been very happy to tell everyone that his daughter is marrying a French. He won't care to eat those words."

"I was told Miss Whitman ran free in this house as a child. And that she was engaged to your elder brother before his death. There must have been a connection somewhere, or Laurence French would have looked for better prospects for his elder son and heir."

"I wasn't for that engagement, but then no one asked my opinion. I thought he could do far better."

"In what way?"

Goaded, she said, "Whatever you heard about Valerie playing here as a child, she isn't one of us. Her father was a Naval officer, that's true. But her mother was the daughter of the firm's chief clerk, Gooding. Because her mother died in childbirth, and her father was always off in the South China Sea or somewhere just as distant, my own mother felt sorry for her and brought her here to play with us."

Rutledge turned away to look out over the garden so that she couldn't read the expression on his face.

It was damning, that bit of news. Valerie Whitman had admitted that she didn't love Lewis French. But if she had married him, she would have become one of the family. No longer *the daughter of the firm's chief clerk.*

She might have been willing to let Lewis French go if she hadn't cared for him. She herself, in Rutledge's opinion, could have done far better than French, judging by what little he'd learned about the man.

But was she as willing to let go that leap into a different world? Wealth. Social standing. A house in London.

Miss French was saying, "I often wondered how she could attract both Michael and then Lewis. It was amazing to me. Yes, she was always underfoot, they were used to her. It's not as if she's actually pretty, like Mary Ellen Townsend." It was said enviously. "I could have understood it if Michael had fallen in love with *her.*"

Rutledge was still considering the ramifications of the connection between Valerie Whitman and Gooding when he realized that Miss French had asked him something.

Turning back to her, he said, "I'm sorry. What did you say?"

"I asked if you thought Valerie was pretty."

What she read in his face brought a deep flush to her own. "You do, don't you? You're just like the rest of them, even my father."

"I'm a policeman," he said. "Involved with a murder inquiry. It doesn't matter what I think."

"But it does," she said viciously. "If I'd killed Lewis and buried him there in my rose garden, you'd believe it quickly enough. But if Valerie has killed him for jilting her, you'll not. You'll make excuses and look for flaws in the evidence, and put off taking her into custody. Why is it," she went on, the venom in her voice pinning him where he was, "that some women can be forgiven anything? There were times when I hated my father and my brothers. They never *saw* me. If I'd suddenly become invisible, they wouldn't have wondered what had become of me until they needed me to look after Mama or keep the house open and ready for them whenever they took it into their heads to come to Dedham—"

She broke off, as if she suddenly realized where her outburst was leading. Breathing hard, she stared at Rutledge, and then turned her back on him, one hand on the railing, the other already groping for her handkerchief. "Go away. Just—go away."

He glimpsed the edge of the pretty square of linen as she gripped it tightly, and saw in one corner the dark red embroidered rose, the petals just open and a drop of white-thread dew on one of them.

Hamish was urgently trying to tell him something, but he turned without a word and walked around the house to the drive, where he'd left his motorcar.

Shaken by the woman's angry words, he wondered if he had indeed been looking for flaws in the evidence, twisting and turning it because he didn't want to believe that Valerie Whitman could be a murderess.

If Afonso Diaz was simply an old man waiting to die and go back to his native country in the only way open to him—in a coffin—then he, Rutledge, had failed to do his duty in a proper and timely fashion.

His doubts and Hamish's violent rumbling in his head carried him all the way back to Dedham and the inn.

And still he sat there in the tiny telephone closet for all of ten minutes before reaching out, taking up the receiver, and putting a call through to the Yard.

Chapter Twelve

Fielding was finally tracked down and brought to the telephone. Rutledge, waiting impatiently, said at once, "Any news?"

"Early days," the sergeant replied. "But there was a bicycle put on the train here in London on the night in question—that's to say, the night after you found the body in Chelsea. We're still looking into that, sir. Male or female, the man doesn't remember, only that the bicycle's rear wheel knocked over his Thermos of tea as he was loading it and sent the tea rolling away. He was afraid to drink it after that for fear the Thermos had broken inside, and he was still angry about that. He does recall that it was a woman's bicycle."

"He's quite sure about that?"

"Oh, yes, sir. I'm looking into who might have bought a ticket to Dedham or the vicinity. But I daresay whoever it was used a false name."

Rutledge suggested it before he could stop himself. "Or put the bicycle on board without any intention of claiming it in the end."

"There's an idea, sir. I'll look into that as well."

Rutledge thanked him and ended the call. Restless and unwilling to sit still, he drove back to St. Hilary and went to find the curate.

Williams had made progress on painting the Rectory. Rutledge followed the wet spills around the side of the house to the kitchen gardens and found the curate just beginning to paint the trim on the porch there.

Williams was whistling to himself as he worked and broke off to see who was coming. "Inspector. You've called often enough that I feel I should offer you a coverall and a brush."

Rutledge laughed. "You've done nice work on your own."

"Yes, well, that's the new description of a clergyman. Jack-of-all-trades. I couldn't ask the church warden to have the Rectory painted when there's so much needing to be done in the church. Not when I'm young and fit."

"Thinking of getting married, are you?"

Williams blushed. "Um—there isn't gossip already, is there?"

"None that I've heard. Are you?"

The curate changed the subject. "What brings you here this morning?"

"I don't really know," Rutledge told him truthfully. "I'm in a quandary about the missing Mr. French. Ever hear of anyone called Afonso Diaz?"

"Who is he when he's at home?"

"He's from Madeira."

"In that case, the French family ought to know. That's where they do business."

"Thank you. The other problem is, what has become of Lewis French? He's been gone away too long, without a word to anyone. Someone must know the answer to that. He's got a business in London that needs his attention. He's expecting his cousin to arrive in England at any moment. He has a fiancée who must miss him."

"It sounds to me rather as if he's dead," Williams said grimly as he carefully descended the ladder. "But that brings us back to the question of who would wish to kill him?"

"Perhaps his sister. She's been left to cool her heels at home all these years while the sons of the family prepared to take their place in the firm."

"Yes, I can see that. But if Lewis were dead, she'd be in London going through the books. Her time come at long last."

Rutledge thought that might well be true, but, devil's advocate, he said, "If she's clever enough to kill him and get away with it, I should think she'd be clever enough to not to show her hand too soon."

The curate grimaced. "I really don't like to think of anyone in my flock being a murderer." Wiping his fingers on rags that were even more flecked with paint than his hands were, smearing the droplets in every direction, he said, "Tea?"

"Yes, thank you."

"I was about to stop anyway. Now's as good a time as any."

"Someone said to me not long ago that Dedham was too pretty a town to harbor murder. Does St. Hilary seem as charmed as Dedham?"

"I don't know that either of them is charmed in that way. Even beauty can cover a multitude of sins. Yet for all you know, the murderer is waiting to be discovered in London."

"Would it were that easy." But Rutledge reminded himself of the clerk, Gooding. Could he have tried to murder Lewis French? Because of his granddaughter? If true, it might go a long way toward explaining why French was afraid to show himself, if he was still alive. The flaw was, Gooding wasn't a young man. Was he still capable physically of putting a deadweight into the motorcar, driving all night to London, leaving a body in Chelsea, then walking away from the

Surrey chalk pit and bicycling back to London? Surely he'd need an accomplice.

Rutledge could hear again Miss French's angry accusation: *You'll make excuses and look for flaws in the evidence, and put off taking her into custody.*

Realizing that Williams had already gone inside and was holding the door for him, he shook himself mentally and followed the curate into the tidy kitchen.

There had been a woman's touch here once. The faded but still pretty curtains patterned with bunches of cabbage roses on a cream background that matched the cream walls gave an unexpected warmth to the plain room. He took the chair the curate offered and watched the man's deft preparation of their tea. Rutledge decided that the curate had been a bachelor for some time and liked his comforts.

"Did Lewis French ever come to you with a troubled mind? Especially over his decision not to marry Valerie Whitman?"

The curate, his attention on counting spoonsful of loose tea into the china pot, shook his head. Finishing, he said, "He might have spoken to my predecessor, if he were still here. He was older, you see. Someone with whom French might have felt comfortable discussing his feelings."

"And Miss Whitman? Did she confide in you when she was jilted?"

Color ran up into the curate's face again. "No. But this I can tell you about her. She has enormous strength of character. I've seen it. She came to Sunday services the day after she had agreed to end her engagement to French. And she sat there, knowing the gossip going on behind people's hands, the speculation, the questions. Then when French announced his engagement to Miss Townsend, she endured their pity. I asked her why, when I saw her that same afternoon, why she hadn't stayed at home. She told me, 'It will be over sooner if they can see me. If I hide in the shadows, it will only encourage them to wonder how I felt.'"

It was clear that Williams was half—probably wholly—in love with Valerie Whitman.

"And Miss French? What did she have to say?"

"You've met her. You know how forthright she can be." Pouring water from the kettle into the pot, the curate kept his face turned away from Rutledge. "I heard her tell someone that her brothers never asked her opinion on any subject, least of all their love affairs."

It was callous and very much in Miss French's style.

As he set a cup in front of Rutledge, and put the sugar bowl and milk jug to hand, Williams said, "I'm afraid we got off the subject. What did you come to see me about?"

"Actually I already have asked you about that. The man Diaz."

"Oh. Well, then I'm sorry I couldn't help."

"You said you believed French was dead. What makes you think so? Aside from the fact that he hasn't made any attempt to contact anyone."

"I was thinking about it the other day after speaking to Miss French. She was buying a small stone. It looked extraordinarily like a rough-hewn tombstone. I asked her what it was for, and she said she felt she should add a little something to her rose garden. That it lacked perspective. I thought that rather odd, and afterward wondered if perhaps she has indirectly faced the fact that her brother is not coming home."

"Why a tombstone for a garden, then, if there will eventually be one in the churchyard?"

"You must ask Miss French. It might have been nothing more than my own fancy."

Rutledge hadn't noticed a stone when he was there. Had Miss French changed her mind about it after her conversation with the curate? Or was it still waiting to be placed?

When they had finished their tea, Rutledge asked one final question.

"What did you feel when the engagement between French and Miss Whitman was called off?"

"I was glad, to tell you the truth. I didn't think they suited at all."

"Is it possible he had a change of heart and decided he wished to marry her after all?" Someone had left—or put—her handkerchief in that motorcar, and if Valerie Whitman believed French was having second thoughts, she might have gone for a drive with him. "Would she, you think, have wanted to marry him still?"

Williams shook his head. "That's unlikely. No, I can't imagine that. She's quite proud, you know. She wouldn't have him back."

If French had had a seizure and hit someone on the road, would Miss Whitman have helped him conceal it? Rutledge wanted to ask the curate that as well, but in the end decided that the man wasn't able to look at Miss Whitman objectively.

Rutledge said, "Thank you for the tea. And the conversation."

"Anytime. Although it might speed up my work if you took up a brush after all."

The words were lighthearted, but Rutledge could see the worry in the curate's eyes. "Look in London, Inspector. St. Hilary isn't hiding a murderer."

London had left a message for him. The clerk at the Sun's desk called to him as he walked in and said, "Mr. Rutledge. Could you ring Scotland Yard as soon as possible?"

He thanked the man and went into the telephone closet.

It was Gibson who answered this time. "Fielding is speaking to someone at the railway station. He's asking for a photograph of Miss Whitman. Do you know where one can be had on short notice? It appears to be urgent."

There was Gooding, of course. But Rutledge would have preferred to speak to him first. And Miss French might well have a photograph, but it would be here in Essex, not London. He thought for several seconds.

"The housekeeper at French's London house. A photograph of the happy couple on their engagement? She might know of something like that."

"Thank you, sir. I'll send a man round straightaway," Gibson said and rang off.

A photograph. And needed urgently. That did not bode well for Miss Whitman.

Rutledge went out into the street, walking without any direction in mind, just . . . walking. He paused at the square to watch the construction going on there, realized that this was to be Dedham's war memorial, and quickly moved on.

He had only a matter of hours. How best to spend them? Where could he find new information that would offset what the luggage van man would most surely say? Or the ticket agent in his kiosk.

Where would Afonso Diaz go to find a killer for hire?

Bob Rawlings? The undergardener with the belligerent attitude? Or one of the other staff, hiding the fact that he knew someone who had killed before and would for the right price kill again? For that matter, where had Diaz found the money to pay such a person?

It was a dead end. There was nowhere left to go with the inquiry into Afonso Diaz, no matter how promising it had seemed in the beginning.

Then why, Rutledge asked himself, had he felt so sure that it was worth pursuing?

Wishful thinking? Or sheer instinct?

Someone spoke to him, and he came out of his reverie to see French's fiancée standing in front of him, smiling.

"Miss Townsend," he said, removing his hat.

"Mr. Rutledge? Have you found Lewis? Is that why you're still in Dedham?"

"Sadly no, I haven't caught up with him," he told her. "I'd hoped he would come to London, if not return to Essex. But there's been no word."

Her expression had been hopeful. Now it fell into worried lines. "But what's become of him? Men don't just disappear. His friends— surely he would be staying with someone. I can't imagine—"

But the trouble was, she could. When he said nothing, she went on. "Is he— Do you think he might be having second thoughts about our engagement? Is he worried because of my father? I know he's strict, I know he is overly protective of me."

With an assurance he didn't feel, Rutledge said, "I don't believe his disappearance is connected with you, Miss Townsend. Rather, I think it has a great deal to do with his firm."

"Do you really? Thank you, that's so comforting to hear. Thank you, Mr. Rutledge. And if you do find him, will you ask him to write to me as soon as possible? Until I hear, I'll worry."

"I promise," he said, and she hurried away, her step lighter, as if she believed him.

He watched her go, then turned briskly back to the inn, his mind made up.

After giving up his room, he drove directly to the French house.

His knock was answered by the maid, Nan.

"Miss French isn't receiving this afternoon," she told him firmly.

"I needn't speak to her. I'd like to borrow a photograph of Miss Whitman. A recent one if you have it. Will you please ask Miss French if this is possible?"

From down the passage came Agnes French's voice.

"The one in the right-hand drawer of Mr. Lewis's desk, Nan."

The maid turned in her direction, but over her shoulder Rutledge saw the door behind which Miss French had been listening shut.

"Just a moment, if you please," Nan said and closed the outer door quietly.

In three minutes she was back, and in her hands was a silver frame.

She passed it to him. "Miss French would appreciate it if you returned this when you have no further need of it."

He told her he would and left. It was not until he was outside the gates that he looked at it.

Black-and-white imagery didn't do her justice. Without the fascinating color of her hair and the ever-changing color of her eyes, Valerie Whitman was just a rather ordinary girl, pretty because she was young, but of no particular attraction.

He turned the photograph facedown on the seat next to him.

Hamish said, "Did ye expect it would be sae different?"

Rutledge replied, "I don't think I considered it at all."

"Aye, and pigs fly."

Chapter Thirteen

Rutledge made good time to London, and he arrived at French, French & Traynor just as Gooding was locking the door for the night.

Rutledge called to him. "Can I give you a lift?"

The senior clerk hesitated, then said, "Thank you. That's very kind."

He got into the motorcar and heaved a sigh. "You've come more quickly than I expected," he said. "Still, we could have talked in my office."

"Yes, I'm sure that would have been best. Why were you expecting me?"

"Didn't they tell you at the Yard? I called because I've had word of Mr. Traynor. I reported it as soon as I'd heard."

Traynor. The other partner in the firm. Expected any day from Portugal.

"Yes, all right. Tell me."

"We've been waiting for word regarding his arrival. With Mr. French still missing, I thought it best— Several days ago I took it upon myself to contact our representative in Lisbon. I had a response today. Mr. Traynor had indeed left Madeira and arrived in Lisbon. Political matters in Portugal are rather uncertain at present, and he and Mr. French had agreed it would be wise to take certain steps to protect the firm's interests."

"What interests?"

"Primarily banking. Mr. Traynor saw to it that the bulk of our funds in Lisbon were transferred to an account here in London, but there was also some concern about the reliability of shipping if the situation grew worse. That too has been resolved. According to our man of business, Mr. Traynor then arranged to travel on to London, and he sailed three weeks ago. It doesn't take three weeks to reach England from Lisbon."

"Go on."

"He'd taken passage on a Greek vessel bound for Portsmouth. Our man of business saw him off, and that's the last word we've had of him. I contacted the shipping line's agent in Portsmouth. There's no doubt Mr. Traynor came aboard. In fact he had dinner with the captain on his first night. When the *Medea* docked in Portsmouth on Saturday morning, as scheduled, Mr. Traynor's luggage was in his cabin, ready to be taken ashore along with that of others disembarking, and there was a gratuity for the cabin steward in an envelope. When it was discovered several hours later that the luggage hadn't been claimed, it was put into storage. A trunk and two valises. Meanwhile the cabin Mr. Traynor occupied was cleaned for passengers just coming aboard, and all was in order."

It was a clear and concise report.

Rutledge turned to stare at Gooding. "Was he carrying the firm's money from the Lisbon bank?"

"No, sir, that came through channels while he was still in Lisbon, as it should have done. But where has Mr. Traynor got to? He hasn't come here, he hasn't arrived at the London house—he's simply vanished. With this information in hand, I contacted the Yard today and asked for you. In fact, I stayed late in the hope that you were making sure my information was correct before coming here tonight."

Rutledge, still sitting in the motorcar in front of French, French & Traynor, asked Gooding to repeat every detail.

Then he said, "Have you been to Portsmouth yourself?"

"No, I haven't. I felt it would be better to let Scotland Yard see to it."

"And you're quite certain the dead man you were taken to see is not Mr. Traynor." But, Rutledge told himself, the timing would be off.

"He hasn't been home since the war, sir, but I'd know him anywhere. I've known him since he was born."

"Have you spoken to Miss French?"

"Indeed, sir, I saw no reason to worry her."

"I've been away from the Yard all day. I'd like to use the telephone in your office, if you don't mind. It will save time."

Gooding got down, unlocked the door, and led the way to his office. Rutledge, sitting in the chair behind the man's desk and reaching for the telephone, said, "If you'll leave me here for a few minutes?"

"Of course." The clerk withdrew, quietly closing the door behind him with the skill of a trained butler.

Rutledge's first call was to Sergeant Gibson, who reiterated what Gooding had just told Rutledge. "The information is on your desk, sir. You'd already left Dedham when Mr. Gooding contacted the Yard."

"Has anyone spoken to the harbormaster in Portsmouth?"

"Yes, sir," Gibson reported. "The missing man disembarked—he wasn't onboard when his cabin was cleaned—and his luggage was offloaded with that of the rest of the departing passengers. When no one claimed it, it was put into storage. A trunk and two valises."

"And every other passenger on the manifest is accounted for."

"Yes, sir. I asked specifically. The records showed that Mr. Traynor had dined at the captain's table the first night out, dined alone the second evening. The night before they docked at six in the morning, the purser saw Mr. Traynor on deck, smoking a cigarette. He spoke to Traynor, who told him he was watching for landfall, because he hadn't been back to England since before the war. The purser didn't see him disembark, as he was busy about his duties, but Traynor's cabin when it was cleaned showed signs of orderly preparation for departure, and no indication of struggle or any other problem. It was assumed he had gone ashore as expected."

"And he seemed to be acting naturally when he was seen moving about the ship? Nothing to show that he was fearful or worried?"

"So it appears, sir."

"Call them back. Ask them to open that trunk. Locked or not."

There was a moment of silence, then Gibson said, "You think he might be inside?"

"Stranger things have happened."

"Sad to say, sir, they have."

When the sergeant had disconnected, Rutledge called the Yard a second time, asking for Fielding. But he was not in.

Hamish said, "Twa men, partners in the same firm, missing. It's no' likely to be coincidence."

"No," Rutledge said. "But how did anyone here in England reach Traynor on that ship?"

"Ye ken, it wasna' necessary. They had only to wait for him to disembark."

Which eliminated Diaz, if he had never left the house in Surrey.

But Traynor would have gone with Gooding. He knew the man and trusted him.

The question then was, why not take the trunk and valises with them? It would have been easy enough to drop them into the Thames later. Possibly along with Traynor's body.

Still, it was foolish to kill both partners so close together, drawing down suspicion on the heads of whoever had done it. Unless it was feared that when the partners got together, some discrepancy in accounts or other misdeeds would come to light.

Back to Gooding.

Rutledge rose, went to the door, and called. The clerk came out of one of the other offices and said, "Did you reach the Yard?"

"They confirmed your account. What I don't understand is why anyone would wish to kill both partners. I can see that one might wish to be rid of the other; it happens. Still, the two men serve very different purposes. One manages London, the other Madeira."

"You haven't found the body of either man," Gooding pointed out quietly.

"Not yet," Rutledge agreed.

"Until you do, I refuse to give up hope."

"Can you continue to manage the firm without them?"

"Not for an extended period, no."

"What about Miss French? Does she have any authority to act on behalf of her brother and cousin?"

"I don't know, sir. The question has never arisen. She's never been to Madeira. She knows nothing about that side of the business, or how the wine is made."

"There must be managers there. Otherwise Mr. Traynor couldn't have left."

"There are. But Mr. French and Mr. Traynor were body and soul of the firm, like their fathers before them. It's different, their roles. It's what's kept this firm alive since the time of Mr. Howard. He was a very unusual man, Mr. Howard. It's his legacy, you see. And he laid it out for his heirs to follow."

Listening to the clerk, listening for any indication that he was capable of taking over French, French &Traynor, Rutledge heard only a man's concern for something he'd given his own life to. But then he'd be stupid to crow too soon . . .

It was the nature of his business, Rutledge thought, to be suspicious. To weigh every expression and every word, to watch the eyes and the way the body betrayed itself. To listen to the voice, a change of tone as a person lied. And still, he would have sworn that Gooding was sincere.

But this had been a very clever scheme, whoever was behind it. And he found himself thinking that Gooding had to be a clever man, intelligent and capable, to have kept his place at French, French & Traynor for so many years.

He said, filling the silence that had fallen, "There's no more we can do tonight. I'll drive you home."

Gooding took out his ring of keys and began to lock the door to his office. He said as Rutledge watched, "My granddaughter has written to me."

"Indeed?"

"She has told me about the handkerchief. While many were made for her, I'm sure Miss Delaney used the same patterns for others."

"She's dead," Rutledge said baldly. "And the woman in the shop didn't seem to think it was likely, as these were particular clients— ones who regularly ordered their favorite patterns. There were other choices available to those who came in off the street."

He saw Gooding glance at the portraits as they made their way to the outer door. The man said, as he turned the last key, "She isn't a murderer. But I suppose now, with Mr. Traynor missing as well, you will consider me one as well."

"Tell me where else I should look," Rutledge answered him, his voice sharper than he intended it to be.

"I don't know. I would have said that the partners had nothing to fear from anyone. But I see too that this business is hard on the heels of Mr. French deciding not to marry Valerie. It smacks of revenge. The truth is, I was glad he changed his mind. They wouldn't have suited. She might have been happy with Mr. Michael. He was a good man. But not with Mr. Lewis."

"Why?"

Gooding got into the motorcar as Rutledge turned the crank. His words were nearly lost as the motor turned over and caught.

"Mr. Lewis wanted someone like his sister, compliant, willing to remain in the background when not required to act as hostess. I'm afraid Valerie has more mettle. Still, she was the granddaughter of a clerk in his firm, regardless of the fact that her father was a Naval officer and came from a very fine family. Miss Townsend is the daughter of a doctor. She has been under her father's thumb and will accept Mr. French's will as her own." He gave Rutledge directions to his house in Kensington, then said, "If you take me into custody, what will become of the firm? I have to ask. The junior clerks are not— They don't have the experience to deal with unexpected problems."

"There appear to be no other suspects. According to you, the *Medea* came in on a Saturday morning. You could have met the ship and dealt with Traynor without anyone suspecting that he'd landed. Unless you have someone who can vouch for where you were that morning."

"I live alone." Gooding took a deep breath. "Well. There is nothing to be done. But I will not let you touch Valerie. She has done nothing wrong. If I must choose between her and the firm, I will not hesitate."

"She was in St. Hilary when Lewis French disappeared. Were you?"

Gooding opened his mouth, then shut it again. Which, Rutledge assumed, meant that there were witnesses who could answer that question—one way or the other—and the man was not going to give the Yard their names.

Hamish said, "Ye've driven him into a corner. It's no' wise."

But Rutledge had already shown the clerk the forces arrayed against him. And that too had been unwise. He said, as they approached the street where Gooding lived, "If you do something foolish, you will not be here to protect her when the burden of guilt falls on her. And as an officer of Scotland Yard, I cannot."

"I have no wish to kill myself. I can still hope that one or the other of my employers will turn up alive and well."

"There's still the dead man from Chelsea."

"Ah yes. But he cannot be laid at my door. Or Valerie's. Not until you know who he is."

With that the man got out of the motorcar, crisply thanked Rutledge for bringing him home, and went inside his dark house without looking back.

Lights bloomed in the entry and then in a room left of the door, and Rutledge, watching Gooding's progress through the house, wondered if he was suddenly afraid of the dark.

Acting Chief Superintendent Markham, weighing the facts at ten the next morning, shook his head. "There's no alternative but to bring in both Miss Whitman and her grandfather."

"There appears to be none," Rutledge agreed. "But we've got a body without a name or a past, while the two missing men haven't turned up alive or dead. How do we charge Miss Whitman or Mr. Gooding, if there is no proof that a crime has been committed? At least not yet."

"On suspicion of murder. It may be that they'll tell us what we need to know, if only to avoid the hangman."

Rutledge was once more fighting a rearguard action. But there was nothing else he could do.

He said, "There's Miss French. She has lived in the shadow of her brother and her cousin and the firm for as long as she can remember. She wouldn't have been the only woman to decide that she would like to take charge of her future."

"She has staff. You've said as much yourself."

"I've yet to determine whether that staff is loyal to her or to her brother, who pays their wages."

"All right then, find out. But don't dawdle over it. I'll give you forty-eight hours."

"Meanwhile, if Sergeant Gibson could ask if any other unclaimed bodies turned up the weekend that Traynor landed in Portsmouth, or after French was reported missing, it might make our task easier."

"Fair enough. But that's all the time I'm giving you. There's a matter in Staffordshire that could well require an Inspector from the Yard. I want you available."

Rutledge thanked him and left.

Markham was running the Yard as he had run his Yorkshire police, taking the lead in examining and solving each case. Without the personal contact with witnesses and suspects, depending on his own instincts to interpret what he read in reports.

He was not likely to succeed in London for very long. But Markham wasn't Rutledge's immediate problem.

Forty-eight hours. That would hardly see him to Essex and back.

He felt trapped.

Hamish said as Rutledge walked into his own office and closed the door, "Ye ken, he didna' give you any more time on purpose."

And that was very likely the case.

Rutledge had warned Gooding. That was all he could do.

Traynor's disappearance put paid to any focus of attention on Diaz. The point could be made that Diaz had never threatened Traynor's family and had had no reason to attack them because it was Howard French who had bought the Diaz property for his vineyards. The Traynors had come into the firm in the next generation.

There was still Fielding and his search for the owner of the bicycle. Rutledge had stopped by the Yard the night before, after setting Gooding down, and left the photograph of Valerie Whitman on the sergeant's desk.

Unable to sit still, he got up and went in search of Fielding. He was told that the sergeant had come in early and then left again.

With the photograph, surely.

Rutledge went back to his own office and sat there staring out the window, waiting for the sergeant to report.

But it was after three o'clock in the afternoon when Fielding finally appeared. He was out of breath from taking the stairs two at a time, his face slightly flushed.

"The man on the luggage van that night—when the bicycle was brought to him—was back in London today. I showed him the photograph. He was quite taken with it. He thought the woman in it had very likely left the bicycle. It was ticketed as far as Thetford, and no one has claimed it. It's still there."

"He was certain—or thought it very likely."

"I don't know. To tell you the truth, he'd said the woman's hair was brown, he thought. And it looks brown in the photograph. He thought her eyes were brown. And they look brown in the photograph. She was pretty. And she appears to be pretty in the photograph."

"Her coloring is rather different. Her eyes, for one, are hazel."

"Yes, well, in a hurry in a poorly lit station, they could have seemed to be brown."

"He must see hundreds of people every week. Why should he remember her, that long ago?"

"He says, because the bicycle fell and broke his Thermos of tea."

"I can see that that might stay in his memory. But the person, after the fact?"

"Yes, I take your point. Still, he says it's Miss Whitman, and there's nothing to be done about it."

"And he's willing to swear that he saw this woman, that she handed over the bicycle?"

"I've sent a constable to take his statement."

"What was she wearing?"

"Dark clothes. That's all he remembers."

Rutledge took a deep breath. "You must give this information to Markham."

"Yes, I know." Fielding frowned. "Is— I need to ask you, sir. Is this woman a friend of yours?"

"I met her for the first time when I interviewed her in St. Hilary."

Fielding's face cleared. "Well, then. I'll be about my duty. As soon as Constable Dean brings me the van guard's statement, I'll take it directly to the Acting Chief Superintendent."

"There's one other link I need to be clear about. Hold up that statement until I get back, will you?"

"If you say so."

"What I intend to learn could reinforce the guard's statement."

"Yes, of course. That's sensible. I'll hold off, then."

"Thank you."

Rutledge waited until Fielding had gone, then quietly left the Yard. He met no one in the passage or on the stairs, and felt like a felon slinking out to his motorcar. He had forty-three hours, and he intended to use every one of them.

Chapter Fourteen

He drove as fast as he dared, but a storm broke just north of London, and he was forced to pull over. Wind tossed tree limbs, littering the streets of the village with leaves and puddles of heavy rain when it came. He could feel the shoulder of his coat getting wet and raced for the door of a tea shop while he could, watching the storm from its windows, then asking for a cup of tea until it passed.

Frustrated at the loss of a precious hour, Rutledge lost another where a tree had been blown down across the road, sent around on a detour that seemed to go on forever before it led him back to the main road.

Finally the outskirts of Dedham were in sight, and the sun came out. He drove on to Thetford, and at the station asked to see the bicycle in Left Luggage.

It was a lady's bicycle, black and ordinary. He had wasted time coming to see it.

Thanking the man behind the grille, he turned back toward Dedham, then went on to St. Hilary.

He stopped first at the French house, and it was late enough that Nan answered the door herself.

He hadn't considered how he would approach the maid. It was not something that he could simply walk in and ask. *How loyal are you to your mistress? Would you cover up a murder for her sake? Would you go so far as to act as an accomplice? And where have you hidden the body of her brother?*

With Hamish humming in the back of his mind, Rutledge smiled. "It's late, I'm afraid, but it's rather important—"

"Miss French has already gone up to bed, sir. Unless it's urgent. She's been that upset, hearing that her cousin is missing as well. Mr. Gooding informed her this morning."

"I understand. As a matter of fact, it's you I've come to speak to."

"Me, sir?"

"Just a few questions that could help us in our search for Mr. French."

"Anything I can do, sir."

"Tell me again about the night Mr. French left."

"There's not much to tell. He came down to dinner as usual, and afterward he and Miss French had a few words in the study. I don't know what it was about, but it ended with Mr. French going upstairs to change to his driving clothes, and then I heard the door slam behind him."

"What did Miss French do?"

"She was in the sitting room, and she ran out after him. I don't know what was said. The motorcar drove away, but she didn't come in. I went out to look for her after a while, and she was in the little Greek temple, and she was crying. I asked her to come in out of the night air. She refused, said she thought he would come back and she wanted to wait. She dismissed me, but I got up again close to two o'clock, and she was in bed."

"Asleep?"

"I couldn't say, sir."

Rutledge considered what Nan had told him. There had been enough time for Agnes French to kill her brother. If he had come home again and found her in the rose garden, if the quarrel had been renewed, she could have rushed to the motorcar and turned it in the heat of her anger and run him down as he walked away.

But then why had the bit of cloth he'd discovered under the French motorcar matched the dead man's clothing, and not French's?

There was the possibility that in his mad need to leave the house behind, French could have hit someone else on the road and suffered a seizure because of it. And his sister had let him die.

That would explain everything.

He said, intending to catch the maid unaware, "Who took the dead man to London, left him there, and then abandoned the motorcar in Surrey?"

She frowned. "I've never been to Surrey, sir. Are you meaning Mr. French? Is he dead, sir? Is that why you've come, to tell Miss French?"

"No," he said, feeling the tension in his shoulders from the long drive and the weariness of knowing he had wasted more of his forty-eight hours than he could spare. "We haven't located Mr. French."

"I'm glad, sir. I didn't want to be the one to wake Miss French and tell her."

He changed the subject. "Did Miss Whitman have a bicycle? Do you remember it?"

"Yes, sir, she and Mr. Michael would go off together, pedaling their bicycles and stopping somewhere for lunch. Just an ordinary bicycle, sir. Nothing special about it. She rather liked it, because Miss French's father had given it to her one Christmas."

"Thank you, Nan. I don't think we need to disturb your mistress after all."

He turned to go, and she wished him a good night.

He drove as far as the dark churchyard and walked for a time between the gravestones. He couldn't help but see that Miss Whitman must be awake because there were lights in one of the upstairs bedrooms.

Standing there watching the light, he said aloud, "He's going to have her taken up for murder. Markham. And her grandfather as well. Where the bloody hell is Lewis French? Or saving that, where in hell is his body?"

Hamish, who seemed to be standing just behind his shoulder in the soft darkness, said, "It'ull do no good to lament. Ye still have half your time left."

But what to do with it?

Rutledge walked back and forth under the trees, barely missing some of the older, sunken stones as he paced.

Markham wouldn't allow him to search for the connection between Diaz and a killer he could have hired.

But there might be a way to do it without prejudice.

The light in the upstairs bedroom finally went out.

Hamish said, "Ye've lost the distance a policeman must keep from his suspects."

"I don't know that I have," Rutledge said. "It's just hard to believe, that's all. There's been nothing—absolutely nothing—that points to her except circumstantial evidence."

"And yon photograph," Hamish said. "The van guard has said so."

At that moment, the cottage door opened, and Miss Whitman, a shawl around her shoulders, came out and walked down the path to her gate.

He stood there watching her. Waiting to see where she might go.

But she crossed the street and came into the churchyard.

"Are you there?" she asked, peering into the darkness beneath the trees. "It's you, isn't it? I saw you from my window as I blew out my lamp. Are you waiting for morning to take me into custody? Is that why you're come to St. Hilary?"

He walked toward her. "I came looking for something that would explain the unexplainable. French isn't the only one who has vanished. Traynor has gone missing as well."

She sucked in a breath. He could hear it.

"Dear God. And you think my grandfather and I have done these things."

"No. I think—I thought I knew who was responsible. But there's no way to prove it. And I've come to the end. I won't be the one to take you into custody. They're sending me to Staffordshire. But it will happen. I'm sorry."

"Yes," she said slowly. "It will happen."

She stood there, a black silhouette against the starlight that lit the street and the front of her house.

And then without a word she turned and walked away.

Rutledge watched her until she had gone inside and closed the door behind her before turning toward his motorcar.

Apropos of nothing, Hamish said, "They burned witches."

But Rutledge wasn't to be drawn. This time he ignored the voice in his head and resolutely turned toward the London road.

Chapter Fifteen

Tired as he was, Rutledge drove all night, and when he reached London he went not to the Yard but to Chelsea.

He stopped the motorcar some distance from the place where the body was found and walked the street again.

Why here? Why had this been the best site to leave an unwanted corpse?

Why not in Bloomsbury or Whitechapel or on the Heath?

Hamish said, "Until ye ken his name ye willna' know."

And there was nothing he could do about it. So far.

He walked on. None of the constables who had interviewed residents of this street or the ones on either side had come up with any information that was useful. If anyone had secrets, they had kept them well. The constables were experienced, men who knew Chelsea. And they had shaken their heads over the collected statements, telling Gibson, "If there's a connection, we haven't found it."

Rutledge had reached the house belonging to Mr. Belford.

It was where he'd been going from the time he left St. Hilary.

The maid who answered the door told him that Mr. Belford was in, but she would have to inquire if he was receiving visitors.

After several minutes, she came back to ask Rutledge to follow her.

It was the same room where he'd spoken to Belford before.

The man was standing by the cold hearth, hands clasped lightly behind his back, his expression bland.

"Good morning." He considered Rutledge. "You've driven how far? Not from the Midlands, I should think. And you haven't been to the Yard, or you would have shaved and changed your shirt. Your expression is grim. Is there another body on this street that my staff has not remembered to mention to me over my breakfast?"

Rutledge smiled. "Not another body, no. But a conundrum, I think."

"You've come for information, then. As I didn't know the man before he was murdered, I can tell you nothing."

"You were right about the watch. It was very helpful. Sadly, it didn't belong to the man in whose pocket it was found. Nor does he appear to have any connection with the man whose watch it was. But now the watch's owner has gone missing and his cousin as well, two men who have no reason to disappear and who seem to have no enemies."

"Interesting indeed." Belford took the chair across from the one he'd offered Rutledge. "Why do you think I should know the answer to this riddle?"

"Because," Rutledge answered, "I have looked into your past. As you must have looked into mine."

"Yes. I've learned to leave nothing to chance. You had an interesting war."

"And you as well. Although you left no footprints to follow."

Belford laughed. "Yes, well, I do try. I had no more success identifying your body than you did. I don't care for . . . messages . . . left near my house."

"If I tell you the entire story, can I do so with the assurance that it will go no further?"

"Of course. It goes without saying. But first I'll ring for tea, shall I?"

When it had been brought in and Belford had poured two cups, he reached into a cabinet to one side of the door and brought out a bottle of whisky, adding a small amount to each cup.

"As a rule I eschew alcohol. But I rather think you can use it," he said.

"Quite."

Rutledge began with the body on the street, the direction the watch had taken him, and what he knew about the French family. He brought in Diaz and what had become of him after the confrontation with Howard French and his son years before. As he went on to describe the asylum and then Mrs. Bennett's charitable endeavors, he saw Belford shake his head. He explained Valerie Whitman's connection to Gooding, and the quarrel between Miss French and her brother.

Finally, considering what he had said, he decided that he had been both objective and fair.

"You've looked into the men who were Mrs. Bennett's staff? Where they were imprisoned, why, and with whom?"

"The Yard felt that there was nothing to be gained by doing that."

"A pity," said Belford thoughtfully. "Because if Diaz wanted to kill, he would have listened to these men, their idle conversation, their experiences during their incarceration, the mates they met in prison, their lies and their boasts and their truths. And gleaned what he needed from them. Finally he would have made his choice as to which person to approach. It's a matter of trust, you see. Diaz cannot afford to be wrong. He will have only one chance."

"He's written no letters, mailed none. Received none."

"But the man who goes to market could easily drop a letter into the postbox."

"How did he come by stamps?"

"Someone cleans Mrs. Bennett's house for her. A single stamp is rarely missed."

"And the response?"

"In the market basket, of course. Or whoever collects her mail could easily pocket one letter appearing to be addressed to Mrs. Bennett herself."

"All right. I expect the man who does the marketing is the primary person he trusts. The man who cleans will not know why the stamp is needed, only that it is. And the man who mails letters and collects return post could be one and the same."

"Exactly my thinking. The fewer who know, the less chance there is of trouble."

It was much as Rutledge had thought. And this was not why he had come to see Belford. He presented his request carefully.

"My problem is finding out who this man may know. Or if he is indeed the contact. There could be another person involved, someone who insists on staying in the shadows. But I think the courier, the man who posts and collects the letters, will try to learn what he can. If only to protect himself."

"In his shoes, I'd do the same. And in the long term this could blow up."

"How would Diaz be able to hire a killer? As far as I know, he has no money. Nor do I think any of the men around him have funds of their own."

As he said the words, Rutledge realized that he had believed Diaz when he said his father had disinherited him. It was worth looking into.

"You have a list of names?"

Rutledge gave them from memory, and taking a small black notebook from an inner pocket, Belford jotted them down.

"I can't guarantee that what I discover will help you," he warned, closing the notebook and restoring it to his pocket.

"Nevertheless, it's worth a try."

"It's a rather nice riddle, this one of yours. I much preferred such cases when I was in the war. I read law, did you know? And found it damned dull."

Rutledge smiled. His own father was a solicitor, and he had not wished to follow in his footsteps. He wondered if, when all was said and done, he'd joined the police for the same reasons that Belford had, lying to himself about his concern for the silent victim.

He had not been surprised that Belford had so quickly agreed to help. That unidentified body on his street, so close to his door, had been the motivation, not any eloquence on Rutledge's part. Rutledge had few illusions about Belford. But he needed the man's help.

He had finished his tea, and now he rose to leave, thanking Belford for his hospitality and his time.

Belford accompanied his guest to the door. "Good hunting. I will let you know as soon as I learn anything useful."

"Thank you." Rutledge had no doubt at all that Belford could find him wherever he was.

It was not a connection he intended to cultivate, but it was going to be very useful in the present circumstances.

Hamish was not in agreement. "Ye've supped with the de'il," he said as Rutledge walked back to where he'd left his motorcar.

"And he who sups with the devil needs a long-handled spoon."

"Aye, ye tak' it lightly. But when he's satisfied about yon body, it's possible ye'll never hear a word of what he discovered."

"On the contrary," Rutledge said, pausing to turn the crank. "He'll want to gloat. He didn't make a career of the Army. I find that interesting. It wouldn't surprise me to learn he's now MI5."

Rutledge's next call was on the solicitor who handled the affairs of French, French & Traynor.

Word had already reached them that Traynor had gone missing, and they were unwilling initially to entertain taking on a request from Scotland Yard.

Mr. Hayes said, "Our first responsibility is to our client, French, French and Traynor. It's a tremendous undertaking. There's pay for the workmen in Funchal, shipping contracts coming due, decisions to be made about the staff here, and a review of the men in charge of the winery out there. I shall be sending a senior clerk to Madeira to ensure that everything continues to run smoothly, but he knows very little about how the wine is made. I shall have to employ an expert to examine the situation there. Added to everything else is the language. It isn't English."

"I understand that this has stretched the limits of your chambers. But I must know if Afonso Diaz has inherited money from his father or if he was disinherited. His father's Will should be a matter of record in Funchal and possibly even in Lisbon. As the solicitors for French, French and Traynor, you have dealt with Portuguese law from time to time. You will know how or where to find the information. And find it quickly. If the Yard pursues the matter, it must go through channels, and I'll be lucky to have an answer in six months' time."

"Yes, yes, I understand. But this man's father sold the property quite legally and the sums due him were paid in full. We have all the paperwork required to show just that. What he chose to do with that money afterward was his own affair."

"I couldn't agree more," Rutledge said. "But this man Diaz is still in England. Your firm handled the business of sending him to the asylum outside of Cambridge. You know that he was treated there. You know also when the fund to keep him there lapsed and he was subsequently released. And you never told me about Diaz. You must surely have spoken to Lewis French about this matter after his brother died and the responsibility for maintaining Diaz in the asylum came up for consideration."

"Yes, and Mr. French decided that he was no longer a risk to the family. The doctor assessed his case and reported that he appeared to be well enough not to be a threat."

"But someone decided that he should remain in England. He tells me that he can return to Madeira only when he dies."

"In fact, that was a provision suggested by Lewis French. He thought it wise to keep the man under his eye. In Madeira there are the winery and the vineyards. Perhaps more temptation than Diaz could cope with."

Rutledge felt like swearing. Lewis French had not understood the threat that Diaz posed to the family. And even Diaz had alluded to the terms of his release, thinking that Rutledge must know them and who had fashioned them. Or else he had tested the waters to see just how much Rutledge did know . . .

Rutledge said to Hayes, "If you don't find out about Diaz's inheritance, then you have done both partners a serious injustice. The police are currently looking at the possibility that Mr. Gooding, the firm's senior clerk, and his granddaughter have murdered the two men."

"Mr. Gooding—" Hayes's intimidating eyebrows shot up with his shock. "But we were counting on him to guide us—his experience—"

"He won't be there, I assure you."

"But Mr. Gooding—*murder.*"

Rutledge had not wanted to bring Gooding's connection to the inquiry into the conversation, but he had had no choice.

"Scotland Yard has nothing to connect Afonso Diaz to what has happened. He is not in a position, as far as the Yard is concerned, to find and pay a killer. If I can prove otherwise, that he has the money to do this, it will go a long way toward persuading my superiors that he should be scrutinized. By the same token, Mr. French and Miss Whitman have recently ended their engagement. This could be seen in some quarters as a motive for murder."

"I have met Miss Whitman," Hayes said starkly, recovering. "If you wish to engage the assistance of my chambers, you will not use her name in this context."

Rutledge was on the point of replying equally harshly when he stopped himself just in time. Hamish, in the back of his mind, was clamoring for his attention, but he ignored what the voice was saying.

"If you care at all for Miss Whitman, you will not take the risk."

Hayes considered him. "If I do as you ask, and then I discover that I have been misled, I shall use all the connections accrued in a lifetime of service to the law to see that you are disgraced."

Rutledge smiled. "You will have to form a queue," he said with a lightness he was far from feeling.

"All right. I will make the necessary inquiries myself. The elder Mr. Diaz used a firm in Funchal to handle the sale of his property. I can begin there."

"Thank you."

"No. I don't want your gratitude. Where can I reach you when I have learned what you want to know?"

"Call Sergeant Gibson at Scotland Yard. He'll find me."

Hayes was surprised. "Very well. I have made a note of it." He jotted something in a small notebook, then set it aside.

"The Yard will arrest Gooding. Whether he goes to trial or not depends on whether there's any way to show that Diaz still wants revenge. He's too old to achieve it firsthand. But he can buy a killer. If there is money, he can reach any number of willing foils. For Gooding's sake, we had better hope that he has got the funds."

"And Miss Whitman?"

Rutledge shook his head. "There is circumstantial evidence against her. Who else could have approached Lewis French after he'd quarreled with his sister? He could have driven no farther than the churchyard, to let his temper cool. When she came to speak to him, he'd have got out of the motorcar and faced her. It would have been easy to kill him then."

"You don't believe that?"

"No. I doubt the K.C. assigned to try her will believe it either, but he will be charged with convicting her."

Hayes shook his head. "You are an odd man, Inspector Rutledge."

"I've learned," Rutledge said, "that sometimes it's the small things that matter most. Do you know what became of the love child that Howard French was rumored to have had when he was only a young man?"

The hooded eyes considered him. "We have handled no such case for the French family."

Again that twist of words that solicitors could offer so easily in place of whatever truth they possessed.

Perhaps there was no love child.

But then again, Hayes could be right. Howard French's father had dealt with the matter on his own, and quite successfully, leaving no records for the future to find. Was that how French himself had learned to deal equally successfully with Afonso Diaz?

"I've a dead man and the motorcar that ran him down. But he isn't French. Who is he? I wish I knew. When I do, I'll know whether Gooding and his granddaughter or Afonso Diaz is responsible for his death. It would save time—and a great deal of misery for everyone—if you would deal honestly with me," Rutledge said. He rose and walked to the door.

Hayes made no move to stop him.

Rutledge left his motorcar and walked through the City, aimlessly for the most part.

He had stepped out of bounds, speaking to Belford. And he had more or less coerced Hayes into finding out what he wanted to know. But he'd meant what he said to the solicitor. That going through channels would take six months. He didn't have six months. Hayes could find the answer in a matter of days. He'd dealt with the solicitor in

Funchal before, and while a request to know the contents of the elder Diaz's Will would appear to be rather odd, Rutledge was sure that Hayes could couch it in terms that seemed reasonable.

And if Rutledge found that Diaz could pay, that murder for hire was possible, then how he had obtained the information was less important than its impact.

Turning, he retraced his steps to the motorcar, the sun warm on his back, his mind clearer. Except for Hamish, whose Covenanter soul was never comfortable with supping with the devil.

Chapter Sixteen

His forty-eight hours at an end, Rutledge presented himself at the door of Markham's office and, after the briefest hesitation, resolutely knocked.

"Come," the Acting Chief Superintendent said, his tone of voice indicating that he was busy.

Rutledge stepped inside the door. "Inspector Rutledge reporting, sir," he said when Markham didn't immediately look up.

When he did, he pushed back his chair and gestured to the one opposite. "That business in Staffordshire? The police there found the murderer this morning, just before dawn. He was asleep, mind you. Soundly asleep after what he'd done. I can't fathom it, can you?"

As he knew next to nothing about events in Staffordshire, Rutledge could offer only "No, sir."

"Well," Markham said, setting aside the papers in front of him. "What are we to do about Essex?"

"I've told you my feeling on that score, sir. We should investigate Diaz."

"Yes, yes, you've made that clear. But I think we must act on what we know, rather than speculate about an old man's dreams of vengeance. I looked over your interview of the doctor at the clinic. He saw no reason to keep the man locked up. And he's the professional viewpoint. I don't hold with all this mumbo jumbo from Austria, delving into a man's mind. But the good doctor has dealt with Diaz for what? Years? And I should think that by now he'd know Diaz better than his own mother and possibly more objectively. We must accept his opinion and go forward from there."

He reached for a file, opened it, and went on. "Did Gibson tell you? The trunk in Portsmouth is empty of bodies. It contained the clothing of a gentleman traveling home. But that was good thinking on your part. A clever way to take a body off the ship without being noticed. But I'd like to know. If Traynor had been in that trunk, who killed him? Gooding was on shore, mind you. He couldn't have done it. Would you lay the killing at Diaz's door?"

"He hasn't left Surrey. But I should think he could have had murder done."

"If that had been the case, I'd be forced to agree with you. But Traynor was not in that trunk, and he isn't aboard the ship. And Gooding was intending to meet him when he arrived in England."

"Put that way, I must agree with you."

"Yes. So here we are. Mr. Traynor missing. Gooding very likely the last person to see him alive. And once Traynor is quietly out of the picture, Gooding can turn his attention to ridding himself of French, if he hasn't already. What we don't know is how involved the granddaughter is. Certainly it appears that she had driven French's motorcar at some point. To the quarry, most likely. And then she went home with her bicycle, only she was clever enough not to claim it at the other end of the line. She could walk home if need be. Less likely to be noticed, I should think."

Rutledge could find no fault with Markham's reconstruction of events. And presented in such a way, almost in the same way a K.C. would open his remarks to the jury, it sounded imminently logical.

Rutledge found himself thinking that Markham should have read law. He would cut an impressive figure, summing up for the prosecution.

He said, "It is most certainly possible. But what if we're wrong? What if this isn't the way it happened? The killer could have met Traynor as he disembarked, told him that Gooding had sent him, and Traynor would have gone with him without suspicion. There are a dozen dark stretches of road or a small wood where the driver could have killed Traynor and disposed of the body. Everyone would assume that Traynor was still in Lisbon awaiting a ship sailing for London. As they did."

"Are you suggesting that we should search Hampshire for his body?"

It was useless to argue about what Markham had already decided was the train of events.

"It would be prudent to discover if there were any unsolved homicides on the road north from Portsmouth."

"As we have no body, I'm agreeable to that request."

That was the only concession Rutledge could wring from the Acting Chief Superintendent.

Rutledge left Markham's office with instructions to take Gooding into custody forthwith, on suspicion of the murder of the partners of his firm. And Miss Whitman was to be taken into custody as an accomplice.

Relieved—for if she was convicted on that charge, she would be spared hanging—he left the Yard and drove directly to French, French & Traynor.

When he was ushered by a junior clerk into Gooding's office, the man rose from his chair and said, "I can tell by your expression. You've come to take me into custody."

"I have no choice, Gooding. We are searching for Traynor's body in Hampshire, and I have asked Hayes and Hayes to look into the Last Will and Testament of Afonso Diaz's father, to see whether he was disinherited or not."

"And Valerie? What's to become of her?"

"She is to be taken into custody as an accomplice."

Gooding sat down heavily. "No. She cannot go to prison. I won't allow it."

"There's nothing you can do."

"There is." He reached into his desk drawer and drew out several sheets of paper. Taking up a pen, he began to write without hesitation, as if he'd already planned what to say. When he had finished and signed at the bottom of what he'd written, he passed it to Rutledge. "A full confession," he said. "See for yourself."

And it was. Gooding admitted to killing Lewis French, transporting him in his own motorcar to the quarry in Surrey, and, having struck a man walking along the road because it was late and he was very tired, deciding to use the man as a decoy. He also admitted to having killed Matthew Traynor, meeting his ship, taking him to a place where no one could hear his cries, and throttling him, as he had French. He ended the statement, *I have acted alone throughout. I did these things because I had worked very hard for this firm most of my adult life, and I felt when the partners got together here in England, they were planning to replace me and give the position to a younger man.*

Rutledge said, "Is any of this true?"

Gooding smiled, but Rutledge couldn't read it.

He thought, *Two old men, Diaz and Gooding. It would be easy enough to walk away, accept the statement at face value—*

Hamish cried, "*'Ware!'* just as Gooding reached into the drawer a second time.

Rutledge was already across the desk, his left hand clamping down hard on Gooding's right wrist and his other hand holding the drawer only half open.

Gooding cried out from the pain but fought hard. The door behind Rutledge burst open, the junior clerk who had admitted him rushing into the room.

"The revolver—in the drawer. *Get it*," Rutledge ordered.

The clerk stopped short, staring at the two men, Rutledge awkwardly across the desk, Gooding struggling to free his hand and pull the drawer wider.

"*Get it*," Rutledge ordered again, this time in the voice that had commanded frightened men going into battle.

The clerk ran forward, came between them as Rutledge let go of the drawer, and reached inside. His face was white, his hand shaking, but his eyes went to Rutledge's face as his fingers touched whatever lay inside.

Gooding gave up the struggle then, leaning back in his chair, his eyes closed.

The clerk pulled out a revolver, an older one but just as lethal as if it had come from the Front. He was handling it so gingerly that Rutledge could see Gooding gathering himself to reach for it, his eyes flying open and almost black with his determination. Rutledge took the revolver out of the clerk's trembling hand and flung himself back across the desk, nearly tripping over his own chair before he got his feet under him again.

Gooding said, rubbing his wrist where Rutledge could see the white marks of his fingers turn slowly to red, "It's easier than hanging."

Angry, Rutledge replied, "It is. You should have done it before I walked into the room."

Smiling wryly, Gooding said, "I had hoped . . ."

He didn't handcuff the man. He said, "You must come with me."

Gooding took his statement, folded it properly, and asked the junior clerk to find him an envelope. He exchanged it for his ring of keys and slid the statement inside. Handing it to Rutledge, he said, "For God's sake, let us go."

He started for the door. The junior clerk, still standing by the desk, said to Gooding, "But, sir—please, sir!"

Rutledge said, "Put in a telephone call to Miss French. Tell her what's happened."

He followed Gooding down the passage and outside to the motorcar.

Without a word, the man got in and waited for Rutledge to turn the crank.

As they were driving through the City, Rutledge said, "You know that if you've lied, it will be found out—because the bodies are not where you tell us they are."

"If I were dead, the police would assume that I'd taken their resting place with me. It was the way I'd planned it."

Naïve, yes, but with the case closed, would the Yard continue to put men and time into the search for the dead? Miss French could of course keep up the pressure to find the bodies of her brother and her cousin, but in the end, it would be one of the unanswered questions of the Yard's history.

Gooding alive could be questioned over and over again. Tripped and confused, he might inadvertently cast doubt on his granddaughter's innocence, on what she could have known, and leave her increasingly vulnerable. He would have to keep a clear head, he would have to keep his wits sharp, and it would mean walking a very thin, dangerous line to convict himself and not Valerie.

Hamish said, "If he had shot himsel', ye would blame yoursel'."

And Rutledge would have done, because he didn't have the evidence to clear Gooding.

"But are ye thinking o' the lass, or the grandfather?"

Gooding said, "Will you speak to Valerie? The police will tell her terrible things and frighten her with threats. I don't suppose they will let me see her. Tell her—tell her that I love her very much, and that I did what I did for the sake of the firm."

"I don't expect they will let me go back to Essex. If I do, I'll tell her."

"Yes. Well. It can't be helped." Scotland Yard was just ahead. "What will you do now?"

"Go where I am sent." Rutledge debated, then said, "If you know where the bodies of French and Traynor are buried, tell them. Or they will use Miss Whitman as a lever. Is her father still alive?"

"Sadly, no. He died somewhere off the coast of Ireland a month before the war ended. And his brother died in France. He was a doctor. His heart gave out."

There was no one, then, to help her.

"I'll do my best," Rutledge promised.

"She isn't guilty. Whatever value you may give to the handkerchief as a clue, she did nothing." Gooding was speaking rapidly now, trying to say what had to be said before the motorcar stopped. "She had no reason to kill Traynor."

They were at their destination.

Rutledge got out and helped his prisoner out of the motorcar. He seemed to have aged in the time it had taken to drive to the Yard, his feet stumbling over the verge as he tried to put a good front on what was being done to him.

Rutledge made a note to ask for a suicide watch.

And then he opened the door, nodded to the Duty Sergeant, and began the process of charging Gooding with murder.

Chapter Seventeen

When it was done, when Gooding had been led away, Rutledge went to his office and sat down to look out at the street.

He believed that Markham was trying hard, trying to clear each case as quickly and efficiently as possible. But the city of York was different from the city of London, where the Yard dealt not only with its serious crimes but with those of the country as well.

Hamish said, "What if ye're wrong, and Gooding is the man ye're after?"

"There may be a way to find out."

Rutledge rose and left the Yard, driving toward the southern outskirts, through Surrey, and to the Bennetts' estate.

He found Mrs. Bennett in the house, the game of croquet long since over, whatever photographs taken and, for all he knew, presently in whatever newspapers had agreed to carry such a story. He himself had seen nothing about it.

She welcomed him, saying that he had come in time for tea and ringing the bell for it.

Rutledge listened once more to her philosophy of helping those who had paid their debts and deserved a second chance to make amends for whatever wrong they had done society and resume a proper role in it.

He said, "Most of these men have a criminal past. Mr. Diaz was in an asylum for attacking two men in their house, while children slept above. He chose not to take up his grievance with them through legal channels. Instead he came armed with a knife and demanded that they deal with him directly. In short, he wanted more than the two men could offer him. He wanted revenge, not justice."

"I expect it was no better nor worse than the other cases. He couldn't understand the language, you see, and was probably as frightened as they were when he confronted them. He's gentle as a lamb now, he loves the gardens, he works so well with Bob. It's time to put the past away and let him live out his years in comfort. I won't allow you to hound him, make him confront the younger man he was."

As if Diaz had done such things as a boy, too young to control temper or bad judgment.

Mrs. Bennett was completely blind to the truth, to what these men were and what they were capable of. Rutledge wondered how her staff viewed her—as a gullible fool they could manipulate or as someone who believed in them. She was counting on gratitude, and it was her bulwark against reality. Why her husband permitted her to go on with this program he couldn't fathom, unless she controlled him as well.

He said, "I'd like to speak to Diaz once more."

"No, I shan't allow you to badger him. He is on my property, he is behaving himself, and I see no reason to bring back the past he's worked so hard to live down."

"I don't wish to badger him, Mrs. Bennett. I should like to tell him that a man has been taken into custody for the crimes I thought he could have committed. It's only fair that I do so."

She frowned. "In that case, I'll have him brought to the house."

"I think I can find him myself. You needn't disturb the rest of your staff."

It took some persuasion, another five or six minutes, but in the end, she let him have his way.

And Rutledge went looking for Diaz.

Hamish said, "If he's the gardener, ye ken, he could ha' buried a dozen men in yon flower beds, and none the wiser."

"God forbid! I shouldn't like to ask the Acting Chief Superintendent for permission to dig them up."

Hamish chuckled. "Ye willna' have a choice."

Diaz was working in the park leading up to the house, some distance from the drive.

He stopped as he saw Rutledge approaching. The heavy secateurs he was using to lop off dead branches were easily able to cut through the flesh and bone of a man's arm. He lowered them and waited.

"Where is Bob today? I thought he was your hands," Rutledge asked in greeting.

"He's taken the first load of brush down to the fire." Diaz looked up at the sky. "A fine day for burning. It will rain before dark, and finish the ashes. What is it you want?"

Here in the wood, with no one to overhear them, Diaz seemed to be having very little difficulty with his English. There was no gallery to convince, and Rutledge was sure the man had long since taken *his* measure.

"I came to tell you that we've made an arrest in the disappearance of Mr. French."

Something stirred in those dark eyes. "Have you indeed?"

Hamish said, "He's worried. Ye havena' told him who it is."

"Yes," Rutledge said smoothly. "I thought I should inform you of this myself. I've already spoken to Mrs. Bennett."

"She will be pleased."

"She was, and she was glad that the Yard had come to apologize."

"Yes."

"There's the small problem of where the body has been buried. But we'll have that out of him in time. The Yard is very good at persuading people to talk."

Diaz turned away to lay the secateurs in the barrow just behind him. "I have no interest in such matters. It is not my affair."

"Yes, I understand. We're having more luck with Mr. Traynor's body. He was in the war, you see, and we can identify him by his scars. Mr. French wasn't in France, which makes it more difficult. I'm afraid I can't give you more details, but it's enough to say that the Yard has matters in hand."

"It is no surprise to me."

"Well, then, I shall bid you a good day." Rutledge looked up. The high boughs overhead crisscrossed and arched like the groins above the nave of a cathedral. The sky was dull, and where the two men stood was gloomy, giving an impression of privacy, of the rest of the world shut out. "Rain is coming? I'm glad to know that. I left windows open in my flat."

He turned away, careful to do so in such a way that he didn't directly show his back to Diaz, but the man kept his distance, and Rutledge walked on, until he was out of sight of the gardener.

He could have sworn that nothing was burning on the property. The wind was light and variable, but it had brought with it no whiff of smoke. Then where was Bob Rawlings?

He had almost reached the drive when he heard someone coming through the trees. Rutledge stepped behind the nearest large trunk, uncertain whether he was being followed or the walker was unaware of his presence.

Waiting patiently, he finally saw the red jumper of a man approaching him not from the direction of the orchard or the back gardens but from the front gates to the estate. He thought at first it must be the man who did the marketing, and then he realized that he was too short, the rhododendrons and other plantings swaying lower as he passed through them.

Rutledge worked his way around the heavy trunk of the tree, staying out of sight, expecting the man to head toward the house. Instead he veered toward where Diaz was working. The faint *snap-snap* of the secateurs could be heard echoing through this end of the park. Overhead a squirrel began to fuss, and Rutledge stayed very still.

He counted to ten, then eased forward to keep the red jumper in sight.

It was then he had a clear view of the man wearing it.

Bob Rawlings.

The man jogged the last twenty feet and called, "It's done."

"Be quiet. The policeman was here. Did you not pass him as you came in the gates?"

"No." Rutledge could hear him thrashing about. "Which way did he go?"

He began to withdraw slowly, carefully, mindful of the secateurs that Diaz had been using. He wanted no part of a confrontation.

Rutledge had reached his motorcar in the loop of the drive before the house and was turning the crank when he heard rather than saw Bob Rawlings burst out of the wood very near where he himself had come out.

He didn't turn but finished what he was doing and got into the motorcar.

As he started down the drive toward the gates, he met Bob Rawlings's eyes and saw the expression in them. It was wariness mixed with anger and something more. A belligerence that seemed to be part of his nature.

Rutledge smiled and kept on going.

It's done. What was done?

He reached the gates and turned onto the road. Not toward London but in the direction of the village serving the Bennett house.

Diaz and his helper worked wherever they were needed to keep the grounds in good order. But that very freedom meant that Rawlings could leave the grounds and return without arousing suspicion.

Either he was meeting someone or he was sending a message to someone.

Rutledge had to ask a passerby where to find the post office. He had already ascertained that there were no familiar red postboxes in the center of the small village.

It was tucked inside a milliner's shop, a tiny square of the British Government hidden away behind a tree of hats and a tall chest featuring gloves and handkerchiefs.

The middle-aged woman behind the grille looked up as his shadow fell across the book she was reading. Marking her place with a rule, she asked politely, "Stamps, sir?"

Rutledge cast a glance over his shoulder, but the proprietor was occupied with a young woman choosing laces, their heads together over a tray of samples.

He took out his identification and passed it through the grille to her.

"Scotland Yard?" She stared at him, her mind busy. He could see her considering and rejecting possibilities. "Is it about those men at the *house*?" The emphasis she put on the word all but identified the Bennett residence.

"I have reason to believe that a letter was posted here. I need to know if that's true."

It was her turn to look around, her voice lower as she said, "There's only one today, sir."

He couldn't ask to see it. But he could ask who had brought it in.

"One of those ruffians," she said, angry. "Walking into the shop bold as you please."

"Can you describe him?"

"Short, fair, wearing a red jumper and corduroy trousers that looked as if he'd climbed trees in them, they were so scuffed and torn."

In fact, Bob Rawlings had been climbing trees.

She went on, "I'm as good a Christian as the next woman, and I challenge anyone to say anything to the contrary. But I don't hold with criminals walking the streets bold as brass. My son tells me they've paid for what they did, but I ask you, why do they have to come *here*, to my village? I saw one of them talking to my daughter, and it quite made me ill."

"They have paid for their crimes," he said.

"Then let them go and live in a city where no one cares who they are."

Rutledge said, "I can't ask you to show me the letter. But I need to know if it's in Mrs. Bennett's handwriting or someone else's. Can you tell me that?"

"It's not in hers. I know her fist when I see it." She glanced around once more and then said, "I must step outside a moment. I'm feeling a little faint from the heat."

Fanning herself with a sheet of paper, she left the post office confines, and as she did a letter caught in her skirts went spiraling the floor. She walked on, ignoring it. Rutledge waited until she had closed the shop door behind her. Then he retrieved the letter and slid it carefully back through the grille.

But not before he had managed to read what an untutored hand had scrawled across the front.

He left at once, and as he walked out the shop door, the postmistress said, "That one's a murderer if ever I saw one. I hope he's taken away from here as soon as may be."

But Mrs. Bennett had assured Rutledge that she had taken in only men who could be rehabilitated. He rather thought she'd misjudged Rawlings.

Or perhaps she hadn't; perhaps Diaz had found something in the younger man that he could mold toward his own ends.

Rutledge thanked the postmistress and walked back to where he'd left the motorcar.

There he took out his notebook and wrote down what he'd seen.

He stopped in Chelsea on his way into London and knocked at the door of the Belford house. He was told that Mr. Belford was not in.

Tearing the sheet out of his notebook, he handed it to the footman. "Would you see that he gets this as soon as he returns?"

"Yes, sir."

Rain caught up with him as he drove down his own street and left the motorcar in front of the flat.

L ater that evening, Rutledge went to the Yard. He had purposely delayed coming in because he hadn't wanted to encounter Markham.

Fielding had left a note on his desk, telling him that the luggage van guard's statement had been collected.

As you asked, I'm holding it until you have advised me to turn it over to the Acting Chief Superintendent.

Not good news at all.

Rutledge wrote a message thanking Fielding, then another asking Gibson for any information he could find on the name and direction he'd taken down from the letter he had seen in Surrey. He disliked depending too much on Belford. A man in his position might easily require the return of a favor down the road.

Finally, he put in for forty-eight hours of leave, setting the request on Markham's desk, then drove through the night to Essex.

He reached it early in the morning, and found the side road that led down to the water meadows at Flatford Mill, where Constable had painted one of his finest works. It hadn't changed much, and he crossed to the other side of the Stour first, moving through the scattered trees, looking toward the mill buildings that Constable had made famous. The village was tiny, hardly more than a hamlet, and he'd had to walk down to it, the way being almost impassable for his motorcar after the night's rains.

The sun had come out, but there were mists still rising from the water, and in the early silence he could hear ducks calling near the weir. Peaceful. That was the word that came to mind. Timeless. He walked some distance before retracing his steps, watching the sun paint the old glass in the windows of the houses opposite a delicate gold. The mill was still there, a hundred years later, and Willie Lot's cottage as well.

He crossed the river again, then went down the lane that led to the mill and the houses. Late flowers grew rampant in the gardens, and bees made a soft humming sound as they worked from blossom to blossom.

Looking back, he could see the angle from which Constable had painted another view, this time of Willie Lott's house. And then the sun was warm on his shoulders as he walked up the long slope to where he'd left the motorcar.

It was time to do what had to be done.

What he hadn't counted on, on his way to call on Miss Whitman, early as it was, was Miss French arriving on her doorstep before he could leave his motorcar close by the church, out of sight.

As he cut through the churchyard, Valerie Whitman had just opened her door to Miss French's knock.

Agnes French's disgruntled voice carried on the still morning air, and he could hear every word. As all the neighbors on either side of the cottage must surely have done as well.

"It wasn't enough to take Michael's love, and then Lewis's," she was saying, "you must kill my brother as well. Oh yes, I've heard from London. It's all quite true, your grandfather has been taken up by the police. And I want to see you taken up as well, as his accomplice. Because you must have been. He's too old, Gooding is, to best Lewis, even with his seizures. He had to have help. I've come to ask for my brother's body so that I can bury him decently where he belongs. I won't take no for an answer. I'll stand here on your doorstep until you tell me." Her voice had risen hysterically, until she was almost shouting.

Valerie Whitman, her face as white as the door she held open with one hand, the other raised a little as if to ward off a blow, stood there listening to the diatribe, uncertain how to answer the charges hurled at her.

"I don't know anything about Lewis—" she began, but Miss French cut her short.

"Don't lie to me. You and Gooding were always close, thick as thieves. He'll not tell the police, but he must have told you. Or did you help to dig the grave? Tell me, *where is my brother?*"

Rutledge thought for an instant that Miss French was about to seize Valerie Whitman's shoulders and shake her.

Crossing the churchyard at speed, oblivious of the traps for unwary feet, he came over the stone wall and across the street.

Miss French turned as Valerie Whitman looked his way, her eyes pleading and then dark with fright.

"He's come to arrest you," Agnes French shrieked. "I knew it."

He opened the gate, came up the walk, and said to Miss French, "That's enough. Go home and mourn your brother there. If you know anything about the firm, go to London and help them sort out what to do now. This is no place for you."

She was about to protest, her cheeks a mottled red in her anger, when he held up his hand.

"No. This is not where you should be. She's not involved. Her grandfather's statement has cleared her."

But for how long? Hamish was demanding, loud in the back of Rutledge's mind.

How long before the police too were at her door?

Rutledge ignored him. "Shall I drive you home, Miss French? You're very distraught."

"I want her to tell me where to find my brother. I want to know how he died. I want to bring him home."

"You never got on with him when he was there," Miss Whitman said. "You can hardly make demands of me in his name."

"I loved my brother, which is more than you can say."

Rutledge said, "Miss Whitman, go inside. Miss French, I'll be happy to drive you home."

She burst into tears then, angry, volatile tears, and stamped down the path, shaking off his arm.

"I'll make her life wretched until I get what I want," she said, slamming the gate back on its hinges. "I will destroy her. That clerk has told me that I am head of French, French and Traynor now, and I will use the power of that position to run her out of St. Hilary. I'll see that she's left to beg on the road, her name anathema to decent people—"

"Stop it," Rutledge said sternly.

Startled, she stared at him. "Does she have you twisted around her little finger too? How am I not surprised? A pretty face, and even an Inspector from Scotland Yard loses his wits."

It was his turn to want to shake her until she stopped, but he couldn't touch her. All he could do was place himself between her and the target of her wrath, forcing her away from the cottage.

She was still furiously angry, unable to stop herself. He could only hope that before they had gone too far, she would wear out her anger and herself.

She raged at him when they were out of hearing of the cottage, shouting at him to do his duty and tell her where her brother was, unaware of the spectacle she presented. Her plain face was distorted, blotchy still, and tears had made tracks through the light dusting of powder that a woman wore when outside her home.

And then, as if a lamp had been turned off, the rage ended. She seemed to know where she was, and with her head down, ignoring him, she began to walk briskly up the road, toward the gates to her house. Her shoulders still shook with her tears, but she kept walking, her mouth set in a grim line.

He stayed with her all the way to her door, turning her over to Nan, saying only that she needed a hot cup of tea and a cool cloth for her eyes. The maid, an arm around her mistress's shoulders, almost lifted her across the threshold, and then hesitating long enough to be sure that Rutledge hadn't intended to follow them inside, she swung the door to. The latch caught.

He wondered if the shock of finding herself in charge of her grandfather's firm had driven Miss French to this outburst. *Beware what you wish for* . . . She had felt left out, ignored, untutored in what brought in the family's wealth, what supported its position, and now she would be expected to show that like the males in her family, she was up to the responsibility. And she'd be doing it in the spotlight of a murder trial.

He didn't envy Agnes French.

Rutledge stood there staring at the closed door, his ears still ringing with her angry words, and then he turned and walked back to the Whitman cottage.

But Valerie Whitman wouldn't come to the door. He called to her and even tried the latch. In the end, he could do nothing more than walk away himself. Back to the churchyard, where he could keep watch.

After an hour or more of pacing back and forth amongst the graves, he gave up and went to fetch his motorcar.

When he drove back toward the main road, he saw that Valerie Whitman had come to her gate, was standing there waiting until he drew even with her.

"Is it true? Has my grandfather been taken into custody for murder?"

"I'm afraid so. He confessed in a statement. In an effort to keep you safe."

"He confessed to what? To *murder*?" Warm as it was, she wrapped her arms around her, and he could hear her teeth chattering from shock. "I don't believe you."

"It's true. As far as it goes. Matthew Traynor is missing as well."

Her eyes flew wide at that. "He's in England? Or is he still in Portugal?"

"His ship docked barely twenty-four hours before Lewis himself disappeared. He disembarked, and that was the last anyone saw of him. His luggage went unclaimed."

"Dear God. And my grandfather is accused of killing him as well?"

"Yes. He knew what he was doing, Gooding did, when he confessed. The original plan was to take you into custody, you see. As an accomplice. You would have gone to prison."

She had begun trembling violently. He wanted to offer comfort, but it was not possible. He was the enemy now.

"I didn't know. I've done nothing wrong, I haven't harmed Lewis or anyone else."

"You must be very careful. If Miss French comes again, she may bring the constable or even the Inspector from Dedham. Keep your door locked and stay away from windows. It will blow over, but until it does, keep a small valise packed and ready by the kitchen door. You may have to leave in a hurry."

"This is my home. I can't leave it. I have nowhere else to go. Not even to my grandfather now."

"Have you no relatives you could stay with for a short time? Until the shock of this news wears off, and people like Miss French come to their senses?"

She shook her head.

"I'll see what I can do. There's the tutor. He lives nearby—"

"No, please. I'm safer where I am."

"Then I'll ask the curate to keep an eye on you."

"Don't make his life wretched. Please, I'll be all right."

But Rutledge wasn't sure of that. Before he could argue the point, she had turned away and hurried back into her house.

He waited until he was sure the door was locked, and then he went in search of the curate.

Williams had heard nothing. Shocked and alarmed by what Rutledge told him, he stared up at the church tower and said, "What am I to do? I can't stay in her house—the gossips would make the worst of that. And she can't come here, for the same reason. If I were as old as my predecessor, it might have been all right."

"Well, then, the least you can do is keep an eye on her. If she's in trouble, if anyone—Miss French included—badgers her, go to the police. Constable Brooks must protect her. She hasn't been accused of anything." Or at least not so far. Rutledge felt helpless and very angry. "She's not her grandfather."

"Yes, yes, I know that. If I could find some older woman— But if Miss French accuses her of knowing more than she ought to know, everyone will have second thoughts. It will be impossible to persuade anyone to come."

Williams would have passed by the man lying beaten and robbed on the road and left him for the Good Samaritan, Rutledge thought grimly. And then he swore at himself, and afterward at Gooding.

"Think of something," Rutledge urged. "I'm needed in London. I'll ask the police in Dedham to send a constable round, but I don't think they will have one to spare."

He had to do something, but until he heard from Belford, there was not much he was free to do.

Frances. He could take her to his sister's house. But even as the thought came to him, he knew it was impossible. He had arrested Valerie Whitman's grandfather. His hands were tied.

He said to the curate, "Keep an eye on her. It's your duty." And with that, he got back in the motorcar and drove away before Williams could argue or find another reason to refuse.

He stopped in Dedham, spoke to the police, and was told that they would take his request under advisement. Miss Whitman had neither made a request for protection nor claimed she was being harassed.

"See that she isn't," he snapped and walked out.

All the way back to London, Rutledge found himself going over every bit of evidence they had so far. He picked up the rain again, and that helped to concentrate his mind. He went first to his flat, shaved and changed his clothes, and as soon as he could, he went to call on Belford.

The man shook his head when Rutledge asked if there was news. "But I hear you have the chief clerk in custody. Surely that's sufficient?"

"Early days," Rutledge said easily. "There's enough circumstantial evidence, yes, but I'm not convinced that he's the right man."

"Hmmm." It was a noncommittal response.

"What do you know about the name and direction I left for you last night?"

"Now that's very interesting. It's a lodgings in the east end of London. The man Baxter, whose name you gave me, is not the brother of this man Rawlings you mentioned earlier. What's more, the woman in whose house he had taken rooms hasn't seen him for several weeks." Belford walked to the hearth and took down an envelope that Rutledge recognized. "This was waiting for him. She was told that any future letters should be held for our—er—colleague, as Mr. Baxter was of necessity visiting friends elsewhere. She appeared to understand that Mr. Baxter was evading the police. There have been no other letters in recent weeks. She rather thought that Mr. Baxter came from Manchester. She had been married to a Manchester man at one time—she recognized the accent."

Rutledge took the letter and put it into his pocket.

"I think it should be opened, in the event there's information there that we can use," Belford said.

Rutledge smiled. "I'll let you know if there is."

He thanked Belford and was about to leave when the man added, "I have a feeling—for what it's worth, mind you—that Mr. Baxter may be your man. He came to London some six weeks ago. He and another man, who didn't stay in London very long, shared the room. The woman was glad to see the back of *him*. She said he was trouble walking if ever she'd seen it."

Bob Rawlings had a half brother. Was this the other man?

And as if he'd read Rutledge's mind, Belford informed him, "I sent someone to Somerset House. Rawlings appears to have been an only child."

If Belford had gone to that much trouble, then the information was correct.

Rutledge said, "I'm fond of lost causes. I think I'll stay with this and see where it leads."

"Then I wish you luck."

Rutledge left and didn't touch the letter until he was well away from Chelsea. He pulled into a quiet lane and opened it carefully.

But to his bitter disappointment, it was not what he'd hoped.

The letter was written by a different hand from the envelope.

It has been a while since I've heard from you. I deserve better, and remind you of promises made.

There was nothing else, no greeting and no signature. It could have been a letter to a lover. Or a reminder of family obligations. Or even a warning that Baxter had failed in some way.

Diaz had been extremely careful, putting nothing down on paper that could in any way be taken as proof that he had hired a killer.

Frustrated, Rutledge returned the letter to its envelope.

Diaz appeared to be a simple gardener. But he had been to university, and he had been in prison, schooling of a very different kind.

And Gooding was still standing in the shadow of the hangman's noose.

Chapter Eighteen

Rutledge was sitting at his desk dealing with the Gooding file when there was a tap at his door and Gibson came in.

"Someone had already been to the lodging house where Baxter lived before the constable got there. A tall man, grubby clothes but polite manner. He took a letter with him. My guess is that it's someone sent by Baxter."

Belford. Or one of his people.

"Did you get a description of Baxter?"

"The constable did. Ordinary looking, those were the words of the woman who lets rooms in the house. Brown hair, brown eyes, nothing to turn your head for a second look. He left the house the Friday before the body was discovered in Chelsea and never came back. He's paid up until the end of the month."

Rutledge considered that. "Do you think he could be our dead man?"

"It's possible that Gooding got him to help with French or meet Traynor in Portsmouth, then got rid of him after he'd done what he was paid to do. If French was already dead and in the back of the motorcar, I can see Gooding running Baxter down, then leaving him where no one would recognize him."

Not Gooding. Not Diaz. Rawlings. Rutledge would have bet on it.

It would be a telling point if the dead man was Baxter. Because he was connected not to Gooding but to Diaz. The letter proved it.

"Clever sod, whoever is behind this business," Gibson commented. And almost in echo of Rutledge's thought, he added, "My money is on Gooding. Which reminds me. An Inspector from Dedham was sent to question Miss Whitman. She barred her door and refused to speak to him."

He had warned her there would be questions. But not this soon, surely?

Rutledge said, "Has Gooding requested legal counsel?"

"This morning. He asked Hayes and Hayes to provide someone."

"Any luck searching for a body along the road north from Portsmouth?"

"Not so far. The Chief Constable for Hampshire isn't best pleased with all his men strung out across the county."

"No. I should think he wouldn't be."

Rutledge thanked Gibson and ten minutes later left the Yard.

It took three quarters of an hour to find the lodging house where Baxter had stayed. Tucked away on a side street, it was easily missed.

Hamish said, "A verra' good place to hide."

And it was. The frumpy woman who answered the door to his knock looked him up and down. "The police have come and gone. I don't need any more of you frightening away my lodgers. And I know my rights. You can't search here without proper papers."

"I don't want to search. I'd like to show you a portrait and ask you if it reminds you of any of your lodgers," Rutledge said with a smile.

"A portrait?" she asked suspiciously. Her hair was still done up in rags, and she put a tentative hand up to them as if she were already considering his request, in spite of her doubts.

"Yes, it belongs to a firm in the City."

"And you'll take me there and bring me back? In that motorcar? I've never ridden in a motorcar."

"Absolutely."

"Then wait here."

She was away for nearly three quarters of an hour. When she came down the stairs again, the rags in her hair were gone and in their place were fair, tight curls that seemed to bob when she walked, despite the ugly hat holding them into place. The dress she had been wearing when she opened the door had been changed to a black one with severe beading at the neck and cuffs. It was better suited to a funeral. But she surged out of the house, walked up to the motorcar, and waited for him to open the door for her. Amused, he settled her in the seat, then turned the crank before joining her there.

She sat up very straight, her purse clasped tightly in her hands, her eyes darting here and there as she took in the passersby, the houses on every street, even the traffic, telling him breathlessly at one point that he was driving far too fast, it made her dizzy.

They arrived without incident at French, French & Traynor. Rutledge handed her down, and she stood there on the pavement like a frowsy duchess while he knocked.

Simmons, the junior clerk Rutledge had seen before, came to the door, stared with open mouth at Rutledge's companion, and then shut it smartly as he ushered them into the outer room.

The woman's gaze swept the furnishings and lamps, the thick carpet and the polished floorboards, not even trying to conceal her curiosity. The junior clerk, confused, asked how he could help Mr. Rutledge.

"I've brought this lady to see the portraits of your founders. I hope that she will find one of them of particular interest."

"The portraits?" If Rutledge had asked to see the giraffe, the man couldn't have been more unsettled. "Er—those in the passage?"

"Yes. It's all right. I've studied them many times. It's the lady who wishes to see them."

The clerk nodded, then opened the inner door, leading the way.

The woman walked ahead of Rutledge, still taking in everything. She would dine out on this excursion for months. The first portrait got her immediate attention. "A fine-looking gentleman," she said of David Traynor, Matthew's father, and moved on.

Standing in front of Howard French's portrait, she tilted her head to one side. "It's not Mr. Baxter," she said. "I mean, I don't see a real likeness. Still, if you squint your eyes just so"—she demonstrated a squint—"you could say it's similar in a way."

"Could they be related?"

"Oh, no, nothing like that. It's the coloring, I expect. Ordinary. Brown. Not like the other gentleman, so fair. You'd take notice of *him* on the street, wouldn't you? And perhaps the shape of this one's face. Not round, not long or square. Just—ordinary." She turned to Rutledge. "Who is this gentleman, then?"

"It's one of the owners here," Rutledge said before the clerk could give her a name.

"Is Mr. Baxter connected to him?" She pointed again to the portrait. "Is that why you wanted me to come here?"

"Not connected. But perhaps someone looking at this portrait and seeing Mr. Baxter later in the day would be reminded of a similarity." He had no intention of speaking of the dead man he'd found in Chelsea.

She gave some thought to his answer. "Well, not if you *knew* them, like."

Satisfied that she had seen all there was to see, she turned back down the passage. "Looking at him from this direction," she said, pointing to Howard French once more, "I don't quite see any likeness, not when his eyes are on me. Still, I understand why you wanted to bring me here. It was clever, better than asking me to tell you what Mr. Baxter looks like."

He thanked the clerk, escorted her to the motorcar, and started back toward her lodging house. It had not solved anything, this visit to the wine merchant's office. But he could take comfort in the fact that Baxter wasn't out of the running.

"How fast can it travel? This motorcar?" she asked.

"Fast enough. Shall I show you?"

She uttered a frightened squeak and shook her head, the curls bobbing in tandem.

When at last they reached her street, she sighed. "Well, I thank you very much for the outing. I dunno as it did you any good, but I was pleased."

He saw her to her door, thanked her, and left.

Back at the Yard, he sat down at his desk, facing the window. It was a rather daunting task, this, he told himself as he stared out at the heavy clouds building in, a dark backdrop to the trees that blocked his view of most of the street.

Hamish said, "Ye're catching at straws."

He was. And getting nowhere.

As the storm gathered, Rutledge sat there watching it, the lightning flaring like the flash of artillery, while the muffled thunder seemed to echo up and down the river. He flinched in the face of it, almost feeling the earth shake as the window glass rattled. He fought against it as long as he could, and then was back in the trenches, struggling to stay alive, to keep his men alive, and as the rain hit the window, propelled by the wind, like machine-gun fire, he clenched his teeth and tried to wait it out. But the room was dark as night at the storm's height, and it was all he could do to stop himself from calling out to men four years in their graves, encouragement, warnings, changes in orders, swearing at the laggards, promising the wounded he wouldn't forget them.

Not here, please, God, not here where everyone will hear me—

And then the storm had moved on, and he was sitting there, hands locked on the arms of his chair, perspiration wet on his forehead and trickling down his chest.

He remained where he was until he was steady again, the worst over.

Hamish said, "Ye should lock yon door before the next storm."

Toying restlessly with Fielding's note as the rain let up and a steamy sunlight tried to push its way through the clouds, Rutledge realized what was between his fingers, and in that instant decided what to do. He would test the sergeant's indictment of Valerie Whitman as the young woman with the bicycle.

He had no reason not to accept Fielding's findings. The man was a very good policeman, thorough, careful, and dependable.

Conversely, if he himself believed that Diaz was the killer, then Valerie Whitman and her bicycle had never been on that train. To show that would surely weaken the Gooding case, even if it did nothing to support his own inquiry.

He opened his desk drawer, took out the frame he kept there, and went down to Fielding's desk.

There were a number of folders on the desktop, and he opened each in turn until he found the one with the statement taken down and signed by the van guard. He made a note of the man's name and then removed the photograph of Valerie Whitman that he'd given the sergeant.

It took a quarter of an hour to locate anyone who could tell him where to find Billy Harden. And then someone said he thought Billy might be in the canteen having a last cup of tea before going on duty.

The station was crowded, noisy, the canteen the same. The station smelled of coal smoke and damp wool from the rain, while the canteen smelled of onions, sausages, and warm bodies, overlaid with cigarette smoke.

Threading his way through the tables, Rutledge finally found a thin, hawk-faced man in the proper uniform, hunched over a pot of tea, nursing the cup in front of him.

"Billy Harden?"

"Depends on who's asking."

"I'd like to speak to you for a moment, if you please. Inspector Rutledge, Scotland Yard." He showed his identification, and the man shook his head. "I've told all I know to yon sergeant," he said, clearly tired of being sought out and questioned.

"It's rather important," Rutledge said, sitting down in the rickety chair across from the man. He took the photograph out of his pocket and set it on the narrow table, careful of the rings from cups and pots and glasses. "You said you recognized this woman, and we have your statement. I'm just double-checking information before we go to trial in this matter."

"Yes, I recognized her."

"Good. It's not a very flattering likeness, but all we had. Her hair is much fairer than it appears to be here. The photograph was taken on a dark day, and the color isn't very clear. I hope Sergeant Fielding pointed this out."

"He did. And that's her."

"She's much taller than she appears here. Nearly five foot nine." Rutledge considered Harden. "Tall enough to look you in the eye, I should think."

"Yes, he told me," the man said irritably. "Quite a tall lady."

"And she's put on considerable weight since this was taken. Two stone, at least."

"I recognized her. All right?"

Rutledge brought out the frame holding the photograph of his sister that he kept in the drawer of his desk, had done since he had come out of Dr. Fleming's clinic and faced his first day at the Yard. A reminder of what he owed her.

"This is another photograph I want you to look at. We have every reason to believe the woman you've identified put a bicycle on the train the night in question, but there's a chance that this woman was with her. Does she look familiar to you? I know it's been some time since you took the bicycle on the luggage van, but it would be helpful to know if she was there as well."

Harden pushed his cup aside to study the photograph Rutledge put down.

"I can't be sure," he said after a moment.

"Yes, I'm glad you are taking this seriously. Take your time."

After about three minutes of staring, Harden frowned. "She was there. Standing just behind the first woman."

"I see. Yes, thank you very much."

Rutledge collected the two photographs and put them back in his pocket.

Turning slightly so that he could see the clock behind the counter, he said, "I left my glasses at the Yard. Can you tell me what the time is? I mustn't be late, there's another interview still to do."

Harden looked up at the clock, squinting. "Nearly half past, I should think."

Rutledge thanked him and rose. Harden poured a last cup of tea out of the pot and nodded.

Rutledge walked way.

The man was myopic, he realized. The time was almost five o'clock. Not nearly half after. And if he couldn't see that clock, barely five feet away, then he could hardly recognize the face of the woman standing by the van or the woman behind her. What's more, Valerie Whitman was not more than five feet six inches tall, she didn't appear to have gained half a stone, much less two since the photograph was taken, and she certainly wasn't fair.

He had reached the canteen door when it opened and a burly man in coveralls came in and called, "Harden. It's time."

Harden looked toward the voice. "Is it?" he demanded.

But the burly man had gone. Harden finished his tea in a gulp and got up.

Rutledge went outside and waited for him. Standing some five feet away from the door, he said as Harden came out, "Safe journey, mate," matching the tone of voice and accent of the burly man.

Harden nodded, "Thankee, Sam." He hurried away, headed for the trains, settling his cap on his head.

Rutledge watched him go, feeling the first surge of hope in days.

He returned to the Yard, set the photograph of Valerie Whitman back into the folder on Fielding's desk, then in his own office, he restored his sister's silver frame to the drawer.

It was then that a second spot of luck came knocking at his door.

Inspector Billings stuck his head around and said, "Are you interested in a bit of game hunting?"

Rutledge said warily, "What sort of game?"

"As in chasing wild geese."

"Come in and sit down."

Billings did, stretching his long legs out before him. "I happened to be there when Gibson was telling our ACS that the Chief Constable of Hampshire was complaining about losing most of his men to your search for a body. Hampshire being rife with crime these days."

"Yes, we've had no luck."

"When I asked the good sergeant what he was hunting for in the wilds of Hampshire, he told me about someone whisked off the *Medea* and then murdered. I hadn't heard about this, having been sent to the antipodes on a case of my own. The odd thing is, when I asked when this man went missing, the date coincided with a rather unexpected bit of information that came my way while I was looking for someone else. Interested?"

"I won't know until I hear the unexpected bit of information."

"I was down along the south coast, sitting in a pub, waiting for someone to appear, when a man came in looking for the local constable. Seems he'd found a body washed up near Dungeness Light. I went to have a look, for fear the man I was after might have run into trouble. By the grace of God, he wasn't my problem because I got back to the pub just in the nick of time to make my meeting."

"What did the body look like?"

"He hadn't been in the water long. No distinguishing marks. Nothing that stood out in my mind. He was dressed well, smooth hands. Not as tall as you, not as dark, strong jawline." Billings shrugged. "I didn't stay. There was too much at stake elsewhere."

Rutledge could understand that.

"Did you follow up later?"

"The local police couldn't identify him, decided he was a suicide, and buried him."

"Why a suicide?"

"He'd drowned. There was a mark across his shoulders, bruising while he was still alive, but that could have been the rail of a ship. They notified the ports where sportsmen keep their boats, but no one was reported missing. I doubt they tried as far as Portsmouth."

"A wild goose indeed," Rutledge said thoughtfully.

"Yes, well, make of it what you like. But if you've lost someone from a docking ship, it's possible he wasn't on her when she docked."

And that was a very perceptive remark.

"I can't quite see how this would fit into what I've been working with. But that doesn't mean it doesn't."

Billings got to his feet. "I don't myself. And I'm off to Staffordshire. The inquiry there is running into difficulties. Again."

"I'll keep this to myself for the moment."

"I thought you might."

And Billings was gone, striding out the door and letting it swing shut behind him.

Rutledge considered what he'd just been told.

The assumption was that Gooding had killed Matthew Traynor and buried his body somewhere on the London road.

Hamish said, "Traynor was last seen by the rail, ye ken, wanting to watch the coast come up."

"It would depend on how close to shore *Medea* was. And how the tides were running. If a man was thrown overboard and he kept his head, he might try to swim. But in the end, he could have tired or developed a cramp."

He got up quickly and ran for the door, after Billings. Rutledge caught up with him just as he was walking out of the Yard.

The Inspector turned and said, "Forgot something?"

"Yes. Two things. Was the body shod? And was he wearing a coat?"

"No to both. But then a coat might be identified. Or else—" Billings considered Rutledge, appraisal in his eyes. "Or he tried to save himself by swimming."

Rutledge smiled. "I would have done, in his place."

"So would I." Billings nodded and walked on.

Rutledge walked back into the Yard, satisfied.

Chapter Nineteen

Rutledge was kept busy for what was left of the day, finishing three reports on cases coming to trial. His mind was half on what he was doing and half on the possibilities tumbling over themselves in his head.

And Hamish too was there, arguing first one side and then the other, a distraction he couldn't escape.

It was nearly eight o'clock when he left the Yard. The days were growing shorter, the long hours of sunlight dwindling toward autumn. He had hated the long days in the trenches, the sun beating down, bringing up the stinking miasma that was always there, until he could smell it even when he'd left the front lines, as if it had been absorbed by his pores. Hot, unable to escape the heat, helmets seeming to burn straight into the brain, thirsty, never enough water, never mind fresh water, and then the final agony, charging across No Man's Land. No chance to bathe, shaving only because the gas mask had to fit, even a fresh uniform filthy before it could be enjoyed, and always the knowledge that if rain came, it would be worse, and sometimes the low-lying mists afterward hiding the deadly gas. He was never sure that winter was any better, the helmet cold, the strap chafing chapped skin, and half-frozen fingers on the trigger of his revolver.

He shook himself, walked to the motorcar, and drove to the flat, grateful to have time to think.

But it wasn't to be.

Frances was there, waiting for him, asking him to take her to dinner.

"All my friends are out of town. Let's go somewhere jolly, shall we, and pretend we're having fun."

He laughed. "It's too late for dinner."

"Well, I haven't eaten, and I'm sure you haven't either. Come home with me, and I'll find something to cook. We can talk."

He had got to the bottom of it. Something was wrong.

"All right. Give me five minutes to clean up and change."

She waited restlessly in the parlor, walking about, touching things, moving them a little this way or that, in constant motion, it seemed to him in the bedroom, listening to her footsteps as they crossed the polished floorboards, then the carpet, back to the floorboards again.

When he came out of the bedroom, she turned, relief on her face, and then managed to smile.

"You're looking remarkably handsome. I like that tie."

"You should. You gave it to me for Christmas."

"Did I? I have good taste."

He took her out to the motorcar, and they drove in silence to the house where they had both lived as children and that now belonged to Frances.

She said as she walked in the door, "Does it ever seem to you that the house echoes when you're the only one at home?"

"I'd never thought about it that way. I suppose it does."

Leading the way through to the kitchen, she began to open cabinet doors and peer into the pantry.

"I'm not particularly hungry," he said after a moment.

"Well, there's soup left over from my lunch and some roast beef, I think. Pickle. Apples. Cheese. Will you make the tea?"

He picked up the kettle, rinsed it, and then filled it with fresh water.

Frances put down the bread she was starting to slice and then said, "Ian. Peter Lockwood? Do you remember him? You were in school with him."

"Yes, as a matter of fact I do," he answered as casually as he could.

"He was a pilot in the war. Came back home to marry the girl he loved—and she had already married someone else. He was quite bitter about it. He left England and went to Kenya. But that didn't suit, apparently, because he's back now. I've run into him quite a lot recently. His father's dead and he's taken over the farm. I think it suits him."

Lockwood's father had been a gentleman farmer. No title, no great estate, but land that had been in his family since the Armada if not the Domesday Book. Old money, a long tradition on the land, and deep roots there.

"Yes, I should think it would." He braced himself for what was to come.

"He's asked me to marry him," she said baldly.

"And what did you say?"

"I told him I wanted to think about it. And I do. Ian, there was someone in the war, someone I cared for very much, but it was impossible. There were . . . impediments, and we agreed not to start something we might both regret."

He'd always suspected it. He even believed he knew who the man was and what the impediment was. And that the man hadn't lived to see the end of the war.

He said, choosing his words carefully, "I shouldn't be surprised. That you'd met someone. For a time I thought Simon might make you happy. But it didn't seem to last."

"No. I like him very much. I really do. But he's—he's not considerate. The way he kept his sister's illness from everyone. He could have said that family affairs had called him away. Instead he simply disappeared from time to time to be with her through the worst of it. I admired that. I felt a little selfish, to tell you the truth, for wanting to know where he was, if there was someone else, if he cared at all. He could have thought of that, couldn't he? A little thing, really, but I wondered if life with him would be full of little things. And if in the end, I could be happy, always waiting for him to tell me what was on his mind. What worried him. What was important to him."

Frances was the least selfish person Rutledge knew. He felt suddenly angry with Simon for making her feel she was.

"And Peter?" he asked after a moment.

"I'm so comfortable when I'm with him. When I'm not, he's still a part of my day, and when he comes to take me to dinner or to a play or just to walk in the park, I feel as if the sun is shining, whether it is or not. Isn't that odd? I haven't felt this way since—since the war. I feel *safe* when he's with me."

The kettle was ready and he made the tea, keeping his back to her, letting her talk.

"Then I don't see a problem," he said finally.

She was busy with the bread again, cutting slices, the knife clinking against the plate in the silence. He waited until the pot was ready and then poured her tea, placing it on the table beside her.

Setting the bread aside, she said, "I don't want to leave you alone in London."

Surprised, he could only stare at her.

"I know how you suffered when you came home from France. Dr. Fleming didn't tell me a great deal—he said it was better for you if I didn't know the whole of it—but he was worried about you, and I've been as well. You've come back to the Yard and done brilliantly. But you aren't happy, Ian, and you haven't found anyone since Jean. I don't know that you've tried. I understand that—I know how Peter felt about the loss of his fiancée, you see, and how long it has taken him to get over her desertion. He told me that it was his fault, he'd spent four years dreaming about a woman who didn't really exist. He just hadn't realized that when he went off to France. He'd come home to *her,* not to the woman who had already married another man without bothering to tell him."

Rutledge didn't know what to say. He'd never told her that Jean had been terrified by the man she'd seen in hospital, and that somehow he'd had the good sense to set her free, however much it had hurt at the time. He'd never told Frances what he'd felt for Meredith Channing, either. It had been too personal, too unexpected, too soon. Too difficult, even to admit to himself that he'd cared.

In a way, he realized, Meredith had deserted him as well.

"I've been too busy to fall in love," he said, striving to speak lightly. "It was hard, returning to the Yard after four years in the trenches. I've had to catch up. And there have been times when I didn't feel very much like going out in the evening. That's the nature of being a policeman."

She knew him too well to be satisfied with that.

"Ian—"

"You needn't worry," he said, summoning a convincing smile. "I'll be all right. When I meet the right person—as you've clearly done—then I'll be as happy as you are now."

He could hear Hamish in the back of his mind. He looked down, busy stirring his tea, so that she couldn't read his eyes.

"Peter is a good man," he said after a moment. "I could see how you would suit."

"Truly?"

"Truly." Ignoring the wave of loneliness that was sweeping him, he added, "Now that we've settled this between us, do you think you could finish those sandwiches?"

She laughed and leaned across the table to kiss his cheek, then picked up the bread again.

Rutledge didn't know if he'd convinced her that he was all right or if she wanted so much to believe it that she would.

The next morning, after a night of little sleep, Rutledge drove down to the coast, to Dungeness Light.

It took him the better part of two hours to find the fisherman who had first discovered the body on the long stretch of stones that passed for a beach.

The man was suspicious at first, facing an Inspector from Scotland Yard.

"What is it you want from me?"

They stood there looking out toward the sea, the Lighthouse behind them.

"We think we may have stumbled on his identity. The question is, could he have come off a passing ship?"

"It would depend, wouldn't it, on how well he could swim." The man turned to squint up at Rutledge. "The sea takes what it wants. If he could fight it and not tire, he could reach a point where he would wash ashore here. Dead, he'd float for a time, bloated and all, then sink to the bottom. This 'un could have made it, I'm thinking, because he was fit enough and the light would guide him the right way. It was just a bit farther than he had the strength to make. Tides are funny things. Predictable as night and day, but the current, see, the current's another matter. It'ull catch a body and spin it, and take it the wrong way, then capricious, it will turn it another direction. This one hadn't been in the current too long."

"His pockets were empty. No identification. Not even a coat."

The fisherman looked out to sea again. "If I were to want to kill a man, I'd do it quiet, just squeezing the back of his neck until he blacks out, then empty his pockets before heaving him overboard. No signs of harm done, see, no way to identify him. And hope that far out, the sea wants to keep him."

Rutledge smiled. "You'd make a good murderer."

The fisherman didn't return the smile. "I killed men in France. Any way I could, so's they wouldn't kill me first. And I didn't hate those I killed. That's the odd thing. I just did it, to be sure I was the one who saw the next day's sunrise. I wasn't proud of it."

"I meant no offense."

"None taken. But I'll never kill again. Not even to save myself. If that's all you wanted, I'm off."

And without waiting for an answer, the fisherman walked away, heading toward one of the little shacks where men kept their gear and sometimes lived when the fish were running.

Rutledge let him go, standing there alone, the wind whipping his trouser legs against his ankles, the whisper of the waves rolling in coming to him, calling to him. He went closer to them, after a while, his shoes crunching through the stones all the long way, trapping his feet in much the same fashion that heavy sand might, pulling at the muscles of the calves until they ached. The tide was out, hadn't yet turned.

He could imagine a man making it this far, tired, almost spent, and then the struggle with the stones would defeat him, and before he could quite reach the safety of the tide line to fall down to sleep, he fell to his knees, and then was knocked over by a wave, drowning because he couldn't lift himself out of the oncoming water.

Not a pretty way to die, within sight of living.

Rutledge stayed where he was a little longer, then turned and made his slow, laborious way back to his motorcar.

I n for a penny, in for a pound.

There was some truth to that old adage, Rutledge thought as he crossed the Thames and headed to Essex.

He had left a note on his desk, saying that he was tying up a few loose ends. And that would have to do.

He reached Dedham finally and then drove on to St. Hilary.

This time Miss French was willing to see him.

She had, he could tell, much on her mind.

"All these years," she said, "we trusted that man Gooding. Out of pity we gave his granddaughter freedom of this house, even allowed her to become engaged to my brothers, and that wasn't enough. He wanted more, and look at the grief he's brought us."

"Are you so sure he's guilty?" Rutledge asked with interest, taking the chair she indicated.

"The police say he is. That's good enough for me."

"What would it gain Mr. Gooding to kill your brother?"

"I expect he didn't think he would be found out. He would go on running the firm, in the hope that eventually I'd have no choice but to make him a partner because I depended on him so. His granddaughter avenged, his own ambition satisfied. Now I must travel to London and try to salvage the firm. I don't know anything about wine, I was never asked if I wanted to learn. It will serve my father and my brothers right if I botch it. But I can't afford to, can I? It's my own livelihood at stake too. And what I shall face on Madeira I don't know. I can't even speak the language. I was never encouraged to learn it."

"Why should Gooding wish to harm Traynor? If it was revenge he was after?"

"How do I know what was going through his mind? He must have thought that Matthew would make choices about the London office that didn't include him. One seldom promotes even a chief clerk to head of firm."

It was a good argument, and would be telling if Miss French was called on to testify.

"I wondered why we'd had no news of Matthew's arrival. So strange, so unlike the man to be so inconsiderate of us. And all this time, Gooding had kept it secret so that he could meet Matthew himself. Odd how things turn out. My father, I think, had hoped that I'd marry Matthew, but he became involved with some woman out there. Perhaps if my father had allowed me to visit Funchal, I'd have had a chance in that direction. Shortsighted, wasn't it? And serves him right."

The diatribe ended. Rutledge thought she was about to cry, but she mastered the urge—if there was one—and said briskly, "You didn't come all this way to listen to me complain."

"Do you remember that when you were a child someone came to the house looking for your grandfather? He caused such an uproar the constable had to be called to restrain him."

"Is that true? Who told you such a thing? Was it Gooding?"

"I don't know that Gooding was told. It was something your grandfather wanted to keep in the family."

"How odd. Lewis had nightmares when he was a child. He said he saw Papa with blood all over his shirt. It was summer, not quite dark, late as it was. Papa was standing below the Nursery window, talking to the doctor and the constable, and Lewis thought they were about to take him away. They kept urging him into the doctor's carriage, and he refused to go. Michael's new tutor was here the next morning. Mama brought him up to meet us, not Papa, and Lewis was frightened that something had happened. Lewis began to cry and ask for Papa. Mama told him not to be silly, he'd see Papa at tea. After she'd gone downstairs again, Lewis asked the tutor if he'd come because Papa was dead. The tutor was quite shocked. He told Lewis that he'd spoken to Papa at breakfast. But we didn't see him until the next afternoon at tea. Lewis refused to go to sleep that night and several nights thereafter, afraid the dream would come back again. I know because he was still in the Nursery and kept me awake as well. But I don't think it did reoccur. Perhaps because it wasn't a dream after all. But who came here? Was it someone we knew?"

"It was someone connected to the winemaking business in Funchal."

"Well then, I expect that was the end of it. Nothing was ever said about trouble with the Funchal part of the business. I'm sure Matthew would know—would have known if there was." She dismissed the matter, returning to her earlier grievances. "I had a note from Miss Townsend. She wanted to know if I'd had news of Lewis. I had to be the one to inform her that Lewis was very likely dead and that Gooding had been taken up for his murder. If she really cared, she would have come rather than write. It would have saved me the trouble of having to explain such things on paper."

He said, "Have you spoken to Miss Whitman again?"

"No, nor shall I."

"If Gooding was Chief Clerk in London, why should he give it all up just because your brother preferred Miss Townsend to Miss Whitman?"

"He dotes on Valerie. Of course he does. Everyone always did. Even my father."

Rutledge wondered, not for the first time, if Agnes French could have killed her brother and purposely prepared for Gooding and Valerie Whitman to take the blame. After all, it was a woman's touch, to leave the handkerchief in the motorcar, to cast the blame on Miss Whitman.

That brought him full circle to the fact that her maid would know if she was away for more than a few hours. The cook, the maids— impossible.

He said, "How long has your maid been in your service?"

"Since I was ten. She was eighteen at the time, and my mother thought I would benefit from having someone look after me. I expect she felt that Nan would keep me out of trouble, but we were soon fast friends."

And fast friends would lie for one another.

Not just childhood peccadilloes but murder as well?

Hamish said, "Did she kill her mother and father? She had the keeping of them, and could ha' rid herself of them when they were too much trouble."

She was just selfish enough that it was possible. And her brothers left the care of them to her. Surely the doctor would have caught anything unusual. Besides, they had been long dead, there would have been no way to prove that suspicion one way or another.

Still—it was an interesting argument. He decided to probe.

"You cared for your parents, in their last illnesses. It must have been very difficult for you."

"It was. My father could have afforded the best nursing care. But he wouldn't put out the money. He told me that I could take over the sickroom and care for Mama. It was very difficult. She was not always the best of patients. But it was my duty, and I did it."

"Again, with your father."

"Oh, yes, Michael and Lewis decided between them that it would be for the best. I was never very close to my father. It was rather nice in some ways for me to see him dependent on me."

She was very open about her feelings. Would she be, if she had been guilty of their deaths?

He couldn't be sure. She was so supremely certain that life had given her less than she deserved, that she might not see the pitfalls of being too truthful about all her emotions.

Rutledge left soon after, still no closer to an answer that satisfied him. All that he had was further proof of Afonso Diaz's presence in the house.

He knew, when he'd chosen to see Miss French first, that he was using it as an excuse to put off calling on Valerie Whitman.

Driving on to her house, he tried to think what he could say that would help Miss Whitman through this dark time, with her grandfather facing murder charges and her own situation more than a little precarious.

But when he reached her door and knocked, he was no closer to an answer to that question.

As she opened the door narrowly, Rutledge could see for himself how stressful the past few days had been. There were circles under her eyes, and their color was less green now, more a dull brown. It wasn't surprising that she hadn't been sleeping well.

"Why have they done this to us?" she asked when she saw who was on her doorstep. "I have had enough of people coming to commiserate. Or so they tell me. Sometimes I think it's more like gloating. Miss Townsend was one of the first, out of kindness. I felt so terrible for her. She was to marry Lewis. It must have been a shock to hear that my grandfather had killed him. She did say that she had come against her father's wishes. He was upset, she told me, because he didn't care to have his patients making comments to him about his daughter's choice of husband."

"He seems to be a rather hard man."

"He's a good doctor. That's why people have tolerated his manners. Or lack of them."

"Do you believe your grandfather murdered Lewis French?"

Her cheeks flushed. He couldn't be sure it whether it was anger or something else.

"Do you wish to gloat too? I thought— You warned me."

"The warning still stands. It's believed he must have had an accomplice."

She made to close the door. "I don't need to hear this sort of thing."

"I'm trying to get to the truth," he said in self-defense, but she shook her head.

"Or hoping that I'll blurt out something that will help you prove he's guilty." She glanced up the street and saw a neighbor watching her. Angrily she said to Rutledge, "Did it ever occur to you that the real truth is that Lewis wanted the whole business, not just the London half? And that he tried to kill Matthew himself? Or have him killed? And the reason you can't find Lewis's body is that he's in hiding somewhere until my grandfather is hanged?"

And then, apparently wishing that she could take back her own cruel words, she went inside, shutting the door with a firmness that was little short of a slam.

As a defense for her grandfather, her argument was sound enough. It would explain both Traynor's death and French's disappearance.

And if that was true, it would mean that the body in Dungeness was Traynor's. But what had she said? *Or have him killed . . .* It would be more consistent with the man French was to hire someone to see that Traynor never landed in England.

Rutledge nodded to the neighbor who had been watching the exchange with Valerie Whitman and drove back to Dedham. This time he found Miss Townsend alone in her father's house.

"My father's at a lying-in," she said, clearly hesitant about inviting him in. And remembering how her father had behaved when he had called the first time, Rutledge could understand her concern as she added, "And my mother is calling on a friend."

"Would you prefer to walk with me? This is police business, Miss Townsend. Your father can have no objection to your helping us in our inquiries."

She smiled tentatively, hiding sudden tears, and invited him into the parlor.

"It's true then about Lewis. And Mr. Gooding. I thought perhaps Miss French was being cruel. I wanted to go and speak to her, but my father felt it would only point up our connection with the family if I did. I even went to see Miss Whitman, taking my bicycle and hoping no one gossiped about that to my father."

"We have every reason to think it could be true. But we have no proof that your fiancé is dead," he said gently.

"I'm sure he must be," she replied forlornly. "Why wouldn't he try to reassure me that he was all right, if that were the case?"

Because, Hamish was pointing out, the man seemed to be as selfish as his sister.

Rutledge answered, "He may be frightened. It's possible that Gooding killed the wrong man, thinking it was Lewis, and he's now in hiding."

"But Mr. Gooding is in custody. Lewis should feel safe now."

"Have you met Matthew Traynor? How did he and Mr. French get on?"

"I was to meet him when he came to England. There was to be a party. But of course that's not going to happen, either. The only comment I remember Lewis making about him was that he was Michael's man and saw things Michael's way still. They were of an age, you see. Matthew and Michael. As Lewis was in charge of the London office, the son of the founder, he felt he should be shown more—I don't know—deference? Mr. Traynor was more isolated on Madeira and should have to change with the times. With Prohibition in the United States, new markets were essential."

It was true, the Act had gone into effect in January of the current year. And exporters must be feeling the loss of revenue rather strongly, with much of Europe still in shambles. Rutledge could see that Lewis French had been discussing this situation with either Miss Townsend or her father. Was that what had been on his mind—the troubling problem he and Traynor would have to address?

Rutledge said, "I'm sorry that I have no information for you now, but I'll send word as soon as I know what has become of Mr. French."

"You're very kind," she said, tears spilling from under her lashes. "I'd even asked my father to speak to Scotland Yard, but he refused." She bit her lip. "He has had one brush with scandal. He doesn't wish to be connected with another one."

"Will you tell me what that first one was about?"

The color rising quickly in her fair skin, she said, "He drank more, during an illness of my mother's. And a patient nearly died. He claimed that he was overcome by worry, but I knew that it had been happening for some time, even before Mama became ill. It was so embarrassing for both of us. Friends turned away, I was taunted by other children. I had even seen my own father too drunk to stand, and that was horrifying. But I lied and told everyone that he had never been overcome by drink. When Mama recovered, he stopped. I was so grateful I'd have done anything for him."

Her father had put her in a very untenable situation. And now, to avoid new scandal, he'd given his daughter none of the support she needed to help her cope with Lewis's loss.

"It was rather awful." She glanced uneasily at the clock, and he knew she was eager for him to be gone before her father came home unexpectedly and recognized the motorcar in front of his door, or her mother returned to find Rutledge in the drawing room. "And then to wonder if Lewis had deserted me as well."

"It isn't desertion, if it's beyond his control."

Thanking her, he left. She had none of the defenses of Valerie Whitman and wasn't self-centered enough to stand up to what was happening, the way Agnes French would survive.

He could feel pity for her.

But *desertion* brought with it a memory of the night before. Of Frances's confession that she was afraid to leave him to his own devices. Of the sweeping loneliness their conversation had evoked.

He wanted his sister to be happy, to have children and a marriage that was all she could wish for. It was important to him—they had always been close, and he loved her very much.

Using her as a shield against the darkness—someone who was always there when he needed her, someone who didn't know the truth, who could cheer him up with a word or sweep him off to join her friends for dinner when he was in despair, who shared a childhood with him, safe ground they could revisit without shadows—perhaps he had lost sight of the woman his sister was.

It would be hard. But he would give her away when the time came and say nothing.

He had seen enough of jealousy in the last few weeks. It was not something he would ever let himself be guilty of.

Chapter Twenty

Rutledge was about to leave Dedham for London when he saw the curate pedaling toward him, the market basket on his bicycle filled with purchases, including a bunch of carrots whose frothy tops swung back and forth in front of him like the bar of a metronome. Williams didn't notice Rutledge at first, his mind clearly elsewhere. When he did, he nearly fell over trying to slow to a stop.

"You aren't here to take Miss Whitman into custody? Are you?" he demanded.

"No. If it happens, the local police will see to it."

"Dear God. I can't take it in. Her grandfather—murder. I tried to talk to her, but she won't open the door. I wanted to ask if I could do her marketing so that she wouldn't have to face the whispers and the backs turning." He gestured to his basket. "It's the least I could do. And I've kept her in my prayers. Her grandfather as well. I don't want to believe that Mr. French is dead. Murdered. It's inconceivable."

Rutledge said, "He hasn't reappeared. There's no other conclusion we can draw."

"He could be in hiding. Frightened, not sure where he can put his trust."

"Then why hasn't he come forward now that Gooding is in custody?"

"I don't know. Perhaps the police believe it was Gooding who tried to kill French, but it wasn't. And that person is still at large."

"How did Traynor and French get on?"

"I have no idea. Mr. Traynor was in Madeira when war broke out in 1914. I was looking forward to meeting him. But I should think, being cousins, that they worked together well. The firm appears to be successful enough. There was even talk of enlarging the house, after Mr. French's marriage." He grimaced. "Miss French was certain he'd expand across her beloved rose garden."

And that would drive Agnes French to murder, if nothing else, Rutledge thought wryly. Everyone had a breaking point.

No matter where he turned, Rutledge could see arguments for and against each possible motive for Lewis French's death.

Where was the proof that he so badly needed to find?

Thanking the curate, he made a decision, turned about, and went back to call on the French family's tutor, Mr. MacFarland.

He knocked at the cottage door, but there was no answer.

Glancing back at the Green, he could see from where he stood that no one was walking there. Marketing?

On the off chance that the tutor was enjoying the fine weather in his garden, Rutledge walked around to the back of the cottage.

There was a small arbor fashioned out of trimmings from the trees that marked the far boundary of the property, and it was set between a pair of apple trees. From where he stood, Rutledge could see sheet music scattered in front of the bench, but MacFarland wasn't there.

Calling, he waited for an answer, but there was none.

Hamish, just behind him, was warning him to take care.

It was all Rutledge needed to go forward, toward the bench. Hamish had always had a feeling for trouble. Some of the men had claimed he had The Sight, but Rutledge believed it was only that finely attuned sense that some men had, honed even more sharply by war.

He reached the bench and saw that the music had not been put down but had been scattered and trampled. As he lifted the sheets, collecting them, he saw a stain in one corner.

Blood. And quite fresh.

He cast about under the trees, but there was no one there. He felt the urgent need to go through the house, but while he was here, he walked on to the high grass just beyond the apple trees. And there he found MacFarland.

The man's white hair was dyed red with his own blood.

Rutledge, swearing under his breath, ran forward, pushing aside the heavy clumps of grass to kneel beside the tutor.

He was breathing. Just. Someone had struck him hard on the back of the head, and the ground beneath him as well as his shirt was wet with blood.

Rutledge lifted him a little, speaking his name.

"MacFarland? Can you hear me? It's Rutledge."

There was no reaction at first, and then the man's eyelids fluttered. He uttered something that sounded like a muffled cry of fear and struggled to free himself.

"You're safe, MacFarland. It's over. I'm from Scotland Yard. Remember?"

The tutor's eyes cleared, focused, and then he said, "Rutledge?" as if the man from London had appeared out of nowhere. "Beware! I think he's still here."

And with that he lost consciousness again.

The attack had only just happened, Rutledge thought. Had his arrival frightened off whoever it was? Looking back toward the house, he could see where the grass had been flattened by dragging MacFarland into cover, to hide his body from whoever had arrived without warning. A hasty attempt, in the hope that the caller would go away again?

Would the attacker come back? Or had he fled when he had the chance?

There was no way of knowing.

Rutledge reached down, collected MacFarland's unconscious form, and with some difficulty, lifted him into his arms.

Despite the need to hurry, Rutledge took his time getting out of the heavy grass with his burden, for fear of tripping. But once out into the open, he moved quickly, through the kitchen garden, around the house, and to his motorcar.

Depositing MacFarland there, he cranked the motor, got in, and started toward Dedham. Looking behind him, he saw that no one had tried to follow him from the back garden, and he felt a surge of relief that he'd got the tutor clear. He had just reached the wooded parkland that surrounded the French family's property when something whizzed past his ear, followed almost at once by the sound of a shot. Hitting the accelerator, he felt the big touring car leap forward, putting distance between him and danger before anyone could aim and fire a second time.

Hamish was urging him to stop and find the shooter, but Rutledge was intent on getting MacFarland to Dr. Townsend. His mind was already processing what little he knew, that the shot must have come from the trees very near the wall that surrounded the French family's park. He couldn't afford to lose MacFarland, his only witness to Afonso Diaz's attack on Howard French. The shooter could wait.

The pieces fit together. It would be very easy to reach the rear of the MacFarland cottage from the place where the shot had been fired. Into the French park, over the wall, through the scatter of trees and high grass, protected from view from most of the village, protected even from the MacFarland house. A killer had only to wait for the tutor to walk into his own back garden on a fine day. It must have been a habit of MacFarland's to sit in that arbor for a time, one the killer must have noted. But why attack him in the first place?

When he got to the doctor's surgery, Rutledge left the motorcar in front of the door and raced inside, praying that Townsend had returned from his lying-in.

He had, coming out to see what the commotion was about as Rutledge demanded to see the doctor at once.

Cutting short Townsend's angry "What do you think you're—" Rutledge turned to him and said, "I've got a dying man in my motorcar. Come at once and help me bring him inside. He's already lost a good deal of blood."

Townsend said, "Who is it?"

But Rutledge was already out the door, and after a brief hesitation, the doctor followed.

"He's one of my patients!" Townsend exclaimed, bending over the man slumped in the seat next to the driver. "Here, take his legs, turn him a little."

It was not easy, getting MacFarland out of the motorcar, but between them they managed, carrying him into the surgery.

"That way," Townsend grunted, jerking his head toward a door down the passage from the entrance. "Examining room."

Rutledge found it, managed to open the door, and helped Townsend stretch MacFarland out on the table.

"What happened?"

"I don't know. I wasn't there," Rutledge said. "I could tell that the blow was recent, and got him to you as quickly as I could."

"Yes, I'm glad you did." Townsend was already running deft fingers over MacFarland's scalp, saying after a moment, "My God, someone struck him. That's not where you usually find injuries from a fall. That's more often here, on the ridge along the back of the skull.

This blow is lower. It should have killed him. I'm astonished he's still breathing."

The doctor continued to work, and after some time straightened up. "That's all I can do. That and cold compresses The rest is up to his constitution. Have you reported this to the St. Hilary constable?"

"There was no time."

"Yes, well, you were there, that's what mattered most. I'll keep him in the surgery. He should go to hospital, but I'm not happy with the thought of moving him again. There's a woman in the village who is very good at nursing. I'll send for her."

"Ask her to write down anything he might say as he comes to his senses. It could help us find whoever did this."

"I'll see to it. No idea why this happened? You were calling on him, there must have been some reason for it."

"I intended to ask him whether he knew anyone else we might contact to track down Lewis French, where he went when he left St. Hilary. Boyhood friends, a particular place he was drawn to. A fresh look at his habits."

Townsend's brows flicked together at the mention of Lewis French. "I can't see why you haven't found a body yet. He must be dead, my wife and I have had to face that. My daughter continues to hope against all hope. Gossip has been unkind to her. The fiancée of a murder victim? The French family in disarray? People seem to talk about nothing else, even my patients. They break off guiltily when I come into the room, then stare. And I know what the topic of conversation must have been."

"I'm sorry. Your daughter deserves better. If you're sure MacFarland is stable, I'll leave him in your hands. There's the constable to find." Rutledge turned to go, then added, "Have you ever heard French say anything about his counterpart in Madeira? How he felt about Traynor's handling of the firm there, whether there were conflicts over decisions or clashes of temperament? Resentment of any sort?"

"I don't see how that can matter now. If they're both dead."

"It could be important. For all we know, French left St. Hilary to meet the ship that Traynor was traveling on."

"I thought it was Gooding who met the ship," Townsend replied, alarmed. "He's been taken up for murdering Traynor, hasn't he, and French as well? Do you think he found the two men together? Or he'll try to persuade the jury that he had?"

"We have to look at every possibility. Otherwise Gooding's lawyers will cast doubt on the evidence being presented."

"We can't have that. The only thing I know about relations between the men was something I read in my predecessor's file. The seizures that Lewis French had—they probably weren't epilepsy. He was injured as a child. He was riding a pony too large for him, and later he told his parents that young Traynor had taunted him into riding it. As a result he was thrown. The seizures began after that, according to his mother. But they blamed both boys equally. Traynor for his taunts and Lewis for heeding them."

"Did Lewis know that they could have been Traynor's fault?"

"I expect he did. He was the one who told his parents why he was riding the wrong horse."

And if Lewis was anything at all like his sister, Agnes, he had blamed Traynor for the fall, whatever he'd told his parents.

Was it a strong enough motive for murder some twenty years later?

They went out of MacFarland's room and were walking toward the door when it opened and Constable Brooks came striding in.

"I was told there was some problem. A neighbor saw a strange man putting Mr. MacFarland into a motorcar and summoned me. I found blood in the back garden and along the road where the motorcar had been standing."

Rutledge said, "He's here, in the surgery. I brought him. I'll drive you back to St. Hilary and tell you what I know."

"It was you, then, Inspector? Mrs. Foster doesn't know much about motorcars. She was worried about Mr. MacFarland."

"As she should have been." Rutledge thanked Dr. Townsend, but Constable Brooks wanted to see the victim for himself. Rutledge left them to it and went out to secure the constable's bicycle to his boot. By that time Brooks had been satisfied that MacFarland would live, and he came directly out to join Rutledge, eager to learn more.

"He said—the doctor—that MacFarland had been struck. If you found him, did you see anyone, notice anything?"

"Only that his assailant could have come from the French property without being seen. And disappeared the same way."

"Why would anyone at the house want to harm Mr. MacFarland?"

Because, Rutledge answered him silently, MacFarland had been at the house when Afonso Diaz had arrived and created a scene. He might remember more than he should about that visit. And if Miss French had killed her brother and left Gooding to take the blame, she wouldn't want anything to interfere with her victory over Valerie Whitman, in whose shadow Agnes French had lived all her childhood. But she knew nothing about Diaz's visit. And why kill Traynor?

He had to come back to a single question. How would Diaz have known MacFarland's name or even where to find him after all this time? He stood most to gain from the death of the tutor, it was true. The last witness . . .

Rutledge turned to Brooks, sitting stiffly beside him, eager to return to St. Hilary and look for MacFarland's assailant.

"Have there been strangers in St. Hilary in recent months asking questions about the tutor? A man you didn't know, who didn't appear to be one of his former pupils?"

"About six months ago," Brooks said slowly. "He told me he was an ex-soldier, looking for a MacFarland who had served with him in Egypt during the war. He thought he might have come home to live with his father. But our Mr. MacFarland had never married, he had no son, and so I told the man. He thanked me and went on his way. I did ask him how he knew we had anyone by that name living here, and he said he'd inquired in Bury, where he'd expected to find his friend, and someone had told him to try St. Hilary, that he might have got the direction wrong. He showed it to me, John MacFarlin, Bury St. Edmunds. I pointed out the difference in spelling."

"You believed him?"

"No reason not to. He left, never came back again. He wasn't the first down-and-out ex-soldier to pass through here since the war, looking for work, somewhere to go, a handout. I've fed one or two I felt sorriest for and sent them back on the road. There was nothing here for them."

There was no way to follow up on the ex-soldier. Or prove that Diaz had sent him. Still . . .

When he had set Constable Brooks down outside MacFarland's house, Rutledge drove to the spot where the shot had come from, got out, and walked to the wall. But there was nothing to be found there. And no way to connect that shot with the attack on the tutor—except for the timing.

Rutledge was tempted to go to the house and ask where Miss French and her maid had been all afternoon. But he would be met with lies if she was guilty and anger if she was not.

He had other business to see to. After that, he would know what to say to Agnes French when he next confronted her.

As he turned toward London, Hamish was there, just behind his shoulder, as he always was. Just as they had watched the enemy, night after night at the Front. But now the young Scot was not the trusted corporal intent on keeping men alive and fighting as efficiently as possible. Now he was the voice of guilt and turmoil, the vivid reminder that Rutledge himself was not yet whole.

Ten miles from London it was Valerie Whitman's voice Rutledge heard, her challenge to him as he stood just outside her door. A reminder that he had not considered the relationship between the two partners. It had stung.

It was very late when he went to call on Mr. Belford.

The man had just come in from dinner with friends and was still dressed in evening clothes, a striking contrast to his coloring. He said, as Rutledge was ushered into his study, "Well met. I have news for you. Whether it is useful or not I can't tell you. But it is interesting."

"I'm glad to hear it," Rutledge said.

"Is that blood on your coat, man? Not yours, surely."

"Not mine. I apologize for not changing, but I feared you might have gone to bed."

"Sit down. Whisky? You look as if you could use it."

"Thank you."

Belford poured two drinks and handed one to Rutledge. "I've had to exert myself on your behalf. Still, it has been a rather interesting puzzle to work with. As a start, I've looked into Afonso Diaz's years in the asylum. The doctors who initially treated him are dead, of course. The latest man thinks he's clever and doing right by his patients. And there's very little information in the files to connect Diaz's reason for being there to the French family. That probably explains why no one was notified that he was being released. And why no one considered him a threat to them. Your visit set the cat among the pigeons, but the upshot was, their judgment for releasing him was still sound. Nor is there anything to indicate Diaz made friends with anyone who would be useful to him in future. I expect he was delighted to find himself among thieves at the Bennett residence. There was the language problem at first, but he's intelligent, he overcame that. He can write in English—there was his request for release to prove it. The fact is, he probably had no expectation of a future, until Lewis French's father died and French himself saw no purpose in continuing payments for the care of a stranger. He must have supposed it was a charity of his father's. Something that could be continued or dropped. He chose to drop it. Two years later, Mrs. Bennett heard about Diaz's imminent release through one of the welfare societies and took him on as gardener. Apparently she had been looking for some time to find a man who knew what he was doing in that direction. She had enough well-meaning pickpockets and forgers, if you like. A *gardener,* mind you, not simply a groundskeeper. And after all, Diaz comes from a long line of farmers. It isn't surprising, is it, that this would turn out to be his skill as well."

"Her gardens *are* quite amazing," Rutledge commented. "She made a good choice."

"Indeed. I also looked into the backgrounds of the men surrounding Diaz now in the Bennett household. Most of them had very ordinary criminal careers. Forgers, for instance, and two men convicted of breaking and entering, another who specialized in cheating lovelorn ladies of their funds, and one who had been embezzling from the man he worked for."

"Hardly hardened criminals," Rutledge said. "But then a murderer wouldn't have been remanded to her care."

"Quite true."

"Anything more?"

"This man Bob Rawlings, who also works for Mrs. Bennett, could well have had a family connection who has never been in prison, but he has associates who have. Any one of them could have given him the name of someone willing to do a quiet murder for a fee. Which one of them we have no way of guessing. If you ask me, Diaz has been very clever."

"He would have to be, to keep his freedom."

"Tell me about the blood."

Rutledge said, "It's the tutor's, MacFarland, the witness to Diaz's attack on Howard French. He'll survive. If I hadn't got there when I did, he would likely have been finished off. And the only person MacFarland's death could benefit is Diaz. There's been another discovery—a body washed ashore close by Dungeness Light. It could be Traynor's. If it is, then he was killed onboard the ship bringing him back from Madeira. Who could have arranged that? Gooding? French? Diaz?"

Belford listened quietly, then said, "Is the Yard still convinced that the clerk, Gooding, is their man?" He was watching Rutledge closely.

Rutledge finished his whisky and set it aside. "Gooding is the consummate senior clerk. Why should he think he could take over the firm by killing the senior partners? It's not ambition, it's folly. As for his granddaughter, he worked with Lewis French, and he would have been more inclined to believe she was well out of the engagement. What's more, he tried to shoot himself after writing that confession. No, I'm not convinced that Gooding is guilty. French could have had Traynor killed. But who killed French? His sister, in a fit of anger? But that doesn't explain our extra body here in Chelsea."

"There's Gooding's granddaughter. The dark horse."

"Her pride was hurt when the engagement was ended. Murder? That's not likely. Still, I rather think a good K.C. will get a conviction. How could he not? Miss French is not equipped by temperament or training to take over the firm and run it successfully. Gooding could have run it for her as his personal fiefdom, and she would have been content to be the titular head, satisfied with money and the pretense of power."

"You're sure no one else remembers Diaz coming to the French house?"

"There was the maid and the boy, Lewis. But she went at once for the constable, and Lewis was thought to have had a bad dream, having looked out the window as Diaz was being taken away. Diaz probably never saw him. He only dealt with the three men."

"You'll never be able to prove this, you know. I have some experience in these matters. All you can possibly do is try to keep Gooding out of the hands of the hangman. Even life in prison offers him a chance to be cleared."

Rutledge told Belford about his experiment with the photograph. "But the man's given his statement. It's in the record," he ended.

Belford got to his feet and offered Rutledge another whisky, but he shook his head.

"Thank you, but I'm too tired."

Belford set their glasses back on the silver tray and went to the window.

"There's only one solution I can see, to draw Diaz out into the open."

"I don't think it can be done. He's been too careful."

"Someone took a shot at you, you said?"

"Yes. I thought at the time that MacFarland's assailant might still be waiting to finish what he had begun, but I didn't expect whoever it was to fire at me. A stone or some other blunt object was used on the tutor. He could hardly fire at MacFarland without half of St. Hilary taking note."

"Do you trust this Dr. Townsend?"

Rutledge considered that. "As a doctor, yes. I'm not sure whether or not I trust him in other directions. What's in your mind? To let Diaz think MacFarland is recovering and about to talk? That sets him up for another attempt. And I have reason to believe that Townsend wouldn't go along with that possibility. Not in his surgery. The man's cottage is too hard to watch. There are too many ways to approach it without being seen."

"Too bad. It would have worked, I think."

"There's another way. I think Dr. Townsend would agree to let it be known that MacFarland is going to recover but the damage to his brain is so severe, he will never be the same man he was. That will keep him safe. But I've been to the Bennett house, I suspect Diaz, and he's well aware of it. He will have to do something about me eventually, whether he likes it or not. And it will have to be carefully done, in no way connected with French or Gooding or the past."

"It's dangerous to be the goat set out for the tiger," Belford warned.

"It will be easier to protect MacFarland in Dr. Townsend's surgery than you, out in the street, as it were. An easy target."

"I'm aware of that."

"I admire your courage. I can't help but wonder why you are willing."

Rutledge thought he knew why. But he wasn't about to give Belford an answer.

Chapter Twenty-one

The next morning, Rutledge bearded the lion in his den, asking to speak to Markham as soon as he arrived at the Yard.

The Acting Chief Superintendent said before Rutledge was quite through the door, "I hope you have something to show for your absence."

"A man was attacked in St. Hilary. He has something to do with the Gooding case."

"I told you that Gooding's granddaughter was involved in this business. It was just a matter of time before we had proof."

"She had no reason to attack this man. He was a tutor to Michael and Lewis French."

"She doesn't need a reason. A new murder casts doubt on her grandfather's guilt. Any victim would do."

"I can see that. It is one answer, but not the only one."

"Still bothered by that Portuguese fellow? He's an old man, Rutledge, he couldn't have killed two men on his own. I looked him up. He's seventy if he's a day."

"Closer to sixty-two. French's motorcar was found in the quarry not far from where he lives."

"Coincidence. Look, he'd have had to take the train to London, then another to Essex, to kill Lewis French. Someone in the Bennett household would have known if he went missing for several days, and they'd have raised the alarm. Mrs. Bennett has been allowed to take in those men in her care, and she can't afford to ignore it if one of them is absent without a damned good reason."

"I rather think he's hired someone to do the killing for him."

"Why are you dragging your heels, Rutledge? Go collect the granddaughter and bring her in. Let the lawyers get at the bottom of who is guilty and who is not. We've made a case, it's sound enough to bring to trial, and I don't see the need to spend any more of the Yard's time on wild speculation."

It was dismissal. Rutledge got up from his chair and walked toward the door.

Markham's voice stopped him.

"Is he likely to live, this tutor? Will he be able to testify?"

"The doctor couldn't tell me yesterday. It was too soon."

"Then find out while you're there."

The hardheaded Yorkshireman having second thoughts?

Rutledge turned. "I'll ring you from the inn when I've seen him."

Markham nodded, and Rutledge went out into the passage looking for Gibson.

The sergeant was in with Inspector Billings.

Rutledge left a message on his desk that he was leaving directly for Essex and would call as soon as he could.

Walking out of the Yard, he made a decision and went first to Hayes and Hayes, solicitors to the French family.

He had to wait nearly half an hour—the elder Mr. Hayes was with another client. Impatient, Rutledge sat in one of the leather chairs in Reception and listened to Hamish's tirade in his ear.

When finally he was conducted to Hayes's office, he asked, "Any news from Portugal?"

"As a matter of fact, I was going to telephone the Yard this afternoon. Mr. Diaz was cut out of his father's Will entirely. You were right about that."

Rutledge had expected no less. Still, it meant that Diaz, without funds to support his vendetta, would have had nothing to bargain with to arrange a murder on land, much less at sea.

Hamish said, "Blackmail?"

It wasn't likely that Diaz had gleaned enough information from the men in service with him at the Bennett house to force a man to kill for him.

Rutledge took a deep breath. Perhaps Markham was right, and he'd been too stubborn to see it.

Hayes was waiting.

"It's a disappointment, your news. The father had threatened, but I needed to know whether he had carried out that threat."

"Yes, fathers often bluster, but in the end, blood tells." The solicitor considered Rutledge. "Was it so very important, this information?"

"It was possible that Mr. Diaz had sought to revenge himself on the French family for his long years in a madhouse. I've reason to wonder if he was ever mad in the true sense, just murderously angry. But the fact that he received no money from his father changes the picture entirely."

"You believe he, not Mr. Gooding, is responsible for the deaths of Lewis French and Matthew Traynor?" The hooded eyes were nearly black.

"Yes. I do. As I told you on my last visit. Diaz is old. He couldn't physically do what Gooding is accused of doing. But he could have hired a killer. And that requires money."

"I was surprised when Mr. Gooding was taken into custody. I've dealt with him for many years, and a more conscientious employee would be hard to find. But then even the most conscientious man can be driven to measures unthinkable in normal situations."

"I'm afraid so. And now the Yard has issued an order for Miss Whitman to be taken into custody." Rutledge rose. "Thank you for your help. I'm sorry it wasn't better news for Gooding."

"Miss Whitman? Preposterous. We acted for her father, you know. Captain Whitman. And a finer officer never lived. Sit down, young man."

Rutledge, eager to be on his way to Essex, did as he was told. Something in the man's voice had changed.

"You asked me for a particular bit of information. I found it for you. But you have just indicated that it was not the inheritance that was so urgent to discover. What you really asked of me was to find out if Diaz had funds at his disposal. Any funds. Is that correct?"

"Yes."

"Then you should know this. I saw no reason to tell you earlier, since it was not included in your request. Mr. Diaz is not destitute. Although his father had cut him off, he had inherited his mother's money while still a young man, and most of it is still in the bank in Funchal, untouched because he was incarcerated first in Portugal and then in England. Here he was never allowed to speak to a Portuguese official, he was never asked if he wished to obtain legal counsel. He was simply locked up. He should have been tried for two attempts to murder English citizens, and so I felt no pity for him. The clinic must have been kinder than prison. And so the money has accrued. It's nowhere near the sums that would have come to Mr. Diaz from his father's Will. But it is most certainly sufficient to hire a dozen murderers, if he so chose. Mr. Diaz is not wealthy—but he could live for another ten years on the income from his mother's bequest without touching the principal."

Stunned, Rutledge could only stare at him, and then as he digested what the solicitor had just told him, he felt a surge of blind anger.

Anger at himself, for not thinking to widen his request. Anger at Hayes for that narrow lawyer's mind, for telling Rutledge precisely what he had asked for, and no more. He would easily have gone away and never known the rest of the story. If he hadn't mentioned Miss Whitman, would Hayes have told him about Diaz's mother?

Swearing silently, Rutledge could only trust himself to ask, "And you are certain about this?"

"I don't as a rule make mistakes," Hayes told him frostily.

"Has he made any use whatsoever of these funds?"

"When he was released into the care of Mr. and Mrs. Bennett, he contacted an agent in Funchal, asking him to act for him in the matter of a cemetery plot near those of his parents. He also has given a large sum of money to the church he attended as a boy, to say perpetual prayers for his soul. And he arranged the transport of his body from London to Madeira, after his death. A stone has been commissioned to mark the place he will be interred. The agent has done just that—and no more."

Rutledge thanked him and got out of Hayes's office before he lost his temper entirely.

At the door, he said, "It's possible you've saved Gooding from hanging."

And with that he turned on his heel and left.

Outside, cranking the motorcar, he gave vent to his fury. So like a lawyer's way of thinking, to hold back what was not in his view pertinent.

As his anger cleared, Rutledge did quick calculations in his head. Leaving the motor running, he strode back into the solicitor's office. Mr. Hayes was already with another client, but Rutledge was not to be deterred.

As Hayes looked up, Rutledge said, "What does Diaz pay this agent of his? And what about the prayers for his soul? I need to find out if that's exorbitant, even for a man who knows he's a murderer. What's more, what is the disposition of the account, once Diaz is dead?"

"I can't—" Hayes began, but Rutledge cut him short.

"Rather you won't. I understand your reluctance to look into that man's affairs again. But if you want to prevent an injustice, you'll find a way. When I leave here, I'm driving to St. Hilary myself to take Valerie Whitman into custody. How long do you want her to stay in a women's prison? It's in your hands."

Hayes was on his feet, shoving back his chair. "I won't be threatened."

"I don't perceive it as a threat. It's a friendly warning that you are in control of her fate. How you feel about that only you can know."

And he was gone, driving out of London at a pace that was a reflection of his mood. Hamish, in the back of his mind, was busy as well. But it was no mistake when Rutledge turned south toward Surrey instead of north toward Essex.

What he'd asked Hayes to do was essential. If the agent as executor was to pay all debts incurred by Diaz at the time of his death, a usual clause in English wills, then he could include any sums that Diaz had borrowed—untraceable—from him before that time. Sums that could already have been transferred to England with ease, from this agent to clients with no apparent connection to Afonso Diaz. An unscrupulous solicitor, paid well for his time, would ask no questions.

Clever indeed. And hopeless to untangle without the help of authorities on Madeira.

But even more urgent was his need now to stake out the goat, and let the tiger know it was unarmed.

Afonso Diaz had had his way for far too long.

Chapter Twenty-two

When Rutledge arrived at the gates to the Bennett property, he pulled over before reaching the house.

Diaz was usually at work in the grounds, and while Surrey was overcast and promised rain, Rutledge rather thought that Diaz preferred his own company to that of his fellows. He would be outside, away from the happy games Mrs. Bennett seemed to enjoy devising or the men's conversations in the servants' hall. Diaz had little in common with any of them. Indeed, he must tolerate Bob Rawlings only because the man was useful to him.

Rutledge found Diaz in the back of the property, wrapped in an old cape of some sort and tending a fire burning the wood the two gardeners had been busy clearing out of the orchard and the park. The scent of applewood was strong, and watching from a distance as the man tossed new fuel on the blaze, he realized that Diaz was far more vigorous than anyone thought, given his age and his wiry build. He had had a way of appearing shrunken, a man who had been defeated by years in an asylum with no expectation of ever seeing Madeira again.

In fact Diaz reminded Rutledge strongly of the painting he'd seen in the French house of a shepherd on a high, windswept hill, watching a flock of sheep.

But here there was no loneliness, no despair. Just a formidable need that had fed on itself for decades. And a mind clever enough to do something about that need.

The thought gave Rutledge his opening, for he hadn't prepared for the encounter, uncertain what the circumstances of their meeting would be.

"Senhor Diaz?"

The man whirled, dropping into a crouch as if to protect himself from attack.

As soon as he saw Rutledge, he slowly straightened, and with that curious stillness that he must have cultivated in the asylum in the face of the madness around him and that was part of his very nature now he waited.

"I've just come to tell you that you've won."

"I don't understand."

Rutledge kept his distance, for he could see as he took another few steps forward the wicked-looking pruning knife for high branches that lay at the man's feet.

"It's an expression," he said. "It doesn't matter what it means. What does matter is that you have succeeded beyond your wildest dreams. French is dead, and although we haven't found his body yet, so is Matthew Traynor. Gooding is sitting in a prison cell awaiting trial for their murders. His granddaughter will be taken into custody this afternoon as an accomplice in those murders. For my sins, I've been ordered to see to it as soon as I can reach Essex. The House of French, French and Traynor is in serious disarray, left in the hands of a woman who is unfit to take it over or run it properly. Give her five years—if that—and it will be worthless. She will be destitute."

He could see the gleam in those dark, unfathomable eyes.

"The only person still alive who witnessed your visit to the French household all those years ago is very likely to be so severely brain damaged that he will be no threat to you. You've wiped the slate clean, and I daresay your English is good enough to appreciate *that* idiom."

Diaz simply stood there, hands by his sides.

"There is nothing I can do to change what you have accomplished or to save Mr. Gooding, who didn't deserve to be dragged into his employers' troubles. But I must admit, it was quite cleverly done, even though I abhor it. I salute you. You have even bested Scotland Yard."

Without moving, Diaz searched the trees through which Rutledge had had to come.

"No, I left no listeners there. We're quite alone. I didn't relish having anyone hear what I came to say."

Rutledge made to go, then appeared to think better of it.

"It was my inquiry from the start. Still, I wasn't sure myself where the truth lay. Whether it was Gooding wanting power or a falling-out of the two partners that resulted in the death of one or both of them. Or even if Miss French had disposed of her tiresome brother. I couldn't find any proof of *your* guilt, no matter how hard I tried."

He met Diaz's gaze. "That is to say, until one of your underlings made the very serious mistake of firing at me as I drove Mr. MacFarland to the doctor's surgery. I can't believe that either Miss French or Miss Whitman is good enough with a revolver to come so close to hitting me. That was when I saw your hand in these events."

Rutledge smiled for the first time. "And so, you see, I have come to congratulate you on a superbly perfect plan. But I am also here to tell you that I will hound you until the day you die, and if I am lucky, I will find the proof I need. However long it takes. I do not care to be made a fool of, Mr. Diaz, and you have made a deadly enemy. In the end, I'll prove to be more clever than you. I live for that moment."

He saw, quick as a flash, those dark eyes flicker toward the pruning knife and back toward the fire. And then they were impassive once more, waiting for Rutledge to finish and leave. Tempted though Diaz was to kill him here and now and burn the body along with the deadwood in the bin, he was unwilling to risk it. He might well kill Rutledge, but this was sanctuary, this position with the Bennetts, and too valuable to lose.

Rutledge laughed. Intentionally. "I'm a match for you, old man," he said with contempt. "The Germans couldn't kill me and neither can you."

Dark color spread into the enigmatic face, and Rutledge saw it before he turned away.

Over his shoulder, he added, "And don't bother to send your underlings to find me. I'm more than a match for them as well. I'm your Nemesis, and there is nothing in the world you can do about it. Nemesis. That's a classical term, one you no doubt studied at University in Portugal. I shouldn't have to translate it for you."

He kept walking, still avoiding the house, until he had reached the gates to the drive. His motorcar was where he'd left it, and he drove off.

He didn't go far.

There was a farm lane just before the village, and he turned down it, following a track that led toward several outbuildings. The war had taken the horses, and their stalls were already in disrepair. At the far end, a new Fordson F tractor had taken their place, its great iron-spoke wheels thick with mud from the late summer plowing. Rutledge pulled his motorcar off to one side, where it couldn't be seen from the road or the farmer's house, marked by tall chimney pots on the far side of an orchard.

And then he walked back to the road, taking up a post behind the shed where the milk cans were left each evening.

It would be a long wait, he expected that. Diaz would have to write his letter and Rawlings would have to find an excuse to carry it to the village for posting.

Settling himself as comfortably as he could against the trunk of a tree, Rutledge tried to ignore the rumbling voice in his head arguing the comments he'd made to Diaz and finding holes in his arguments.

"He willna' risk everything to come after ye. It would cost too much. He missed his chance by yon fire, and he kens it verra' well. And ye'll be faced with a man ye've niver seen. It will be when ye least expect it that he'll strike."

But this wasn't the first time that Rutledge had set himself as the goat to draw out a killer. Once it had been necessary to protect the next victim. Another time he had seen it as the only way to bring a suspect back to where he could take him in. In Diaz's case, the man had achieved what he had set out to do and was in the clear. Their relationship had had to be reduced to a personal challenge. Not hunter and hunted, but a test of nerve. Would Diaz choose the prudent course and rid himself of the last threat to his schemes? Or would he cut his losses and take the chance that there was nothing Rutledge could find in the way of proof, however long he might go on searching?

"I don't think he'll trust a surrogate. I believe Diaz would prefer to kill me himself to be sure nothing goes wrong."

"He hasna' put a foot wrong. Ye told him that."

"Yes, but his underlings have. I think the man we found in Chelsea was intended to be French, but something went wrong, and another man died in French's place. The mistake was rectified, and the other man became a decoy, complete with French's watch."

"Then where is French? Why has he no' come forward?"

"Because he knows Gooding isn't the killer. Either that or he's dead."

"The tiger ye've angered is no' a man to toy with."

"We'll see."

"And if he does come for ye, where is the proof that he ordered the deaths of the ithers? He willna' speak."

"No, but Bob Rawlings will talk, faced with the rope as an accomplice in murder. He's arrogant. And behind that is weakness."

"Then why not tak' him up for murder and see what he has to say."

"I have no reason to take him into custody. Only my suspicion."

It was a vicious circle, and Rutledge had thought it carefully through.

The minutes turned into hours. He glanced at his watch several times, knowing he should be halfway to Dedham by now.

And then, coming down the road, whistling in a monotone under his breath, was Bob Rawlings. Frowning, apparently deep in thought, he was swinging the stick he was carrying rhythmically back and forth, back and forth in an unconscious counterpoint to whatever tune was in his head. In his left hand was an envelope, and as Rawlings got closer, Rutledge could see the stamp affixed to it and the black scrawl of a name.

He waited for Rawlings to come back again from the post office. And it wasn't long before the man appeared, for he'd wasted no time in the village. The frown had deepened into a scowl, and he was wielding his stick like a scythe now, viciously whipping off the heads of the wildflowers along the verge of the road. Taking out on them the mood he was in.

Hamish said, "If he's no' a killer now, he'll grow inta one."

As Rawlings passed Rutledge's vantage point, Rutledge could see the edge of an envelope sticking out of his pocket.

A reply to previous letters? Or one for Mrs. Bennett? Impossible to tell, but something had happened to infuriate the man.

Rutledge made certain that Rawlings was well out of hearing before cranking the motorcar and driving quickly toward the village.

The postmistress was reluctant to let him see the letter, but her feelings about the men at the Bennett house overcame her scruples once more, and Rutledge recognized the direction on the letter as the same one he'd seen on his last visit.

The postmistress glanced around, then leaned toward Rutledge.

In a whisper she said, "And I just handed him one from that same address."

"Has he had replies before this?"

"Not one. But someone wrote this time, and when he tore it open, he didn't like what he read. He went out of here looking like a thundercloud."

And that, Rutledge thought, explained what he himself had witnessed.

What had been in that letter?

"I telt ye," Hamish railed as Rutledge drove toward the Thames and the crossing for Essex. "He isna' coming for ye himsel'. And you willna' know the face of the man who will shoot ye."

"It's a risk I must take. And even so, that man will lead the Yard back to Diaz."

"The tail of the tiger can be as dangerous as the teeth."

Rutledge said, "It's always possible for the goat to outsmart the tiger."

"It doesna' happen verra' often," Hamish said dourly, and blessedly fell silent for several hours, leaving Rutledge alone with his own thoughts.

It was very late when Rutledge reached Dedham, and a summer storm was breaking over the town, the flashes of lightning illuminating the stone face of the handsome church, the windows of the shops across from it, and the tall façade of the inn.

He found a room, slept hard, and in the morning, made his way to Dr. Townsend's surgery.

It was three quarters of an hour before Townsend came in, late for his hours because of an early call from one of the outlying farms. He apologized to the patients waiting to see him, and then nodded to Rutledge.

"Will you come into my office, Inspector?"

Rutledge followed him, and as soon as the door was shut behind them, Townsend turned to him. "Mr. MacFarland has no recollection of what happened to him. He was sitting in the arbor studying something by Liszt, and the next thing he knew he was awakening in my examining room."

"I had hoped for better."

"I'm sure you had. It's a wonder the man's brain functions at all. He could have suffered irreversible damage."

"That's the other matter I came to discuss. It's important for several days that you tell anyone who inquires that MacFarland has suffered just that. It will save his life. He knows something that has already proved dangerous once."

"Miss French came to inquire, when she'd learned MacFarland was here. I told her he was still not stable, but I thought it possible that he'd make a full recovery."

"Then let it be known that the man suffered a massive stroke as a result of his injuries."

"I can't do that. I can't tell people he's had a stroke, and then tell them I was mistaken, that he's recovered completely. I'm a doctor—"

Rutledge remembered that Townsend had already been involved in a scandal because of his drunkenness and a missed diagnosis.

"Then tell them that you were asked to help the police in their inquiries. If you don't," Rutledge said, "someone will walk through that door determined to kill him, and you and your staff will be at risk with him."

Alarmed, Townsend said, "Surely no one would carry this business so far?"

"Will you take that chance?" Rutledge asked. "Your wife and daughter are just next door. If there's shooting and one of them comes running, what then?"

"Leave my family out of it," Townsend answered, angry.

"I'm only saying—"

"Yes, I know what you're saying. There has been enough un-
pleasantness for them to deal with already, and I won't add to their
troubles. People believe what they hear first, and don't always accept
what they're told about it afterward."

Rutledge thought it was more likely the father who was having
trouble with the whispers. And he suspected that Miss Townsend
might have accepted Lewis French's proposal of marriage at her parents' behest. She had been very concerned for him, but there had been
none of the tearful pleas for information that usually followed a much
loved fiancé's disappearance.

Dr. Townsend was finally persuaded to see the advantages to
himself of protecting the tutor, and then Rutledge went in to visit Mac-
Farland. He was still pale and shaken, but he was quick to grasp what
Rutledge had proposed. "I can't think of any of my pupils who held a
grudge. I don't know what this is about."

Rutledge made certain the door was closed and no one was listening outside it. Coming back to MacFarland's bedside, he said in a low
voice, "I think this has to do with the man who came unannounced
into the house the evening you interviewed for the position of tutor."

"But that's decades into the past. I can't imagine what it has to do
with me."

"You were there. You knew what had transpired. You could therefore point a finger at the man responsible."

"Yes, but he is in an institution. Surely they knew why. There must
have been some sort of treatment or the like. I'm not the only source of
information. Am I?"

"They did know at the time why Diaz was there. But it wasn't fully
laid out in his records—perhaps to protect the French family. You are
the last link with the truth. You could tell the police why Diaz came to
St. Hilary and what he did that night that sent him to the asylum. You
are not a member of the family, your evidence would be objective and
accepted. And so you became a target."

"Dear God. I'd not thought about it in years. It wasn't until you came and asked questions that it popped back into my mind."

"Do you remember anything at all about the attack on you?"

"Nothing. I seem to recall hearing a rustling in the high grass just beyond the arbor. I thought it was an animal foraging. We have quite a number of squirrels and other creatures that come quite close to the house. I sometimes watch them from my dining room window. And so I paid no heed," he ended, regret in his voice.

Rutledge left soon after.

He found Agnes French at home, and reported to her that Mac-Farland had had a stroke as a result of his injuries. "I'm told you got a favorable report this morning. A sad turn of events."

"Well, in a way it's Mr. MacFarland's fault," she replied. "I've mentioned to him several times that he should clear out some of the undergrowth beneath the trees and open up the section of his property closest to our park. He harbors stoats and hares and heaven knows what else there, and we have trouble on our side of the wall because he refuses to do as I ask."

Rutledge smiled. He had learned to expect Miss French to feel that other people's problems were of their own making.

She thanked him for his news, sad though it was, and he left, glancing up at the painting above the Queen Anne table. He thought perhaps it had been painted in Madeira, which explained its pride of place there by the door. And he was struck again by the strong emotions caught by the artist.

He had put off the reason for being here in Essex as long as he could. Turning the bonnet of the motorcar toward the church and the cottage where Valerie Whitman lived, he prepared himself for what had to be done.

Walking up the path to the door, he remembered how she had reacted to visitors coming out of curiosity rather than compassion. He would pay her the courtesy of taking her away without making it obvious that she was his prisoner, destined for a London prison.

Hamish said, "She willna' care for that either."

And Rutledge thought Hamish was right.

Knocking at the door, he waited patiently for Miss Whitman to answer his summons. When she didn't, he knocked again, a little louder this time. She still refused to come to the door. He was reaching for the latch when it opened just the barest crack.

"Go away. I've nothing more to say to you."

"Will you walk with me? I've left my motorcar on the far side of the churchyard, as usual. I'd like to talk to you where your neighbors can't hear us."

"Unless you've come to tell me that my grandfather has been released from prison and his name cleared, I don't want to listen to anything you have to say."

"Then let me in, and I'll tell you why I'm here."

"No!" Her voice was sharp. "Please, will you go away and leave me in peace?"

"I can't, Miss Whitman. I'll stay here on your doorstep until you agree to come with me."

Her voice changed in an instant, low and hurt. "Have you come to arrest me?"

"Yes."

"But why? I've done nothing. I can't leave St. Hilary just now. If I do—if I do, I shan't be able to face any of my neighbors ever again. Haven't you caused enough trouble?"

"I'm sorry. I'm a policeman, Miss Whitman. I do what I have to do for the sake of the law." Surprised at the depth of his apology, he added, "I don't want to do this. But I've been given orders, and I must obey them."

She made to close the door, but his boot was in the crack, preventing it.

"Give me time to pack a few things," she pleaded.

"Once this door is shut, I can't rely on its opening again."

Suddenly angry with him, her eyes a blazing green in her pale face, she reached behind her for a shawl, then flung the door wide enough to step out in front of him before pulling it shut with a snap behind her.

"I'll go as I am," she told him, and set off down the path toward the churchyard.

"Miss Whitman—"

Catching her up, he walked beside her in silence until they had crossed the road and entered the churchyard. He wanted to take her arm and make her face him, to tell her that he was trying to free her grandfather and keep her out of prison. But he couldn't do either of those things.

They were beside the church when she finally spoke. "I daresay they won't let me have my own things in a prison, anyway. I've read about the way the Suffragettes were treated. It was inhuman. I don't expect conditions have improved in ten years."

"A little" was all he could say. The warders would be cold, distrustful, and inured to pleas of innocence, and the other inmates would be of a class she had surely never known.

The curate was coming toward them as they rounded the apse, a broad smile on his face. "Well met. I've just finished the painting. How does it look?"

And only as he finished his greeting did he realize that there was something wrong.

Rutledge said easily, "I've come to bring Miss Whitman to London. I'm afraid I can't stop. But from here, it appears to be quite good workmanship."

The curate turned to Miss Whitman. "Is everything all right?" he asked.

"Nothing has been right since my grandfather was accused of murder."

"For what it's worth, I can't imagine that he— I mean to say, I don't know him well, but it seems impossible . . ." His voice trailed off in embarrassment.

"Thank you. That was kind," she rallied enough to say.

He walked with them the rest of the way to the motorcar and, with an expression of concern on his face, watched as Rutledge helped Valerie Whitman into her seat. As if mindful of his duty, he sprang forward to turn the crank. "Is there anything I could do? Please tell me."

But she looked away, not answering him.

And then Rutledge was driving down the lane toward the main road, his face grimly set. Beside him, for the first time, Valerie Whitman's calm cracked, and she began to cry, turning away to look out the window, so that he couldn't see the depth of her despair.

Chapter Twenty-three

Rutledge found the turning for Flatford Mill and stopped up the hill from the river as he had before.

Valerie Whitman, alarm in her eyes, asked, "Why are we here? I thought you were taking me to London."

"I am. We can afford a few minutes of grace. I shouldn't worry if I were you. Let's walk, shall we?"

He had to persuade her to go with him. They had reached the farm when he heard another vehicle stopping where he'd left his own. He thought it might be a motorcycle.

Someone had been following him at a discreet distance ever since he'd left Dedham behind, and he was worried. He had felt the presence, seen flashes of sunlight on metal, and yet no one caught up with him whether he slowed or sped up. He hadn't expected Diaz to act so quickly. Not when there was a witness in the motorcar with him.

He urged her across the bridge and to the far side of the river, where there was a little more protection. The way they had just come was in the open. The reflection of the brick mill and the miller's cottage was so perfect that it might have been a photograph. Not a ripple stirred it, and despite the age of the building and the need for repair, it was still a scene Constable would have recognized. But Miss Whitman ignored it.

They had just reached the trees when she stopped and refused to go on.

"What is it? I won't go another step until you tell me."

"The trees just there," he said harshly, taking her arm and forcing her ahead of him. She turned on him, ready to struggle against his grip, when he saw something—someone—move to the top of the slope across the stream. But he had reached the shadows now, no longer a target for anything short of a rifle.

"Someone has been following us. I don't know who it is. But I have made enemies during this inquiry. And I don't want to drag you into my trouble."

She stared at him, then turned to look back toward the slope they had come down. It had twisted and turned, shaped by oxen and drays and wains, but she could see no one.

"Are you certain?" Turning back to him, she studied his face. "I don't see anyone. Is he waiting by the motorcar, do you think?"

"It's possible." He was still holding her arm, and he released it, stepping back.

"How did you make enemies?" she asked. "On my grandfather's account? Or on mine?"

"I was looking into Howard French's past. There was the possibility of an illegitimate child, and that was worth pursuing. But it led nowhere. And so I began to look at the other relationships in the family. That led me to something quite unexpected. One night a stranger came to the house and threatened French and his son.

It was quickly covered up, the man taken away. I explored that link through MacFarland, and learned that the man not only was still alive but had been released from the asylum where he'd been locked up. I had little to work with, a hunch, the nature of the man himself, the feelings he must have harbored against the French family."

"I'd never heard anything about this. Not from the family, not from my grandfather, no one," she said. "Why haven't the police arrested him, questioned him?"

His eyes still on the road, Rutledge gave her the briefest explanation, adding, "The problem is, whatever I want to believe, I can't prove any of it. And the Yard requires proof. Evidence. Something to be going on with. In the eyes of the police, this man has not done anything wrong, and what's more, there's no real proof now he ever threatened anyone. Twenty years has seen to that."

"Would what you believe clear my grandfather . . . and me?"

"Very likely. Yes, I think it would."

Sunlight, filtering through the leaves, brought out the honey gold in her hair, and he found himself thinking that she should be painted this way.

Clearing his mind of anything but Hamish's voice, he said, "Stay here. I'm going back to the motorcar. If no one is there, if the motor hasn't been tampered with, I'll come back for you."

"No, I don't want to stay here alone."

"He couldn't have reached the outbuildings over there without being seen. He'd have had to cross that patch of open, sunlit ground."

"I know. But if you can circle around him, whoever he is, then he can circle around you. I'm safer if I go than if I stay."

"If I give you an order at any point, you'll obey it instantly, do you understand?"

"I do. I promise."

"Then stay behind me."

"He must know I'm here."

"I'm sure he does. But any shot at me could hit you instead."

"He's armed?" That shook her, but she said stoutly, "I'll stay clear."

He walked briskly back around the millpond and over the bridge toward the clearing, his shoulder blades twitching as he waited for the shot that miraculously didn't come. And then they began to climb the sloping, rutted track that led to the high ground where he had left the motorcar.

And still there was no challenge, no shot being fired.

Nor was there anyone there when they came in sight of his motorcar. It stood alone on the knoll. And although he looked the motorcar over carefully—tires, under the bonnet, and even under the frame—it appeared to be untouched.

Valerie Whitman, watching him search, asked, "Was it because of me? Was that the reason whoever followed you went away? After all, I should think that killing me would make the police wonder if my grandfather was guilty or not."

Rutledge dusted off his knees, straightened his coat, and went to turn the crank. "I think he was here to verify certain information. That MacFarland was no longer able to testify to the past and that you were being taken to London."

All the same, he was watchful on their way back to the main road, and most of the way to London.

Valerie Whitman was quiet the last twenty miles, her face pale and set.

"I'm frightened," she said finally as the traffic grew heavier and the streets of London led inexorably closer to her incarceration.

"I'm sorry," he said inadequately, and wished Markham at the very devil.

He stayed with her through Magistrate's Court, where she was remanded to Holloway, and the last things he saw were her wide eyes as she was led away, half hidden by the prison matron who had taken her in charge.

I t was a long night, spent with Hamish's voice in his head and a glass of whisky, untouched, in his hand.

Who had followed them to Flatford Mill? It was far too soon to expect Diaz to have orchestrated an attempt on his life. And so someone had simply had a watching brief. Had Rutledge himself led the man to MacFarland? Quite unintentionally? Or had that ex-soldier passing through already made certain where the tutor lived?

There was a telephone at the inn in Dedham. If someone had been waiting for further instructions, it would have been easy to reach him. Rutledge wished he'd set the Dedham police to find out, but it would have required too much time, too many explanations, and no certainty of success in finding the contact. At least Miss Whitman was safely in Holloway, and the goat could confidently expect to hear again from the tiger.

Hamish said finally as Rutledge managed to fall into a restless sleep, "Ye claimed ye were his match . . ."

He reported to the Yard the next morning, told Markham that his orders had been carried out, and watched the man nod enthusiastically.

"Well done. Write up your report and see that it's on my desk by the end of the day. Any trouble?"

"Someone followed us out of Dedham. I didn't recognize the motorcar. It stayed with us even when I pulled off at Flatford Mill. And then it was gone."

"Does Miss Whitman have any friends who might take exception to your bringing her in, hoping for a chance to intervene?"

Rutledge thought of the curate, but the man had only a bicycle.

"None that I'm aware of."

"And you weren't followed to London."

"No. I made certain of that. It prolonged the trip, but I believed it to be a wise precaution."

"Then I should think it was coincidence. Or mere curiosity."

But Rutledge had spent four years in the trenches. He had smelled danger there at the mill. He had known that the shadowy figure had come most of the way down the steep slope of the track, before changing his mind and turning away.

Coincidence be damned.

He finished his report and set it aside to be picked up and carried to Markham's office.

Restless, he looked out the window at the gathering clouds and the rise in the wind, lightly touching the leaves on the trees, then beginning to shake them in earnest.

Hamish was worrying the fringes of his mind, trying to bring back a memory that was elusive, almost imagined rather than true.

Rutledge tried to ignore it, but it was persistent, and he found himself going over every step of his arrival in Dedham, from the doctor's surgery to Agnes French's house, thence to the cottage where he'd taken Valerie Whitman away. And still whatever it was eluded him.

There was a knock at the door, startling him, and Gibson came in. "It's dark enough out there to light a lamp," he said, and Rutledge realized that he had been unaware of the gloom. As he reached over to turn on the lamp, Gibson went on. "A call from Maidstone. The Allington Lock on the River Medway. A body washed up against the fish pass. There's a knife still in it. Markham wants you to go there. He thinks it could well be the man we've been searching for upriver at Aylesford."

"I thought that was MacDowell's case."

"So it is, but he's in Gloucester, and you're in London."

Any excuse to get Rutledge away from the Yard until his attitude toward the closed case had changed . . .

He said, "What else did Maidstone tell you? Am I to swim down and bring him up?"

"Just that their man is already on the scene. He's asked for ropes and men to haul in the body, and Inspector Chambliss thought the Yard would wish to be present when they did. You can identify the man. You saw him before MacDowell did."

"For my sins," Rutledge answered. He picked up his hat and his umbrella and followed Gibson out of the office and down the passage.

"Do you need a map?" Gibson asked.

Rutledge knew the Lower Medway, where the river widened enough for boats to come down to this final lock and sail out into the Thames Estuary.

"Thanks, no. I can find it."

The storm suited his mood as he stepped out the door of the Yard and walked toward his motorcar. The wind lashed him with rain, but he couldn't open the umbrella, holding on to his hat as he ducked his head against the sting of the raindrops.

He thought as he got into the motorcar, relieved at being inside, that he was just in the mood for something, anything, taking him out of the claustrophobic Yard.

Moving slowly through the downpour, his eyes scanning the road in front of him, he made his way across the Thames and turned to pick up the road to Rochester, Canterbury, and Dover. The storm followed him, lightning flashing and nearly blinding him a time or two. He considered pulling over, then decided to keep up a slow but steady pace, watching darkness overtake him before he got to his destination.

After a while he saw the turning he was after, left his motorcar at the top of the low ridge, and walked down the long slope to the path along the River Medway. Behind him he heard a tree groan and then begin to fall. He whirled, expecting to see it crush the motorcar, but it landed with a *whoosh,* jarring the ground, not twenty feet behind the boot, blocking the track out to the main road. He swore. What if Maidstone had already retrieved the body and gone home, thinking he might not come in the teeth of this storm?

The Medway was popular with boaters along this stretch, and the lock was a fair size, allowing access upstream for pleasure craft and even the occasional rowboat. A few barges moored along this side offered a different way of life for those who preferred to live on the water, leaving the less accessible far bank open for boats coming into or out of the lock. Ahead of him across the river was the lockkeeper's house, all but invisible in the pounding rain. There were lamps on inside, a beacon against the storm.

Hamish said, "It's na' use, the river's in spate. Best to wait out the storm."

But Rutledge was wet to the skin already, and watching the trees overhead bend and sway, he thought his chances were better going toward the river than sitting in the motorcar just as uncomfortable, waiting for the next tree to come down. "I can at least judge if the body is still there, and if it isn't, I'll go directly to Maidstone. It will save time."

He kept to the path that led to the small dam. The roar of water from the sluices was deafening. The fish pass was on this side, and must be a whirlpool by now. Anyone caught in that had no chance, and the body would be battered before it could be brought out. He hoped like hell that it had been retrieved, or the identification would be all that more difficult. And he wanted a look at the knife.

There was no sign of the constable on duty. Either he'd gone, as Rutledge expected, or he'd taken shelter with the lockkeeper while he waited to report to whomever London was sending. But Rutledge glanced into the small gray stone building he was passing, on the off chance that the local man was in there. Somewhere among the trees upstream, another tall one came down, and Rutledge could feel it rather than hear it hit the ground. He was grateful the worst of the lightning had passed.

Moving on toward the dam, he fought the wind gripping him, and he kept well away from the water already lapping at the stones that set off river from land.

There was a steel bridge over the dam, and he went up the steps with a hand on the rail, trying to look down into the debris that had collected by the fish pass. If he saw nothing he would cross to the lock-keeper's cottage. The man would know what had been happening on his turf.

Even Hamish's voice was shut out by the roar of the sluices, and Rutledge cast a glance up at the bridge above them, searching for the constable.

Then leaning over as far as he dared, he pointed his torch down into the maelstrom that was the fish pass, where limbs and branches, leaves and whatever other flotsam the storm had picked up tried to get through the grating and into open water beyond. But there was no outlet for anything of any size, and the debris simply launched assault after assault against the immovable iron.

Something was down there.

He could see what appeared to be a sleeve, but he couldn't tell as it rolled and went under and then surfaced again whether there was a hand in it. The beam from his torch struggled to penetrate the thick tangle, and he leaned out farther, pointing the light directly at the last spot he'd seen the sleeve tossed. The wind twisted and pushed at him, and the beam bounced badly.

Looking again to the top of the stairs, Rutledge thought there might be more shelter from the buffeting if he stood up there. He climbed to the walkway, but there wasn't much relief to be had, for here the wind tried to spin him around. He made one more attempt to direct the beam of the torch into the water below, and he was rewarded with another look, better this time, at the sleeve.

A coat, there was no doubt about that. Waterlogged, it still tumbled about like a mad thing. He had yet to glimpse the man. But the coat was enough to tell him that the body was probably still down there, that the storm had prevented any attempt to reach it.

He was on the point of turning to cross the bridge and walk to the lockkeeper's house when a flash of something white stopped him. A face? Or a piece of the flotsam of the river? Impossible to say.

He leaned out as far as he could, braced against the railing, the torch pointing to where he'd last seen the white object. It had been brought to the surface once. It could still be in the top layer of the tangle. He was too far away to hope to identify a face, but if that's what it was, it would solve the problem of what to do next.

Concentrating on the small, round circle of his torch beam, he waited.

" 'Ware!"

The word appeared to be hardly more than a whisper against the sluices and the storm's wrath. But Rutledge heard it.

There was movement on the bridge at his back, he could see it out of the corner of his eye, and his first thought was that the constable had spotted him and come out to meet him.

Then he realized that the man wasn't wearing a helmet or even a hat, in spite of the rain.

Whoever he was, he wasn't a policeman. Surely the lockkeeper hadn't ventured out this far just to see what Rutledge was doing.

All too aware of how precariously he was stretched out, he made to turn, but the shadow was already leaping toward him, taking advantage of the chance to push him over. The man caught Rutledge's ankle and viciously raised it, throwing him even further off balance.

There was only one move left to him. Rutledge swung the torch with all his strength in a backhanded arc that brought his body around as well. He couldn't hear the torch strike flesh, but he felt the blow in his wrist, and the shadow staggered.

But the attacker recovered quickly, and with an openmouthed roar that was lost in the torrent of water under their feet, he rushed at Rutledge before he could shove himself clear of the treacherous rail.

Neither man could find a foothold on the wet decking as they fought in a silent and desperate pantomime. Rutledge held on to his torch, the only weapon he had, but it was a grave disadvantage.

It was touch and go, and then Rutledge's boot slipped, and he fell against the rail. Before he could recover, the other man slammed into him, bending him backward toward the swirling water below. Unable to find purchase for his feet on the decking, Rutledge was losing the battle. A fist in the abdomen knocked the air out of him, and he lost his grip on the torch. He could feel the man's hands drop to his ankle, grunting as he lifted Rutledge's right leg, the rail hard against his spine and his weight inexorably shifting.

Hamish was shouting in his ear. Rutledge jerked his body hard to the left, managed to break the man's grip on his shoulder, and felt his hand brush the torch as he went down, his knee crashing into the decking. He caught the torch up just as the shift in momentum went his way. The other man, still holding Rutledge's ankle, was pulled forward and then shoved back as Rutledge flexed his leg. His opponent was thrown against the rail, letting go, and Rutledge was on his feet, swinging the torch a second time. He missed the man's head, his wet fingers slipping as he brought the torch around, but it struck the man's ear solidly.

At the same time the light threw his attacker's features into high relief. In that split-second glimpse as the man reared back, a hand to his head, Rutledge recognized him.

Breaking free, Rutledge brought his left fist down on the side of the man's neck.

He staggered, just as a strong gust of wind caught him, turned him, and spun him backward. Reaching wildly for the rail, he caught it and, as Rutledge came toward him, lifted his feet and lashed out at him. But he judged it wrong, overbalanced, and hurtled over the rail.

Rutledge caught at his wrist to stop him, but their hands were wet, and there was no real grip. The pull of gravity was too strong, and the man pitched down into the swirling water, nearly pulling Rutledge with him.

Wheeling the torch toward the water, Rutledge saw Bob Rawlings's face, eyes wide with fear, mouth open in a soundless cry, as he tried to reach the side of the pool. And then Rawlings was sucked under.

Rutledge waited, but his attacker didn't come up. He circled the small pool with the beam and finally saw Rawlings. He was no longer struggling, his eyes fixed now, even as the light swept across them.

Rutledge stood there, his chest heaving from the effort he'd made to hold on to Rawlings. And then he turned and walked across the bridge, hatless, the rain pouring down his face.

It was a long way to the house, across the bridge over the sluice gates, then down the lock and over a smaller bridge to the far bank, and another forty feet to the cottage.

He had to pound on the wood to be heard. The keeper opened the door, said, "Good God. Come in," and slammed it behind Rutledge as soon as he was inside.

"I'm dripping," Rutledge said as water ran off his hair and clothes to puddle around his feet on the polished floor.

"Wait here."

The keeper came back with several towels, and Rutledge did what he could to dry off enough to walk into the front room.

"Sit down," the man said, then looked around as if to find a suitable place to offer his unexpected guest.

"I can't stay," Rutledge said. "Is the constable here? Or did he leave when the storm broke?"

"Constable? What constable? There's been no one here since the last boat came through at noon."

Rutledge said grimly, "There's a man drowned in the fish pass. I need to report to the nearest police station."

"Wait until the storm passes. There's nothing anyone can do now. I'll make tea."

Rutledge let himself be persuaded, but he hadn't been in the cottage for more than twenty minutes when the wind dropped and the rain was reduced to light showers. To the west the sky was brighter. Toward the Channel and France it was still an ominous purple-black.

He stood at the window of the front room, thinking about Rawlings.

The man couldn't have followed him here unless he had been waiting outside the Yard for Rutledge to appear. And that made no sense.

What did make sense was a false call to the Yard. Markham had leapt to the conclusion that it was in regard to an inquiry in progress, an inquiry that had been thoroughly covered in the local newspapers, giving MacDowell's name, Chambliss's, and even Rutledge's.

A few words—*This is Chambliss in Maidstone. That inquiry in Aylesford? I think your man's dead. He's in the fish pass at the Medway Lock with a knife in him. Better send someone to have a look. A constable will meet your man there. We've got ropes and hooks coming. I've got to go, they're waiting for me.*

And if Rutledge hadn't been sent, no harm done—it could all be put down to a vicious prank. A dead man in the fish pass? Just an old coat, and someone's vivid imagination.

It could have been done. It had Diaz's mark on it, simple, without a trace.

And it had almost worked.

It was a rather daring way to draw him out of London. But why was it Rawlings had been there, and not Diaz?

Rutledge set down his teacup, thanked the lockkeeper, and went back out into the rain, his clothes hardly dry from their earlier soaking.

He crossed over to the bridge above the sluice gates, and saw that the river was still in spate, the heavy rains upstream still rushing toward the sea.

Rutledge wasted no time searching for Rawlings's body. His concern now was the downed tree blocking his motorcar. He discovered there was just—only just—enough room to drive out past the uprooted trunk. He walked around it, judging it, then went to the crank. His tires slithered and slipped in the torn, wet earth. Then the offside front wheel nearly came to grief, and for an instant he was certain he would lose control entirely. But the others stayed on firmer ground, and he shot up to the road in a spurt of speed that nearly took him across it and into a ditch.

By the time he'd managed to reach the main road, the rain had nearly stopped.

Just as Rutledge had expected, the Maidstone police knew nothing about a knifed man in the fish pass. Indeed, no one had telephoned the Yard.

Chambliss was furious that his name had been used in that connection, angrier still that he now had to deal with the aftermath of the hoax.

"We've had no luck in Aylesford. I'd have reported to the Yard if we had. The fool's gone to ground. He could be in Chatham or Rochester. Or anywhere else. He knows he'll be safer in custody, but he's too frightened to come in. And if the dead man is who you tell me he is, he's got nothing to do with our little problem."

"London had no choice but to investigate. And I should have been in that fish pass, not Rawlings."

"Yes, yes, I see that. And there was no way of knowing how bad that storm would be, was there? I don't like my turf used for a spot of revenge. What sorts of cases have you been dealing with, then, that you've made enemies like this one?"

Chambliss didn't expect an answer. He turned and began to issue orders, then said to Rutledge, "Are you staying? Until the body is brought out?"

It was the next morning before they could try to reach Rawlings's body, and it was difficult at best, even with the river down, to hook the clothing and bring the body up the steep walled slope onto the earthen bank above.

Rutledge was interested to see that their first efforts had brought up an old Army greatcoat. He squatted beside it, looking at the sleeve. It would have been easy for anyone seeing it to think a man had fallen in. Had Rawlings tossed the coat in for verisimilitude? Something to catch Rutledge's eye when he arrived and make him believe that the summons had been real? After all, as Chambliss had said, no one had expected the storm's fury, and Rawlings had had to find some way to draw his attention away from the figure lurking in the shadows, waiting for him.

Such careful planning was, Rutledge thought, more a hallmark of Diaz's plotting than of Rawlings's methods. And rather diabolical.

One of the constables shouted, and Rutledge turned to see the pale, dripping body coming up over the lip of the wall, heavy with water. One arm flopped, almost in a macabre greeting, and the men fell back.

But once laid out on the ground, the body was small and very dead, the face and hands scraped from their battering against the grating of the fish pass.

"Sure of your identification?" Chambliss asked, coming up to stand beside Rutledge.

"Yes. Robert Rawlings. Late of Surrey, the household of a man called Bennett and his wife. She collects men just out of prison. They serve as her staff."

"Foolish business, that. You owe me, Rutledge. But from the look of you, you've already paid. Get that lump on your forehead seen to."

"I will," he replied. He hadn't known it was there or even that it had happened until he'd taken a room at a hotel close by the police station, and realized why he had had to show his identification to the clerk before he was allowed to sign the register. His clothing damp, wrinkled, filthy, blood in his hair, he looked like anything but a representative of the Yard. "Can you see to the body? I want to go directly to the Bennett house before news of Rawlings's death reaches them."

Chambliss considered him. "If you'll give me what I need to write my own report."

"Done," Rutledge answered.

He looked down at Rawlings's body.

What role did you play last night? he silently asked the dead man. *A surrogate for Diaz? You fought too hard, you went too far. What had I done to you to make you stand there waiting in that storm for me to come? It wasn't for him that you wanted my blood. Why?*

Hamish said, "He was tricked. As ye were tricked."

Rutledge thanked Chambliss and his men, then walked away up through the trees to where his motorcar was waiting on the main road.

Half an hour later, he was well on his way to Surrey.

Chapter Twenty-four

Rutledge stopped briefly at a country hotel on the border with Sussex for lunch. He'd missed his dinner the night before, was up before breakfast this morning, and was very likely to miss his dinner again. He had made some effort before joining Chambliss at the lock to remedy his appearance, paying the desk clerk's wife to press his coat and trousers. He was still well below the standards of a hotel. He smiled wryly when the waiter led him to the corner table nearest the service door to the kitchen.

On his way to the dining room, he'd discovered that the hotel possessed a telephone.

He put in a call to London while waiting for his meal to be brought to the table, and he caught Sergeant Gibson just coming on duty after a long night hunting for a murderer in Islington.

"I've run into a small problem concerning the drowning in Kent,"

Rutledge told him. "There's a link to Surrey, and I'm on my way there now."

"I'll pass along the word, sir. Meanwhile, there's a message for you. Marked urgent. It's from Mr. Belford. Came in last evening, late. If you remember, he lives on the street where the first body in the Gooding inquiry was found."

Rutledge thanked him and put up the receiver. Still standing there in the small telephone closet, he considered going to London first to see what Belford had to say, but there was the time factor. The later he reached the Bennett household, the less likely he was to be there before news of Rawlings's death preceded him.

Belford would have to wait. And it was possible that his information was already outdated.

Rutledge set out for Surrey as soon as he'd finished his meal. A watery sun was shining when he reached the village just before the Bennett house, but clouds had moved in before he turned in to the long drive through the park.

There was no immediate answer to his knock, and then one of the staff came to the door.

"Mrs. Bennett is resting," Rutledge was told. "I doubt she'll be receiving visitors before tomorrow."

"It's urgent."

But he was adamant that Mrs. Bennett couldn't be disturbed.

Rutledge left his motorcar halfway down the drive, out of sight of the house, and went in search of Afonso Diaz.

It was possible, just, that Diaz had gone to Kent with Rawlings, to keep him to his purpose. But Rutledge wasn't convinced of that.

"Ye canna' count on the men who work here to tell a policeman the truth about the ithers. It's like the Army, they'll no' talk to an officer."

That was very true. A brotherhood, and he was the outsider.

He went first to the place where the fire had been burning.

Diaz wasn't there. Rutledge began a systematic search of his usual haunts: the gardens, the orchard, and finally the barn. They were all empty.

A time or two he suspected he was being watched from the house. The men there knew who he was, possibly even knew why he was there, but there was no way he could avoid being seeing from upper windows. Still, no one came out to challenge him.

Rutledge had left the park until last. Under the canopy of the trees, where sunlight dappled the ground, a now-aging collection of rhododendrons and azaleas had been planted. Exotic and very popular, their spring blooms gave an airy beauty to a woodland, and Jean had always admired that.

Walking quietly through them now, he kept watch for Diaz, remembering too well that pruning knife. It had a long reach, it could strike him before he saw it coming. But as he swept the area, moving steadily back toward where he'd left the motorcar, Rutledge had the strongest feeling that he was alone in this part of the park.

That changed suddenly, and he stopped walking to listen. The wood was silent. There wasn't so much as the patter of rain on the leaves overhead. The mist was too light. And then he glimpsed the dark red of a man's coat some forty feet away, and he knew he'd found his quarry.

The question was, had Diaz found him first?

Rutledge walked on, cutting the distance between them in half, then stopped.

"I've been looking for you," he called.

The red coat took on the shape of a man as Diaz stepped out from behind a shrub.

"You seem to have nothing better to do than to haunt me," he said levelly. "There's a story, you know, about the voices of dead shepherds coming from the cliffs above the sea. In Madeira. You can hear them at night. I have done this. My father took me there as a boy. It's a very high cliff, the highest on this side of the Atlantic, and seabirds nest there at night. It's their voices that sound like the shepherds. I was quite frightened. Are you a dead shepherd?"

It was a long speech for Diaz.

"I might have been, at the Allington Lock. I've come to report to Mrs. Bennett that Bob Rawlings is dead. In my place."

If this was news, Diaz showed no sign of it.

"A pity. He was very good on the two-man saw. Mrs. Bennett will be upset."

"Why did he try to lure me there?"

"Who knows? I was not in his confidence. But his brother is missing. He has been for some time. I expect Bob heard me thinking aloud one evening. Wondering if you were the one who had consigned the body to a pauper's grave."

"He doesn't have a brother. According to Somerset House." And according to Mr. Belford.

"You are misinformed. The boy was taken in by Bob's mother when his own mother died. No one bothers much with the arrangements of the poor. No lawyers come to smooth the way. But they grew up as brothers, and it was enough."

Rutledge remembered the scowl on Rawlings's face coming back from the village only a few days ago. What had been in the letter he'd received? News he didn't want to hear?

Was it Baxter who had been found dead in Chelsea? Had he been the man hired to kill Lewis French? It must have seemed to be an easy way to earn the money on offer, attacking an unsuspecting target.

But how did Baxter come to die? And where was French?

Who had made the decision to leave the body in Chelsea?

There was no time to consider whether Diaz was lying or telling the truth about Rawlings.

Rutledge said, "Did Rawlings go to the rooming house in London before he went to the Allington Lock? He must have done, to be so angry. He waited for me to come, you see. In spite of the storm. He didn't want to miss his chance. But he wasn't clever enough to impersonate a Maidstone Inspector on the telephone. Someone else did that. Still, it was sheer luck that I went to Kent, that someone else wasn't sent instead. How did he persuade Mrs. Bennett to allow him to leave the estate?"

Diaz smiled. "She has a soft heart."

Or hadn't been told.

"How many other brothers did Rawlings have?"

"I have no idea. You could have asked him, if you hadn't let him die."

There had to be at least one other person at Diaz's beck and call. Because if Baxter had been killed in Essex, who had brought his body to London and then hidden the motorcar in the quarry? Who had struck MacFarland on the back of the head and then taken a shot at Rutledge? Who had been watching to see if Rutledge left the Yard and headed for Kent? If it wasn't Diaz himself, who was it?

Perhaps Belford knew. That would explain his urgent message.

Watching him, Diaz said, "You claimed you were my match. I have proved you are not."

"I was Rawlings's match," Rutledge replied grimly.

"As you say, I have had trouble with underlings. But that has been . . . remedied."

And Rawlings was dead; whatever he knew or had been a part of had died with him. Baxter was very likely dead. Rutledge was certain Diaz wouldn't mourn his tools. If they knew too much, he might even be grateful to be rid of them. But would their loss make it more difficult to hire others?

With a nod, Diaz walked off in the direction of the orchard, angling away from Rutledge rather than moving past him.

Rutledge started toward his motorcar. Diaz had come to gloat. From some vantage point he'd seen Rutledge searching for him and must have guessed that Rawlings was dead. But he had been in the shrubbery for several minutes before he'd come forward into view.

Why?

Rutledge skirted one of the larger rhododendrons and was about to round the second when he heard a soft *chink!*

And in the same instant, Hamish shouted "*'Ware.*"

Rutledge stopped where he was.

Diaz had not taken the last opportunity to kill Rutledge with the pruning knife. Had he regretted that, and today taken advantage of the new chance Fate had unexpectedly provided him?

Rutledge looked around, saw nothing, and then moved his foot very gently forward.

There was that sound again, like a chain . . .

He could feel the cold sweat on his body.

Somewhere here there was a mantrap. And he had accidentally nudged part of the chain that held it in place. If he hadn't heard that slight *chink* . . .

He saw a short stick under the azalea beside him, squatted with great care, and reached for it, swearing as he almost lost his balance.

Getting to his feet once more, he poked gently on either side of where his feet were planted, then nudged the stick ahead a few inches.

Nothing.

He dared not move.

Was that what Diaz had been busy about? Smoothing the leafy ground so that the trap couldn't be seen?

He leaned a little forward, poking again. And then a little farther still, barely twelve inches from where he was standing.

Seeming to leap out of nowhere, the mantrap sprang shut. The jagged row of steel teeth closed on his stick, biting it in half with a vicious metallic snap that made Rutledge wince.

One more step—and his foot would have been mangled or his

ankle broken. Would anyone have come to his aid, or would his calls have been ignored? In the house, out of hearing, Mrs. Bennett would have gone on with her day, and the men who served her would have said nothing, for fear of becoming involved in something that could have sent all of them back to prison.

Rutledge doubted Diaz would return before morning, leaving his prisoner to suffer.

Let him come then, and find nothing.

Rutledge was about to move on when he thought better of it.

Diaz considered himself to be very clever. And expecting Rutledge to find the first trap, he might well have set another where an unsuspecting foot would step straight into it.

There was nothing for Rutledge to do but retrace his steps, where he knew the ground to be safe, and cut through the trees in a different direction, coming to the motorcar in a roundabout fashion.

He set out, tense, expecting to hear another trap close just as he put his foot down. There had been time for Diaz to set one trap, perhaps two. But no more than that. Still, he couldn't put his trust in any logic when it came to Diaz.

Rutledge reached the low outer wall of the park, swung himself over it, and walked down the main road until he came to the gates by the drive.

And still he looked over the motorcar, fairly certain that it was all right, but again, putting no trust in the man who had set that diabolical trap.

As he drove toward London, he carried with him the feeling—indeed the certainty—that he had not heard the last of Afonso Diaz.

Rutledge went directly to Chelsea, calling on Belford.

When the man came into the room, he looked his guest over and said, "If I didn't know better, I'd say you went bathing in your clothes."

Rutledge smiled, glancing down at the wrinkles in his coat and trousers. "I was caught out in that storm last night."

"Were you indeed? No wonder I never heard from you. We lost a tree just along the street. A small one, but I'd have preferred not to be under it when it came down."

Belford went over to pour two glasses of whisky, saying, "Once again, I think you need this. Unless you're concerned about that blow to the head?"

Rutledge laughed as he accepted his drink. "I can't tell you how I got it. It was just—there—this morning."

Belford stared at him for a moment, then realized that he was joking.

"I've finally got a foot in the door, so to speak. Or a man into that lodgings. The address you gave me. The former occupant of the room hadn't paid his rent this week, and nor had he appeared. The owner was quite happy to store his belongings in the cellar. Not much there—my man had a look. Clothing, a photograph of two boys, a few books."

"This was Baxter?" Rutledge asked.

"Yes. There had been another man with him that first night, but he was gone the next morning."

"You mentioned him before. An accomplice? Or someone who needed a bed for one night?"

"Mrs. Rush, the owner of the house, didn't know. He had little to say for himself when he arrived, and she was still in bed when he left. She remembered that someone called him Ben."

"Interesting. But so far not useful. Baxter, by the way, was a foster brother to Rawlings."

"Was he, by God. There was no official record of adoption."

"He was never officially adopted. His mother died and Rawlings's mother simply took him in."

"Well, well." Belford emptied his glass and set it back on the tray. Standing by the hearth, he said, "Something has happened. You'd better tell me."

Rutledge said, "It's a long story."

"I have the time. And the patience to hear it."

Beginning with the decision to taunt Diaz, Rutledge gave Belford an account of the arrest of Valerie Whitman, how they were followed, and then the journey in the rain to the lock at Allington. Belford said nothing, but he frowned as Rutledge described what had happened on the footplate of the bridge. When Rutledge told him about the mantrap, Belford whistled.

"You'd best look under your bed at night."

"Believe me, I shall," Rutledge replied grimly.

"I don't think my man can learn much more where he is, but I'll leave him there a day or two longer."

"It wouldn't hurt." Rutledge turned his empty glass one way and then another, catching the light in the deep cuts in the crystal, watching the prism effect. "Was this the urgent message you left for me? That you had put someone in the lodging house?"

Belford smiled. "After I left that message, I wasn't sure whether or not I was ready to tell you. I've been searching for it on my own."

"Searching for what?"

"Baxter had a motorcycle with him the night he arrived. He left with it early in the morning on the day he disappeared."

"A motorcycle!" Rutledge exclaimed and nodded. "Yes, I'd been wondering—it makes much more sense than a motorcar. The question is, where is it now?" He stood, put down his glass, and said, "You have a telephone, do you not?"

Belford hesitated, then answered, "Yes, of course."

"I'd like to use it."

Belford took him into the study and showed him the instrument on the desk, then was about to leave the room when Rutledge said, "No, stay."

He put in a call to the Maidstone Police and asked for Inspector Chambliss.

"He's just been called away, sir. Is it important? Should I try to see if I can stop him?" asked the constable who'd answered.

"It's urgent."

"Very well, sir. Won't be a moment." The constable put down the receiver, and Rutledge could hear him hurrying out the door.

It was nearly five minutes before someone returned. The receiver was lifted, and Chambliss's voice said impatiently, "This had better be important, Rutledge. I have another murder on my hands—domestic matter."

"You searched the area around the lock, after I'd left?"

"We did and found nothing. By the way, they pulled your hat out of the water. I'll send it to you."

Rutledge ignored the comment. "Have you found a motorcycle?"

There was a silence. Then Chambliss said, "We found one down by the barges. It was chained to the posts on the gangway of the *Lucy Belle*. Appeared to belong there. The owner is away, we couldn't question him. But the local constable tells me that he'd had houseguests over the weekend, and we think the motorcycle belonged to one of them."

"It could have belonged to Rawlings. Will you send someone to bring it in and secure it?"

"I can. But if you're wrong, I'll take the blame from the owner of the *Lucy Belle*."

"In which case I'll apologize in person. But I think that's how Rawlings got to Kent so easily."

"I'll send someone along. Right now, I'm needed elsewhere," Chambliss said.

And he hung up.

Rutledge leaned back in the chair behind the desk, relaying the conversation to Belford.

"Very good. I hope it belongs to your man."

"So do I." Rutledge rose. "I must clean up and then return to the Yard. Thank you for your help."

"My pleasure."

But was it? Rutledge again wondered why Belford had been so helpful to the police in an inquiry. He'd claimed he hadn't cared for a dead man showing up on his street, and that had been logical, an acceptable reason for involving himself. But was there something more?

Rutledge drove to his flat, changed his clothes, and went on to the Yard, closeting himself in his office to write a report. He did not link Rawlings to the Gooding case, but otherwise gave a full account from his arrival in Allington to his discussion with Inspector Chambliss on the telephone that morning.

He finished the report, handed it to a constable to put on Markham's desk, and then took out a sheet of paper.

Where was the missing man? There had to be another man in the picture.

Who had watched the Yard while Rawlings was in Kent?

If Baxter was the dead man in Chelsea, who had driven him there and later left the motorcar in a chalk quarry?

Who had tried to kill MacFarland and, when the opportunity arose, had taken a shot at Rutledge as he drove the tutor to Dr. Townsend's office?

It couldn't be Diaz, even though he had masterminded all that had happened. The man was too foreign in his appearance to pass unnoticed in a place like St. Hilary. The xenophobic villagers would have reported him to the police straightaway, suspecting him of every unsolved crime within twenty miles.

The man Baxter had brought to the lodgings for one night?

Where was he now?

Hamish was silent, having no opinion to offer.

Rutledge stood, stretched his shoulders, and decided to walk down to the river. Action of any kind was better than being cooped up in this room, in the shadow of the Acting Chief Superintendent.

But the river failed him as well. He walked over the Westminster

Bridge and back, and it wasn't until he was within shouting distance of Scotland Yard that he made a decision.

He went in search of Gibson.

"I need information on a Mr. Bennett, who lives in Surrey. The one who is married to the lame woman who takes in newly released convicts with nowhere to go."

"Yes, sir. Meanwhile, Inspector Chambliss called while you were out. The motorcycle wasn't there when he sent one of men to collect it."

Rutledge thanked him, left the Yard again, and went to Chelsea, to beard Belford in his den.

"You look much better," Belford said approvingly. "Sit down. It's too early to offer a whisky, but there's tea. Or coffee, if you prefer. I've come to like Turkish coffee."

"Thank you, no. I need to know what you can find out about a Mr. Bennett."

He explained the connection, then said, "It will take the Yard some time to discover what I want to know."

"Come into the study."

There, while Rutledge stood by the window, Belford put through two telephone calls. When he had finished the second, he turned in his chair and nodded to Rutledge.

"Very interesting. Percy Hargreave Bennett was in Berlin when war broke out. He was there to visit a friend in banking circles. And he was interned at the Ruhleben civilian detention camp just outside of Berlin. He tried twice to escape, and during the second attempt suffered internal injuries from a fall. He was repatriated at the end of the war, and resigned from his position at the Bank of England. He was rather bitter, I think, about Ruhleben. He felt the bank should have warned him in time to get out."

"Was he one of your men?"

"Good God, no. But we had a list of the internees, you know. It was a rather odd time. The internees ran the camp themselves, even published a newspaper. Unless they tried to escape, they were left to themselves. We wanted to be sure there were no . . . Trojan horses . . . among them, someone put there to spy on them."

"Did you find such a spy?"

"That's not for you to know, Inspector."

"Where is Bennett now?"

"Our last report had him at that house in Surrey. Inherited property, old family. A younger son even went to the New World on one of the earlier colonization attempts. Virginia, I believe it was. We were satisfied that Mr. Bennett was no threat to anyone."

"Was it his own incarceration that led him to take on these ex-convicts with nowhere else to go?"

"Possibly. Who knows? It didn't concern us, and so we left him alone."

"I think it's time to inform Mr. and Mrs. Bennett that one of their lambs has strayed from the fold. It will be interesting to see what they have to say."

Rutledge thanked Belford and drove directly to Surrey.

This time he knocked at the main door and waited to be received by Mrs. Bennett.

"Good morning, Inspector. Or is it afternoon?"

"Only a little after twelve," he told her.

"Then I haven't missed my luncheon. You must stay and join me."

"Thank you. But I've come on a sad errand."

"Indeed?" There was alarm in her eyes.

"Bob Rawlings has drowned in the River Medway."

"Bob? But he's in the gardens as we speak, helping Afonso Diaz. You must be mistaken."

"I'm afraid not," he said. "I saw the body for myself. And I'd met Rawlings here. I recognized him."

"I don't understand. He's been worried about his brother. I know he slipped away once to look for him. I didn't say anything. I felt that his love for his brother did him credit. But his brother lives in London. Not Kent."

"Nevertheless. Has anyone else gone missing? That's to say, has anyone else been given permission to leave because of a family matter? An ill mother in Essex, a sister with a sick child in London?"

She smiled. "Inspector, I trust my staff, and they come to me with their worries. But Bob has been very steady, very conscientious. He's even confessed to me that he was very much aware of how he'd ruined his life and how grateful he has been for this second chance. If he broke his parole to me, it was done out of love for his brother. I will not hold that against him."

Her description of Rawlings was very different from Rutledge's encounters with the man.

"She's blinded by her good deed," Hamish said. "She willna' see that she's been betrayed."

"There's another matter of some importance, while I'm here," Rutledge said. "I'd like to speak to your husband, if he's at home."

"Alas, he's in Glasgow. Something to do with a prize bull he was interested in buying. Could I help you?"

"Does he own a motorcycle?"

"A motorcycle? Yes, of course, he used to race before the war. A very dangerous sport. I was happy when he gave it up. But he kept the beast, I think to pretend he might someday take up the sport again." There was a sadness in her eyes. "Men seldom like to grow old, Inspector. Or infirm. That was his youth, that motorcycle. And so I said nothing."

"I understand he was interned during the war. In Berlin."

"Yes indeed. It kept him out of the war. He's some years older than I, but he would have been one of the first to enlist. They took men of forty, you know. If they had a useful skill. And he spoke German, because he was sometimes there on business. Perhaps it was wrong of me, but I knew my husband was safe where he was, for the duration. The Germans didn't mistreat their prisoners. Still, he never wanted to go back to Germany when the war ended and he was sent home. He said it had changed too much and he was afraid the changes boded ill for the future."

"Do you have cows, Mrs. Bennett? I've never seen them."

"Of course we don't. That's why he's in Glasgow, to look into starting a herd."

Rutledge was listening to Hamish, who for once was agreeing with him.

"Thank you, Mrs. Bennett. Could you call your staff together? I'd like very much to speak to them."

"Whatever for? I can answer any questions you might have. They don't care for policemen, which isn't surprising."

"Nevertheless."

In the end she had him ring the bell, and one by one her staff appeared.

Rutledge waited until they were all present, even Diaz, before saying quietly, "It's my sad duty to inform you that Bob Rawlings has died. I know this will come as a shock to you, and I'm sorry. But I know you would want to be told."

Mrs. Bennett gasped, as if finally taking in the news. Then she said, "We must bring him here. To his home. He would want that."

"How did he die?" one man asked, frowning. "He didn't—he wasn't here last night, but we didn't know he was ill."

The accent was Cornish.

Rutledge said, "He had gone to Kent on a private matter. Perhaps Mr. Diaz can tell you more about that. He was caught in the storm and drowned."

Another man, this one very much a Londoner, said, "I didn't know he knew anyone in Kent."

Rutledge turned to the man, who had been pointed out as Mrs. Bennett's cook when he had come here the first time. "Was he worried about anything? Not eating well?"

The man coughed and said hoarsely, "He ate well. Always."

Rutledge thanked them and let them go.

As the door closed behind them, he said, "I don't remember—what was your cook's crime?"

"Harry? He was a junior clerk in a law firm. He told me he'd embezzled a sum of money to help pay for his mother's care. Wrong of him, I know, but a man who has nowhere to turn can be tempted. He served his sentence in full."

He had also most certainly been the voice of Inspector Chambliss on the telephone call to the Yard. Well spoken and convincing, however hard he'd tried to conceal that just now.

"Do you have a telephone?" Rutledge asked.

"Yes, we do. My husband had it installed after the war."

"Perhaps Mr. Bennett could call me at the Yard and clear up the small matter I'd come to ask him about."

"You must wait until he returns from Glasgow. And there's poor Bob to see to. We have a responsibility, you see." She reached for a handkerchief. Rutledge tried to see what was embroidered on it. Lilacs? "I can't quite believe . . ."

"I understand."

With that he took his leave.

Harry the cook might have made that telephone call, but he was not the third man in the plot. The household could do without a gardener, but the cook? Never.

The net was closing on Diaz. But not fast enough.

When Rutledge returned to the Yard, Gibson met him in the first-floor passage and said, "You should know. Gooding's trial begins Monday morning."

"So soon?" It was a shock.

"Mr. French was a prominent man in some circles. And the case against Gooding is strong. There appeared to be no reason for further delay."

"The bodies of the victims haven't been found."

"The hope is, once he's tried and convicted, he'll tell us where they are. To keep his granddaughter from being tried as his accomplice. If he's condemned, he has nothing to lose. He'll do anything then to save her from the gallows."

But if he hadn't killed French or Traynor, then Gooding had nothing to bargain with for Valerie Whitman's life.

Chapter Twenty-five

Rutledge cursed Diaz all the way back to his office.

And he knew, without the insistent voice of Hamish in the back of his mind, that the fault was his.

Rawlings was dead. There had been no way around killing him, but Rutledge had wanted him alive. Still, someone had gone to Kent and brought back the telltale motorcycle. Diaz still had a henchman he could rely on.

Turn it around, Rutledge told himself. Upside down.

He found the sheet he'd been working on, crumpled it, and tossed it aside.

Taking out another, he began to draw diagrams.

He could see before him the evidence against Gooding and his granddaughter, very solid, except for the missing bodies.

He heard an unexpected sound in the corridor—the mew of a cat.

Gibson tapped on his door, then opened it, carrying a young white cat in his arms. One eye was pale blue, the other a pale green. Under the sergeant's elbow was a sheet of paper.

"What are you doing with a cat?" Rutledge asked, amused. He hadn't pictured Gibson as an animal fancier.

"She was up a tree, and a constable brought her in. The owner will be here in half an hour to claim her. She was in Fielding's office but set him off something fierce. His eyes are red and weeping, and he's sneezing every breath. I volunteered to take her away. Here's what I've discovered so far about your Mr. Bennett."

Rutledge came around the desk to take the sheet from him, and for good measure smoothed the cat's fur.

He stopped, his hand in midair.

"Not you as well?" Gibson said, turning quickly toward the door. "I'll take her away."

"Yes, go on," Rutledge said absently, his mind elsewhere. "Thank you."

He was scanning the sheet as he spoke. It was almost exactly the same information that Belford had given him. Except for the last line.

According to the constable whose rounds included the Bennett property, Mr. Bennett had not been well after his return from internment. He'd finally been reduced to being pushed about in an invalid's chair for weeks. The constable hadn't seen him for some time and assumed that he was now bedridden.

The eyes of the police—constables walked their rounds and filed away information that was often invaluable when a crime occurred.

Still, what if no crime had occurred here? What if Mr. Bennett had finally died of the injuries incurred in Germany while he was making good another escape attempt? And his wife, for unknown reasons, had kept his death a secret?

So that she could hire a staff, even without the money to do so? If her husband hadn't returned to his position in the Bank of England, what had they lived on? A good many families with lofty bloodlines back to the Crusades were nearly penniless . . .

And the cook could answer the telephone as Mr. Bennett, just as he had pretended to be Inspector Chambliss.

Mr. Bennett hadn't been a party to anything that had happened, because he hadn't been there.

Rutledge left in a hurry, driving as fast as he could back to the house in Surrey. It was after the dinner hour when he arrived, the late summer evening already drawing to a close.

Mrs. Bennett wouldn't bury her husband in the orchard or under the compost pile. She would find a way to honor him.

Rutledge took out his torch, shielded it, and set off for the gardens. There was the terrace above the croquet pitch, with formal borders boxing in a broad, sloping lawn, at the bottom of which was a narrow pond. Pretty, open, offering a handsome view from any of the formal rooms that overlooked it. The beds had been planted to reflect three seasons with maximum effect.

Here? He thought not. Too open, too public, not somewhere to grieve in private. Where, then?

On the far side of the house, Rutledge found what he was after. The main bedroom wing looked down on a more or less private garden, set behind a wall some four feet high but not solid, the bricks forming a lacy diamond pattern that offered light and air as well as seclusion. At the far end, an allée of shrubbery protected it from storms, with access through an ornate wrought-iron gate. Above the garden was a small balcony, and a light showed in the room connected to it.

The master suite?

He found a place where he could climb the wall and let himself down easily on the far side.

Even in the darkness it was lovely. An old garden, old as the house, very likely, but given new life and color. Roses and other flowers formed patterns that led to the center of the garden. There only white flowers had been planted, and they gleamed in the ambient light like sentinels, marking the circle where a small statue of an angel in white marble held pride of place.

No churchyard could have provided a more touching memorial to the dead. Looking out from the balcony above, Mrs. Bennett could find her husband's grave even in the dark of night, and be comforted. In the mornings she could see it when she sat on the long terrace outside her private sitting room, or in late afternoon when she took her tea there.

Had Diaz done this? If so, it showed a side of the man that no one else had seen. A thoughtfulness, a kindness, a sense of beauty and compassion.

Rutledge stood there for a moment, staring up at the serene face of the angel.

Mrs. Bennett was not the person to question about this. But he thought he could find out what he needed to know from Somerset House.

He left the garden in the same fashion as he had come in, over the wall, then threaded his way back to the drive. He walked down it and out the gates, to where he'd concealed the motorcar.

Hamish was saying, "Ye canna' know for certain the woman's husband is under yon statue. No' until ye dig it up."

"I will stake my reputation on it."

"Aye, ye may verra' well have to do just that."

Strike Bennett off the lists of those in league with Diaz.

By morning Rutledge would know more.

Somerset House was quiet when he arrived. He found the clerk he usually turned to for information. There was, as he'd expected, no will for Bennett. He was not officially dead.

But Bennett's father's Will was there.

The house, surprisingly for such a small property, was entailed. The implication was, once it had been far larger.

It was left to Mrs. Bennett's husband as the only son of Henry George Albert Bennett. If he should predecease his father or have no living male heirs, the house went to a distant cousin.

Rutledge stared at the name.

It wasn't Gerald Standish. It was his father, William.

And a swift search showed that William had died in 1902, leaving one son, Gerald.

Gentle God. Early on, Rutledge had investigated the disappearance of one Gerald Standish of Norfolk.

That was why Bennett's death had never been made public. The house and property would have gone to Standish, and unless he was a compassionate man, Mrs. Bennett, crippled though she was, would have only the money her husband left her in his will. And if the estate had already fallen on hard times, to the point of having to let her previous servants go, Rutledge could understand how Mrs. Bennett had tried to find a way to keep the house staffed by turning to the likes of Afonso Diaz and Bob Rawlings.

"Did they also hasten the husband to his death?" Hamish asked. "If he didna' care to have such men in the house?"

"I doubt it," Rutledge answered silently, only just catching himself in time. "If he was also ill, there was no need. But I'll lay you odds that Standish is dead."

He thanked the clerk and left Somerset House, of two minds about what he ought to do next.

A brief stop at Galloway's produced unexpected confirmation.

"I just posted a letter to you," the jeweler said, looking up from a tray of diamond rings he was about to put away. "I found the artist. The one who painted that exquisite miniature. His name was Mannering. Henry Westin Mannering. The subject was his neighbor's young daughter. She married a Standish and disappeared from the record. He painted her on her sixteenth birthday as a gift. I shouldn't be surprised that he was in love with her. He never married, went on to fame and fortune, and died of cholera before he was forty-five." Galloway reached into a private drawer and brought out the miniature. "You'll want to return this to the owner. I'm glad I saw it. Such a beautiful piece."

Rutledge took it, thanked Galloway for his efforts in tracing the workmanship, and went to his flat for a valise before setting out for Norfolk.

Standish had never come back to his cottage, and the general view of the village was that his war had overturned his mind and he'd done away with himself.

"So sad," the woman in the pastry shop said, shaking her head. "He was such a nice young man. Quiet, yes, kept to himself, but I liked him. My own son died in the war. But I often found myself thinking, if he'd come home, he might be the same as Gerald Standish, shut off from everyone and everything. And so I was kind to him."

It seemed to be a fitting epitaph.

Rutledge thanked her and was about to leave when she said, "I asked him for a photograph once. He thought it forward of me, I'm sure. A middle-aged woman? But then he came back in the shop the next day, as if he'd known what I was feeling. And he gave me one he'd had taken in France. I put it in a frame next to Tommy's. My two boys."

"Would you show me this photograph?" Rutledge asked.

"I'm finished here at three. If you can wait that long?"

Rutledge could. He found the constable, and together they returned the miniature to Standish's cottage.

"Although what's to become of this lot, I don't know," the constable said, surveying the front room. "Sad, isn't it?"

There had been nothing here that connected Standish to the Bennett family. No letters, no entries in the family Bible, no paperwork in the desk that pointed to the entailment. If Gerald Standish had known he was a distant relation, he had had no sentimental feelings about it.

No photograph of the house, no letter of condolence from the Bennetts on the death of his father. Of course the Bennett estate was hardly wealthy, stately, or famous. It had probably been half forgotten with the years, an anachronism, from a time when keeping property intact ensured money and power, retainers to fight at one's side and a voice at Court. Still, Rutledge would have expected the grandmother to have kept his father's papers for him. But then perhaps she had, reminding Standish of ties to a distant future. And after his war, he had not cared.

Rutledge knew how the man had felt. Perhaps his death had been a blessing to him.

But it was still murder, if what Rutledge suspected was true.

At a quarter past three, the woman in the pastry shop stepped out the door and looked around for him. She had changed into street clothes, and he almost didn't recognize her in the upswept hairstyle and a becoming hat. She said, "Perhaps it's best I don't know what happened to Gerald. I can always hope he'll come back one day. But if the constable had found his body, I'd like to lay him to rest where my Tommy would have been buried, if he'd lived a long and happy life at home. It's important for all of us to know that someone cares."

Her cottage was not far from the pastry shop, with pretty curtains at the windows and matching chintz on the chairs. He followed her into the front room, and she passed him the photograph.

"That's my Tommy," she said, her fingers lingering on the frame as if reluctant to let it go.

He could see the likeness, the same straight nose and firm chin, the same short, stocky build. Tommy smiled for the camera happily, and Rutledge thought the photograph must have been taken just as the young soldier arrived in France, before he knew what war was.

"A fine young man," he said, giving the photograph back to her.

She held it for a moment longer and then set it down. "Yes, he was. I couldn't have asked for better. It was just that I had him for such a short time. He was only eighteen when he enlisted."

With a sigh, she set the photograph back by the chair that must have been her favorite, because her knitting was beside it on a small stand. She took up the next frame and handed it to Rutledge.

And he recognized the dead man in Chelsea. He was standing by a gun carriage, one hand resting on it, the other on his hip. He was smiling, but not as Tommy had done, still free from the shadows. Standish was already showing the strain of battle, although he was trying to keep it at bay. Any likeness to Howard French was tentative at best here. The way one might see a stranger on the street and ask, *Did I know that man? He looked familiar . . .*

Rutledge wondered who it had been meant for, this photograph. His grandmother? A girl back in England who cared? What had become of her?

"I was here before, asking about Standish in the village. I don't remember seeing you in the shop then."

"I was in Norfolk with my sister. She'd had kidney stones, and I went to stay with her until she was well again."

Would it have shortened the long, tangled road to the truth if he had found this woman here in the village and talked to her then, seen the photograph?

There was no way of knowing.

Rutledge wasn't quite certain what she would feel if he told her how Standish had died. Or that his body was already in a pauper's grave in London.

He said simply, "Another fine young man."

"Indeed." She looked at him, her head to one side. "You were in the war. You remind me of Gerald somehow. Not in appearance, just . . . something."

He smiled. "We were both soldiers."

"Yes, that's true."

He thanked her and left.

Driving out of the village, Rutledge said aloud, "I don't believe

Standish would have cared about the Bennett house or been in any hurry to send Mrs. Bennett packing."

Hamish answered, "Sae it would seem. To her, it would be verra' different, a cloud that blotted out the sun."

Nor would anyone who had come to live in the Bennett household and knew it as sanctuary want to count on the kindness of a stranger. Still, Rutledge thought that Diaz had protected himself and his plans, not Mrs. Bennett.

As he drove to Essex, and St. Hilary, Rutledge considered what this meant to Gooding's case, now that the dead man in Chelsea had been identified.

Hamish said, "The motorcar that killed the man is still the motorcar of Lewis French."

And so it was, straw with which the K.C. could make bricks to wall up Gooding. The connection to Diaz was too slender a thread.

Where the hell was Lewis French?

If Gooding's trial was to begin Monday, Rutledge was bound by duty to tell what he knew about the corpse found in Chelsea. He would have to testify, like it or not.

Rutledge drove into Dedham late that evening and went to look in on MacFarland.

Townsend, still unhappy with the pretense that his patient was suffering damage that was irreversible, said, "I hope you're here to release both of us from this charade. My patient's well enough to go home. And he's no happier here than I am to have him here. I have to smuggle in his meals, pretend my daughter is helping me nurse the man around the clock, keep my staff in the dark." He shook his head. "Surely you've brought us some answers."

"Not yet. Gooding's trial begins Monday. This is Thursday afternoon. I'm doing all I can."

"Well, then, you must tell MacFarland that he can't leave yet."

Rutledge walked back to the small room where the tutor was being kept and said as he opened the door, "I'm sorry. This is difficult for you. It is difficult for all of us. Give me a few days more."

MacFarland said, "If someone would bring my books to me, it would help. Staring at the walls, nothing to keep my mind busy—no way to pass the time. It's difficult. My head aches, and the doctor says I shouldn't read. But if I read, perhaps it wouldn't ache at all."

"Tell me what you need."

Rutledge handed MacFarland his notebook, and the man made a list for him. "You shouldn't have any trouble. I've only asked for titles you will see straightaway."

"Give me an hour."

"Yes, of course. Thank you."

Rutledge left, drove to St. Hilary, and went into MacFarland's cottage.

The tutor's reading glasses were exactly where he'd left them, and the books were relatively easy to find. A satchel under a window provided transportation, and Rutledge had just finished adding the last title when someone flung back the door and said, "Whoever you are, step outside and identify yourself!"

"Constable? Inspector Rutledge. I was just . . . looking for anything that might help us find out who attacked MacFarland."

Constable Brooks stepped inside and saw the satchel in Rutledge's hand.

"I'm sorry. We've had a rash of petty theft lately. I thought I might have caught the culprit."

"Petty theft?"

"Small things. Someone went into a neighbor's henhouse, milk was missing from a porch, another woman put a pie on the windowsill to cool—"

Rutledge interrupted. "Did this begin when MacFarland was attacked?"

"No, later on. I suspect it's one of the lads I've had trouble with before. He'll be in borstal before the summer is out, if he keeps on the way he's going."

"Thank you, Constable. Sorry to have given you trouble."

"Any news of Miss Whitman?"

"None so far."

"I don't like thinking about her in prison."

"Nor do I."

"She's not a killer," Brooks persisted, taking up the satchel and following Rutledge back to where he'd left the motorcar. "Whatever her grandfather has done. Why didn't you drive down to the cottage?"

"Because I didn't want to draw attention to where I was heading. Since the cottage is empty."

"Mr. MacFarland is better, isn't he? You've got his spectacles there. I went to look in on him yesterday, and the doctor forbade me to see him. If he'd taken a turn for the worse, the doctor would have wished me to add it to my report."

Rutledge smiled grimly. "Keep that to yourself. I think he could still be in danger."

"Here, not my petty thief, hanging about for another chance at the tutor?"

"Not very likely. But someone went to a great deal of trouble to kill him, and the next try might succeed where this one failed."

Brooks nodded. "I'll keep that in mind, and see that the cottage is watched."

Rutledge drove away, heading not for Dedham but for the village church, leaving his motorcar out of sight by the Rectory. Walking through the churchyard, he observed Miss Whitman's cottage for a time, and then crossed the road once the sun had set.

Hamish said, "Ye have no right to search here."

"I don't intend to search. I can't shake the feeling that she was hiding something before she left. She wouldn't let me in—she was willing to go to prison in what she stood up in, no toothbrush, no comb, no change of clothes. It's been worrying me, but now I think I may know why. If Standish was killed by French's motorcar, French may have got away and eventually come to Valerie Whitman for help."

"It's no' likely. They parted on bad terms."

"Still, he couldn't go to his fiancée, could he? She lives with her father, in the center of Dedham. And perhaps he isn't up to dealing with his sister's uncertain temper."

"Then why did she no' tell everyone that he isna' dead? It would save her fra' prison."

"I don't know. But I'm going to have a look." Rutledge let himself in through the gate carefully, so it would not squeak, then walked up to the door. She had not locked it then—and it was still unlocked. He opened it quietly, stepped inside, and then pulled it closed.

Using his shielded torch, he walked from room to room, and he could smell her scent, he thought, in each of them. Lilacs? It was as if she had only just left. She had good taste in furnishings, fine pieces, with a few paintings that her father must have bought. China dishes in the cupboard, a pretty porcelain shepherdess on the shelf above the hearth, next to her an ormolu clock. All in their places, waiting silently for their owner to return.

The torch picked out a square of white linen lying on the table, flashing for an instant across the rich colors of embroidered pansies. How easy it would have been for someone to walk in here and take one of Miss Whitman's handkerchiefs for later use. A handkerchief was very personal, dropped in a moment of intense anxiety or anger at the scene of a crime, or left under the seat of a motorcar after wiping one's fingers. And this was known to be her favorite pattern. A simple thing, and so all the more readily damning.

He reached the stairs to the upper floor and hesitated. He didn't feel comfortable going through her bedroom. And the house was silent. No one was here after all. He had misunderstood her reluctance—that strong sense of privacy that seemed to come so naturally to her—to open her door even to Scotland Yard, and he wanted to make amends by leaving as quickly as he could.

And then he heard a foot brush against something over his head.

Someone *was* there.

He waited, holding his breath so that he could hear better.

He'd been right.

There was another sound, as if whoever it was had heard him as well, and was trying to stay still. And the harder he tried, the harder it became.

Rutledge called, "Scotland Yard. I know you're there. You might as well come down."

Nothing, not even the sound of breathing.

Mice? Scenting him and looking for cover?

He said again, "I'm here to help. If you won't come down, I shall have to come up."

He waited for a whole minute, counting off the seconds in his head.

And then he turned for the stairs, starting warily up them, prepared for anything.

A window went up, and he could hear someone struggling to get out.

Rutledge went back down the stairs, raced through the front room, and reached the door as a foot came into view.

He caught the foot and pulled, and with an oath, someone came down almost on top of him and lay there for an instant, winded.

Rutledge turned the torch on the man's face—and didn't recognize him at all.

"Constable Brooks's petty thief. Come on then." He reached for the man's collar and prepared to bring him to his feet.

"Get your damned hands off me. If you're a policeman, I want to see proof."

Rutledge reached into his pocket for his identification, and as he did, the man came to his feet, hit Rutledge with all his strength, and turned to run.

Rutledge still held the torch, and he swung it, intent on stopping the intruder any way he could. And then he remembered using the torch on Bob Rawlings just before he went over the railing, and he tempered the strength of the blow.

The intruder fell, gasping for breath, then struggled to rise.

"Now listen to me. I'm from Scotland Yard, and you're coming with me to the police station—"

Breaking off, Rutledge stared.

The torch couldn't have done the damage he saw in the man's throat. He had aimed higher. But the ugly gash had broken open and was bleeding heavily.

"My God," Rutledge said, jerking out his handkerchief and trying to stem the flow. "Hold on to that." He pressed the man's hand to the handkerchief, turning quickly back to the house. "Stay where you are, or you're likely to bleed to death."

A voice in the darkness said, "Rutledge? Is that you? What's happened? I saw your motorcar."

And the curate stepped through the gate into the pool of brightness that was Rutledge's torch. Just then he saw the man on the path, and the handkerchief already dark with blood. "This man has been injured—Rutledge, did you do this?"

"I found him in the house. When he ran, I stopped him."

The curate looked quickly to the houses on either side. No one had come to the door. "Let's get him to the Rectory. We've got to stop that bleeding. Take his other arm."

"Wait here." Rutledge disappeared into the house, back in a matter of seconds with a small pillow, which he added to the handkerchief. "Keep it there," he ordered and then took the man's other side, all but dragging him down the path and toward the gate.

The curate had it open, and Rutledge got the man through. "There's no time to bring up the motorcar. We've got to hurry."

His senses returning, the man managed to stumble along between them. It seemed to take ages to reach the Rectory, tombstones and plantings catching at their unwary feet as they made their way around the church to the Rectory gate. The steps were hardest, and then Rutledge had the door open and pulled the man into the lamplight of the Rectory parlor.

He nearly stumbled over a chair, hooked it with his foot, and brought it around to push the man into it.

The curate went into another part of the house and came back with a wooden box.

"Bandages and the like," he said. "Altar boys always have skinned knees and stubbed toes."

Rutledge had removed the pillow and the handkerchief. The bleeding had slowed, clotting over. He could see that the gash was an old one. Very likely, in the man's attempt to climb through the window, he'd reopened it because it had never healed properly.

"Who are you?" the curate asked gently. "Are you hungry? In need of work? I can help you."

The man's temper flared. "I'm—" He stopped short, eyes on Williams's clerical collar. "Is this man really from Scotland Yard?"

"Yes, of course he is. He's been in St. Hilary conducting an inquiry."

The man turned to Rutledge. "You're the bastard who took Valerie away. Where is she?"

"In prison," Rutledge said shortly. "Charged along with her grandfather in the murder of Lewis French. Are you French? If you are, why didn't you show yourself and keep that young woman out of Holloway?"

"Damn you, she said she was going to bring home her grandfather. She told me it was finished, and I let her go."

"But he's not French," the curate was saying. "I tell you, he's *not* Lewis French."

"Then who is he?"

"My name is Traynor. Matthew Traynor. French tried to kill

me—he sent someone to make sure I never reached England. I got away from him, just, and I've been in hiding ever since, not knowing where to turn, who was against me. I'm in no condition to survive another attempt."

"Where have you been since your ship docked?"

"My parents' house. It's been closed since before the war. The problem was food. I'd walk to another town and buy what I needed, until the money I had in my pocket ran out." He grimaced. "I'm a wealthy man, and I couldn't pay for my dinner. I've had to forage—steal—dig in gardens at night. I was chased by a dog one night, and had to sleep in a barn. Miss Whitman found me when I'd fainted from hunger. I was out of my head for two days, and she had to keep me in the cottage. She wanted to call in Dr. Townsend, but he's the father of Lewis's fiancée. She left food for me when you took her away, but that's gone and I've been forced to steal again."

"You never went to the police? Or to the authorities at the port?"

"I never even showed my passport. I got off the ship by carrying an elderly woman's luggage for her. Her son come to fetch her, as far as anyone could tell. I knew perhaps twenty people in England, most of whom hadn't seen me since before the war. My neck was inflamed, I was so feverish the driver of the first omnibus accused me of being drunk. I walked for miles before taking the next omnibus, for fear of being followed. And there was someone in the grounds of my parents' house when I got there. I thought he was waiting for me. I watched as he tested windows, doors, looked in all the outbuildings, then waited, sitting on his motorcycle in the drive until well after midnight. He left finally, and I got in the way I sometimes got out as a boy. What was I to tell the police—this scruffy stranger, a knife wound in his neck, no money, in England without the proper papers—if they brought Lewis or Agnes in to identify me and were told that I wasn't Matthew Traynor, what then?"

"You'd have had to come to the police in the long run."

"Yes, I know. But on my terms, when I could stand on my own two feet and not faint from hunger or pain. And then Valerie—Miss Whitman—told me that someone had tried to kill Lewis, and that Lewis had disappeared. I didn't know what to think then. Now *you* tell me she's in Holloway Prison. For what?"

"Her grandfather is about to go on trial for killing French and you."

"She never— My good God. That's what you meant earlier. That I could have saved her from that."

"What did you do with the man who tried to kill you?" Rutledge studied the man, fairly certain that his account was truthful. But there were gaps all the same.

"He came up to me as I was standing at the ship's rail, watching for the white cliffs. I should have been able to see them; it was a clear night and we weren't that far out to sea. We spoke, the way strangers do, and then he took out a cigarette, asking if I had a match. I was looking down, finding it, when suddenly he bent over, grabbed my ankles, and had me half over the rail. I somehow managed to beat at his head and shoulders until he let me go, and I fell hard to the deck. He had a knife then, and he went for my throat. We fought—I was in the Army, I knew a thing or two about that—and in the end, it was he who went overboard, not I. We were coming up on Dungeness Light, but I never waited to see. I was bleeding badly and hurried down to my cabin to take care of it. I stayed there, afraid of questions, until we docked."

The man at Dungeness Light.

"Was he English? The man with the knife?"

"Oh yes. A London accent, I should think. I asked the purser, and he said he thought the man had got on in the Azores. I went down to his cabin, searched it, found nothing, and packed up his belongings for disembarkation."

"Did you learn his name?"

"I did. Benjamin R. Waggoner. Whoever he may be."

The other man in the lodging house. The one called Ben . . .

"I tell you, it has to be French who is behind this. He'd told me that when I came to England, we'd talk about some changes he had in mind. I wouldn't be surprised if my death was one of them. And who else would know to look for me in the grounds of a house closed for six years?"

"He could have been looking for French," Williams suggested.

Satisfied that the wound had stopped bleeding sufficiently to bandage, Rutledge put on a field dressing and then said, "He ought to eat."

"I have a little leftover soup from my own dinner, and some bread, some cheese," the curate offered.

"That will do," Traynor said. "I've had nothing today."

Rutledge and Traynor left for London soon after Traynor had eaten and Rutledge had looked again at the wound on his throat. It had sealed, but the flesh around it was inflamed. He needed medical care, and sooner rather than later.

Traynor slept for the first two hours of his journey, his head cushioned on the bloodstained pillow from Miss Whitman's parlor. Rutledge waited until his passenger was fully awake, then told him about Diaz.

Traynor said, "Are you telling me that I was nearly killed because of something Howard French, my grandfather, did years ago?"

"I'm afraid so."

Traynor whistled. Then he turned to Rutledge and demanded, "If you know all this, why is Gooding standing trial? Why is his granddaughter in prison?"

"Proof has been hard to come by. This could just as easily have been a feud between you and French that Gooding was caught in the midst of. The police believe Gooding will tell them where the bodies are buried, to keep his granddaughter from going to trial. But he doesn't know, you see. He has nothing to bargain with. And so she will have to suffer as well."

"But I'm alive—I can testify."

"To what? That someone tried to kill you? You can't prove it wasn't Gooding's plan in the first place. And whoever attacked you can't testify as to who hired him, if he's drowned."

"What can I do? There must be something. I can't wait for the jury to bring in a verdict."

"I'll find a doctor to look at that wound. And then I'm taking you to Hayes and Hayes. They'll deal with the trial by asking for a postponement on the basis of new evidence. You. And Inspector Billings saw that body at Dungeness Light. It can substantiate your story of being attacked while on board the *Medea*. I can also show who the dead man in Chelsea was. And why he was killed. But there's still Diaz. There are still the charges against Gooding. Lewis French is still missing."

"He's got to be stopped. Somehow. This man Diaz."

"Meanwhile, Hayes will see you safe. I could put a constable on his door, but it would only serve to draw attention to the house."

"Watch your own back, meanwhile," Traynor told him grimly.

Hayes greeted Traynor like the long lost Robinson Crusoe, calling him "my dear boy!" over and over again. Rutledge thought that the fact that someone able to run the firm had actually survived was more important to the elderly solicitor than the fact that it was Traynor.

"I'll start proceedings straightaway to halt the trial. And I'll find a safe place for you to stay, Mr. Traynor. Meanwhile, my own house is at your disposal, and I'll see that your baggage is retrieved from Portsmouth." He went on, laying out solutions to every problem but that of Lewis French. And that he tiptoed around.

At length Rutledge was free to leave. Traynor thanked him profusely, and Hayes promised to keep him informed.

"But what do we do about Mr. Standish?" Hayes asked. "He isn't a client, I have no authority to settle his affairs."

"Leave him to me," Rutledge said.

He went directly to the Yard, wrote a full report on Traynor's experiences and the probable postponement of the trial, and handed it to a constable to be put in the Acting Chief Superintendent's basket. He was in no mood to wait for Markham to come in, even though it was close on dawn already.

As he left the Yard, Rutledge searched for a motorcycle anywhere in the vicinity, and again on his own street, and there was no sign of one.

Ben Waggoner was dead, Rawlings as well. If Standish was the man in Chelsea, then there was Baxter still to contend with.

And Diaz.

Rutledge let himself into the flat, and almost at once knew that he was not alone.

Something in the stillness had changed. And there was the faintest scent of applewood fires.

Hamish said, "The bedroom."

Rutledge put on the lamp by the door as he always did, and went through the post that had been come in his absence. Working his way slowly toward the bedroom doorway, he reached the hearth and stopped.

His service revolver. It was in the chest beneath his bed. Had Diaz found it?

That changed the odds.

He said, well to the side of any shot from the half-open bedroom door, "I know you're there. Let's finish it."

After a moment, Diaz walked into the sitting room lamplight. He appeared to be unarmed.

"I've rather spoiled your plans," Rutledge said easily. "Traynor is alive, and MacFarland will live. We've taken steps to halt Monday's trial. I now know why Standish had to die. You'd be wise to take the next boat to Portugal or the Azores. While you can."

"Standish was Bob's decision, not mine. He grew very protective of Mrs. Bennett. I had only to tell him that you would see her punished for what he and I did to make him want to kill you."

"Where's Baxter?"

"I have no idea. He is of little interest to me now."

"Then you've come to say good-bye?" Rutledge smiled.

"I've come, as you said, to finish this." Diaz reached into his pocket and drew out a pale green scarf.

Rutledge had seen Frances wear it many times over the summer. Diaz had been inside her house. Baxter. Was he there? Had something happened to Frances?

Feeling a surge of anger that was red hot in his blood, Rutledge crossed to where Diaz was standing and, without hesitation, knocked the older man down.

Diaz, stunned for a few seconds, raised himself on one elbow and put out his tongue to taste the blood on his lip.

"Without me, she will die," he said simply.

"You won't know whether she will or not," Rutledge said, standing over him. "Now get up." When Diaz didn't move, Rutledge reached down, caught the man's collar, and hauled him to his feet. He pushed Diaz ahead of him across the room, and through the door.

He held on to Diaz while turning the crank, shoved him into the motorcar, and was in beside him before Diaz could recover.

Diaz sat up, smiling, certain that Rutledge would drive to his sister's house.

But Rutledge did not. He went directly to the Yard, marched Diaz up the stairs, and went to find Billings, who was in his office.

The Inspector looked up, startled, as Rutledge came in with Diaz.

"What the hell?" he began, and then saw Rutledge's face. "What's happened?"

"There's something I have to do. This is Afonso Diaz. I want you to keep him here, and if I don't come back, take him to Markham. He's killed before, and he will kill again. Don't trust him."

He shoved Diaz into a chair, then unfolded the scarf so that it spilled across Billings's desk.

"He's just given me the proof of guilt I've been searching for. He was in my flat threatening me. And he's been inside my sister's house. I want him up on charges for that. We'll sort out the rest later." He faced Diaz. "On Mrs. Bennett's property, I was the trespasser, and whatever happened to me could be explained away. You should have left it at that."

"Who is Mrs. Bennett?" Billings demanded, but Rutledge had turned on his heel and was leaving.

He heard Billings say, as the door swung closed, "Now, then, Mr. Diaz. Why don't we have a little conversation while we wait."

Back in the idling motorcar, Rutledge drove to his sister's house.

A motorcycle rested on its stand just down the street.

He'd found Baxter.

Leaving his motorcar where it couldn't be seen from the house, he got out, went through the back garden of a house next but one to where Frances lived. Out the gate at the bottom of the garden, he walked down to her back gate, quietly let himself through, and then stood for a moment, listening.

The garden was quiet, save for a few crickets by the little pond. He circled it and made his way toward the rear of the house, keeping to the shadows of trees and shrubs.

No lights showed.

Where was Baxter, and where was he holding Frances?

Hamish was silent in the back of his mind.

Reaching the terrace door, Rutledge tested the latch. Locked.

Swearing under his breath, he walked quietly across the grass to the servants' door. This he found unlocked, and he stepped inside, letting his eyes adjust to the gloom of the passage that led to the servants' hall. The rooms were empty—the live-in staff was a thing of the past. Instead, dailies came early in the morning to do what was required.

He made his way to the servants' stairs and chose that route up to the bedrooms. They were narrow, and he was a tall man. It took a little time to reach the first floor quietly, and there he stood in the passage once more, getting his bearings.

If he were Baxter, where would he be?

Not in the ground-floor rooms, surely, where he would be cornered if Rutledge had already dealt with Diaz.

At the top of the main staircase, then.

The passage was carpeted. Still, Rutledge took off his boots and left them in the servants' stairwell. Walking in his stocking feet, he stayed close to the wall, a few steps at a time. The main stairs were just ahead.

Movement caught his eye. Someone was there, sitting on the top step, watching the main door. Waiting for him to unlock it and walk in.

But where was Frances? In one of the bedrooms? It was likely—she wasn't the target, he was. And hurt or unhurt, she must wait. His first duty was to deal with Baxter and keep him alive, if it was humanly possible to do so. If the anger racing through every nerve ending would let him stop in time.

Baxter had a split second of warning, no more, wheeling in time to see Rutledge hurling himself forward in a tackle that pinned Baxter just as he was rising.

They rolled, and Rutledge saw the flash of a knife. Silent, deadly.

He was on his feet first, Baxter just that second slower, and they closed, Rutledge keeping the knife hand well away from his face and throat. But Baxter had recovered, was quick now, rearing back for better purchase, and Rutledge felt the blade cut through the cloth of his coat and plunge toward his chest.

The wound wasn't deep, but it was bleeding, the breastbone hurting. Rutledge threw himself at Baxter before the knife had been fully withdrawn, catching the man's wrist and turning the blade back, forcing it toward Baxter's throat.

He had a fleeting thought, that Frances wouldn't care for blood on her carpet, and the knife slid sideways into Baxter's shoulder instead. The man yelped, twisted away, and Rutledge went after him, catching the knife wrist once more and pinning it to his side. Baxter, smaller and more agile, twisted away again, just as Rutledge landed a very solid blow. It caught Baxter on the side of the head rather than the jaw, and it sent him reeling backward.

Rutledge had a flashback to Rawlings, turning in the air, just as Baxter lost his balance and went backward down the stairs.

Rutledge went after him. Baxter hit the landing and stayed where he was, lying on his side. The knife was near his free hand, and Rutledge kicked it the rest of the way down the stairs.

"Help me," Baxter said, his voice a thread. "Something's wrong." He frowned, tried to move, and cried out instead. "It hurts."

Bending over him, Rutledge couldn't judge how badly the man was injured, but he took no chances, keeping well clear of Baxter's feet. He said roughly, "Where is she?"

Baxter misunderstood. "He's in the roses. When the French woman went to London. The staff's half day. For her to take the blame if the rest went wrong." He coughed, and blood frothed on his lip. Raising frightened eyes to Rutledge's face, he whispered, "I can't breathe." He tried to clutch at Rutledge. "Don't let me die. I'll do anything. Please."

For putting Frances in danger, dying was what the man deserved, Rutledge thought grimly. But the Yard needed him alive. And so did Gooding.

Judging Baxter's weight, Rutledge picked him up. Baxter writhed, screaming in agony, and Rutledge almost dropped him. "Be still. I'm trying to help you." He managed to carry him down the stairs, got the door opened.

Pausing there, he called, "Frances? I'm here—I'll be back."

Baxter was in Casualty ten minutes later, under the eye of a constable Rutledge dragooned into guarding him. He waited only long enough for Baxter to be examined.

"He'll live," the doctor said. "Broken ribs, possibly a punctured lung—"

"He is in charge and will have to stand trial. Make certain he lives," Rutledge ordered.

Before the doctor could answer him, Rutledge was racing out of Casualty to his motorcar, driving at speed to the house, pulling up by the door, and dashing back inside, cursing himself for not having taken five minutes to find Frances. If she'd heard the fight and Baxter's fall down the stairs, she would be frightened alone here.

It took more than five minutes. It took him nearly three quarters of an hour.

He began searching on the first floor. It was where Baxter had been waiting, and he would have been guarding his prisoner as well. But there was no sign of her in any of the bedrooms. In her dressing room, he saw at once that she must have packed several bags. They were missing as well. Spaces in her closets confirmed this.

Where had they taken her?

He went through the bedroom a second time. No signs of a scuffle, no overturned furniture, the bed showing only the indentations of the valises. *Who had packed them?* Was she still in the house, or had they already taken her away?

Frantic, he went downstairs, calling her name as he opened the door to the small drawing room.

And the first thing he saw was an envelope resting on the mantelpiece. His name, her handwriting.

He crossed the room in three strides, took down the envelope, and tore it open. He could feel the cold fist in the pit of his stomach as he unfolded the notepaper.

Ian, darling,

You're away again, and Sergeant Gibson wasn't there to tell me where. I'm off to spend the weekend with Peter and his parents. Wish me well.

Much love,
Frances

She hadn't been at home.

They hadn't found her here. But they'd taken the scarf to convince him they had.

Rutledge could feel himself shaking, first with relief, then with helpless laughter.

She need never know how frightened he'd been. She need never know what had taken place in the house she considered her home and her sanctuary.

Hamish said, "Can ye be sae sure she's no' under duress?"

The niggling doubt was there. Along with his need to hear her voice.

He told himself that if she'd been forced to write that note, she'd have given him Simon's name, not Peter's. A warning. All the same, he would think of an excuse tomorrow to call the Lockwoods.

He was turning away, the note still in his hand, when he saw the blood on his shirt. He had forgot that he'd been stabbed.

Going out to the motorcar, he retrieved his torch and spent the next half hour on his knees, making certain there was no telltale blood for Frances or her maid to find. He marked the few spots and scrubbed them out himself.

Finally satisfied, he left the house.

He spent another hour dealing with Baxter, then reported to the Yard that the man was in custody and asked Billings to see to the paperwork.

"Where is Diaz?" he asked the Inspector.

"He's under lock and key. Not without a struggle. He told me you were a man tormented by ghosts. What did he mean by that?"

For an instant Rutledge could think only of Hamish. Not a ghost, but a haunting nevertheless of the living by the dead. And then he remembered the ghosts of dead shepherds calling from the edge of the cliff. The piping of seabirds coming in to nest at night. He said, forcing amusement into his voice, "It's a legend of Madeira. Meant as a taunt. That I was chasing a will-o'-the-wisp."

"He's a nasty piece of work, I'll say that for him," Billings told Rutledge.

And then Rutledge went home.

The flat felt stuffy, but there was no lingering scent of applewood smoke.

He dressed the thin cut on his chest and went to bed.

L ate in the afternoon of the next day, Hayes arranged for Miss Whitman to be released. Gooding was to remain in custody until Monday morning, when all charges would formally be dropped.

Hayes himself was present when she walked through the gate. Traynor had come with him, and he went forward quickly to greet her and lead her toward freedom and Hayes's motorcar.

Rutledge was there as well, standing a little distance away from the lawyer's motorcar.

She looked very tired; there were dark circles under her eyes, which seemed more brown than green from where he was watching. Her hair, usually so lovely in the sunlight, was dull, without life.

She saw him, stopped for a moment, and their eyes met. But she didn't acknowledge him. After all, he hadn't kept her out of Holloway.

He waited until Hayes's motorcar was out of sight before walking back to his own and driving away.

Ahead of him still was the knotty problem of what to do about Mrs. Bennett and her household.

And whether to leave Mr. Bennett in peace in that quiet garden.